Y2K

D1707563

218-JAME

Y2K

The Millennium Bug

Don L. Tiggre

Library of Congress Number:		98-87822
ISBN#:	Hardcover	0-7388-0117-8
	Softcover	0-7388-0118-6

This book was printed in the United States of America.

To order additional copies of this book, contact:

Xlibris Corporation
PO Box 2199
Princeton, NJ 08543-2199
USA

1-888-7-XLIBRIS
1-609-278-0075
www.Xlibris.com
Orders@Xlibris.com

I DEDICATE THIS BOOK TO MY BEST FRIEND
AND PARTNER, WITHOUT WHOSE SUPPORT
I WOULD NOT HAVE BEEN ABLE TO WRITE IT:
SUNNI MARAVILLOSA!

ACKNOWLEDGMENTS

The first person I would like to acknowledge is you, the reader: without you, I wouldn't have people to share my stories with, and that'd be an unhappy thing. So, thanks! Next, I would like to thank my beautiful beloved partner, Sunni Maravillosa for her indefatigable good cheer, charm, and willingness to read my manuscripts at 3:00 a.m. while 8 months pregnant. I also thank my sons, Thales, Logan, and Alec, for their patience and understanding—and their amazing efforts to play quietly while I was working on this book. Special thanks also go to Debbie Moeller, Lizzie Manning, and the Hobbyt for their excellent suggestions and input on ways to improve this book, and to my published friends James P. Hogan, L. Neil Smith, and F. Paul Wilson, for their support. And Dassa—thanks for reminding me to follow my dreams!

A special acknowledgment also goes to all the wonderful musicians in the bands listed in the attributions beneath all the lyrical quotes that begin the chapters in this book. Your music has inspired me and I offer my "fair use" of a few of your words in this book as a tribute to the wealth your work adds to all of humanity.

Also, an apology is in order to the people of Rifle, Colorado, for the imaginary overpass. I could have sworn there was one there the first time I drove through!

FOREWORD

"Just around the corner is a brand new century
Now we'll keep the fire burnin'
and this ol' world will keep turning round and round
I think we're ready for a change in the weather."
—Tesla, *Change in the Weather*

Many things described in this story are real, but set in fiction. This much is NOT FICTION:

In the late 1990s, all across America and around the world, people began receiving their replacement credit cards in the mail, as usual. The credit cards looked normal enough, but they expired in only one or two years. This was because the issuing banks' computers were not set up to handle dates in the year two thousand and beyond. So people whose cards expired in 1997 or 1998 received new ones that expired in 1999.

Technically, this was a 'century lapse' problem, but it was a part of a much larger programming nightmare that involved countless computer and electronic control systems. It was called 'The Millennium Bug,' or 'Y2K' (for Year 2000).

Most people did not understand the problem. Confident that it didn't matter, or that the experts would fix it, people largely ignored the Millennium Bug. The few who thought about the problem at all were divided into two camps: those who began preparing for the apocalypse, and those who thought of it only as an intellectual curiosity.

It was just a computer glitch, right? How much trouble could a date cause? It's not like it could actually *hurt* anyone...

Chapter 1:
January, 1998

"There's a bad moon on the rise!"
—Credence Clearwater Revival, *Bad Moon Rising*

The man passed unobserved, wearing a nondescript hat pulled low over his eyes, and a gray trench coat. The people who noticed him at all paid him as much attention as passing drivers might give a vacant billboard. He slipped into the dim interior of the building early, choosing a seat where he could be near enough to the stage to see well, but far enough into the shadows between lights to offer concealment from casual glances.

He had cased the club before going in, and knew not to go near the back door; there were cameras there.

He sat at a small table, erect and alert, slowly nursing a drink with no alcohol. In a specially sewn pocket on the inside of his coat rested a double-edged knife—thin, narrow, and deadly. He had spent many hours sharpening both sides of the twelve-inch blade, honing both cutting edges to a sharpness that would have inspired the envy of the finest maker of Samurai swords. Touching the knife handle reassured the man—he did so from time to time as the club filled with patrons and the show began.

There were two girls featured that night: one with long hair the color of a rich golden honey, the other with shorter hair colored an improbable cherry red. Both had brown eyes, but where one pair was soft and reflected caring, the other was hard, and reflected hatred.

The dancer with the angry eyes noted the man when a gyrating light flashed across his face. He was not too close, and didn't try to stuff money into her G-string—it was the way his gaze slid over her body that stood out. He didn't exactly leer, didn't merely lust. His look was more predatory. It was a look of ownership— perhaps the way a lion might look at a gazelle it had just downed.

After closing time, the two dancers let themselves out the back door, trusting the peaceful image relayed by the cameras. It was unusually warm for a January night, so the pair wore lighter jackets over their street clothes, rather than the quilted coats they had bought for each other as Christmas presents.

"Well Prue, another day, another dollar."

"Yeah." Prudence frowned. "Kat, I really hate this job!" She leaned her head on Kat's shoulder as they strolled across the parking lot, paying scarcely any more attention to their surroundings than she might if they had been in a sunlit park full of people. "I get so tired of it!"

Kat ran her fingers through Prudence's long hair. "My offer still stands, Prue. You know it doesn't bother me—I'll keep at it and help you finish school. You don't have to do it anymore."

"It sure is tempting, Kat, but I want to do this myself. It's important to me." There was a van parked between Prudence's gray Saturn and the building. As they rounded the front of the van, Prudence fished her keys from her purse and handed them to Kat. "Here, you drive toni—"

The van's sliding door was open and the man was there, with the same look of ownership he'd worn inside the club. Prudence was sure he wasn't doing anything that was new to him. She could tell by the calm way he held his knife, his confident posture, and the look on his face that spoke of his certainty regarding what was about to happen. He gestured with the knife. "Get in. We're going for a ride."

Prudence stood still, frozen with shock. Kat looked wildly about for help, but before she could scream, the man growled, "The cameras aren't wired for sound and there's no one around, so there's no point in screaming. Now *get in!*"

Neither woman moved to obey, but Kat began to tremble and dropped the car keys. She lunged after them reflexively, a move the man interpreted as an attack. As she lurched forward, he swung low, driving the long knife between two ribs and upward through Kat's chest.

The sight of the knife tip poking out of Kat's back snapped Prudence out of her paralysis. She balled her fist and swung at the man's head with all of her adrenaline-boosted strength. She missed, landing a solid blow to the larynx. She could feel cartilage breaking as the windpipe collapsed.

The man let go of the knife and Kat's crumpling form. He clutched at his throat, gasping and gurgling as he collapsed against the van.

But Prudence was not done with him. "You... *Man!*" She screamed and kicked him in the groin, then kicked his head as he slumped to the ground. "*Man!*" She couldn't think of a worse insult, so she kept screaming and kicking until the raw burning in her throat forced her to stop.

Her vision cleared a little with the pause—to the sight of Kat lying on the ground, the knife still protruding from her back. "*Man!*" She stomped one last time with all her weight on her former attacker's damaged throat and ran back to the club to get help.

Many hours later, at a south Atlanta police station, Prudence rubbed her weary eyes. She had no more tears to soothe the stinging in her eyes that grew stronger with every hour they kept her up. "Look officer, I've told you all I can remember." She knew she sounded tired and unconvincing, but Kat was dead—it was hard to care how she sounded. "This guy was waiting for us. I know he planned it because I spotted him in the club first, and then he avoided the cameras by the back door. He had the sliding door open on his van and had it parked so no one could see what happened from the building. He killed my friend and I kinda went nuts." Remembering the knife sticking out of Kat's back brought more heat to her voice. "I can't say I'm sorry he's dead, but if he is, it isn't because *I* was the one planning a crime. For crying out loud, my friend is dead too!"

"So," the officer across the table from Prudence doodled on a note pad as he spoke, "you just happened to accidentally kick him hard enough to crush his windpipe and asphyxiate him?"

Prudence glared at him and made no other response.

Before the officer could press his point, another cop entered the interrogation room. "Take a look at this, Jack." He handed over a manila file full of faxes. He had come on duty with the morning shift and had been asked by Prudence's interrogator to run a check on the deceased.

Jack whistled softly. "Well miss, according to this, the man you...dispatched...last night had a long history of attacking...exotic dancers. He was serving a 30 year sentence for a string of rapes and possible murders but apparently got released because of a computer error. Sez here that the program that looks ahead for the upcoming years' parole hearings screwed up because it couldn't chew on dates after the year 2000, or something like that."

There was more, much more, that Prudence had to endure before they released her, but eventually they did. The sun was high over the eastern treetops when a Fulton County police cruiser dropped her off by her Saturn. It felt much colder now than when she'd left the club the night before with Kat, so she pulled her jacket tight around her. The van was gone, but there was a double stain—Kat's blood must have pooled under the man too—outlined in chalk on the asphalt. There was a metallic odor in the air that hadn't been there before.

"Fucking men." She stepped over the stain and unlocked the car.

*   *   *

Dr. Jared Christensen was sitting at his desk when he opened the letter. It was a normal-looking envelope from his credit card bank and he was preparing to pay his bills. His three older daughters had gone to a Tallahassee ward meeting with their mother, and his two younger daughters were watching TV with his youngest—a son, thank the Lord—in the family room.

Normalcy reigned until he slit the envelope open. He usually paid his credit card company in full every month—credit card interest being such a waste of money—but this time he'd let half the balance ride because of all the Christmas purchases the family had made. It was less than a thousand dollars and he was intending to pay it off. When he read the bill his jaw dropped; the balance due was $19,981,979.17.

"Holy..."

The doctor put the paper down. He gazed around the room—as if to assure himself that he was in the right room in the right house—and picked it up again. The statement still read almost twenty million dollars. A mistake! It had to be a mistake...but what a mistake!

He could feel his heart racing as he pulled out his wallet and slid the card out. The numbers on the front and the magnetic strip on the back now suggested something sinister to him. Over the strip was a twenty-four hour service number. With trembling fingers, he dialed the number and sat back to wait for an answer. It was busy. He tried again and got the same result.

That was the moment his son—a five-year-old incapable of sitting still—chose to burst into the study. "Dad, you've gotta see this, you're on TV!"

"Show me, Val." It was an old joke in the family and the boy was overacting his innocence, but Jared went along with it. It was no less absurd to him than his credit card statement! In the family room, the children were watching 'Mr. Rogers' Neighborhood.' Fred Rogers had already donned his cardigan and was tying his sneakers.

"See Dad," Val beamed, "it's you!"

Everyone knew it was coming but laughed anyway. Jared Christensen *did* look a lot like Mr. Rogers.

"Remember when Kathy thought that the house with the little

trolley was where you went to work, Dad?"

"I remember, Val, but you weren't even born yet!" Jared hugged his children and mentally thanked Jesus—and his wife Emily—that he had such a wonderful family. The girls smelled of bubble-gum from a new kids' shampoo they were trying, and all three wriggled to evade his embrace so they could watch the show un-impeded. Thus far, Jared's family had been his greatest challenge in life, and his greatest joy.

When he returned to his study, the bank service number was still busy. "Humph! Well, no wonder, if they did this to other people's bills!"

He wasn't able to get through for several days, and by then he had received another letter. This one stated that a major computer glitch at First Federal Bank & Trust had produced erroneous bill-ing statements for a number of customers, and that the bank apolo-gized for any inconvenience. Special hot-lines had been set up to handle customer complaints and the billing department was work-ing overtime sending out new statements to cardholders.

The error had something to do with a problem they were try-ing to fix at the bank, something called 'Y2K'. FFB&T computer programmers, working while the bank was closed, had made a mistake that had resulted in more than 19 million dollars being added to the credit balances of every cardholder the bank had. The mistake had been discovered the next morning, but by then thou-sands of incorrect account statements had been sent out.

Amazing! It was the sort of thing that happened in the science fiction Jared had read as a boy—not the sort of thing that one would expect to crop up while going through the monthly bills!

Sitting at his desk, Jared brought his web-browser up on screen and clicked on the Search button. The Excite search engine brought back more than 20,000 hits when he typed in 'Y2K'. There was more information on the Y2K problem than he'd ever want to read, but browsing a few pages made two things clear: 1] many computer experts had been warning about 'The Millennium Bug' for years, and 2] few people had been listening.

The Web seemed full of references to a book by a couple named Ed and Jennifer Yourdon, entitled *Time Bomb 2000*. Apparently, after writing the book, the authors had become even more concerned about how many vital systems would fail because of Y2K problems and had moved to a remote and relatively low-tech part of the southwestern United States. Jared located many other resources, including government web sites, dedicated to the problem—it was mind-boggling how many things, from power companies to banks, could be affected.

Now that early problems were manifesting themselves, more people were beginning to take note. Credit card company executives had been among the first non-programmers to realize that the Millennium Bug could cause serious damage—as those at FFB&T were now all too painfully aware! Unfortunately, realizing that there was a problem was not the same as solving it, and many companies had only gotten as far as the temporary fix of not issuing cards that expired after December 31, 1999.

A major part of the problem, according to what Jared read, was that the year field in a computer program was not always obvious. This meant that *every* line of code needed to be checked—and there were millions of lines of code to check and fix in a single bank or large company! An average novel might only have about 10 or 15,000 lines... Imagine having to read each line carefully for suspicious combinations of two letters, and then imagine that this had to be done 100 times! That would be similar to looking for Y2K problems in a single bank's computer code.

What was more alarming was that among those most vulnerable were governments; they were the biggest users of the kind of old mainframe systems prone to Y2K problems. Some U.S. government agencies claimed to have completed reviews of the software that needed fixing, but there were very few that made that claim, and none claimed to have actually fixed all their Y2K problems. The state governments were all over the chart, with some saying they had the problem well in hand, and others admitting they had not even started a review.

The consequences of unpredictable shutdowns in government computers would vary in importance by agency, but all the experts agreed that it was serious. While some hysterics were predicting the end of the world with the arrival of the year two thousand, government officials were saying that the problem would be handled. They grudgingly acknowledged the truth that there were not enough people familiar with the outdated programming languages where the problem was worst, and not enough time to train new people, but maintained that all the critical systems would be fixed on time. The rest would have to be taken care of on a prioritized basis.

Jared laughed upon reading this. As though bureaucracies accustomed to cost overruns and flexible time schedules would be able to solve a problem that had an absolutely fixed deadline! He stopped laughing abruptly. What would happen if they *couldn't* fix the problems?

Before logging off the internet, Jared came across an unrelated story about the Governor of Utah, who'd had a skiing accident and passed away the previous night in a hospital. The Lieutenant Governor was being sworn in as Governor that day. After finishing, he stared at his screen for a while without seeing. Disturbing news.

Being a devout member of the Church of Jesus Christ of the Latter Day Saints—a Mormon—Jared Christensen believed that the world was indeed in its latter days. The gloomy news was frightening, but... Surely the latter days were not coming this soon?

*   *   *

Lt. Colonel Alexis Thomas was well aware of the Y2K problem. Thank Life she was not actually assigned to try to fix it—just trying to keep track of it was bad enough!

The press was right about the possibility of "unpredictable" problems occurring because of the Y2K bug, but they had no idea. It was classified, of course, exactly how much of the military's software was not Y2K-compliant, and Alexis was not kept informed of all the various internal reviews, but she knew it was bad. All the jokes she'd heard about 'military intelligence' came back to her now and didn't seem funny at all.

It wasn't so much that the tanks and airplanes that had computers on board would stop working after the year two thousand, or that they would decide to start dropping bombs on their own—that couldn't happen. To be sure, modern warfare was computer-intensive and places that had the most computer equipment, like the Strategic Air Command (SAC) and the North American Defense Command (NORAD), would be hit hard. But the average infantryman would also be affected, as many manufacturers of parts and supplies were vulnerable, and the machinery those infantrymen depended on needed a *lot* of parts and supplies.

And then there were all the 'supercomputers' that surrounded her, more than one hundred feet below the Pentagon building, across the Potomac River from Washington, D.C. She knew that many of the systems were not Y2K-compliant, but no one would tell her how many. It was not supposed to be her place to worry about such things; her job was to monitor the capabilities of other countries, not her own. But that didn't stop her from finding out what she could!

As it turned out, most countries were either not aware of the problem, or were ignoring it. If this kept up, she estimated that more than 95 percent of everything that had anything to do with mainframe computers overseas—military or otherwise—would stop dead in its tracks not long after the year 2000. Even in Europe. The Europeans were aware of the problem and were taking it seriously, but not seriously enough. They were concentrating their efforts on Y2K-compliance among the computers that ran their government systems from their capital cities and they were as behind as everyone else at actually implementing fixes.

It scared the hell out of Alexis just how interested her superiors were in the Europeans' strategies for dealing with Y2K problems.

She threw her pen down and stood up to stretch, bending so

far backward that she made an up-side down letter J out of herself—a slender letter J with long chestnut hair that she wished she could wear unrestrained when she was alone under the ground with her machines. Damned Army regs! It made no sense that she had to have her hair all tied up when she was utterly alone. But hers was not to question why...

She wondered for a few seconds how long it had been since she had flown anything and, looking at the work on her desk, decided to get away from her electronic dungeon for a bit. She needed to think. She always thought better when she was *doing* something, something that forced her gears to get moving, something like flying. Why hadn't she joined the Air Force?

Sacrilege!

Perish the thought!

Alexis laughed. She didn't share in the feeling of inter-service rivalry that was so important to everyone else around her, but that didn't mean she would actually *want* to be in the Air Force—they hardly had any choppers and she'd never get to fly one! In many ways, Alexis was not like most of her peers. Leaving the military was a daily thought for her, but staying in the Army was her ticket to flying the machines she loved, so she kept her thoughts—and her differences—carefully hidden from her fellows and especially from her superiors.

Hmmm. There was that major whom she'd beaten in a fencing match—what was his name? Metsky? Letsky? Gretsky! Major Gretsky had promised to let her practice on his chopper. She suspected that the promise was actually an attempt on his part to get closer to her when she wasn't helmeted, padded, and keeping three feet of flexible steel between them, but, of course, the major would never even hint at such a thing to a lieutenant colonel. She sighed and shook her head.

Alexis didn't get that many chances to fly anymore, now that her work in Signal had taken over so much of the time she'd once put into Aviation. What the heck! She picked up the phone and called him.

He was a little surprised, but definitely pleased to hear from her. "Colonel Thomas! You're calling to cancel our re-match—can't risk anyone finding out that you won by pure luck—right?"

"You wish!" She snorted. "Major, you promised to take me up, so how about it?"

"You serious?"

"Sure I'm serious!" She laughed. "I've been flying a desk for too long. I miss it."

"Well, as it happens, I'll be taking my baby up in about two hours. If you can get here in time, you can come along. Ma'am."

"Today?"

"Yes, ma'am!"

"I'll be there, Major. Where do we meet?"

"You know Fort Belvoir? It's the Cobra hangars, immediately to the right of the fixed wing hangars."

A Cobra gunship! Now she was really getting excited; female combat helicopter pilots were against Army regs, so she rarely got a chance to get in—let alone fly—an attack chopper. "What do I need to bring?"

"Just yourself and your clearance."

"Great! Let's see, at this time of day, I should be there in about an hour. I sure appreciate this, Major Gretsky!"

"My pleasure, ma'am... And, it's Gishesky."

"Oh. Gishesky. Sorry."

"No problem—happens all the time."

"Well, thank you, Major."

She smiled and hung up the phone. This was going to be fun. She'd made every effort to log as much flight time as she could, but she'd never flown a Cobra before!

*   *   *

Michel Gerard frowned. His computer had frozen up on him. He had been updating his calendar and had entered the dates he planned to go skiing in the Alps in '99 and '00. It was a routine thing—he updated his calendar daily—and he didn't see why the system should crash over something so mundane.

"Merde alors!" He grumbled and punched a worn intercom button on his phone. "Grace, my computer, she is frozen again. Warn everyone zat I am rebooting please, yes?"

"Will do, Inspector!" Grace clicked off her phone and buzzed the others in the offices of Gerard Investment Management who might be affected by the reboot—Michel's machine had the most memory, so it doubled as a server for the office's local area network.

Michel stared at the phone with the mixture of annoyance and amusement he always felt when Grace called him Inspector. He'd never understood why the *Pink Panther* movies had been so successful, until he'd moved to the United States and become Americanized enough to grasp that Inspector Clouseau had a comic French accent. He knew that he should work harder to rid himself of his own accent, which was still very strong. Still, people understood him well enough—so working on it never made it to the top of his 'To Do' list. After Grace had pointed out how similar to Clouseau's his accent was, he realized that he was something of a walking cliché to many Americans, but he couldn't help it. It was just the way the words came out, and he didn't really mind Grace's teasing. It was actually part of what made their working relationship as fun as it was efficient.

He only hoped she wouldn't slip up and call him "Inspector" in front of a client. How could anyone take his investment advice seriously if they kept seeing Peter Sellers in their minds when he spoke with them? It was bad enough that he resembled Gerard Depardieu, to a degree—something several clients had remarked upon now that Depardieu was making movies in English.

The advisor muttered to himself, pressed the reset button on his computer, and stared out the window while the machine shut itself down. It was late, almost time to go meet Natalie for dinner, and the sun was painting the bottoms of the afternoon altocumulus clouds various shades of red, orange, and gold. Central Park was beginning to fade into shadows, more than forty stories below.

Rectangles of fire sparked off panes of glass that were angled to reflect a sunset whose golden light hid the city's blemishes and allowed Michel to imagine himself atop Mt. Olympus, before it plunged into the night.

The display of color reminded him of the current price of gold and his mind drifted… The way central banks around the world were selling off their gold reserves, it might be a good time for investors who could afford taking the chance to buy some gold. After the sell-off, the price was likely to head back up again, and might do so sharply if the trouble in the Asian markets continued spreading to the rest of the world.

Michel's computer bleeped and he turned away from the window. Instead of displaying his electronic desktop, the screen was black with white block lettering.

Mumbling "merde" again, he checked the machine's floppy drive to make sure nothing was interrupting the start-up routine. Nothing was. He hit the reset button again and watched the machine as it shut itself off and attempted to come back on-line. It displayed several error messages he'd never seen before and ended up stalled in the same place. What could it be? This was a fine machine, not the product of a rickety socialist economy like the one he'd left behind in France!

After 25 minutes of trying to get the recalcitrant machine to work again, Michel Gerard was in a foul mood. He stabbed at his telephone and missed the intercom button, bending his fingernail back in the process. "Shit!" he cried out and cradled his hurt finger. Then he burst out laughing. He must be truly turning American; he'd said it in English!

Deciding that his stubbed finger was a clear sign that he should wrap it up for the day, he carefully pressed the button and asked Grace to have someone come look at his computer in the morning.

Grabbing his hat and coat, Michel headed for the door. His mind was already on how he might use this extra time before dinner to come up with some kind of surprise for Natalie—maybe theater tickets?

He didn't give his computer another thought until he returned in the morning. When the elevator doors opened on his 42nd-floor offices, Michel had completely forgotten about his computer woes. Natalie had loved his surprise and had put on a production of her own at her place, after the show. It had made him forget about *everything* for quite some time!

Now, stepping out of the elevator a little later than usual, he was in a great mood. Grace lifted a stack of mail toward him, but he waved her off with a laugh and turned up his accent. "Neht now Cato! Eh em trying to defuze zis behm!!"

Grace laughed. "No bombs in the mail Inspector, only money and bills. You might as well take them; you won't have anything better to do this morning."

Michel dropped his hammed-up Clouseau accent. "What do you mean?"

She inclined her head toward his office. Through the open door, he could see a young woman—obviously a computer repair person—disconnecting all the cables from his CPU and placing the unit in a padded box for safe transportation.

Never one to conceal his feelings, he left Grace with a "zut alors!" and ran into his office. "What is it? Surely she is not zat broken? I was not even doing anysing unusual!"

The young woman smiled and patted the ill machine where it lay in its box. "I'm afraid your computer's been bitten by the Millennium Bug."

"What?!?" Michel was a well informed man and didn't like being blind-sided. "I sought zat problem only affected mainframe computers!"

"Mostly mainframes, yes, but not exclusively." She adopted the clipped phrasing that computer people often use when speaking to other people who show signs of knowing something about computers. "It affects some micros too, but usually it's something that can be fixed with new software. Yours is a pretty rare case—I have to replace the motherboard. It's uncommon, but it does happen. Would you like me to put the newest Pentium in while I'm at it? It should be significantly faster than what you have in there now."

"Okay... Yes. But when can you 'ave her back?"

"Tomorrow morning. I have everything I need to fix it back at the shop today, but I'll want to run some tests before returning it. I could also get you a hard disk drive that'll hold about ten times more data, if you want it."

"No, sank you." He grinned. "We do not even use all ze space I 'ave. Just bring her back to me as fast as you can. Yes?"

"Okay," she answered.

Michel was shaking his head as she left. He had a bad feeling about this Y2K thing. He didn't like anything that could catch him so completely off guard!

*   *   *

Angel checked his gun. He pulled the magazine out—ten cartridges were visible inside, through the nine holes that were there for that purpose, and the one at the top. His stomach churned and he cursed himself for his weakness, hoping no one else could see it. El Cabron would never feel so squeamish before an execution— hell, he'd enjoy it! But Angel was not Cabron, and checking his gun always helped him to calm his nerves. He'd taken it from the first policeman he'd iced. It had become his good luck charm, a symbol of power in his mind.

The others were staring at Angel with rapt attention. Mario was on his knees before him. Cabron had 'tenderized' him in preparation for his execution, and the bound teen was bleeding from several lacerations, some visible, some not.

Angel smiled for his audience and spoke in Spanish: "Mario, tell me the truth and I'll go easy on you." The actual words were in an impenetrable barrio dialect that even native Spanish speakers from places other than Los Angeles would have a hard time understanding.

Silence filled the abandoned factory—a suffocating fluid that drowned thought, stilled minds. But that didn't mean the watchers could not empathize with Mario; they could imagine themselves in his position all too well. They could feel his trembling in their own hearts.

"Mario, I know it was you. Your girlfriend's brother is a Black Thunder. How'd those skinheads know we were gonna hit the electronics store if you didn't rat on us?" Angel's voice dropped to a stage whisper, carried by the liquid to the onlookers with crystal clarity. "Tell me... Did they threaten her?"

Mario shifted on his knees, the intertwined manacles on his wrists and ankles preventing him from moving far. He said nothing. The silence thickened, making it nearly impossible for the audience to breathe.

"Last chance. Tell me!" Still no response.

Angel's gang—everyone except Cabron—leaned forward imperceptibly. They knew it was coming, but the loud report of the 9mm autopistol still made them jump. The liquid in which they were suspended had crystallized and shattered in an instant. Mario keeled over, refusing to cry out in spite of the agony, his right knee a mangled ruin.

"Tell me!" Angel shouted, not as coolly as he intended. But the silence had been broken by the gunshot and the uncertainty in his voice was masked by Mario's ragged breathing. Angel raised the gun again. "Tell me and I'll have you taken to the hospital— you can still live!"

"You...can't...let me live." Mario finally broke his silence, panting with the effort of fighting his pain. "Go...ahead...and get it...over with!"

"You wish. First tell me what I want to know."

Mario did not answer, but the silence did not return; the wailing of approaching sirens pushed the liquid back.

"Lucky shit." Angel shot Mario in the head and turned to the others. "I am Angel Jesus Ramos Ortega and no one betrays me, or the Ejercito del Norte, *NO ONE!*"

The gang responded with barrio cheers and catcalls.

"¡Vamonos!" Angel gave the order for tactical withdrawal and his soldiers gratefully melted into the sharp-edged shadows of Los Angeles in the evening, mindful of the lesson they had just learned.

Angel Ortega had never heard of the Y2K problem and couldn't have cared less.

*   *   *

In northwestern Colorado, between the towns of Craig and Rifle, hid the Dollar Ranch. It occupied all of a startlingly green valley—now covered with snow—about two miles long and a quarter mile wide. The ranch also encompassed the surrounding rocky hills and several thousand acres of arid land, sparsely dotted with sagebrush and juniper trees.

Merlyn T'bawa loved the Rocky Mountains. His pride in his ranch showed on his craggy sun-baked face, as he sat on his horse contemplating his valley. The sun was fierce this high up, but it was no match for the sharp cold winter air. Even behind his sunglasses, the raw wind made his eyes water as he viewed the fresh blanket of diamonds the previous night's snowstorm had left on his land. He and his partner, Anna Wu, had built up the Dollar Ranch from little more than dust, dried bones, and a seasonal stream. It now prospered and he was well pleased.

But that prosperity was not to be counted in heads of cattle. The Dollar Ranch's value lay in its strategic location and in its natural and man-made features that made it easily defensible. It was a number of these features Merlyn had in mind as he surveyed the land, thinking of ways to improve upon it.

He wished that Anna were with him so he could talk his ideas over, but she'd insisted that time was short and she still had much to do before the fire-control software she was working on would be ready. She was right, of course. The year 2000 could not be delayed or rescheduled, but he still wished she were with him. He never tired of her company—never had since she had rescued him from being in the wrong place, Tienamen Square, at the wrong

time. Exactly where she'd come from, and why she'd risked her life
to save a foreigner who had taken forbidden pictures, was something that she alone would ever know.

Hmmm... An outer perimeter fence would attract too much
attention, he decided. If he built it at the base of the hills surrounding the valley, it could easily be overrun by anyone driving a
4x4, let alone military equipment. If he built it along the top of
the valley rim, it would be visible against the sky and give away
their location. What was needed were hidden defensive emplacements that could cover overlapping fields of fire all the way around
the valley. Machine guns? Lasers? No. Not lasers—too many problems trying to make them lethal. And they'd take too much power,
anyway. Besides, machine guns would be easier to keep working in
hard times.

Merlyn urged his horse forward and turned the question over
in his mind as he rode back toward the ranch buildings. He dismounted at the fence bordering the pasture surrounding the main
house and opened the gate. The horse stepped through on its own
and Merlyn closed the gate behind them. In the spring, the field
would blossom with many wildflowers, providing a beautiful and
fragrant setting for the house. Now, and during any season, it also
provided a clear field of fire against unwanted guests.

When Merlyn entered the house through the kitchen door,
Goya Siqueiros was cooking up a batch of something that smelled
too good to ignore. "¿Que es?"

"Enchiladas Suisas," she answered and shooed him away from
the oven. "¡No estan listas! You go. Wash up. Talk-talk to you
machine. I call when ready!"

Merlyn complied. He teased her occasionally by snatching
morsels of her aromatic creations before they were ready, but he
never made her truly angry on purpose. He had found her on a
ventilation grate, slowly freezing to death on a Denver street a few
years back. Taking in homeless people who were willing to work
was something he'd ended up doing without ever intending to
make a habit of it, though he tried to be very careful about who he

let stay on the ranch. Goya had turned out to be an outstanding cook, and to have experience valuable to a mountain ranch—she had run away from a village high in the Andes, somewhere deep in Peru.

Tromping up the stairs, he found Anna waiting for him in their "study." The room did have several floor-to-ceiling bookcases, but was dominated by two state of the art computer work-stations and more closely resembled a computer store than a study.

Anna's hair was darker than Merlyn's longer-than-stylish afro, in a silky sort of way. He bent to kiss her, where her locks parted in the middle, but she tilted her head backward and took the kiss on her forehead, right between her distinctly Oriental eyes. "You need to work on your stealth, Beloved," she mock-scolded him, "I could hear you stomping around before you even got in the kitchen!"

"I don't think so!" He took a step back in mock fear. "I know how dangerous you are!"

"Oh... You know I didn't mean to kill him!" She was referring to one of the homeless people Merlyn had given shelter to a year earlier. The man had attacked Anna when they had been alone, mistaking her slender build for weakness. In all the time Merlyn had been helping homeless people, that individual had been the only one to cause any serious trouble. Nevertheless, the Dollar Ranch didn't take in homeless people anymore; they were approaching times when tighter security would be necessary. Anna's tone softened with genuine regret. "He didn't give me enough time to hurt him more carefully."

"My sweet love, I didn't mean to tease you about that. Your mind is certainly a more dangerous weapon than your physical skills. Besides, you know he wouldn't have given you the same consideration."

They held each other silently for a while.

"You'd better check your e-mail. There's been a lot of activity today—seems that people have picked up on the FAA's quiet admission that a lot of their computers aren't going to work after 1999. Unless they get more money, of course. I think it may prompt some of our fence-sitters to make up their minds. It could bring in the rest of the money we need for our defense perimeter."

"Okay, but not until I get another kiss."

She smiled and granted him his wish. Not really satisfied, but well contented, he sat at his computer and clicked the "check mail" button. He could never get enough of Anna!

CHAPTER 2:
MONDAY, FEBRUARY 2, 1998

"Look in—to the eye of the storm
Look out—for the force without form."
—Rush, *Force Ten*

Michel Gerard paced in his office, occasionally stopping to eye his computer and think about the implications of his recent experience with it. The machine was faster now, as promised, but different in another way he couldn't quite put his finger on. Grace told him he was being silly, but he swore the thing *smelled* different!

He needed to talk to someone about this Millennium Bug thing. Making up his mind, he sat at his desk and hit one of the speed-dial buttons on his phone. "Max? Michel here!"

"Bonjour Monsieur Gerard." The cheerful tone of the voice on the line belied the formality of the greeting. "To what do I owe the pleasure, you old scoundrel?"

Michel chuckled. "Is zat any way to address ze man who has taken your already substantial assets, my dear Max, and made zem even greater?"

"Oh, don't play hurt. So what is it? A new joke?"

"Well, I did 'ear a good one on ze ferry ze ozer day."

Max didn't bother asking what it was—he knew he was going to hear it whether he wanted to or not.

"So, why did ze man stop at a radiator shop instead of a gas station to go to ze basroom?"

Max let out an exaggerated sigh. "I don't know Michel, why did he?"

"Because it was ze best place around to take a leak!"

Max obliged his friend with a loud groan. "Now I know you're up to something. That joke was too bad to be the reason you called, so what's up?"

"Oh, I 'ave been sinking about ze future." Michel hesitated, a little embarrassed to bring up the real reason he'd called. But he wasn't going to find a better source of information who would also understand his interest and reasons for asking, so he forged ahead. "Max, what do you know about ze Y2K problem?"

Max whistled. "I know that you will be doing a lot of diversification of my portfolio, including the purchase of precious metals, before mid-1999. Why do you ask?"

"Eh, you might not want to wait zat long on ze precious metals, but, well, you more or less put your finger on it. What is likely to 'appen has profound implications for how I advise my clients. I am not sure I understand all ze ways zis Y2K sing will affect businesses and ze economy, so I want to know what you sink will 'appen, yes?"

"Why ask me? You're the advisor!"

Michel didn't answer.

"Okay, okay. You know the markets like nobody else, but we both know you're not a computer genius. I'll tell you what: nobody really knows what will happen, but it's pretty scary to think about."

"What are ze worst and best case scenarios?"

"Even that could be hard to peg. I've read estimates that say that if the current pace of fixing things holds, some 600 billion dollars in international trade would come to an immediate standstill on New Year's Eve, 1999. But it gets worse. Everyone who gets a government check—welfare recipients, retirees, government employees, soldiers, *everyone*—stops getting paid. What happens when they get hungry? They can't even borrow money if the banks are all shut down. There are some folks predicting the biggest bank run in history, but even that assumes the banks have any idea how much money their depositors have. There could be food riots in the streets by February or March of 2000. Very few people live off the land any more, Michel. What happens to them when commerce comes to an abrupt halt?"

Max paused to let his friend think about the question. "The worst case scenario is that this thing could send us back to a new dark age."

Michel started to protest, but Max rushed on. "Mind you, I don't think that will happen, but you asked what the worst case scenario might be. Many companies are working on fixing their non-Y2K-compliant systems and replacing those they can't fix. I think there will be a lot of stuff that stops working on the morning of January 1, 2000, but most businesses will keep going. What makes it hard to say for sure is that even if a business might get all its systems Y2K-compliant, some of its critical suppliers might not, or the suppliers' critical suppliers, and they're in trouble."

Michel could hear Max's chair creak as the man leaned his considerable weight back and thought more about what he was saying. "Anyway, to try to look at the bright side, let's assume that the business world basically marches on without stumbling too seriously. The big question then becomes: how prepared can the government get?"

Another pause. More creaking. "Unfortunately, they don't even know where all of their Y2K problems are, and the people who can fix them are getting snapped up. There's not enough time to train new people, so, even if they do figure out everything that needs to be fixed, there won't be anyone left to do the fixing! Still, for a best case scenario, let's assume they get in a panic early next year and start hiring whatever help they can find, at whatever price is demanded. I think it'd be pretty safe to say that the military will do everything possible to make sure all the really, really important stuff gets fixed—I mean, nukes won't start going off, or anything like that..."

"What!" Michel had never imagined that a computer 'bug' could be quite that dangerous.

"I said I didn't think they'd let any of those systems have any critical malfunctions."

"But... It is possible?"

"Anything's possible, Michel."

An uncomfortable silence descended.

"On the civilian side," Max continued, "they'll probably place the highest importance on keeping the IRS running, though how they'll pull that off, I don't know. Remember a few years ago when they had to scrap the new computer system they'd spent hundreds of millions on?"

"Yes! Zey 'ave spent billions over ze last sree decades and 'ave not been able to upgrade. Zey will never be able to beat ze Y2K deadline!"

"Right. They've shown that they simply don't know how to upgrade, but let's assume they do, if only because—as hard as it is to imagine the government fixing something on time—it's even harder to imagine them letting their money supply dry up."

"Zey could do like sird world countries and print more paper money to pay for sings."

"The automated printing presses the Department of Treasury uses are exactly the kind of old dinosaur systems that will be hardest to fix. For heavy manufacturing stuff like that, the companies that made the equipment are often no longer in existence or are completely retooled for a newer line of products, so there isn't any way to get a new control unit that's Y2K-compliant. And buying a new system, if they can afford it, can be just as big a headache."

"Oh."

Max drummed his fingers on his desk. "They'll come up with something, but I'm really not sure what'll get fixed and what won't. They might try going back to paper on some systems—there may even be some folks still around who remember how things were done before computers—but government programs weren't that big then."

"Zat was before Lyndon Johnson's Great Society programs, yes?"

"Right. And the computers track everything—even print the checks! I have a hard time seeing how they'll manage if they can't get the computers to print the checks. They'd have to hire thousands and thousands of clerks, and thousands of people to check up on 'em! I suppose they could try setting the date back the night before midnight, but then they'd end up with all kinds of problems with people getting paid too much, or not enough... I suppose they could try direct depositing money, but that assumes that the computers that keep track of payments are working, and that all the recipients' banks systems are working—not to mention the recipients that don't have bank accounts!"

"So, wait... Are you telling me zat ze best case scenario is still chaos?"

"No. Well, yes. But there's chaos and there's chaos. I guess I could say that, in the best case scenario, we'll have a severe recession."

"Zat is ze best case?"

"It can't be any better than that. Businesses would be mostly okay, but the government would have to, say, double its payroll—or even triple it—in order to do what it is committed to doing. That will either set off high inflation or an unprecedented devaluation, depending on what they do about it. Spending will skyrocket, no matter how they do it. One thing is absolutely for certain: it's going to be a huge tax on the economy. And that will, at the very least, kick off a recession."

"Okay, I can see zat."

"But I'd say that was pretty unlikely. I think it's more probable that we'll be looking at a depression, maybe even a depression to make the 'great' one look like a slow day at the mall."

Michel was silent for some time. He didn't want to believe his friend, but as far as he could tell, there was nothing obviously wrong with his analysis. Finally, he asked, "What about overseas banking? I could 'ave my clients spread zeir assets across many systems and jurisdictions."

"That's probably a good idea, but it doesn't look like any countries are doing particularly well at preparing for the year 2000. Even the most backward country in the world, one with negligible reliance on computers, will be hurt bad if its trading partners are hurt by the Y2K bug. And what good is money overseas, if you can't get to it?"

"Can you recommend to me some reading on ze subject? I had no idea how urgent zis will become, and so soon! As more people realize what is about to 'appen, I will need to be able to advise zem—well in advance of actual changes. I am ashamed to admit zat I should 'ave been sinking about zis years ago!"

"Don't be too hard on yourself, Michel. Think about how the bankers and bureaucrats in charge of the failing systems must feel about their foresight! Anyway, no sweat. I'll fax you a few things I have around here, and e-mail you some web addresses to look up. I'll even lend you my copy of Yourdon and Yourdon's *Time Bomb 2000*."

"Sanks. Want to get togezer over dinner and discuss your port-folio?"

"Be glad to! I'll bring the book. Will you bring Natalie along?"

"Not unless you promise not to slobber all over her zis time!"

They laughed and made the arrangements before hanging up.

Michel Gerard ignored the fax machine and didn't check his e-mail for hours. Instead, he sat looking out of his window, think-ing about what to tell his customers—and how. It was clear that many would simply refuse to listen to such doomsdayish talk, but others would. He'd need to have different recommended strategies for different kinds of clients, but all of them would have to have an eye toward commodities.

Commodities.

Such a strange word: commodities. What commodities would have the greatest value after the Y2K problem had done its worst?

An image of guns, gold, and dried food came to his mind, but he pushed it away. Surely it wouldn't get that bad...

CHAPTER 3:
MONDAY, MARCH 9, 1998

"I've seen the world through a bitter stare
But my dream is still alive
I'm going to be the best I can."
—Queensrÿche, *Best I Can*

Prudence never picked up hitch-hikers, but this was different. The girl on the side of the road was practically wearing a sign saying, "Please rape me!" She couldn't have been there long and certainly wouldn't last there long.

It was a nice day for March, but the girl's skimpy clothes were really too light for the weather. She had dirty blonde hair that might actually be natural and emerald green eyes. At a guess, Prudence would have said she was about eighteen. The dancer pulled up, a few yards beyond where the girl was standing. If it had been a boy, or even an older woman, Prudence would not have bothered. But after her recent loss, she just couldn't leave such an obvious innocent to the lions.

The girl trotted up to the passenger side of the Saturn and waited. Prudence hesitated, pushed her doubts aside, and pressed the button that lowered the window. "Where're you going?"

"Li'l Rock."

"You're in luck! Get in!" Prudence unlocked the doors.

The girl had a small suitcase, the kind you can roll onto an airplane, and a backpack. She opened the back door and tossed her bags in, then slammed it harder than it needed to be shut and wrenched open the front door. She slumped heavily into the passenger seat.

There was a silence in which the only noise was the whirring of the passenger side window, rising to close out the not quite warm air.

Deciding that it would be better to let the girl speak when she was ready to, Prudence put the car in gear and eased back onto the road. She tried to smile reassuringly while looking unconcerned and respectful of privacy, all at once.

It didn't take long.

"Mah name's Trish. Thainks." Her voice was clear and strong, but tired. She pronounced her name as though it had two syllables: 'Tree-ish.'

"Prudence. You're welcome." Prudence waited a while and then decided Trish could handle a little prodding. "So, where are you really going?"

Trish froze. "How'd you know Ah'm not goin' to Li'l Rock?"

Prudence grinned, partly because of the way Trish pronounced 'you' more like 'yew' and partly because of her naiveté. "Let's just say that you don't look like you've been on the road long, but you do look like you want to go someplace far, far away, so it can't be Little Rock."

"You're right. Ah wanna go as far west as you'll take me."

"Well, you're still in luck. I'm going to Vegas, so I can take you most of the way."

"Vegas! Ah thoughta goin' there, but Ah thought somewheres in California would be bettah... But how did you know?"

"How did I know that you're trying to leave some kind of problem far behind you? Kid, you're dressed like a girl who's just decided to become a hooker and is trolling for her first trick. You couldn't have been there long. And you're all packed up, so you sure weren't going to Grandma's house to take her milk and cookies! You were definitely running from trouble." Prudence laughed. It was an abrupt hacking sound, devoid of humor. "Hell, maybe it was obvious to me because I'm in the same boat!"

"You?"

Prudence nodded, but didn't elaborate. She'd lost her job at the club, after...after the incident...because the police kept coming around to harass her. The club owners had told her that it was bad for business to have cops showing up all the time. Besides, she didn't really have her heart in the act after losing her partner.

"Well, thanks all over again, Prudence. Ah've got some money and Ah ken help pay for gas."

"Keep your money ki—Trish, you're gonna need it. You really are in luck. I'm going your way anyway and you won't cost me much more than I was already going to spend. And besides, it feels good to save someone from being raped."

Trish grew silent again, and they drove on for a quarter of an hour before Prudence noticed that Trish's eyes were brimming with tears. "Hey, are you okay?"

The girl wiped angrily at her eyes. "Do you really reckon Ah was in danger?"

"Dressed the way you are?" Prudence snorted. "I wouldn't think it'd be more than five minutes before some *man* came along and decided to make a meal out of you!"

Trish noted the way Prudence emphasized the word *man* as though it were the worst insult imaginable. It made her think of her own situation. "Ah... Ah was tryin' to git away from that. Ah'd only climbed over the fence and put out mah thumb a few minutes before you came along. And Ah... Well, Ah wasn't lookin' for trouble *ahead* of me."

"Shit! Is that what you're running from? Did some bastard—" Trish buried her face in her hands and Prudence cut off what she had been about to say. Pulling over onto the shoulder again, she slipped out of her seat belt, popped Trish's belt free, and did her best to console the whimpering girl in the confined space.

"Mah Daddy..." Trish tried to explain, but couldn't find the words for some time. "Mah Daddy, he..." The girl held on to her Prudence the way a drowning person grabs a life preserver, sobbing freely now. Her tears had dampened her hands and her whole body felt feverish. "Ah got used to it after a while, but lately he's been drinkin' more an' more. He started beatin' on me and...and Ah just couldn't take it no more."

"Shit," Prudence repeated, and rocked the girl against her chest. "It'll be all right," she whispered. "You're safe now. You can stay with me as long as you like."

Trish's shaking calmed and she probed Prudence with bleary eyes. "You're very kind," she snuffled, "but Ah ken take care of mahself."

"Sure you can!" Prudence sought to reassure her. "I wasn't proposing to take care of you. You're your own woman now! I'm thinking that life's easier with a roommate you can trust—a partner—but I wasn't even saying that; I only wanted you to know that you can stay with me as long as you want. You don't have to take your chances on some fucking *man*!"

"Thainks! Ah really don't have anywhere in particular to go."

"Well, there's good money to be made in Vegas, and you've got the looks!"

Trish blushed, but didn't demure. Prudence's remark about her looking like a hooker had been more true than she wanted to think about. "What d'you have in mind?"

"I'm not exactly sure myself, but I have some experience as a dancer, and I know we can make good money without having to spread our legs, if we play it smart."

"Ah'm listenin'!"

"Well... Remind me to tell you more about Kat sometime. For now, I'll just say that she was someone very special. She found me when I was lost—gave me my life back, really..."

Trish could see Prudence going back in her mind, pulling out dusty old memories she hadn't meant to ever look at again. Being let in, being so...*present*...to someone else's pain helped her to ignore her own—for the time being. She waited for Prudence to continue.

"I was a parasite, Trish; a leech swimming in filthy water, waiting for the next man to come along so I could suck his blood as long as he'd let me... No, I was worse than that. I was some low creature that hasn't even been named, something sick that crawls in the mud and lives by letting herself be exploited and discarded by others. I lived by letting men use me—letting them suck on *my* blood!"

No one had ever spoken to Trish in this way before. Prudence, a total stranger, was opening her heart to Trish and letting her see into its darkest corners. And in those shadowy places full of broken and wounded things, she saw herself.

"And then Kat came along. You'd never know how special she was by looking at her... She used to do the wildest things to her hair!" Prudence submerged herself in memories of Kat for a short while, unaware of the time passing. "But Kat was like that; more to her than met the eye. She got right down in the filth with me and took my face in her hands and turned it up until my eyes were looking into the sky, where the birds fly free. She was the first person who ever looked at me as more than a truck-stop slut. She told me I was never meant to wallow in the muck, but to soar with the birds. She believed in me, Trish... I don't know if I can explain it, but in that one moment, she changed the course of my life. Instead of living—if you want to call it that—by letting men use me, I decided to use men to get what I want."

To Trish, it was as though Prudence had poured a burning solvent on her soul, stripping away years of gunk that had accumulated on it. When she examined the shining thing revealed, she was amazed at what she found in herself; a free being—truly free! "*Ah understand!*" It was a revelation! *She could do whatever she wanted, make whatever she wanted of herself.*

In an instant, Trish changed from being a girl running from fear to being a young woman seeking a future she wanted to live in. Still gripped in a semi-religious ecstasy, an unexpected and sudden rebirth, Trish turned to Prudence and announced, "Ah want to fly with you!"

Prudence was momentarily taken aback. She had never opened up to anyone in that way, except Kat, and couldn't have explained what had made her do it, if anyone had asked. She had been talking because... Because it was the right thing to do. She had not expected such a strong reaction from Trish, not expected her to choose a new path right then and there. But she could see the earnest look in her eyes, and would not yank back the helping hand she had offered.

Neither of the two were aware of the impact their encounter would have on Prudence, but she too had changed course and—whether she realized it or not—would never be the same person again.

"We may have to fly up through some storm clouds," Prudence told Trish, "but I'm sure we can break through to the clear blue sky, if we try hard enough! Kat was going to stop dancing when she sold her first novel—I am going to stop when I've saved up enough money to go to college and get a degree. Would you like to do that with me?"

"Ah sure would! But...what happened to Kat? Did she sell her first novel? Ah'd like to meet her some day."

"You can't." Now it was Prudence who could not control her tears. "I... I can't talk about it now. I'll tell you later."

It was some time before the two could resume their journey westward.

CHAPTER 4

March 23, 1998
Tallahassee, Florida

Dear Elder Young,

I am writing to you because I don't personally know anyone else in the Church who has the standing you do and who would listen to what I have to say with as open a mind. I remember well from when you were my mission president in Japan the way you always had an open mind and a willingness to listen to people.

I've done some checking, and I know that the Church is aware of the so-called Y2K problem. However, recent personal experience has alarmed me a great deal about the situation, and I want to make sure the church is ready for what may lie ahead. My credit card company charged me about 20 million dollars because of a Y2K problem. The mistake was cleared up, but I've had to go through a great deal of trouble to ensure that my credit record was not permanently harmed. Imagine what headaches such problems could cause the Church, an organization hundreds of thousands of times more complex than my household!

As I said, I'm glad the Church is already working on the problem, but our efforts are all internal. I'm more concerned about the governments under whose jurisdictions we operate. Governments use more of the old vulnerable mainframe computers than anyone else. What happens if they fail to fix the problems before December 31, 1999?

I checked on a U.S. government World Wide Web site that reports on the federal government's progress preparing for the year 2000. I found that almost all agencies, with the possible exception of the Social Security Administration, are unlikely to be ready on time. This includes the Department of Defense and the Department of the Treasury. It is frightening when the U.S. government admits that they are not going to meet a deadline that cannot be moved and that there will be "unpredictable" failures.

I was also able to look into what state governments are doing. Utah seems to be working hard on the problem, but I cannot really tell from their web site whether or not they think they'll have everything critical fixed on time. Other states don't even seem to have started reviewing what their problems might be.

And then there are the overseas governments—it is hard to tell whether any of them are doing anything at all! The problems could be quite extreme in third world countries that own very old computer systems and have no means to repair or replace them.

I believe it is important for the Church to prepare for consequences that range from the possibility of needing to increase relief efforts beyond church members(in the case of breakdowns in the computerized government welfare system), to dealing with widespread chaos (if all the millions of people who depend on various governments for their livelihoods are suddenly cut off and things are not fixed before they start getting hungry).

Now, I realize that it may seem hard to believe that there could be riots in the streets in America in the year 2000. Indeed, I hesitate to bring it up, but it is a possibility—what else could all those people do if they were suddenly without means? The more frightening scenarios might not be very likely, but from the look of things, there *will* be disruptions of some kind and I think the Church should be prepared to step in and help.

I am not suggesting that the Church has the resources to stop or even significantly reduce the impact of whatever will happen in the year 2000, but I think we ought to be prepared to help out. What I suggest is that the Church appoint a committee of experts and formulate a set of contingency plans.

This way, whether the disruptions are mild or serious, the Church can protect its own interests and possibly extend a supporting hand to the communities in which we operate.

If we are prepared to support people in their time of need, it could be an unprecedented opportunity to share word of our Heavenly Father with people who might be more willing than ever to listen to Him in their hearts.

I pray it does not come to some of the more frightening possibilities I have read of in my research on this topic, but we should be prepared. I hope you will agree and will forward this suggestion on to the appropriate authorities within the Church. Please feel free to call me if you have any questions. You can also visit some of the web sites I've listed below for more information on the Y2K problem.

Thank you for your time and attention.

Sincerely,

Jared Christensen

Jared Christensen, MD

P.S. Did you see the <u>Business Week</u> article on Y2K entitled, "Zap! How the Year 2000 Bug Will Hurt the Economy"? It was in their March 2, 1998 issue and has some pretty

frightening things to say about possible
power outages.

Some relevant web sites (there are many
more):

1] http://ourworld.compuserve.com/homepages/
   roleigh_martin
2] http://www.yourdon.com/books/fallback/
   fallbackhome.html
3] http://www.webleyweb.com/y2k/y2k.html
4] http://www.yardeni.com/y2kbook.html
5] http://www.baproducts.com/y2knl.htm
6] http://www.y2ktimebomb.com/
7] http://www.euy2k.com

CHAPTER 5:
TUESDAY, APRIL 14, 1998

"Every day we're standing in a time capsule,
racing down a river from the past
Every day we're standing in a wind tunnel,
facing down the future coming fast."
—Rush, *Turn the Page*

"En garde!"

Alexis raised her epee and began probing Major Gishesky's defenses. She enjoyed fencing because it favored dexterity and skill over brute strength, an advantage she needed against most of her male opponents—and she wasn't about to restrict herself to competing with only women. She knew that she was no amazon, and not so young anymore either, but she'd take brains over brawn any time!

Precision shooting was also enjoyable, but that wasn't a way to get a good workout, which was her objective just then.

As with flying, both sports helped her to settle her thoughts. *Bzzzzt!*

She glanced down and groaned. She had stepped out of bounds—off the side of the mat—and Gishesky hadn't even attacked!

"Ground control to Major Tom! Can you hear me Major Tom?"

"Shut up and fight, Gishesky. I can whip your butt in my sleep!" Did he know that when she had been a major some of the other majors had nicknamed her 'Major Tom'? Probably not. How could he know?

"Yes, ma'am!"

"En garde!"

Shuffle, slide, lunge. *Bzzzzt!* "Hey!"

"Score one for the good guys. En garde!" Back at the center line, Alexis pressed her attack immediately, aggressively beating Gishesky's epee aside and charging inside his defenses. He was forced backward until he ran out of mat. *Bzzzzt!* "That's what you get for talking too much!"

"Geez! I mean: yes, ma'am!"

Attacking again without delay, she caught Gishesky right over the heart with the tip of her epee. *Bzzzzt!*

He was breathing hard now, when they faced off at the centerline again. Before raising his blade, he commented: "If I may say so, ma'am, you seem unusually savage today!"

"Thank you, Major, but compliments won't win you any slack." In her mind, Alexis knew he was right. What was it? Was it the disturbing lack of year 2000 preparedness in the military? Or that they were now admitting to it in public? Or was it the glee her superiors had shown over her last report on European Y2K measures?

Bzzzzt! Gishesky forced her off the mat again. She could feel sweat trickling down her own back now. Concentrate! She brought her mind to bear on her immediate problem.

Bzzzzt! Bzzzzt!

"Nice try, Gishesky. Next time, ask me what the hell is going on in my department and you might distract me enough to win!" They took off their gauntlets and shook hands.

"So, what is going on in your department?"

"It's classified." Besides, I don't want to talk right now, I want to get home—I've got a date! "But any time you want to talk choppers or let me fly that Cobra of yours again, just let me know!"

"You think I'm crazy? They aren't meant for that kind of stress, and neither am I!" They both laughed and then he realized the informality with which he had addressed a superior officer. Belatedly, he added, "Sir—I mean ma'am. I mean, I didn't mean..."

"Relax, Major. I know what you meant and what you didn't mean. And I do appreciate you letting me fly with you."

"Any time, ma'am!" He retreated while he could.

Alexis tisked sadly and headed for the shower. She was as rank-conscious as the major—it was a necessary survival trait—but she hated it that military people couldn't simply...talk to her, like normal people. And why was she thinking of an on-line appointment as a date? Does an encrypted computer chat with a rancher out west really count as a date?

Alexis, she told herself, you're a bit old to be trolling the internet for dates!

It really wouldn't hurt to actually spend some time with a flesh and blood man again... If she could find one who wasn't an idiot. And, actually, she was very young for a Lieutenant Colonel, only thirty-eight—for a few more days, at least!

She hadn't always been a recluse, but the world and the people in it had seemed friendlier when she was younger. Life knew how long it had been since she'd—

Never mind!

She stripped and entered a shower stall, turning the temperature of the pounding water up as high as she could take it. It didn't distract her long. Isn't it a bit weird to prefer the company of people you never meet, except as words on a screen?

The question was still on her mind an hour later, as she settled into her 'electronic nest' in her apartment. She sipped on some tea and checked her e-mail, while waiting for the time she and Merlyn had set. A message from him was the last thing in her in-box, having arrived after some work-related mail and some junk mail. She pulled it up and read:

> Hello Princess,
>
> This was floating around on the internet a few years ago and I thought I'd lost it. I just found it on an old floppy and I don't think you've seen it, so I'm

pasting it below. I hope a good laugh will help you relax after your long day.

Type at you soon!

M

————————8<————————————8<—————————

Attached is some correspondence that actually occurred between a London hotel's staff and one of its guests. The London hotel involved submitted this to the Sunday Times. No name was mentioned.

———————————————————————————

Dear Maid,

Please do not leave any more of those little bars of soap in my bathroom since I have brought my own bath-sized Dial. Please remove the six unopened little bars from the shelf under the medicine chest and another three in the shower soap dish. They are in my way. Thank you,

S. Berman

———————————————————————————

Dear Room 635,

I am not your regular maid. She will be back tomorrow, Thursday, from her day off. I took the 3 hotel soaps out of the shower soap dish as you requested. The 6 bars on your shelf I took out of your way and put on top of your Kleenex dispenser in case you should change your mind. This leaves only the 3 bars I left today as my instructions from the management are to leave 3 soaps daily. I hope this is satisfactory.

Kathy, Relief Maid

Dear Maid — I hope you are my regular maid.

Apparently Kathy did not tell you about my note to her concerning the little bars of soap. When I got back to my room this evening I found you had added 3 little Camays to the shelf under my medicine cabinet. I am going to be here in the hotel for two weeks and have brought my own bath-size Dial so I won't need those 6 little Camays that are on the shelf. They are in my way when shaving, brushing teeth, etc. Please remove them.

S. Berman

Dear Mr. Berman,

My day off was last Wed. So the relief maid left 3 hotel soaps as we are instructed by the management. I took the 6 soaps that were in your way on the shelf and put them in the soap dish where your Dial was. I put the Dial in the medicine cabinet for your convenience. I didn't remove the 3 complimentary soaps that are always placed inside the medicine cabinet for all new check-ins and which you did not object to when you checked in last Monday. Please let me know if I can be of further assistance.

Your regular maid, Dotty

Dear Mr. Berman,

The assistant manager, Mr. Kensedder, informed me this A.M. that you called him last evening and said you were unhappy with your maid service. I have assigned a new girl to your room. I hope you will accept my apologies for any past inconvenience. If you have any future complaints please contact me so I can give it my personal attention. Call extension 1108 between 8AM and 5PM. Thank you.

Elaine Carmen
Housekeeper

Dear Miss Carmen,

It is impossible to contact you by phone since I leave the hotel for business at 745 AM and don't get back before 530 or 6PM. That's the reason I called Mr. Kensedder last night. You were already off duty. I only asked Mr. Kensedder if he could do anything about those little bars of soap. The new maid you assigned me must have thought I was a new check-in today, since she left another 3 bars of hotel soap in my medicine cabinet along with her regular delivery of 3 bars on the bath-room shelf. In just 5 days here I have accumulated 24 little bars of soap. Why are you doing this to me?

S. Berman

Dear Mr. Berman,

Your maid, Kathy, has been instructed to stop delivering soap to your room and remove the extra

soaps. If I can be of further assistance, please call extension 1108 between 8AM and 5PM. Thank you,
Elaine Carmen,
Housekeeper

Dear Mr. Kensedder,
My bath-size Dial is missing. Every bar of soap was taken from my room including my own bath-size Dial. I came in late last night and had to call the bellhop to bring me 4 little Cashmere Bouquets.
S. Berman

Dear Mr. Berman,
I have informed our housekeeper, Elaine Carmen, of your soap problem. I cannot understand why there was no soap in your room since our maids are instructed to leave 3 bars of soap each time they service a room. The situation will be rectified immediately. Please accept my apologies for the inconvenience.
Martin L. Kensedder, Assistant Manager

Dear Mrs. Carmen,
Who the hell left 54 little bars of Camay in my room? I came in last night and found 54 little bars of soap. I don't want 54 little bars of Camay. I want my one damn bar of bath-size Dial. Do you realize I have 54 bars of soap in here? All I want is my bath size Dial. Please give me back my bath-size Dial.

S. Berman

Dear Mr. Berman,
   You complained of too much soap in your room
so I had them removed. Then you complained to
Mr. Kensedder that all your soap was missing so I
personally returned them. The 24 Camays that had
been taken and the 3 Camays you are supposed to
receive daily (sic). I don't know anything about the
4 Cashmere Bouquets. Obviously your maid, Kathy,
did not know I had returned your soaps so she also
brought 24 Camays plus the 3 daily Camays. I don't
know where you got the idea this hotel issues bath-
size Dial. I was able to locate some bath-size Ivory
which I left in your room.
   Elaine Carmen
   Housekeeper

Dear Mrs. Carmen,
   Just a short note to bring you up-to-date on my
latest soap inventory. As of today I possess:

— On shelf under medicine cabinet - 18 Camay in 4
   stacks of 4 and 1 stack of 2.
— On Kleenex dispenser - 11 Camay in 2 stacks of
   4 and 1 stack of 3.
— On bedroom dresser - 1 stack of 3 Cashmere
   Bouquet, 1 stack of 4 hotel-size Ivory, and 8
   Camay in 2 stacks of 4.
— Inside medicine cabinet - 14 Camay in 3 stacks
   of 4 and 1 stack of 2.

— In shower soap dish - 6 Camay, very moist.
— On northeast corner of tub - 1 Cashmere Bou-
    quet, slightly used.
— On northwest corner of tub - 6 Camays in 2
    stacks of 3.

Please ask Kathy when she services my room
to make sure the stacks are neatly piled and
dusted. Also, please advise her that stacks of more
than 4 have a tendency to tip. May I suggest that
my bedroom window sill is not in use and will make
an excellent spot for future soap deliveries. One
more item, I have purchased another bar of bath-
sized Dial which I am keeping in the hotel vault in
order to avoid further misunderstandings.
    S. Berman

Alexis was chuckling out loud by the time she got to the third
note in the soap saga. She was laughing by the time she got to the
sixth. By the tenth note she was laughing so hard she couldn't
wipe the tears away fast enough. It was actually hard to read the
eleventh one, and she had to take a break before reading the final
note.

Life, it was great to have friends like Merlyn! With one simple
message, a joke or a poem, he could make a great day out of one
that had been tedious up to that point.

Alexis blew her nose and dabbed at her still-damp eyes. It was
time to activate the privacy software she had written to carry on
electronic 'chat' sessions in private.

She entered the commands, and then typed: **Hello Merlyn!**

Her screen showed an immediate response: *Hello, my Warrior Princess!*

Alexis smiled. It wasn't merely a matter of words on a screen;
somewhere, there was a man with a warm and humorous personal-
ity that she really enjoyed 'talking' to. When she was 'with' Merlyn,

the keys were warmer under her fingertips. So what if she didn't get to see him? He still touched her inside, where it mattered most, and made her feel warm and happy. And she thought she had the same effect on him, too.

Break any laws today?

If I did, do you think I'd tell a government goon like you?

She laughed, and typed back:

Hey, we ought to get hooked up with one of those internet telephone applications, one of the encrypted ones. I've got a lot on my mind I'd like to talk to you about, but I'd wear my fingers out typing it all.

I'm already set up. All you have to do is download the software and we can talk. :-)

I don't have a computer microphone. :(

You don't need one—don't need anything fancy, at least. If you have a microphone you use with a cassette recorder you can use that.

I think I might have one of those.

Great. Why not download the software and we'll hook up again in, say, a half-hour?

Okay!

Merlyn recommended a web site where Alexis could get the software and they logged off, Alexis feeling a vague uncertainty. After all they had shared, it didn't make sense to get all jittery like a teenager on a first date, but what if she didn't like the pitch of his voice? What if it was different actually talking to him, like normal people on the phone? Oh, well; too late to back out now!

She set her computer to download the software and dashed off to search her closet for the microphone.

This was going to change the nature of their friendship.

CHAPTER 6:
FRIDAY, MAY 22, 1998

"You're joking, You're joking!
I can't believe my eyes
You're joking me, you gotta be!"
—*Nightmare Before Christmas* soundtrack,
Oogie Boogie's Song

"No! Max, zis cannot be true. You are calling to pull my leg, yes?"

"Michel, I swear it's true—I just heard the president announce it. They've created a new layer of bureaucracy designed to help prevent the things I'm saying the Millennium Bug could cause, and it's called Critical Infrastructure Assurance Office."

"But Max, even *this* president must know that 'ciao' means 'good-bye' in Italian! Did no one in the White House see the irony?"

"He delivered it with a straight face, Michel. I honestly don't think any of them have a clue."

Michel laughed. "Zis will not inspire confidence."

Max chuckled as well. "No, I don't think it will. The internet is already buzzing with jokes about the appropriateness of the name."

"Speaking of which, I got a good joke today in my e-mail. Zere were sree socialists stranded on a desert island, and—"

"I've already heard it, Michel, and it wasn't that funny. Why do you hate socialists so much anyway? Personally, I just kinda feel sorry for them."

"Zey are ruining my country. Why should I not despise them?"

"Well... I guess I could say the same thing about America, but

I don't take these things personally. Anyway, I don't want to get into another debate on politics, I just wanted to tell you the news. Talk to you later, okay?"

"Okay. And thanks for sharing zis joke wis me!"

"You're welcome. Bye."

"Bye, Max."

CHAPTER 7:
WEDNESDAY, JUNE 17, 1998

"Eastside meets Westside downtown
No time the walls fall down
Can't you feel it coming?
EMPIRE!"
—Queensrÿche, *Empire*

Angel and his counterpart from the Golden Dragons left their guns outside the meeting room, as did their lieutenants. Cabron was loath to part with his weapon, but subsided at a warning glance from Angel—a vicious dog that had to obey its master, but did so reluctantly. As agreed, an equal number of Ejercito del Norte and Golden Dragon gang members stood watch over their leaders' weapons, as well as the meeting place itself—another abandoned factory.

Angel offered his hand to the Asian gang leader. The latter took it confidently, but his palms were sweaty and Angel could feel it. The Latino grinned broadly, sensing that his opponent knew he had the advantage, and the two sat at a folding table that had been brought for the meeting.

"Chang, I won't waste your time with small talk." Angel assumed the initiative and started the conversation in English, the language the two gangs had in common. He was much more articulate than Chang had expected, and that too was an advantage he pressed. "We took out Black Thunder and we took over their turf. Now, I know some of it may look unguarded, but you're moving in on *us* now."

Chang gave the appearance of being completely at ease, but he hesitated before answering. He knew that Ejercito had grown by more than half since smashing Black Thunder, making them bigger than the Dragons. "An-hel, how can I move in on you if you're not there?" Being third generation Chinese-American, Chang spoke without an accent and even tried to use the proper Spanish pronunciation of 'Angel,' but it did not seem to impress the Latino. He licked his lips nervously. "We're only moving into the area next to our own, which—as you say—looks unused anyway."

Angel held up a placating hand. "We are using it, but I have an idea. Fighting won't help either of us; it's too expensive. We've never had anything against the Dragons, and now that the idiots who ran Black Thunder and attacked our turf—and yours—are out of the way, I think we could make a lot of money if we joined forces." Rather than elaborate, he fell silent and allowed the idea to sink in. After a few seconds, he added, "Ejercito Dragon, or Dragon Army, would then be the biggest gang in southern California."

Chang was clearly taken off guard, but also clearly relieved. He noted again that Angel spoke much better English than the typical Chicano street kid, and wondered where the well-known high school drop-out had come by his education. This idea—joining forces—went against the way of things among gangs, and he wasn't particularly fond of Hispanics in general, but the potential for profit was enormous. He made his mind up quickly, but he made a show of thinking it over. "That will probably scare some of the smaller gangs around us into joining as well. Without the *expense* of fighting between us, we'll get a lot more out of our businesses. It would only be the police we'd have to worry about, and they've never really been able to stop us anyway..."

The deal went down more easily than Angel had expected. Chang had been much more worried about a gang war than he had been, and that had put him in a weaker bargaining position. No wonder, Angel thought with pride, he would have beaten—possibly even destroyed—the Golden Dragons. Instead, Chang had found himself offered a deal that would make him a rich man. It might even be possible, after a few more consolidations, to completely dominate the entire L.A. markets on street dealing in drugs, fake IDs, and other lines of business both gangs were into. Asians always did have more sense for business than guts for a real fight anyway!

"Equal partners, right?" Chang held out his hand, now cool and dry.

"Of course." Angel shook on it and the two stood.

They both knew that Angel would carry more weight, as he had more men. Chang worried about it, but thought that there would be time to deal with the problem, perhaps through additional deals made with newer members of the coalition.

For his part, Angel could now see that the time would not be too far off when he would have the strength and resources to strike at his real enemies.

Chapter 8:
Sunday, September 13, 1998

"I believe there comes a time
When everything just falls in line
We live and learn from our mistakes."
—Pat Benatar, *All Fired Up*

The Dollar Ranch was preparing for guests. Merlyn and Anna were very busy, even though most of their guests were not to arrive until late in 1999—because they were getting ready for friends that would be staying for a *long* time. They were not merely cleaning the guest bathroom and turning down the sheets; they were drilling wells and building barns.

The fifteen wells had been finished the week before and the barns were now going up, one near each well. Each of the fifteen lots on which the structures were being built was spaced evenly around the circumference of an oval that covered perhaps one half of the little valley at the center of the ranch.

To any neighbors who happened to see them built or to look inside, the barns would have seemed rather peculiar. Each had heavily insulated walls, a chimney that could be connected to a wood stove, its own well right beside it, and wiring that ran back to the main house's Allied Signal 500 kilowatt turbo-generator.

None of the barns had stalls for animals, nor bales of hay. Instead, as they were completed, they were filled with construction materials: cement, lumber, pipes, wiring, nails, screws, conduit piping, electrical switches and circuit boxes, prefabricated triple pane windows, prefabricated doors, shingles, sheet rock, joint compound, paint...and many prepared logs. Each assortment was a complete set of materials needed to build a respectable rustic 'log-style' ranch house with three to six bedrooms. Enough room was left in the barns that a family could 'camp' among the building supplies comfortably, in both winter and summer.

Half of the barns had already been sold, including contents and the 40-acre wedges of land on which they were built, each radiating out from the central oval. These had been bought by 'investors,' all good friends of either Merlyn or Anna, who wanted someplace safe to be during the troubling times they were sure would come with the year 2000. The reason for the barns was to avoid letting the county authorities—especially the tax authorities—know that the Dollar Ranch was, in essence, being subdivided. If their worst fears came to pass, there wouldn't be any county authorities to worry about when the time for building houses came around.

Anna was riding with Merlyn this day. The air was cool, dry, and calm. The sun warmed the two as they rode. They were traveling the elliptical road Merlyn had cleared with a bulldozer along the common area between the future home-sites. Anna brought her horse to a stop where she could see the construction crew working on one of the last barns. From the varying ages and genders of the crew members, it was obviously a family working together. Their lean and tanned bodies gleamed in the sun. "It's a good thing Dreamer was willing to come out early and help with the building. These barns will be useful, even after the real houses are built."

Alone with Merlyn, Anna was much more talkative than when others were around. It wasn't that she didn't trust her friends, nor that she lacked confidence as a public speaker. She had a deeply-set emotional aversion to gregariousness that stemmed from her childhood in Tibet, and whatever traumatic horror the Chinese government had wrought upon her village. She never spoke of it, even to Merlyn, but he had come to understand that she was the only one to make it out alive—and that she had been forced to do unspeakable things in order to do so.

Merlyn laughed. "Some of them might even be used as barns!" He tipped his cowboy hat at the working family and nudged his horse back into a slow walk along the road. In spite of her past, Anna was an essentially joyful person, in love with life. When they were alone, that side of her came out, like the sun from behind the clouds. It was too bad not many people got to see it. Merlyn pointed, "Look, there's Jimmy!"

It's difficult to get a bulldozer to skid around a corner, but Dreamer's oldest daughter—a willowy platinum blonde of seventeen—was doing her best to try. She appeared from behind the barn the rest of her family was working on and turned to follow the property line between its land and the land that would go with the next barn. She was leveling a road that would start at the oval driveway and continue all the way up to the valley's rim. She laughed and waved when she noticed Merlyn and Anna.

The two waved back, Anna with a bemused expression. "I can understand her tom-boyishness—she's been given a lot of responsibility and had it pretty tough since her mother passed away—but why does she call herself Jimmy?"

Merlyn shrugged. "Who knows? She's a teenager! But I'm not complaining; she works as hard as Dreamer does and it's fun to have her around the house." He laughed again. "I don't know which I enjoy more, Dreamer's children, or the library he brought—I don't think the Vanderbilt House has so many books!" Grinning, he urged his horse to pick up a little more speed. "It was a great deal on both ends. Dreamer and his family get 40 acres of land and a nicer house than the one they left in West Virginia. We, and our investors, get free labor and the building know-how to build 15 houses and associated structures. It saved us all a bunch of money, and brought some of our friends out here sooner than we might have otherwise had the pleasure."

Anna agreed. "It's interesting that Dreamer turned out to have exactly the kind of knowledge and experience we needed—an amaz-

ing coincidence that he was looking for a new job when we needed
a contractor who could keep his mouth shut."

"Not nearly as amazing as you are!" Merlyn was rewarded with
a look that, while not extravagant, had the same effect as a blown
kiss. "Really, how many friends do we have in cyberspace? Thousands of people know us, hundreds are friends, and maybe fifty
individuals and families are close enough that we've met in realspace.
There's probably expertise in everything we need out there on the
Net, if we ask for it. It's knowing who we can trust that's the trick,
and getting to know people through the ideas they express in
cyberspace before meeting them is a big help in finding ones we
can trust."

"You're right, of course," Anna smiled. "I know it as well as
you, but seeing it come together here on our ranch
is...uplifting...exciting." She spurred her horse into a trot and
Merlyn matched her. "I remember feeling a little uncomfortable
last year when Dreamer came west to camp with us at Flaming
Gorge and wouldn't tell us his real name. We've known him as
'Dreamer' on the Net, but I assumed he'd share his real name—
his realspace name, as you call it—with us when we met in the real
world. I was unsure of how things would work out." She sighed as
she scanned the little valley and all the work Dreamer and his
family had wrought. "He's been a great help. I'm really glad it's
working out—I don't know how we would be managing without
someone with his skills... And I do trust him. If he wants to be
known only as Dreamer, I won't be the one to tell him he can't
be."

"Yep."

They rode back toward the main house in silence. At the gate,
Anna turned to look over the ranch wistfully. "It's too bad I can't
get my family to come live with us out here." She was referring to
the Chinese family that had taken her in after her natural family
had been murdered.

"You can lead a horse to water, but you can't make him drink.

Have you made sure they understand what kind of water it is we're offering?"

"You know how Father is." Anna usually spoke of members of her adoptive family as though she had never had any others. "He doesn't see why we need computers at all when we have abacuses. He wouldn't believe that something as silly as a date in a computer could cause any serious harm, let alone send the country into chaos."

"You can only lay the possibility before him. If he will not accept it—or our invitation—there is nothing more you can do."

"I know, and I have tried to make the different possibilities clear to him. He simply doesn't want to see them. I've accepted that, but I still worry. They live on the Florida panhandle: retiree heaven. When those folks haven't received a government check for a few months and start getting really hungry, it could get very ugly there. It won't be safe."

"I know. And it'd be a real shame if something happened to them, especially after all the work we did getting them out of China." They had arrived at the stables and Merlyn leaned over to kiss Anna before dismounting. "You know that even though I'm not all that close to my family, I have many dear friends who won't even consider the possibility that the bureaucrats might not be able to beat this deadline. Or they imagine that the serious problems can be avoided by simply turning the clocks back. They have no idea of what is about to happen, and don't want to know. What can I say to them? They don't believe me about the coming storm, and I wouldn't force them to come weather it with us if I could."

After tending to their horses, they made a circuit of the main house. The new wing was about halfway built. It would be mostly single room apartments, but a larger meeting room was also being made out of the existing dining room. In spite of how few of their loved ones took their fears seriously, Merlyn and Anna hoped that many of them would come to the Dollar Ranch before it was too late. Done with their daily tour, the partners entered the house through the kitchen, greeted Goya, and headed up the stairs.

For her part, Goya didn't care about convincing anyone of

anything. She didn't care about anyone else in the world, except Merlyn and Anna. But she was a good sport and put up with the sawdust and other growing pains with only good-natured grumbling.

On their way up to the study, Merlyn and Anna came to the same conclusion they always did on the subject, and both spoke the same thought at once: "I hope everyone gets here on time!"

To which Merlyn added: "I'd bet you money that *something* will happen that scares a lot of people. There *will* be warning signs, and the smart ones will pay attention. Those are the ones who will make better neighbors, anyway."

CHAPTER 9:
TUESDAY, OCTOBER 27, 1998

"And another one gone,
and another one gone,
Another one bites the dust!"
—Queen, *Another One Bites the Dust*

Chang, who never showed much emotion on purpose, had the distinct shadow of a smile on his face as he drove home. It was rainy and cold—an utterly miserable night. But the latest financial reports he'd received from his lieutenants on the profits Ejercito Dragon was making were good enough to make any weather seem fine. The icy drumbeat that rattled on the roof of his Ferrari was drowned out by the loud music playing on the car's stereo.

It bothered him how quickly the increased profits were creating new loyalties among his men for the larger organization over their original gang. It was clearly dangerous that all the new arrivals were swearing loyalty to Angel. Chang now had few truly loyal men left to him.

He pushed the thought from his mind and concentrated on the road. It was winding up into the Chino Hills—fortunately, there was little traffic.

How to strengthen his position within Ejercito Dragon? If things kept up they way they were going, Angel would end up with undisputed dominion over an organization with more than three times as many members as there were police officers in Los Angeles!

Just as he had this thought, Chang became aware of the headlights behind him. They were moving fast and almost upon him. Before he could do anything, he felt a jolt and a sudden acceleration, as the Ferrari was pushed from behind. In seconds, he was through the guardrail and tumbling end-over-end. The sports car didn't explode, but the lightweight frame offered scant protection as it crunched on the rocks below the road. He was dead before it stopped moving.

Chang's accident wasn't questioned by his men. They were making more money than they had dreamed of, and gave Angel the credit for making it all possible. No one wanted to rock the boat.

Ejercito Dragon continued to grow.

Chapter 10:
Wednesday, March 31, 1999

"She's a midnight mover, never misses a beat
Watch her dance, she's a savage dancer."
—Ted Nugent, *Savage Dancer*

Razor and Rapier were winding up their act. The audience was silent and attentive as the two fought out the final scene on the steps of a space-age Aztec pyramid. Faceted glass prisms and mirrors lined the set, adding to the dazzle of their dance, as the two combatants clashed in a mixture of laser, strobe, and spot lights.

The costumes, which had been a skin-tight body suit for one and a revealing arrangement of black leather straps and chrome armor plates for the other, were now slashed and tattered. Razor lunged, and Rapier parried, but not before a slice of her costume fell away, offering yet another carefully planned glimpse of what lay beneath.

After a few more cuts, stabs, and cloth-ripping moves, the dancers would have appeared less naked if they had been wearing nothing at all.

Razor was choreographed to be the more skilled fighter, but Rapier, who fought with the weapon after which she was named, had more reach. Razor's weapons were metal gauntlets with semicircular razors on both sides. The design was taken from a comic strip by the same name, in which the heroine had wrought havoc with such wrist-razors. They made both of her hands into battle axes.

Now, at the end of their painstakingly precise routine, both dancers were dripping with fake blood, but Razor was panting harder.

She gave the audience a look meant to convey her refusal to be worn down, and feinted to the right while dodging to the left. Her foot slid out from under her and she went down hard. Rapier pounced immediately, but took time to gloat as she angled her blade for a fatal strike... In that instant, Razor snapped her gauntleted hand closed around Rapier's weapon. With a twist and a kick, Razor pulled Rapier down and sat astride her, pinning her to the ground.

Rapier struggled violently, but to no avail; she too was tired, and could not dislodge her enemy.

Razor bracketed Rapier's head with one pair of blades, her armored left fist holding her victim's chin. The lights dimmed as the twin points of Razor's right hand blades descended toward Rapier's eyes, and there was a bloodcurdling scream in the dark.

When the lights were out, Razor kissed Rapier and the two dancers hustled quickly off stage.

"Hot damn, girls!" The manager of the Golden Chalice Club was waiting with a towel for each of them. "We had to turn men away at the door again! I've never seen a routine with the appeal of what you do—sex and violence, right in their faces! It's been, what, a couple months now, and our cup still runneth over!"

"So give us a raise, Larry, and just hand me the towel, don't try to rub me."

"Now Prue, you know you two already make more than any other dancers in the club!"

"Don't call me Prue! Don't *ever* call me that! Our relationship is strictly professional—it's 'Prudence' or nothing. Got it?"

Larry scowled. But he backed off and stopped trying to grope the girls under pretext of offering them their towels. "Fine, fine, Prudence and Patricia. Whatever. You know, I wouldn't put up with your shit if your show didn't pack the house every night."

Trish smiled sweetly. "Would you like us to take our sheeit somewhere else?"

Larry started on a hot retort but stifled it. He cared more about making money than getting the last word in. Only idiots let their dicks do the thinking in business. That was why he was so successful; he knew that having the best girls in his club was better for business than having the best girls in his bed. "Aw, c'mon, you know I didn't mean it!" He spoke with all the sincerity of a used car salesman. "I didn't come over here to fight with you two. I like you. And I've never held it against you that you're dykes, never tried to include any extra services in our arrangement, right?"

Prudence was impatient to get back to the showers and clean off the fake blood. "Right Larry, so what *did* you come back here for?"

The manager in him reasserted itself, and he couldn't quite suppress his glee. "Oh, there's been some real big screw-up at the airports. I mean *real* big. I just heard it on the news. All the airplanes are grounded. All of 'em! Not just here in Vegas, but all around the country, and even around the world. I was listening to the radio back in my office and some guy broke in—right in the middle of a song!—to say that something's gone haywire with the computers and all the airplanes are grounded. He says it'll probably take 'em weeks to clear it up."

Stunned, the dancers made no answer.

"I know you two were really looking forward to that vacation in Mexico, but it don't look like it's gonna happen now. So, I was wonderin' if you'd like to extend the show one more week and see what happens with the airplanes then. Okay?"

Prudence shot her employer a look of pure hatred, which he ignored, and headed for the private dressing room she shared with Trish. The younger dancer followed quickly, as though she and Prudence could escape the bad news in their room.

"Well, think it over and let me know," Larry called after them, "after you see the story for yourselves on the news, okay?"

When the dancers reached their dressing room and turned on the little black and white TV perched on their dresser, they found that Larry was telling the truth. For once in her life, Prudence wished that a man had lied to her.

She also thought she'd heard the expression "Wye-too-kay" before. It had something to do with what had happened to Kat...

Trish was mesmerized by the talking head, who was giving some preliminary estimates on how many hundreds of millions of dollars this computer problem was going to cost the airline industry and entire economies around the world. "Ho-ly shee-it," she murmured softly.

Prudence remembered: Y2K! "There's nothing holy about this shit," she answered.

Chapter 11:
Thursday, April 1, 1999

*"You can't go on
thinking nothing's wrong."*
—The Cars, *Drive*

Jared put down his paper with mixed feelings. On the one hand, people were finally taking the Y2K problem seriously. On the other, this thing with the air traffic control computers was proving incomprehensibly costly. Thank God no one had been hurt!

He rubbed his eyes, tired of staring at the newspaper folded on his desk. It sat there, pretending that nothing had changed, folded neatly in its place: away from the other tidy stacks of papers and bills. So why did the soft gray sheets lined with their curved black ranks seem so threatening? Why did the rows of letters and words look like columns of soldiers marching off to war over the contours of an uneven battlefield? Because he knew the story they told, of course, and understood the implications.

And people who should also understand were making jokes about it!

Even though the breakdown had occurred on the night of March 31st, the story had hit the papers on April 1st. There was no end to the jokes and comments being made about the Federal Aviation Administration, CIAO, and April Fool's Day.

The trouble had started with the Dallas/Fort Worth regional control center and then infected neighboring regions. From there, the problem had spread to National Flow Control in Washington D.C. This had eventually resulted in a complete shutdown of all automated air traffic control in the United States. The computer problem had not extended overseas, as early reports had indicated, but the American paralysis had made a complete hash of most flight schedules around the world.

There were people stranded the globe over and airline companies were absorbing millions of dollars in losses. Federal Express was shut down and UPS was crippled. Businesses and individuals of every description were threatened with closures, layoffs, and bankruptcy if things didn't get going again soon.

There had been no accidents, partly because the problem had not affected all systems simultaneously, partly due to the FAA's decision to field test its new software late at night, and partly due to the truly heroic efforts of the country's air traffic controllers.

The interconnected systems were still not yet up and running, lending some truth to the April Fool's jokes. "Life-flight" helicopters, small planes cleared for similar emergency services, and certain military aircraft were the only things flying.

Apparently, the FAA had loaded some new Y2K-compliant software on the computers at the Dallas center. The software had been thoroughly tested and approved by the FAA's 'end-to-end' testing center and was supposed to be compatible with other systems linked to it, but something had obviously gone wrong. The new software had worked correctly at first, but breakdowns in compatibility protections had resulted in corrupted data that flowed from the test computers to others downstream. The FAA defended itself, arguing that it had not wanted to implement the new software system-wide until it had been proven in one of the regional centers. The current disaster might have been avoided if the rollout had been nationwide, or it might have been worse if other problems had developed. Even the most thorough testing can miss something...

Further thoughts on the debacle were interrupted by the shrilling of Jared's phone.

"Hello, Christensen residence."

"Dr. Christensen?"

"Yes, this is he." Jared tried to sound friendlier than he was feeling just then.

"Er... This is Hyrum Behle, at Elder Young's office."

"Ah, yes." He sat up straighter. "What can I do for you?"

"Well, you wrote a letter to Elder Young about a year ago, and, frankly, we didn't take it too seriously at the time—it seemed so alarmist! But, well, with recent events..."

"Elder Young didn't take my letter seriously?"

"Well, not exactly, no. You see, he gets so much mail—being one of the Quorum of the Twelve—that I have to sort through it for him. He can't possibly read it all, so he relies on me to bring the most important or personal letters to his attention, and since the Church already had people working on the Y2K problem..."

"I see." The doctor let his tone convey that he was too polite to say exactly what it was he saw.

"Ah, yes. So. Anyway, Elder Young has read the letter now and would like to involve you in an effort to prepare the Church for possible contingencies. You obviously understood the full magnitude of the kinds of problems this thing can cause well before any of our people here did, so he wants you on the team charged with dealing with them."

"I'm honored, but I can't leave my patients and return to Salt Lake City without some kind of warning. I'll need some time."

"Oh, no! That won't be necessary. The Church is assembling a virtual task force. You can stay right where you are and continue what you're doing. For now, all you would need to do is exchange ideas with the others via e-mail. Occasionally, there might be a need for a teleconference. Would that be okay?"

"I suppose so... Who is the task force chair? Whom should I contact about this?"

"Actually, Elder Young says that we are overrun with experts here and none of them can agree on anything. He says the task force needs a chair who can see the big picture, not just the computer programs. So he wants you to be the chair."

"Oh..."

"Don't worry, it shouldn't take up too much of your time."

"You misunderstand me, it is an honor to serve, but I'm not sure I'm the man for the job. Why should all those experts listen to me?"

"Well, besides the fact that you've been appointed by one of the Quorum of the Twelve, Elder Young thinks you're a natural leader. He says he has full confidence in your ability to give the group the direction it needs."

The doctor thought for a moment before replying. "Very well then. I suppose you will send me e-mail addresses and background material on the team members and what the team has done thus far?"

"I've already got it prepared for you."

"Great. I'll be expecting it then."

"Yes. And...thank you, Doctor!"

"Tell Elder Young that he is very welcome."

"I will. Good-bye."

Chapter 12:
Thursday, April 8, 1999

"Pull me under, Pull me under
Pull me under I'm not afraid
All that I feel is honor and spite
All I can do is set it right."
—Dream Theater, *Pull Me Under*

Alexis Thomas frowned at her new insignia: silver eagles. They were heavy, the metal cold in her palm. She felt as though the April Fool's joke had somehow fallen on her.

"A promotion, sirs?" She had thought they were going to demote her!

"Yes, Colonel Thomas." In addition to Alexis, there were three generals, an admiral, and a letter from the president in the room. It was her superior officer, Major General Herbert Hudgins, who was doing most of the talking. The generals from the Air Force and Marines and the Admiral watched, their faces inscrutable. "You must have a rank that will make people jump more quickly when you tell them to jump. The authority that will make this inter-service task-force work is ours, of course—the president has asked the four of us to coordinate the efforts of our services. But after talking it over for a while, we agreed that a single expediter who knows what everyone is doing with regard to Y2K preparedness in all four branches would really help accelerate the process. You know, alert people to dead ends, let people know about particularly successful efforts. You understand?"

Alexis tipped her head once and put the eagles on her collar.

"We expect results, so we must give you the authority, staff, and budget to enable you achieve them—set you up for success, as it were. With your new rank, the inter-service authority being given you by the president, through us, and the Y2K mandate from the joint chiefs, you should get as much cooperation from the Air Force, Navy, and Marines as you do within the Army, right gentlemen?"

The other three agreed.

"But... Permission to speak candidly, sir?"

"Yes, yes, by all means!"

"I don't understand, sir. I submit a report everyone tells me is the end of my career, detailing exactly why we are heading for the edge of a cliff with no way to stop, and now you want me to solve the Y2K problem for all four branches of the military?" The joke was certainly on her!

"Let's not exaggerate, Colonel. We don't expect you to solve the whole problem yourself. Our offices and staffs will be working on solutions within each of our services. Your role will be to expedite and coordinate, and, yes, it was because of your report that we picked you! You are completely uncompromising and realistic about this situation. As the recent experiences of the FAA demonstrate, Y2K solutions need to be developed with the utmost skepticism and attention to detail. We simply cannot afford to fail—even once—the way they did. You're perfect for the job because you won't approach it with an over-inflated ego, convinced that you'll take care of it. The resources we are placing at your disposal should convince you that it's not impossible, but your natural skepticism will drive you to try harder. You'll be better at helping us to solve the problem than anyone else."

"Well, impossible is a strong word, sir, but it's not only one problem that needs solving—the big problem is that there are billions of little problems that all needed to be fixed, and some of them don't even look like problems."

"Colonel, we won World War II and put a man on the moon.

Surely we can manage to fix our computers!" This was from the Marine.

Typical Jarhead! We put a man on the moon, so we can do anything! If that were so, how could rag-tag bands of rice farmers in Viet Nam kick our butts? The most powerful army in the world! Just as rag-tag shepherds in Afghanistan taught the second most powerful army in the world a lesson in humility... Some problems don't have perfect answers, and some people never appreciate their own capacity to fail.

"Sir," she tried to explain in her most reasonable voice, "even if we could fix all the hundreds of millions of lines of code in every mainframe computer in every branch of the military, some of those computers would still go down. An embedded system, like a sensor with a computer clock that no one thought to test because the machine doesn't use dates, could have logic hard-wired into it that is not Y2K-compliant. This in turn could introduce corrupt data that could affect the whole system—as with the FAA. Or we could get the whole system clean, only to have something else take it out, like an air conditioning system that no one knew had a microchip in it. And even if we could make sure everything got taken care of—on time—we would still have trouble. The civilian services are going down, or most of them are, and the Department of Treasury will for sure."

"You see, Colonel," the Air Force general chimed in, "you have a better grasp of the problem than anyone else. Who could do a better job helping us to prepare?"

Not to be upstaged by the other services, the Admiral had to add his own comment: "Your concern about the Department of Treasury is well founded, but I'm sure we'll find a way to make sure every sailor—and soldier!—gets his pay...maybe we'll issue scrip of some kind. Don't you worry about that; all you need to do is help coordinate our efforts to stay in business. You just tell us what you need—more staff, whatever—and we'll get it for you."

Damned Zoomie and fool Squid! They weren't listening. "Very well, sirs. But I'll need three teams. One team will work on expediting the fixing of the code in the mainframes. Another will continue gathering intelligence on what other countries—and particularly their militaries—are doing. And a final team will take care of everything else. I'll need the authority to reassign the best programmers and system analysts from all the services—Army, Navy, Marines, and Air Force—and authorization to fly my teams out to different installations to examine their problems firsthand."

"Excellent! We'll set up a protocol to expedite the reassignments. We're counting on you, Colonel!"

"Thank you General Hudgins. I'll do my best, sir!" She saluted and left the office.

On her way home, Alexis allowed herself to flow with the evening traffic, instead of engaging in her usual 'pilot the car' games. She couldn't get over the enormity of the responsibility she'd been given. It was the 'everything else' task that was going to be impossible. She had accepted anyway, in part because orders are orders, and in part because she didn't know anyone who could do a better job.

Besides, every problem she could help avert was one less disaster to worry about. And there were plenty of pending disasters to worry about! The burden was being thrust upon her because her superiors were frightened. There was no other word for it: they were frightened. World War II and men on the moon, hah!

Hmmm...

There was another possible explanation. Maybe her report *had* sealed the fate of her career; there was no way she—or anyone—could make sure everything got taken care of. There simply wasn't enough time! Maybe she'd gotten the promotion and the job because no one else wanted it, and the blame was going to fall on her when things got bad. The term 'meteoric rise', she realized, is an oxymoron: meteors don't rise. They are only visible because they are burning up as they fall! Maybe that's what someone had in mind for her...

Arriving at her apartment later than usual, she tossed her jacket with the new silver eagles on her bed and headed for the shower.

Usually, the water helped wash away her worries, but not this night. Instead of massaging fingers on her neck muscles, the water was more of an irritating tapping on her shoulders. Full colonel less than two years after making lieutenant colonel...good grief! Her closest friends were still calling her Major Tom—and some of the non-military ones might still do so—but this mission was going to change her whole life!

Government agencies and large companies were trotting out their Y2K solution plans and telling everyone that they would never make the same mistakes the FAA had made, and that everything would be fixed well before the deadline. The top brass in the Pentagon was no different. They had set out charts and action plans where the TV cameras could see them, even though her report on the difficulties other countries were having made it clear that there was no possible way to get all mission-critical systems fixed on time. The U.S. had more computerized systems, and hence more Y2K problems than anyone else. What a charade!

Alexis dragged herself out of the shower, feeling no less tense than before. Slipping on her bathrobe, she settled into her computer nest with a cup of hot cocoa.

She ran another of her own programs to access an anonymous forwarding server and pinged Merlyn to see if he was still on-line.

The response was immediate: *You're up late tonight, my Warrior Princess!*

Hook up the encrypted voice function, please. I need to talk to you.

Okay Princess.

She backed out of the anonymous relay and activated the encrypted voice mode. Merlyn's call came quickly.

"Hello Princess!"

Alexis smiled. She just loved that warm baritone voice! The slight island accent made it all the more interesting.

"Merlyn, I'm scared."

"You!?"

"Yes, me. The top brass are all acting like they don't know how bad the problems are and that everything will get taken care of on time, but they can't be that stupid. They must know that there is no way even the mis— Uh, there is no way the military will get everything fixed. And even if we did, the country as a whole is not going to make it. They're bullshitting the public—not to cause unnecessary panic—or some such nonsense."

"That bad, huh?"

"Worse!" She stood and paced, still in range of the microphone. "They promoted me, gave me a bunch of money and people, and basically ordered me to fix the problem!"

"A promotion? Didn't you just get one, not too long ago?"

"Yeah. It's pretty uncommon. I was already at a very high rank for someone my age—it helped getting a Ph.D. the Army wanted and starting out with a commission straight out of school—but this is... I've never heard of anyone making full colonel at my age. I feel like there's more politics to this than I care for. I'm not sure exactly what, but these things never happen for no reason."

"Is it not even a possible explanation that you're doing a great job?" Merlyn found Alexis' often acid observations of the military way of life fascinating, in a morbid sort of way.

"Hah! Not a chance! You don't get promoted for doing a good job; you get a pat on the back and a decoration to hang on your uniform."

"A medal?"

"Yeah, something like the ARCOM, the Army Commendation Medal."

"Oh." To Merlyn, it was like hearing about a strange tribal ritual his ancestors in Africa had practiced. "So, what was that about *you* having to fix it, Princess?"

"It's the assignment from Hell." She drummed her fingers on her mouse-pad absently, imagining her friend doing the same thing. "It's like the brass can't bend their minds around the idea that rank and money aren't what we need. What we do need is more time, or more experts on decades-old COBOL programming techniques, but there aren't any more of either and they can't order them to appear!"

"Are you supposed to be telling me this?"

"Well, what I've told you is only an opinion; I haven't said anything classified about specific systems. But this link is secure. They don't have any crypto hacks who can beat me! And I trust you. There is no one else I talk to about my work—no one else I can!" She chuckled. "Besides, you often give me good ideas, ideas that help me in my job, ideas that—I hate to say it—may soon save lives."

"I'm honored. But should you really trust someone so completely whom you have not really met?"

"How long have we been corresponding? I may be foolish, but I feel that I've come to know you." Alexis' cheeks colored, but it was true, dammit! She'd never been more sure of anyone in her life. "The man behind the words on my screen and the voice in my ear is trustworthy. There are a lot of things that can be faked easily, but a way of thinking is not one of them. I just can't believe that a person of anything less than the highest integrity could think the way you do."

"I'm blushing!"

"Good! Maybe you'll give me a good deal on some land!"

Merlyn hesitated. "You want to buy into the Dollar Ranch?"

"Yes." She had made the decision without realizing it, but she never hesitated once she made a decision. "It'll take all my savings, but I'm convinced that the shit is going to hit the fan and I can't think of any place I'd rather be—or any people I'd rather be with—when it hits."

"Alexis, that's terrific!" There was the scrape of a chair being pushed back. "Hey, Anna, Major Tom says she'll be joining us!"

Anna's voice came through. "That's wonderful! Merlyn has become very fond of you and has been hoping you'd come out here before it's too late."

Anna's comments threw Alexis' thoughts off on a tangent. They were an intrusion into the warm space she'd been sharing with

Merlyn. She found herself surprised by a strong emotional reaction. It couldn't be jealousy—could it? She knew about Anna, of course, and had not thought of herself as being romantic about Merlyn. He was a dear and trusted friend—no more than that!

She realized that she was letting a pause in the conversation get uncomfortably long and pushed her muddled feelings aside. "So, you do have some land left? I was thinking I might be too late. I know you've invited other people—I was thinking the FAA disaster might have made up their minds."

"It has. Even my father, who doesn't understand the Y2K problem at all, has decided to move out here and stay with us. But there's one plot left—Merlyn's been saving it for you."

Alexis felt something electric pulse up her spine. It was Anna who answered, but Merlyn who'd saved the spot. There was no sign of jealousy on their end, only excitement. They could probably have sold that last spot for a great deal of money. Saving it for her was an incredibly generous thing to do. "You've been saving one for me?" She didn't doubt her hearing, but...

Merlyn laughed. "I've got a barn with your name on it. But you know, I'm thinking now that that might not be the best way for you to go."

"What do you mean?"

"I mean that you're single and don't have any family that you'd bring with you, so you don't really need a house to yourself. We're adding more rooms onto the main house here, each one a complete studio apartment. You could use one of those and invest your savings in the kind of hardware and supplies that we both know would be valuable. I'd even let you have the room at no charge if you'd take charge of our security and help out with our computer systems. I'm not the military type, as you know, and neither are most of the people I trust enough to let in on what we're doing here. Anna is a computer whiz like you, but she doesn't have the experience in cryptography and military tactics you do. We've got some ideas for securing our perimeter and our IT, but I'm sure we could use some input from an expert."

"Merlyn... You know I'm not a Green Beret or anything like that. And even though the taxpayers slaved so the Army could pay for my fancy degree and feel good about starting me out at a higher rank, we both know that some of the best programmers in the world were high school dropouts. I'm a computer analyst who'd rather be flying choppers, with most of my experience in communications."

"You're still my Warrior Princess!" Merlyn laughed again.

"And, while what you say is true," Anna added, "it is also true that your experience has taught you a great deal about the things we need help with."

"Well..." Alexis' cheeks were burning again. "You realize that I can't leave the Army right away. I'm going to be really busy trying to prevent fires, and then running around trying to put out the ones I don't prevent."

"We understand that." It was Anna again. "But let us know if your fire-fighting brings you to Utah, Colorado, or Wyoming. We'll arrange a meeting and settle the details then."

"Okay. I'll be pretty busy, but I should be able to find a way to squeeze a meeting in."

"We look forward to it, Princess!"

When they broke the connection, Alexis wondered how such a meeting might go. She would love to get to meet Merlyn at last, but she didn't quite know what to make of Anna.

Hmmm. Utah, Colorado, or Wyoming? Communicating through the internet was such an anonymous thing, and she liked it that way, but where the hell was the Dollar Ranch anyway?

CHAPTER 13:
SATURDAY, APRIL 10, 1999

"Then what's to stop us, pretty baby
But what is and what should never be."
—Led Zeppelin, *What is and What Should Never Be*

Angel sat impatiently in an armchair and waited for Rosalia to wake up. He hadn't wanted her brought up sharply, with smelling salts or the like. She'd take it better if she awoke as from a normal sleep. This was no lost runaway, no drugged child that was to be used and then disposed of.

This was *Rosalia*.

The chair was behind a one-way mirror that afforded a clear view of the whole room. Angel was irritated by the wait—no one ever dared to keep him waiting! Or so he told himself. The idea that his nervousness might be caused by a fear of what might happen when Rosalia awoke was not one he could admit to conscious thought. So he waited, tormented by fear and longing, telling himself it was annoyance he was feeling. Nevertheless, it was about the time the narcotic was supposed to wear off that the source and object of his anxiety began stirring.

At first, she stretched and turned over, as if she were still in her room at home, where she'd gone to sleep. Her long sable hair rippled as she pulled it back from her face with one hand, revealing the delicate jet arches of her eyebrows and eyes of a deeper black than the dark side of the moon. The eyes were sad pools of care, wiser than their years should have made them. Abruptly, she sat bolt upright in the bed and tried to look in all directions at once. What had happened? Where was she?

Angel smiled; she would never know! Then he frowned. He'd never had so many conflicting emotions at once, not since... No, better not to go there.

Rosalia got up and started to wrap a sheet around her slender body, until the thick terry cloth bathrobe laid out for her at the foot of the bed caught her eye. It had excited Angel tremendously to find out that his captive slept in the nude. Who'd have thought it of sweet, shy Rosalia?

She donned the robe and gave her surroundings a more careful examination. The room was opulent beyond anything she had ever imagined. And it was a *big* room. A floor-to-ceiling entertainment center with an enormous TV and enough electronics to control a mission to the moon covered most of one wall. A door opened onto a sumptuous bathroom with gold and crystal fixtures. The bed was a huge wrought-iron four-poster, big enough to hold wrestling matches on. The rug swallowed up her feet in a white fleecy shag that cushioned like real sheep's wool.

And there were books! A set of bookcases with at least 5,000 books on them covered an entire wall. She couldn't help herself. She moved toward the bookcase and ran a hand over the spines of more hard-backed books than she'd seen anywhere, except in a library. There were classics, poetry, and—better than anything else—shelf upon shelf of advanced texts dealing with the basic sciences. Someone who knew her well had stocked this bookshelf.

Unseen, Angel smiled. He knew the books would work! But then Rosalia drew back from the books, suddenly horrified. She dashed for the door and did not seem overly surprised to find it locked. Then she ran to the bathroom, but stopped in the doorway when she saw that it had no windows. No windows—none in the main room either.

For a several long seconds, she did nothing. Then she marched slowly to the center of the room and started screaming at the top of her lungs. She screamed and screamed. Hysteria edged into the screams and they rose in pitch. She continued far beyond the point where her voice became hoarse. She continued until she collapsed, sobbing soundlessly on the floor.

Angel made a disgusted face and pried himself from his chair. In the hallway, he found the guard outside Rosalia's door with his gun drawn, facing the door nervously. "¿Que paso?" he asked as his boss approached.

"Nada," Angel grunted, "se puso histerica." *Nothing, she went hysterical.*

The guard holstered his pistol.

"Find Yasuka and tell her to bring some tea and something to eat. And aspirin. Quickly!"

The guard hurried off and Angel returned to his chair. Shortly, a frail, battered Asian girl entered Rosalia's room, bearing a tray with tea, pastries, and aspirin.

Rosalia didn't move.

Yasuka set the tray on a night table by the bed and turned to leave. She knocked softly, and as the door opened, Rosalia leapt up and sprinted straight for it. But the guard caught sight of her coming and jerked the door shut after Yasuka, before Rosalia could cover the distance. She crashed against it full-tilt and crumpled to the floor again.

Angel was not amused. This was not going as planned. In fact, the timid love of his boyhood was showing signs of violence and cunning. How else had she changed?

A movement brought his attention back to his prisoner. She picked herself up slowly and began making a slow circuit of the room. She paused at several places, but didn't stop until she came to a free-standing lamp that had a long tubular metal body—it was one of the tall kind, meant to reflect off the ceiling. She unplugged it, wrapped the cord around the base, and removed the lamp shade and light bulb.

Not yet understanding, Angel made no move. What the Devil?

Rosalia took the lamp to the entertainment center and swung it carefully so that the base hit right in the center of the television.

The loud implosion of the picture tube sent rebounding glass shards in every direction. She smiled and shifted to a higher gear. Swinging the lamp again, she bashed the stereo. Then she caved in the speakers.

Now Rosalia was getting her whole body into it. Clocks. Vases. Framed prints. She was panting with effort when she smashed the tray with the tea.

Angel watched in absolute dismay, unable to move or even say anything—until she started toward his mirror. Then he wrenched himself from the chair and flung himself back out into the hallway.

The guard's manner telegraphed uncertainty, even fear—the crashing reverberations emanating from the room were quite loud, even through the heavy steel door. He'd heard the clamor of violence from such rooms before, but only after Angel had gone in and had his fun with whatever white urchin—never a Hispanic—they'd brought him that day. This was something else...something more like the sustained fury of a hurricane.

Angel pulled his gun from his waistband and jerked the door open. "Rosalia!"

She was about to pull over the last of the bookcases when he entered, evidently having tired of the lamp before getting to the mirror. Her hands now empty, she balled them on her hips and faced him squarely. The room smelled of tea and ozone.

"Rosalia..."

"Bastard! I knew it was you!" She spat on the floor. "Let me go or you'll be sorry!" Her Spanish, unlike Angel's, was no barrio dialect. She spoke with the precise, quasi-Castillian enunciation of a highly-educated Latina.

Angel was used to submission and fear, not defiance. He was momentarily taken aback, but the threat activated an automatic response. He raised the gun and pointed it squarely at her head.

She glared.

He stood.

Both were trembling.

"Rosalia, I didn't bring you here to hurt you. I brought you here to show you that you were wrong. Jorge was wrong. I've made it. I'm big. I can give you anything you want!"

"Can you give me Jorge back?"

"Daughter of a whore! He's dead, and I rule Los Angeles. Can't you admit that you are wrong when the proof lies all around you?"

Rosalia laughed, reminding him without looking that what lay around her was a shambles.

Angel did not miss the point and scowled. "Do you have any idea how much this stuff costs?"

"No. And I don't care. Angel, we grew up together. You were such a sweet boy until your parents were murdered. Can't you see that none of this will bring them back? Can't you see that all of this shames their memory? Jorge told you, warned you, but you wouldn't listen. Your stupid gang wars killed him—your best friend!—and now all you have left around you is destruction."

"Destruction? I make millions! Every month!!"

"You make nothing." The answer was calm, devastating. "All that you have is taken from those who make things, those who can create. You are like a hole in a bag of gold dust. Everything you do leaves less in the bag. Tell me Angel, what will you do when there is nothing left in the bag? How will you feed your appetite when there is no one left to steal from?"

"You fucking crazy idealist whore!" Angel was the one screaming now. "Jorge ruined you! You were like me. I loved you! He ruined you!"

"No, Angel, he saved my life. And it's not too late for him to save yours, if you'd just listen to what he told you—"

"No! I didn't bring you here to make me feel guilty! I brought you here to show you real power, real wealth, real life. Rosalia, I will be king here soon, and I wanted you to be my queen." He stopped, not sure what he wanted now. His chest was heaving and he was closer to crying than he had been since the day his parents... "Rosalia, I wanted to give you so much!"

"You have nothing I want!"

It was too much. Angel closed the space between them in three strides and backhanded her across the face. The blow knocked her all the way around and brought her up against the wall. She hit and slumped to the floor. Angel stood over her, indecision twisting the muscles in his face. Then he reached down with his left hand and yanked her hair so as to force her to look at him. He moved the gun across her field of vision and pressed the muzzle against her right temple. "I have your life in my hands." The gun pressed harder. "*This* is power. Now, admit that Jorge was wrong, or I'll kill you."

She clamped her mouth shut.

"*Admit it!!!*"

"No. There is nothing but death in your hands. You have no power over me."

"I have the power to kill you!"

"Then do it!"

The words lodged in Angel's heart, an icy arrow that froze him solid. He couldn't move or think or speak.

His stricken look penetrated deep inside Rosalia, and she reached out with her fingers to smooth the pain engraved on his face. "Oh Angel, it's not too late, let me..."

"*WHORE!!!*" Angel's vulnerability vanished in a white flash of fury. He clubbed her with the butt of his gun. "*WHORE!!!*" He hit her again, above her right eye, and then again. Blood spurted as she folded, but that was the only thing about Rosalia that moved.

The sight of the crimson flow dripping on the bathrobe, seeping through the white terry cloth, brought Angel up short. He stood over his love, scarlet spatterings on his gun, on his fist clenched around it, on his silk shirt. Animal wailing escaped from his clenched throat—inarticulate testimony to his anguish. What had he done? What had *she* made him do!?!

CHAPTER 14:
FRIDAY, JUNE 11, 1999

"Ain't nobody gonna take my car
Eight cylinders, all mine
I'm a highway star!"
—Deep Purple, *Highway Star*

"Mon cher Monsieur Gerard, I have a surprise for you!"

"Max, I am busy..."

"This won't take long, Michel. Ten minutes, max. Meet me downstairs."

"Downstairs? You are coming over?"

"I'm already here. I'm in the lobby. Take the elevator down and I'll show you. Indulge me, okay?"

"Well, I suppose it is ze least I can do for one of Gerard Investment Management's best customers... I will be right down." Michel reached forward to hang up the phone then had a second thought. "But if zis is one of your practical jokes, I am going to sell all your stocks and put your money into government bonds!"

"That isn't funny, Michel. Just trust me. You'll like it."

When the elevator doors opened on the ground floor, Max was positively bouncing with anticipation. "This way Michel." He led the way toward the second set of elevators that descended to the parking levels. Inside, Max punched the button for the lower-most floor of the parking deck. The building was not full, so no one parked on the bottom level. Michel had never been there.

On the way down, Michel remembered something that he'd thought of the night before and had been bothering him ever since.

"Max, I 'ave been in zis country for more zan ten years, and zere is somesing I still do not understand."

"What's that?"

"Why do zey call zem 'good old boys'? It is a contradiction, no?"

Max rolled his eyes. "That's not even a pun, Michel!"

"No, I am serious! A boy is young, is he not?"

"I don't know—I mean, yes, boys are young. It's a southern thing. An expression. Culture. Something..." Max eyed his friend sidelong. "Does it matter?"

Michel was about to answer, but was cut off by the elevator dinging. The doors parted to reveal an empty garage deck. Some of the lights had gone out and no one had reported them to maintenance—and apparently maintenance had no more reason to come down here than anyone else did. Save a nondescript sedan of indeterminate color covered with a thick layer of dust, off to the right, the place was entirely vacant.

"We are here... Why?"

"This way!" Max assumed the air of a conjurer about to do his best trick, swirled an imaginary cape, and led the way around the elevators.

When they cleared the corner, a white ice cream truck came into view. It was not new, but it had a new coat of paint, complete with images of ice cream sandwiches, drumsticks, and popsicles. A row of bells over the cab sat ready to announce the sale of frozen treats to the children of New York.

Michel turned to his friend, to ask if the surprise was behind the truck, but Max was no longer beside him—he was unlocking the truck's back doors! The conjurer took the latch in hand, swung one of the heavy doors out, and bowed to an imaginary fanfare. "Ta-da! Take a look inside!"

"You are kidding, yes?"

"Nope! This is it. Trust me, and take a look inside!" Max grinned smugly and waited for applause.

Michel peeked gingerly through the door, as though afraid a

giant whipped-cream pie might spring out of it, as from a monstrous jack-in-the-box. No pies sprang out, but what he found was even more surprising: the inside was outfitted with RV fixtures. There was a range, a sink, a refrigerator, and a table that presumably folded down to make a sleeping surface with the benches beside it. The back area opened into the driver and passenger area. There were various cabinets, carefully arranged so as to allow access to little openings that resembled the narrow slits from which arrows were once shot from castles. And there were two well-stocked gun racks, with drawers and an open cubby holding several army-green ammo boxes below each.

"What is zis?" Michel Gerard was flabbergasted.

"It's an armored camper, of course." Max feigned innocent hurt. "No intelligent person should be without one in the year 2000!"

"But...but..." The Frenchman couldn't get his mental gears back in motion. "No ice cream?"

Max laughed in absolute delight. "No ice cream. This is an old Brink's truck—an armored car! I had it painted to look like an ice cream truck. Pretty good disguise, don't you think?"

For once, Michel had nothing to say in response to Max.

"This thing has a special engine—uses gasoline instead of diesel. I had double wheels put on the back so it won't sink into dirt so easily, if you ever have to drive off-road. And if they get shot, the tires will take you a hundred miles before they wear out. I also had the transmission custom built; give it a long flat road, and this thing'll get up to a hundred!" With a final magician's flourish, Max held out the keys. "And now it's yours. I know you'll never think of it beforehand, so it's fully stocked with extra gas, dried food, water, and plenty of ammunition for the six rifles and two handguns. I even put some Tyvek clean suits in that cabinet there, in case you and Natalie ever have to get out of the truck in a place that might be contaminated."

"Max... I do not know what to say." Michel didn't know

whether to laugh or be horrified. "Zis must 'ave cost you a for-tune!"

"Oh, not really. These trucks don't usually get that many miles put on them, shuttling between banks and supermarkets, and what-not—I bought it for a steal! Had the new engine put in and the work done on the interior, of course. It's got two brand new extra heavy duty batteries, to make sure it'll start, even if you forget to come turn it over before you need it. I had other stuff done too, but it all set me back less than twenty grand—chicken feed next to the money you've made for me, and saved for me by telling me when to pull out of airline stock."

The praise was gratifying, of course, but the gift was ridicu-lous. "Ze airline sing was easy. Ze FAA has been behind all ze ozer federal agencies in trying to fix zeir Y2K problems for so long, zat zere was a pretty good chance zat anysing zey tried would crash 'big time,' yes? But zis! What am I supposed to do wis zis? Do you know what zey would do to me if zey found me wis all zeze guns? Each one would get me a long jail sentence, and I am not planning any vacations to war zones!"

"Relax. Who's going to look for guns in an ice cream truck?" Max laughed and then became more serious. "Besides, in less than a year, there may not *be* anyone to enforce those gun control laws—or victim disarmament laws, as I call 'em. Before that happens, you should take the time to learn how to use them. Go to a private range. Practice. You don't want to have to figure them out in a hurry. My friend, I know you don't believe me when I tell you how bad it's going to be. I know you know it, but don't really believe it. Michel, the war will come to you. So just leave this here and keep the keys near you. One day, you'll need to get out of this city, and it'll be ugly out there. With this, you'll have a chance of getting out alive. You'll remember it when you need it."

"You," Gerard leveled an accusing finger at his friend, "are completely insane. But I love you. So come on up and 'ave a drink wis me, and let us talk no more of apocalypses."

"I can't." Max hung the key ring on Michel's still extended

finger. "I've got to get to the airport."

"Anozer vacation, so soon?"

"Not this time. Y2K is still a ways off, but the fiscal year 2000 is going to be hitting all kinds of companies soon—governments too. They'll be hit harder than they'll admit, mark my word! The balloon is going up, Michel, and I'm getting out while I can. I'm going to stay away from computer-intensive societies for a while. I've bought a nice little house in Costa Rica and I'll be managing my affairs from there. Except that we won't be able to do lunch so often, you won't even be able to tell that I'm gone—until the phone system goes down."

Michel studied his friend long and hard. He was serious. He really had come to believe the worst predictions concerning the Millennium Bug! It was frightening that a person who had always been so solid and upbeat could now be so certain that society-as-we-know-it was about to come to an end.

In spite of his trust in his friend, Michel could still not quite bring himself to believe such visions of doom and gloom. But he pocketed the keys to the truck and thanked Max.

CHAPTER 15

The Washington Herald

Friday, September 10, 1999

INSIDER REVIEW

Edward Switcher

Y2K Panic in Washington

A strange thing has been happening in the capitol city lately: Y2K protesters are outnumbering the political protesters in Lafayette Park, across Pennsylvania Avenue from the White House. Y2K protesters have become so numerous in Washington that one can barely see the hunger strikers and other dissidents. Park Service officials estimate that there were more than 2,000 protesters present on Thursday.

These people come from all walks of life. Some are former line workers of closed factories, others are former pre-sidents of companies that fell to the so-called Millennium Bug. Others still have their jobs, but are worried that they may lose them soon, if the government doesn't do something to fix the problem.

The nation has been reeling from one economic blow after another, since July and August, when numerous businesses entered into the fiscal year 2000. Many executives failed to have their companies' computer systems prepared for Y2K, and many more did not realize that the problem could hit them before January 1st, 2000. This created the first economy-wide wave of crises, causing the Dow to drop over 1,500 points in a single day.

Secondary and tertiary waves of bankruptcies and closures hit weeks later, as companies that depended on the first victims could no longer remain in business.

Now, with less than four months to go before the year 2000, people are starting to show signs of panic. If so much economic chaos could come from just the failure of companies with non-Y2K-compliant accounting software, protesters ask, what will happen when the actual deadline strikes?

Earlier this week, the president issued a widely publicized statement, calling for calm. He did not answer questions about how many U.S. or state government systems were affected by the fiscal year 2000, but said that the Critical Infrastructure Assurance Office's best experts were working on the problem, and that he was confident that all vital systems would continue functioning after January 1.

There is great speculation as to what exactly the president meant by "vital systems." The White House maintains that all the people that depend on the government for their livelihood will be taken care of, but this has only added fuel to the speculations.

Continued on page D8.
Also, see related story on A1.

CHAPTER 16:
SATURDAY, SEPTEMBER 18, 1999

"We're taking our chances
Gonna do it our way
Pedal to the metal shooting down the highway."
—Mr. Big, *Alive and Kickin'*

Merlyn T'bawa and Anna Wu sat at opposite ends of their new table. In truth, it was the same oak table they'd always had, but it had been rebuilt so that more leaves—many more leaves—could be added. This time, there were only about a dozen people seated at the table, so only one new leaf was in use. Everyone had pushed their chairs back after finishing an enormous meal, except for those having a second serving of blueberry pie and vanilla ice cream, and the group was discussing the next phase of building in their valley.

"Well," Anna broke her silence when the conversation started going over the same ground again, "I think that if we're going to have wires running from here to the gun emplacements, we ought to dig the trenches first." As always, when she spoke the others quieted and listened. Given how rarely she spoke in group settings, it was a natural response—what little she did say was always precisely on the mark.

"Makes sense to me," Merlyn agreed, "with all due respect to my beloved partner's efforts, the fire-control software for the automatic weapons is good, but not infallible, so a central override is a must. We need to be able to control our defenses from here and radio signals can be jammed, so that leaves us with wires. Jimmy, you know how to operate a backhoe, don't you?"

"Sure, but aren't automatic weapons illegal?" The girl sat up straighter when the attention shifted to her. "Aren't they a risk?"

Merlyn spotted Ed, a young man who had recently arrived as a boarder at the main house, hiding a smirk with his napkin. "That's a good question Jimmy," Merlyn pinned Ed with his gaze while answering, "because if we were buying illegal guns, some of them might get traced here and we could have federal entanglements we're not ready for."

Jimmy leaned forward, crossing her arms on the table.

Ed was a good man, if a little quick to judge. Anna had met him somewhere on the Net, and he had met them several times on trips to Utah, before deciding to move to the ranch permanently. He was young, headstrong, and not highly intellectual, but his heart seemed squarely in the right place. He dropped his napkin and gave Jimmy a thoughtful second look. His interest in her increased, for more than one reason.

Merlyn smiled slightly as he continued. "But these guns aren't automatic in the sense of 'full-auto' machine gun firing. They are high-powered TJC-30 rifles, a sort of clone of the Browning .30 caliber machine gun, except that they're semiautomatic. TJC-30s are perfectly legal to own, and we bought them before it became a crime for anyone to sell them to us without getting our social security numbers. So there's no reason for anyone to try to trace them, or to think of looking here if they did try to trace them."

Jimmy nodded, uncrossing her arms.

"What we're doing to make them automatic isn't even illegal. It probably would be if the government knew we were doing it, but it's not something commonly done. The difference is semantic. You see, they think of automatic weapons as being weapons that fire continuously as long as the trigger is held down. If we were to alter our guns to do that, it would be illegal, but that's not what we have in mind. We're not the government and we can't afford as much ammo as they can. What we're doing is putting a computer in each gun emplacement."

"I get it!"

Merlyn believed she did, but elaborated anyway, for the benefit of anyone else at the table who might not. "The guns will be automatic in the sense that they will be automated—the computers will shoot them. And they won't simply spray bullets down the hillside; they'll use infrared sensors and motion detectors to shoot single targets at a time. They'll still be pretty fast, but they won't waste ammunition. They'll shoot only moving targets that are about man-sized and warm. And *our* computers won't crash on New Year's Eve."

Jimmy thought about it for a moment. "Are you telling me that precision robot guns are legal, but fast-firing guns you have to aim yourself are illegal?" She laughed.

"Well, yes and no. Machine guns in the normal sense are legal for some people in some places, but you have to get government permits and pay them licensing fees. You're right that it is a less dangerous kind of weapon that the government has been trying to take away from people. After Y2K takes out the bureaucrats who would try to stop us, we'll turn up the speed on the computers. That'll make our guns almost as fast as normal full-auto .30 Browning machine guns, but a lot less wasteful. What we're doing isn't something people normally do, so they haven't gotten around to making laws about it. Not that I want to make excuses for elected officials who violate their oaths to uphold the Constitution and its second amendment!"

"Oh." Jimmy tossed her long hair and flashed a smile that happened to slide over Ed. "Well, yeah, I can dig trenches with a backhoe, and I can see why we'd want people with safe cover up there in case of real trouble, but what about the rockier areas? Backhoe won't dig into solid rock."

Ed jumped in. "Hey, I could use my truck to haul the dirt you dig up to the rocky places and make... What do you call 'em? Breastworks! We can make dirt and rock breastworks where we can't dig trenches between the automatic gun emplacements. They wouldn't even look like defenses from the outside!"

Dreamer interrupted, his voice devoid of emotion. "You want

to make breastworks with my daughter, son?"

Jimmy was horrified. "Daddy!"

Ed blushed furiously and experienced a sudden urge to examine the blueberry stains on the napkin in his lap in great detail.

Dreamer couldn't hold it in any longer and burst out laughing. Merlyn joined in and Anna laughed with her eyes.

"Dreamer, that was wicked!" Merlyn regained his composure. "I don't see that Jimmy objects, and it's an excellent idea, Ed."

Ed was still blushing, but he managed to find his voice again. "Aw hell... It was nothing. We can start tomorrow, if you like, Jimmy."

"Okay." She graced him with a smile that could melt icebergs. "Where should we start, Mr. T'bawa?"

"I'd say you don't need any help figuring that out." Merlyn smiled at the renewed laughter and blushing. "Just keep track of your progress on the map in my study. That way we'll know when it'll be safe for us to start rigging the guns."

From there, the conversation turned to the new families expected to move in over the next months. Jimmy's sister Dawn—two years younger than her sister and nearly as blonde—and her brothers wanted to know if any of the new families had children their ages. Dreamer himself was interested to know that there were single women among the incoming, though he didn't mention it. His children were never happy about it when he dated someone, even though he reassured them that he was not trying to replace their mother.

Merlyn was pleased. In spite of the fears bringing the residents of the Dollar Ranch together, he could see that they were excited and happy. Creating something is always fun, but creating a community has warm human rewards that go beyond any other kind of creation... Except, perhaps, for the joyful and deliberate creation of a child.

CHAPTER 17:
MONDAY, NOVEMBER 8, 1999

"You've got fins to the left, fins to the right
And you're the only bait in town."
—Jimmy Buffett, *Fins*

"How about yonder thicket of plants with the big leaves? Ah don't think anyone could see our mopeds from the beach or from the road."

"Perfect!"

After hiding their rented mopeds, Prudence and Trish pushed their way through the plants down to the seaside and spread their towels. The sand was bone white and ground fine by the Caribbean waters, which were banded into shades of blue that one would sooner expect to see in the sky than in the sea. A quick check revealed no one else on the beach. They doffed their bikinis and settled down to the serious business of soaking up the sun from the cloudless vault above. The rhythmic reverberation of the tumbling waves washed over them and made it impossible to keep their eyes open.

"Can you believe this, Prudence? Ah cain't. We finally made it! Cozumel is even better than Ah thought it'd be!" Trish stretched on her towel, enjoying the sensation of the warm sand under her feet.

"I don't remember anything in the brochures about all the trash and craters in the streets, but the sun sure feels good." Prudence also stretched and toyed with the sand between her feet. "I can't get over this heat—in November!"

"Yeah, and Ah sure need the sun; lookit me, all fishbelly white!"

"Do all fish have white bellies?"

"Now, don't go teasin' me about mah southern talk again..."

The two chatted for a while longer, until a shadow fell across the sun. Opening her eyes, Prudence beheld a brown-skinned man with a toothy grin and black hair leaning over her. He had a machete over her neck. "You no move!" he ordered.

Prudence grabbed his wrist with both hands and yanked down and to the side. Her reaction was instantaneous, executed without conscious thought. The machete stabbed into the ground and the startled man, who had already been leaning forward, toppled. He fell on Prudence, arms and legs flung wide.

That was a mistake.

Prudence kneed him in the groin with a fury accumulated through years of unexpressed hatred. The man rolled off her, balled up in agony. With the speed of Razor on Rapier at the end of their act, Prudence was on him, straddling him, holding him to the ground. She stared at the *machetero* for an unmeasurable stretch of elastic time, uncertain of what to do with him.

He recovered somewhat, and, seeing her nakedness spread below his face, made licking motions with his tongue.

That was a bigger mistake.

Prudence's fury engulfed her in such a flood of acid heat that she was barely conscious of pulling the machete from the ground. "Animal," she hissed and drew the sharp blade across the man's throat. His eyes flew wide and he tried to get loose, but it was too late. She sliced again, opening a ragged hole in his windpipe. Air rushed in and out through the hole... In and out, in and out. With each rush, the flow diminished in strength.

When the man was completely still, the acid receded and Prudence glanced over at Trish. She was still sitting where she'd frozen, the second she'd realized what was happening.

Prudence sighed and heaved the machete out over the water. It spun and hit flat, skipping once before sinking beneath the waves. "Trish, help me drag him out into the water. With luck, some kind barracuda will take care of him for us."

Trish didn't move.

"C'mon Trish, we need to get rid of him before someone sees!" Still no movement. "Trish!!"

Trish finally blinked and jumped to her feet. "Ah don't... Prudence, how could you do that?"

"Oh, it was easy." The older woman misunderstood her friend's question. "The idiot was leaning so far forward, he could have fallen all by himself—it only took a little tug to knock him off his feet. You've got to react without thinking. Men always expect you to be shocked, to freeze. And they expect you to try to get away later, but by then it's too late. Because he's anticipating it, he'll have you tied up, or something. The instant reaction is the only chance you've got to surprise *him*, and make *him* freeze. Then he's yours!"

"That's not what Ah mean! Ah mean, how could you just keeill him like that? You had him pinned. We could have tied him up and taken him to the police, or something..."

Prudence scrutinized Trish coolly, trying to fathom her friend's squeamishness. "Well, we could have done that, but they would have let him go. He would have told them that he was only going to take our purses, or some such lie, and they would let him go after a few days. Then he'd be out again, doing what we both know he was about to do to us, to other women. This way he'll never hurt anyone again."

Prudence regarded the dead man, feeling no remorse whatsoever, then shrugged at Trish—who was wondering how anyone but the man could 'know' what he was going to do. "But I'll tell you Trish, that's not why I did it. I wish I had, but it wasn't. I was just pissed. He is everything I hate—a fucking rapist—and I got mad. So I killed him." What she didn't say was that she had enjoyed it. It was the closest she'd ever come to having a sexual thrill with a man. "Now, are you going to help me get rid of this body, or what?"

Trish didn't answer, but she bent to help. They dragged the body out into the ocean as far as they dared. The blood was attracting the interest of something with fins even before they left the water. With the body no longer in sight, they took the time to dress, and then scooped up the blood-soaked sand and tossed it into the water. Before leaving, they erased the marks left in the sand by the struggle and the dragging of the body.

As they were pushing their mopeds back out onto the road, Prudence stopped Trish. "If anyone asks, we didn't see or hear anything. *Nothing*. Okay? If we try to make up any kind of stories or excuses, we can get caught in a lie. We tell the truth, but only part of it: we went riding, we did some tanning. We don't remember anything about any guy with a machete. Got it?"

"Got it." After all, Prudence had warned her that there might be some thunderheads to fly through before they reached blue skies. Trish supposed that they had to get hit by lightning sometimes, but that didn't mean she had to like it.

They kicked their engines into life and set off down the road.

CHAPTER 18

Return-Path: <jchristensen@floridalink.com>
X-Sender: jchristensen@pop1.floridalink.com
Date: Wed, 10 Nov 1999 14:29:03 -0500
To: "Bill Appleton" <bapple@utah-inter.net>
From: jchristensen@floridalink.com (Dr. Jared Christensen)
Subject: Re: External Problems
Cc: Y2K task force

Gentlemen,

In Bill's last message, he wrote:

>Jared, I'm as pleased as you are that the Church seems to
be ready for Y2K. >But I don't understand why you're so concerned about the favorable reports >from the various governments in whose jurisdictions we operate...

Well, you weren't here when we got this task force together, so you can't remember the discussions we had then.
Basically, we're dealing with bureaucracies that have no history of completing projects on time and on budget—and there
was neither enough time nor budget to begin with. To make
matters worse, even here in the U.S., government agencies
have a long history of lying to the public when they think it is in
the public interest, or just don't want to admit the truth.

So, we have a situation where we are being told that the
most serious challenge the U.S. government has faced since
the Cold War has been dealt with and that everything will be
fine. Have you noticed the way the CIAO director never seems

to give a straight answer in an interview? Doesn't that make you nervous?

>You don't believe all that doomsday nonsense in the tabloids, do you?

I don't know that I do, Bill. But the problems caused by the arrival of the fiscal year 2000 are real and very serious. Wouldn't it be prudent to have contingency plans in place, just in case? I'm not suggesting that we commit major Church resources to any new operations, but I think we should have plans in place for helping out, in case the worst does happen. That's it. All I'm talking about is paper.

So far, the Church's only investment has been the time our "Worst Case Scenario" committee has put into drafting plans. Now those plans are before the full task force, and I want them forwarded to the Quorum of the Twelve and the president's office as soon as we can clean them up and get them ready.

As you pointed out, the Church's own computer systems have been tested. We should be okay. But we live in community with other people, and we need to think about them as well.

So, I'm scheduling a full task force conference call for this Friday, the 12th of November, at 4:00 p.m., eastern time. That should give everyone in different time zones time to finish lunch first. Please do your best to be there—we need everyone's input!—and let me know if you can't make it. With luck, we can wrap this up with few changes and be done after Friday.

Gentlemen, it's been a pleasure working with you, and I hope our efforts will prove sufficient. We'll know in a very short time!

Warm regards,

Jared Christensen

CHAPTER 19:
TUESDAY, NOVEMBER 30, 1999

"The waiting is the hardest part
Every day see one more card
You take it on faith
You take it to the heart
The waiting is the hardest part."
—Tom Petty & the Heartbreakers, *The Waiting*

Alexis felt sick. She imagined herself standing on the bow of the *Titanic,* watching the iceberg looming closer, taller, blotting out the stars... Ever so slowly, and way too late, the bow begins to swing to the left. The ship is going to hit and there is nothing that can stop it.

Only, this time, it wasn't a matter of a few thousand people on a boat. It was the whole fucking planet, and there was *nothing* that could stop the collision!

Sighing, she got up from her desk in her underground office and decided to hunt for a coffee pot that had something liquid left in it.

Shit, maybe she ought to quit and go join Merlyn. *And Anna?* There were feelings there she still didn't want to explore. Besides, she couldn't give up. She wasn't a quitter. And the Pentagon would need its best people on hand to deal with the problems when the Millennium Bug bit for real.

At least they had gotten the mainframes at the Pentagon fixed— she hoped. It had been harder than even she had expected, but her mainframe team had come up with some excellent procedures.

Some of their ideas had come from the team monitoring progress in Europe, though this success was overshadowed by the rather disturbing news from Russia. The tests on the systems they'd debugged ran clean, but there was no way to know if the fixes would really work until Y2K actually hit. Most of the mainframers were now flying around the country, supervising repairs and training others to do the same.

Unfortunately, things weren't going so well elsewhere. NORAD and SAC both insisted that they already had all of their systems fixed. Alexis didn't see how that could be, especially since each satellite in orbit required its own unique Y2K debugging. There had been an unusual number of military launches recently, and even a few extra space shuttle missions, but there was no way they could have them all checked out. And none of that even began addressing the problem of compatibility between Y2K fixes!

Alexis didn't know whether to look forward to, or to dread the arrival of the Y2K preparedness reports from NORAD and SAC.

In spite of the authority she'd been given from the officers supervising Y2K preparedness in each of the armed services, the support of the joint chiefs, and the mandate from the president, there was even more inter-service foot-dragging than she had feared there would be. They all cooperated, eventually, but the clock was ticking down, and there was no way to replace the wasted time.

To her surprise, Alexis found a freshly brewed pot of coffee on her first try—must be other folks burning the midnight oil too. She closed her eyes and savored the hot liquid as it burned its way down, reinvigorating her as it went. Opening her eyes again, she searched up and down the hallway and spied dark hair, khaki pants, and a blue shirt—pulled tight over a muscular build—receding to the south. "Mr. Allen? Is that you?"

The man turned. It was him; his civilian clothes were easy to spot. "Yes, Colonel Thomas? What can I do for you?" He turned and came back toward the coffee machine as he spoke, seeming quite happy to see her. Perhaps he too needed a break.

"Oh, I just need a break from pulling my hair out over inter-service rivalry. Tell me something new. Any late breaking news from the 'everything else' team?"

John Allen chuckled. "The 'everything else' team is doing a great job. Once I got them to understand that they need to look in the wrong places—equipment that doesn't use date information, or where there aren't any microprocessors at all—you know what I mean—they started coming up with more lists of components to be checked than you could believe. Maybe we're getting more cooperation because we're not seen as telling folks from other branches how they should do things; we just send them lists of components to check and replace."

"Sez you." Alexis grinned wryly. "We'll have to do some inspection tours to see if they're actually doing the replacements."

"If we sent a list of stuff to a soldier and told him it had a pretty good chance of failing in a month, he—or she, sorry, no offense—wouldn't replace it?"

"Oh, they'd want to, if they weren't busy playing cards. But if the CO isn't convinced that it's an emergency, he—and relax, most times it is a he—might not make it his first priority to get the replacements, because of budget or other concerns. Even if everyone jumped to implement our suggestions, there might not be enough time to get to them all. And I doubt we have enough supplies of Y2K-compliant components or substitutes to take care of everything, anyway."

Allen grimaced. "There isn't a person on the team who feels confident enough to give me a decent estimate on what percentage of the problems they think we've got licked. Those reasons must be a part of why. Some say as low as 40 percent, others as high as 70 percent, but none of them are willing to commit to those numbers as outside limits. We're still working on bringing those percentages up higher, of course, but you're right about us not being able to get to everything. I'm actually working on a progress report right now. This cup of coffee should see me through to the end of it. I'll drop it off on my way out."

"Good. I look forward to seeing it." Alexis liked talking to Mr.

Allen. He spoke to her with the respect he'd accord any decent person, not with the artificial and rigid civility of military decorum. Besides, he smelled good—not the kind of heavy use of cologne she couldn't stand, but a slight trace of after-shave mixed in with the man's own masculine scent. She found herself wanting to prolong the conversation.

He obliged: "Colonel Thomas, if I may say so, you look very tired. Why not go home and get some rest?"

"I'd like to," she straightened her uniform, "but I can't. There's so much to do! I know I can't do it all, but every thing I can get checked off my list is one less thing that might go wrong and get somebody hurt."

"Well, you're probably right about that, Colonel." He sipped his coffee.

"It's Alexis, please. You've been working as a consultant here for more than six months, and you didn't have to salute me to begin with, so please call me Alexis—at least, when there's no brass around. I like to be reminded that there is a human being under this uniform."

"Fine. Alexis." Her comment about what was under her uniform sent his mind off in a direction that flustered him. She was clearly very fit, and even though her uniform did its best to hide her curves, Allen suspected that Alexis had curves aplenty and all in the right places. Embarrassed, he stuck out his hand, as though they were meeting for the first time. "And my name's John." He winced for having made such an awkward gesture, but pressed ahead. "Please call me John."

Alexis shook his hand and graciously took no note of his embarrassment. "Well, John, I brought you on because you were the most knowledgeable person on embedded systems I could find. I'm sure you know how few like you there are. The civilian agencies, contractors, and suppliers that we deal with have hired mainframe programmers to fix their big computers, but none of them are working on embedded systems the way you and the 'everything else' team have been doing. I keep trying to warn them, and they keep saying they have their hands full with the mainframes—we'll just have to see what happens!"

"Like coming up against a brick wall, huh?"

"You know it!" She chuckled, in spite of her frustration. "Or, in the immortal words of Charlie Brown: Aaaaargh!!!!!!!"

They both laughed and headed back to their respective offices.

There was no doubt about it; Alexis' teams had done far better than she had thought they would. But even if the armed services made it, their effectiveness would definitely be severely crippled. And there was no question that the civilian authorities were going to have a hard time pulling through with any ability to function at all. She didn't want to think about martial law, but the idea wouldn't go away.

Back in her chair, Alexis reviewed the summary report she was preparing at the president's direct request. How to work in what would be in John Allen's report? What about whatever was in the NORAD and SAC reports? She wondered idly about what her counterparts in the CIA, NSA, and other agencies were saying in their reports. And what about the poor sucker they conned into taking charge of CIAO—he must be having nightmares while preparing his reports!

Well, no point in wasting time wondering about it; she knew she'd tell 'em exactly like it was, as she'd always done.

Her superiors, agency heads, and even the president were feeding the public forecasts of smooth sailing. If she was completely blunt and to the point, she might be the scapegoat picked for blame when things crashed, but at least they'd know in their own little minds that they had been warned. What's the worst they could do? Kick her out of the Army? At least then she'd be free to join the folks out at the Dollar Ranch.

They were almost upon the iceberg. Nothing much to do now, except brace for the impact, and be ready to scramble to the pumps afterward.

Chapter 20:
Wednesday, December 8, 1999

"You sell the copy like the cover of a magazine...
The things that they see make the daily reviews
You never get free—everybody wants you."
—Billy Squier, *Everybody Wants You*

Michel Gerard had scarcely any time for speculation. He'd never been so busy in his entire career as a financial advisor. Everyone—*everyone!*—had gone skittish and was constantly wanting their portfolio rearranged, not to mention the new customers!

Michel was one of the few advisors to warn people to pull out of airline stock before the FAA disaster. When word got out that Michel's clients had also made huge amounts of easy money when the fiscal year 2000 had hit, new customers had begun flocking to his business. He was not so certain that he deserved the accolades, and was under a great deal of pressure to shelter his clients from the Big One, now less than a month away.

His task was not made easier by people reading new 'expert' advice in the papers every day. They called, always in a near panic, directing him to buy this or sell that. It was ridiculous! He could serve them far better if they'd just leave him alone and trust him.

The office was turning into a madhouse—it was worse than Macy's the day after Christmas!

All the extra transactions were making him an enormous amount of money, but few of them were doing his clients any good.

The phone rang—again.

"Merde," he mumbled and took the call. When he got done explaining to the caller that buying stock in gun manufacturing companies *was* a good idea, but only *if* they could certify Y2K preparedness, he punched Grace's intercom button.

"Yes, Mr. Gerard?"

"Eh ham Inspecteur Clouseau, yeu fuel!"

Grace burst out laughing. "Thanks Inspector, I needed that!"

"You are welcome! But please, hold my calls for ze next half 'our. I need to sink."

Grace giggled. "Well, don't sink too low, or Natalie will be disappointed tonight!"

"Natalie! Mon Dieu! I was supposed to meet her for lunch!"

"She called, Inspector, and I told her what kind of day you're having. She understands and says she'll meet you at your place after work tonight."

"Grace, ze woman is a saint. I do not sink I deserve her!"

"You're probably right Inspector, but, if you don't mind my saying so, she really does love you."

"Sanks Grace." And then, on an impulse: "And I love you too— never worked wis anyone better!"

Grace's voice caught, but she managed to answer, "Now don't make me cry. You just go do your sinking."

"Yes Grace."

Chapter 21:
Wednesday, December 8, 1999

"Tell me lies, Tell me sweet little lies!"
—Fleetwood Mac, *Little Lies*

"And you're sure these chips are Y2K-compliant?"

Angel smiled. "Absolutely! They came from a new company that filed for bankruptcy last month and sold off its assets. They were made this year and are one hundred percent Y2K-compliant. I'll show you the paperwork." This was to be a big deal, and the profit would allow him to buy some very special toys he thought he might soon be able to play with.

It was one of his Asian lieutenants who had hit upon the idea of using their fake ID business to make fake Y2K compliance certificates and sell cheap microprocessors at premium prices. This was Ejercito's biggest deal yet and would bring in a profit in excess of $1.3 million. Computer companies were getting so desperate for ways to keep up with the demand for Y2K-compliant circuitry and software that many had become willing to turn to the black market.

Today's dupe was an older white man—obviously an engineer and not a businessman. He had actually brought the money in a suitcase, just like in the movies!

The authenticity papers were examined and accepted. The cash changed hands and the truck drivers were told where to deliver the merchandise.

Nice and neat.

CHAPTER 22:
FRIDAY, DECEMBER 24, 1999

"I get by with a little help from my friends
Gonna try with a little help from my friends."
—Beatles, *A Little Help from my Friends*

"The Dollar Ranch looks so different!" Anna reined her horse to a stop. Alone with Merlyn again, her more vibrant side was showing.

"Well," her partner pulled up beside her, "there are more people living in the valley now, but we haven't started the serious building yet. If you ask me it's all those holiday decorations they set up on our house."

Anna laughed. "I didn't even think about what would happen at this time of year, with so many families here. It was only natural that they'd want to decorate the Big House."

"Yes, but did they have to cover it so thoroughly? Every window I look out, all I see are wreathes, lights, and ribbons. I'm glad your family hasn't fallen for all that madness!"

The two laughed together, holding hands, then Anna took on a more serious tone: "I'm sorry your family has not decided to join us, Beloved."

Merlyn shrugged. "I suppose it may be for the best. Your father had no problem signing the Contract, once he understood the logic of it. I doubt any of my family would really see things our way, no matter what logic we brought to bear. They wouldn't mesh well with the community we're building."

From up on the valley rim, where the two sat on their horses surveying that very community, the holiday decorations were hardly visible. The most discernible differences in the little valley were Y2K-related.

Breath steaming on the cold air, the pair urged their horses forward along the snow-clad road Jimmy had made immediately inside the defensive perimeter. Smoke came from the chimneys of all but two of the barns. Half of the studio apartments were occupied as well. The roads radiating out from the central oval were all completed, so that people anywhere within the valley could race to defend any part of the perimeter that might be attacked. When the houses were built, along with the watchtowers Alexis had suggested they add to their perimeter defenses, the valley would look even more transformed.

Merlyn slowed his horse and indicated a spot with a gloved finger. "When there aren't any more building inspectors, we'll build watchtower 14 right there."

The armored watchtowers would look too conspicuous to pre-Y2K authorities, so they would have to wait. However, other less conspicuous suggestions Alexis had made—she being the closest thing to a security advisor the Dollar Ranch had—were already being implemented. Planting remote-controlled explosives under the road that led to the ranch, and under the radial roads within the valley had been the easiest to do. Fougasses—home-made napalm sprayers—had also been easy to install at key places where enemies might amass.

"You know," Anna remarked, knowing what her partner was thinking about, "Alexis was right about the watchtowers, and she's right about the redoubt too. I don't know why we didn't think of those things."

"She is our Warrior Princess, after all!" Merlyn chuckled, and then grew more serious. "I know she's right about the redoubt. The valley won't be secure as long as we have to rely on one central hub; if it falls or malfunctions, we'll all end up dead. But building an easily defensible backup command center will be difficult, and it will take time. I'm afraid we'll have to wait until the disappearance of the building inspectors before we can build that kind of heavy-duty bunker."

Anna regarded Merlyn soberly. "You're not thinking outside your nine dots, dearest partner. Why *build* a redoubt when the west side of the valley has a perfectly comfortable abandoned mine in it? Were not the mine's defensive possibilities one of the reasons we bought the Dollar Ranch? It certainly isn't the best grazing land!"

"Why, that's...brilliant!" Merlyn blinked. "I haven't told Alexis about the mine, or I'm sure she'd have thought of it too. I've been thinking of it mostly as a fallout shelter, and a low-visibility warehouse." He shook his head. "I must be getting old—it's perfectly obvious! The mine already has a backup generator, so installing a backup computer system would be relatively simple. Even digging an escape tunnel from the mine to the basement command center in the Big House could be pulled off without anyone noticing. We can use the empty shafts and tunnels to dump all the dirt from the digging. Won't have to lift a single pail above ground, where it could be seen. With an underground redoubt like that, anyone who overran our perimeter would be in for a nasty shock."

Anna nodded, and the two rode on until they arrived at the next gun emplacement.

Merlyn dismounted and stooped over a rectangular cement slab on the ground—the wind had swept the snow off this one— and punched a combination into a keypad recessed into its surface. There was a beep and the whining of heavy duty electric motors as a portion of the cement slab rose, exposing the computerized weapon.

The TJC-30, its solenoid actuators, its firing computer, its sensors, and its neatly folded 300-round ammo belt were all in good order. The belts were assembled from regular 30.06 ammunition, scrounged by Merlyn and Anna at bargain prices at gun shows over the course of several years. Because of the mixed sources, some of the rounds of ammunition had armor-piercing bullets, some had incendiary bullets, and others had various kinds of soft-point and jacketed bullets. In a sustained conflict, the trench and breastwork gunners might have to change the belts, so each gun had two 300-round backup belts.

Merlyn smiled at the memory of Dollar Ranch's children earning extra pocket money by helping to assemble the belts. "Who'd have thought that kids would make such great machine gun belt linkers!"

Anna smiled in return. "It was amusing to see them with all those piles of bullets and links. They did a great job, and saved us from a lot of tedious work!" Her thoughts turned to the purpose of the belts, and her tone hardened. "Do you think two backup belts are enough?"

"That's 900 rounds, my dear Soulmate—per gun! More ammunition than that would assume an attacking force numbering in the thousands, and that doesn't seem very likely out here in the middle of nowhere."

"No, I suppose not... Unless the Ferals decide to come after us for hoarding, or some such charge, when things get rough." Anna always referred to Federal agents as Ferals.

"We'll keep an eye out for Ferals then. The watchtowers should help. And if things really fall apart, we could hole up in the redoubt until they starve out here."

The sixteen watchtowers, when built, would be spaced about every half mile—depending on the terrain—a short distance inside the valley rim. The north, east, and west towers, and the south tower by the gate, would be manned twenty-four hours a day when times were bad, and all sixteen would be manned in case of an alert. All the towers would have a Barrett semiautomatic long distance sniper rifle—a huge high-powered gun, spartan-looking and black, that shot fifty caliber Browning Machine Gun ammunition.

The .50 BMG cartridges—also scrounged in whatever variety could be found at gun shows—were enormous, about six inches long and nearly an inch across the base. Each tower would have a rack of ten extra magazines and a large ammo can with a hundred

more rounds, so that tower guards could aid the breastwork defenders, especially if the attacking force was wearing body armor.

Merlyn smiled at his mental use of the word 'breastwork'.
Ever since that night at dinner, the word had taken on new meaning to most of those living in the valley. Dawn never ceased teasing
Jimmy about it. Dreamer's eldest daughter usually ignored it all,
having reached an age where it was beneath her dignity to respond
in kind.

It was also true, Merlyn reflected, that the others were slack-
ing off a bit on the teasing, as new arrivals were providing romantic opportunities of various kinds for all but the youngest. He
punched a second code on the pad and sent the cement slab back
to its resting place. Back on his horse again, he leaned over to kiss
Anna, and the two headed for the next emplacement. Everything
was in order. The little valley was becoming a fortress.

The owner of the Dollar Ranch and his partner were not anticipating things to get really bad for a few more months, but were
not sure of the timing, and didn't want to take any chances. Everyone who could had either moved onto the ranch permanently, or
was taking an extended vacation with them.

All they needed now, after chaos broke loose and the above-
ground buildings could be completed, was to wait for the fireworks.

Chapter 23:
New Year's Eve, 1999

"What ya gonna do
Time's caught up with you
Now you wait your turn
You know there's no return."
—Black Sabbath, *Hand of Doom*

10:00 p.m., EST

Michel usually enjoyed going to New Year's Eve parties, but the Millennium Bug had him in a funk. So many variables! So many things to consider in advising his clients! So many ways it could all turn out...

And now it was finally here.

The news from France and the rest of Europe did not look good. It had to be admitted that nothing had blown up yet, and there were no reports of massive accidents with large numbers of fatalities... But the advisor was still uneasy—Max had warned that some of the immediate failures would be small and take a while to cause larger, more visible problems. It could also be that everyone with any sense was staying away from computers on this night. If so, then perhaps nothing really bad would result from the failures that had already been reported. Time, and the news, would tell.

Natalie had wanted to go to a party, but Michel had been unable to shake a feeling of impending doom, and had told her to go ahead without him.

Now, watching the domestic news reports unfolding on his

television, he was glad that New Year's Eve 1999 had arrived on a Friday night. Nothing major so far, and a couple days to sort things out before the markets opened... Max's war had not come. Maybe Michel should go join Natalie after all. He switched the tube off and pried himself off the sofa—there was still time to look for something he could wear to the party.

*　　*　　*

11:59 p.m., EST

Jared and Emily Christensen sat in the family room of their Tallahassee home. The kids were all asleep—or at least in their rooms, in the case of the older ones. The couple sat with their arms around each other, watching the ball drop in Times Square.

The turn of the millennium and the unusually warm weather—barely freezing—had brought out millions of native New Yorkers as well as visitors to the city. Large projection screens had been set up in nearby parks to accommodate the overflow from Times Square. The commentators on the Christensens' screen were saying that the crowd—estimated at between four and six million—was the largest ever recorded on film and possibly the largest single gathering in history. Similar crowds were gathered in Los Angeles, Chicago, Atlanta, and other cities, but none were as large as the one in New York; everyone wanted to be in the Big Apple to watch the year 2000 ball drop...

And drop it did!

"Well, Brittany," one of the talking heads was saying to the other, "it would seem that the ball is working like a charm."

"It sure is Bob!" She turned to look directly into the camera. "As you know, a very special ball was built for this year." Her script scrolled up her TelePrompTer, right above the camera lens. "It has two thousand high powered strobe lights controlled by a small on-board computer. The computer has been *very* carefully tested for millennium bugs. We shouldn't have any problems like the ones that have been reported in countries that were less prepared for the year 2000 than the United States is!"

On screen, as the ball descended, shapes, lines, and curves of brilliant light swirled over its surface, faster and faster, until the frenetic microsecond when the ball reached the bottom of the pole. The new ten-foot-tall numerals lit up with "2000," and a volley of fireworks leapt into the air. The uproar from the crowd was so deafening that the fireworks seemed to explode silently over their upturned faces.

The scene of jubilation carried on for several minutes, while the commentators made inane noises of relief that the year 2000 had gotten underway without any problems.

Then Bob frowned and pressed his ear-piece deeper into his ear. In fact, the ear-piece was a prop: he too was reading off a TelePrompTer. "Hold on Brittany, I'm getting some breaking news over the wire." He frowned again and pretended to be listening while he read his new script.

The camera zoomed in on his face. "Ladies and gentlemen, I'm receiving news that sporadic power outages are being reported all over the eastern seaboard. The first details are only beginning to come in, but it seems that several cities, including Tampa, New Haven, Charlotte, Jersey City, Bangor, and many more lost power at the stroke of midnight."

The Times Square scene behind Brittany and Bob was replaced by an east-coast weather map with red dots appearing every few seconds where power outages were being reported. The two newscasters spent some time speculating on the possible causes of the problem while waiting for more information to come up on their prompters.

Finally, Bob got a new script and started reading it into the camera. "Reports are now coming in of major regional black-outs and brown-outs spreading westward, all the way to California." He fiddled with the ear-piece again as the new script scrolled farther up. "Ladies and gentlemen, electrical power along a significant portion of the west coast has gone down and seems to be staying down. The extent is not yet known, but San Diego is out, as are Los Angeles, San Francisco, Sacramento. Even Reno and Las Vegas, in Nevada, are without power."

The weather map expanded to show the entire country. Splotches of red appeared and disappeared in various places. Most of California and Nevada were bathed in red. Bob and Brittany took turns listing major affected cities.

"An official CIAO spokesperson has not been located for comment yet," Bob resumed his commentary, "but our correspondent in Los Angeles says he spoke with someone at Pacific Power, the largest electric power utility in the west, who said that the problem did not originate in their system. He says a neighboring system had some kind of problem and that a failure at something called an 'intertie' caused major problems in the pacific grid. Apparently, one section after another has shut itself down in order to avoid being overloaded..."

"Oh my God!" Jared turned to Emily, no longer listening to the television. "All those people out celebrating New Year's Eve! Those crowds will turn to mobs in the dark!"

*　　*　　*

11:59 p.m., EST

"Colonel Thomas, where would you like the extra monitors?" The man addressing Alexis was an Air Force captain, arriving through the door with two enlisted men who were trundling a portable array of screens. The two enlisted men were chuckling over some joke.

Alexis frowned. "This isn't a game, boys, a lot of people could die in the next twenty-four hours."

"Yes ma'am!" The two sobered up.

"Put them over here to the right of the satellite feed monitors." Why had she scolded them? There was no reg against sharing a joke in a hallway, and everyone needed to release their tension somehow—the approaching onset of Y2K had everyone on edge.

The two didn't seem perturbed, however, and set to work hooking up the new monitors and reconfiguring the ones already in place. When they were done, one screen in the expanded collection showed CNN, a number showed newsfeeds from other networks, a few showed live feeds from various military installations, and several showed real-time orbital views.

The scariest scenes were the orbital views. These were showing mostly on the monitors that had already been set up in Alexis' Y2K Tracking Center. She had been watching them all night. By the time New Year's Day hit the prime meridian, she had seen more cities disappear into darkness than she could count.

Things had started with the Pacific Islands, Japan, and Asia, where the first parts of the earth had entered the year 2000. Unfortunately for Alexis and other watchers, a large weather system was covering most of the far east. Occasionally, as midnight moved westward through a gap in the cloud cover, cities and other light sources would go out. This had become quite pronounced as Y2K hit Europe, especially when the entire country of Belgium had vanished from sight. You couldn't miss Belgium's disappearance; virtually all of their highways were lit up at night, making Belgium one of the brightest places on nocturnal earth, as seen from space. When its power grid had gone down, it was as though the cold waters of the North Sea had poured into the heart of Europe and obliterated the country.

Now it was the United States' turn.

Even as Alexis was monitoring the satellite feeds, four of them went blank. On the remaining views from space, she could see electrical problems start on the East Coast and spread to the West Coast in a matter of seconds. It wasn't her focus, but something similar was happening in Canada, while Mexico hadn't been hit yet. Power started coming back on in some places in Central, Mountain, and Pacific time zones, but at locations already in the year 2000, the electricity stayed out. And in California.

She and her team leaders were gathered to track the results of their labors, but what was happening in the civilian world drew their attention, and the power outages were not a good sign. A somber mood suffused the group as they waited quietly to see what would happen next.

"Captain Smith," Alexis addressed the Air Force captain, "run a diagnostic on our machines here and get me a report from every command center in this time zone. See if NORAD thinks they'll be able to get those satellites back on-line."

"Yes, ma'am!"

She turned to the CNN monitor, resisting the temptation to slump in her chair. They didn't seem too badly hurt by the power outages, but they couldn't get reports from within affected areas. The problems were obviously Y2K related, but none of their talking heads could say for certain what was going on. This left them with little intelligent commentary to make.

John Allen, sitting behind a console to Alexis' right, remarked on this: "Well, at least the quality of the reporting seems normal."

Alexis turned to him, ignoring the joke. "Mr. Allen, what's the latest from our bases in Korea and the Pacific Islands? They've had the most time for secondary Y2K problems to manifest themselves—the kind of embedded systems failures your team was working on—any new situations reported yet?"

"I've don't have a complete report on that yet, ma'am, but it looks like they are having sporadic failures, even in mission-critical systems. I think commo gear is being particularly hard hit, so it's taking time to get the information. They've had problems with power too—some installations have had to switch to backup power, and I have at least two reports of that failing as well."

The Colonel sighed and leafed through some reports she'd been handed earlier. Her team leaders and specialists all worked in silence, the glowing images on the screens making the stillness seem all the more eerie. She closed her eyes and rubbed her temples—the combined tang of burnt coffee and ozone was giving her a headache.

A phone warbled.

Ensign Beck, a young computer specialist on loan from the Navy, picked it up. "Y2K Tracking Center, Ensign Beck speaking." He listened for a short while. "Colonel Thomas, it's General Hudgins' office for you."

"Thank you, Ensign." She picked up the call on her own phone. "Colonel Thomas here... Yes, I'll wait. Yes General Hudgins. No sir. Yes, our preliminary information is that there will be more random failures. I'm especially concerned about the satellites we've lost. Communications seems pretty hard hit, and other mission-critical functions may be at risk... Excuse me, sir? That projection is based on the experience of our installations overseas that began experiencing Y2K problems hours ago. We're still waiting for reports from installations in this time zone."

She gestured to John Allen to bring her what he had and began reading some of the details into the phone. Then she stopped abruptly. "The president wants what, sir?" She gaped at Allen and rolled her eyes. "We'll need some clerical support staff down here to write that many reports... Yes sir, I'll keep you posted. And, sir? May I suggest that Ft. Meade, Langley, and some other non-military facilities with tracking centers might be able to give us independent assessments of the situation? No... No sir. Thank you, sir!"

She hung up the phone and watched her people's faces for their reactions. "Well, it's going down. It doesn't look great for us and it will certainly be worse for the civilian agencies. The phones are still working, but power is going to be a major problem. And who knows what folks will find when they go to work Monday? I suspect that we'll all be a lot busier pretty soon!"

"It's possible to get busier?" It was Allen again. "How?"

"Never mind that now, it's almost time for Y2K to hit Central time—let's see what happens."

On the screens, more cities were disappearing. In less than a minute, most of Mexico vanished, and then more screens blanked out as more satellites died.

*   *   *

8:59 p.m., PST

Razor and Rapier had finished dancing a new variation on their routine and were out among the patrons of the Golden Chalice Club. Both were hating it, but it was in their contract—as it was for all of the club's dancers—that they had to mix with the guests during the club's New Year's Eve party.

The whole reason Prudence had created the sexual/combat dance gig was so that she and Trish could be seen without being touched. Now there were men pressed all around her and she couldn't breathe without inhaling their sweaty musk. The sexy costumes achieved their purpose on stage, but now their effectiveness was working against the dancers. The situation was made worse by the very success of Prudence's strategy: men who had hungered for the pair—from a distance—for months were now pressing close, supposedly for autographs.

Things had been manageable to begin with, in spite of a room occupancy that would give the fire marshal a coronary, but then some blockhead had thought up the idea of having Prudence sign her autograph on his skin. Larry had obligingly gone to his office to fetch a box of permanent markers and now even the men who'd already received autographs on paper were pressing close again, presenting various parts of their anatomy for signing.

Prudence and Trish were back to back, fending off the press with markers, trying to take some satisfaction from making sure the autographs would show where the men's wives could see them. Prudence took to making a slash mark underneath her stylized 'Razor' with the tip of one of her blades. To her disgust, the men loved it.

Trish could see that Prudence's temper was beginning to fray. "Ah cain't stand this, but at least it's only for one night!" she whispered.

"Right, partner. Just a few more thunderclouds to fly through!"

She paused in her scribbling to kiss Trish lightly on the cheek.

The countdown from Times Square was showing on several of the Golden Chalice's projection televisions. The club wasn't scheduled to do its own countdown for another three hours, but everyone had wanted to watch the big one in New York City. The final countdown brought a merciful reprieve from the jostling, as the men turned toward the screens and began counting out loud: "Five, four, three, two, one... Happy New Year!!!"

The lights went out.

And came back on.

And went out again.

Then came back on before going out and staying out.

"Shit!" Someone muttered in the dark.

The word broke a spell, and everyone started talking at once, grumbling and complaining. At first, the people in the crowd thought the lights would come right back on, so none of them moved. After a while, however, the air began getting musty, and people began looking for a way out. There were emergency lights, but they were few in number and cast sharp-edged, confusing shadows.

Prudence and Trish were still back to back, but some moron managed to get his hand between them and stroke Prudence's ass. "Whoever you are, get your hand off me if you want to keep the hand!"

The hand was snatched away, but Prudence's voice reminded the men that they were in a room in which they could not be seen, with nothing between them and the women they had been lusting after for so long. Consciously or not, they pressed forward. A finger here, a hand there, and...was that a tongue?

Prudence screamed and began stabbing about her with her razor gauntlets. She felt the now-familiar acid rising and was not gentle. The men gave way, cursing.

Sensing that her partner was about to let the heat take her again, Trish turned and placed a restraining hand on Prudence's shoulder. "Prue," she whispered, "let 'em go. They're pullin' back, and there ain't no fish heah to take care of the bodies."

Prudence tensed as if to spring, then laughed. "No fish!" After she calmed a bit, she hugged Trish—mindful of her gauntlets. "You're right, little sister." She tried to look into her eyes, but there wasn't enough light to see.

People cleared out of the room as they found their way to the exits, making it easier for the dancers to see. Instead of heading out onto the street or parking lot, where all the men would be, they made their way back to their dressing room. They locked the door and stripped out of their tight-fitting costumes.

"You know," Prudence pulled Trish's hand until the two were sitting on the floor, holding one another, "Kat called me Prue. It has always sounded wrong coming from anyone else's lips, but it sounded right when you said it. I think Kat would have liked you."

*   *   *

11:57 p.m., PST

Angel decided it was a gift from God. The city was plunged into darkness three hours before he'd planned for it, giving him more time to set up. Add to that the blessing of having every cop in the city trying to control the rioting, and it had to be a sign from God.

When he had told Rosalia of his plans, she had called him a devil and had actually attacked him with her fists! Well, there would be time for taming the shrew later. Right now it was time to play with his new toys.

"¡Cabron," he motioned imperiously, "dame uno!"

Cabron opened the suitcase that rested on the bed of the pickup truck the pair had stolen for use that night. In the gloom, only the vaguest outlines of the rocket-propelled grenades and their launcher could be seen, resting in wadded newspaper cradles that had been fashioned for them. Cabron couldn't read the Cyrillic lettering stenciled on the outside of the tubular launcher, but there were pictures as well, and he had already practiced with the weapons at a time when he'd been able to see better. He took one of the lolli-pop-shaped grenades and fitted it to the end of the tube. "Ten, Jefe." He handed the weapon to his boss, as well as some ear plugs. Donning ear plugs himself, he took out a second RPG.

Angel shouldered the primed weapon and sighted on the po-lice station across the street. All around the city, two-man teams with RPG-7s were doing the same thing. He waited until his watch read 11:59:50, and then began counting down as he sighted in on the doorway. A police officer started coming out, holding the door open while she spoke to someone inside.

"Tres, dos, uno..."

The streak of fire and accompanying explosion were gratify-ing. The grenade lanced through the open door and exploded in the foyer. Gouts of flame surged back out the doorway, knocking the policewoman to the ground and blowing the doors themselves off their hinges.

Glass was still tinkling down when Angel held out his hand. "¡Cabron, dame el otro!"

Cabron's ears were ringing so loudly he couldn't hear the or-der, but he knew what was wanted and handed the second gre-nade over.

Angel slid the RPG into the launcher, sighted on the window he knew was the police chief's, and pressed the trigger. The gre-nade rocketed up into the window, leaving a trail of smoke and creating a another explosion every bit as gratifying as the first.

"¡Vamonos!"

The two gangsters hopped into their truck and tore off down the street, before the few people in the building even knew what had hit them.

A message had been delivered to the LAPD: they were no longer in control of the city.

Chapter 24:
New Year's Day, Year 2000

"You can feel the waves coming on
Let them destroy you or carry you on
You're fighting the weight of the world
But no one can save you this time."
—Dream Theater, *Take the Time*

01:23 a.m., MST

Merlyn sat at his computer, reading messages from friends around the country and the world.

Anna came up behind him and began massaging his tired neck and shoulder muscles. "What do they say?"

"It's bad, but not as bad as it could have been. The World Wide Web is full of holes where servers have gone down—lack of power or other Y2K problems—but since the phones are working most places in Europe and North America, I'm getting a lot of news. Most businesses are closed for the holiday, so we won't begin to know how bad they're hit 'til late Monday. The governments probably won't tell the truth, so who knows when we'll find out what's going on there. Right now, the biggest problem seems to be power outages, especially the big one in California."

"So, no one's written about L.A.?"

Merlyn turned to face her. "You mean something besides the power outage?"

"It's not clear yet what's going on. The news keeps repeating so much that I fall asleep and miss the new stuff! Anyway, there's been a series of explosions throughout the whole metro area. Downtown L.A., Glendale, Pomona, Long Beach, Newport Beach, the works. Earlier on they thought it might be gas lines exploding because of something to do with the power outage, but they're finding that a lot of police stations have been hit. Now they think it might be something deliberate."

Merlyn whistled softly. "Do they think it might be international terrorists or are they blaming domestic criminals?"

"Too early to tell. They weren't even thinking that it was deliberate until a few minutes ago."

Anna settled on Merlyn's lap and the two sat together for a long while, saying nothing. When she bent to kiss him on the forehead, his eyes were wet. "What is it, Beloved?" She kissed each eyelid, tasting the salt.

"My best friend and most wonderful partner, I love you so!" He leaned his head against her chest. "It's going to be bad, my sweet, very bad. Maybe not right away, but I know things are going to get very, *very* bad before they get any better. And people are going to die. And many of the ones who don't will turn on one another with fear and hatred in their hearts."

"It is what we have prepared for, my love."

"We've prepared, yes, but I guess I was still hoping it wouldn't happen." He sighed. "And so few others have prepared! What will they do when things fall apart? I still don't know."

*   *   *

07:36 a.m., EST

"Hello? Yes. Elder Young?"

Jared motioned to everyone in the breakfast room to be quiet so he could hear. It didn't work. "Can you hold on a moment while I switch phones? Thank you." He handed the handset to Emily. "Hang up when I pick up the one in the study, please, Honey? Thanks!"

In his study, Jared sat at his desk and lifted the receiver. "I've got it!" He heard the click and then resumed his conversation. "Yes Elder Young, what can I do for you?"

"You can start by dispensing with the formalities, brother Christensen." The voice was old and gravelly, but full of warmth and charm, like Earl Nightingale's. It was the kind of voice that made you want to believe in every word it uttered. "Call me Richard, please, and I'll call you Jared, if that's all right with you."

"Yes Elder—I mean, yes, Richard. So, I've heard from some of the Y2K task force members today... I understand that the Church is weathering the storm with relatively few difficulties?"

"Indeed, Jared, indeed. And that is due in no small part to your efforts. The embedded system threat you picked up on has turned out to be one of the most important things we did right. It is embedded system trouble that is causing the power companies so much difficulty, and even the military seems to have had a lot of trouble with that side of things. Thanks to you, the LDS Church may well come through this better than any other organization of our size."

The doctor blushed and could think of nothing to say.

"So, congratulations are in order, but that's not the only reason I called."

"Oh?"

"Yes. It seems that the power outages were the first big problem, but there will be more. It was very fortunate that so many things were closed for the holidays, but from what we can tell here in Utah, things are going to be quite chaotic come Monday morning."

"How so, El—Richard?"

"Oh, we hear from Church members in the military, members who operate businesses, members in government... From what our people are telling us, a *lot* of things are not going to work right for some time. And that's not all. Arlene Waller has asked the Church to be prepared to help with additional relief efforts, if the state government should prove unable to perform certain functions."

"The governor said that?"

"It is strictly confidential, but yes, she did."

"Hmmm... Well, these kinds of things were among the reasons I insisted on having the extra contingency plans drawn up."

"And that's why I'm calling. I know you have a successful practice there in Tallahassee, but the Church needs you. *I* need you to come back to Utah and help us manage our implementation of those contingency plans."

"Ah... I'll need some time, Elder." Jared made a face as though he had bitten his tongue. "Richard."

"I understand." The sympathetic voice disregarded the slip-up. It resonated with smiles and understanding. "Please take all the time you need. It will take time for us to see exactly what kind of contingencies we're dealing with anyway. But please hurry and get here as quickly as you can. It is your blessing and your burden, son, to be able to serve the Church in this way."

"I am honored to be called upon."

"All right then, ring up my office when you're ready and talk to Hyrum Behle about taking care of moving expenses. We'll go ahead and get a house set up for you, and some space here in the Church office building, so you can hit the ground running when you get here. And, Jared..."

"Yes...Richard?"

"Thank you, son. I believe that what you did for us has saved lives, and surely that means that our Heavenly Father is looking out for you. I look forward to seeing you here in Salt Lake soon!"

*   *   *

10:53 a.m., EST

"Are you sure about this?" Alexis knew it was an unnecessary question, but she couldn't keep herself from asking.

"Absolutely, Colonel. Ma'am."

"All right, get me everything you have on it, fax a summary to

General Hudgins and the White House, and then get me the president on the line."

She was handed a phone about ten minutes later. "Mr. President?"

"Yes Colonel Thomas, what can I do for you?"

"You asked to be informed directly if anything came up that could be a threat to national security while our defensive systems are crippled. Have you seen my fax yet, sir?"

"It's coming through now, Colonel..." There was a pause and then Alexis heard the president whistle softly. "Holy... Are you certain of this information, Colonel?"

"Yes sir. My overseas monitoring team has been keeping an eye on all international traffic dealing with Y2K problems, and this situation has been confirmed by numerous intercepted transmissions. The Cubans have been trying to reach Moscow about it with increasing desperation, but the former Soviet republics have been the worst hit in telecom. Castro's been reduced to using short wave radio and he's having a hard time getting anyone to respond to his requests."

"Damn! You know, we tried to get Yeltsin's crew to stop him from bringing that reactor on-line in the first place. How bad do you think their problem is?"

"It's bad, sir." Alexis glanced down at one of her own summary sheets. "From what we can tell, something went seriously wrong as soon as Y2K hit them at midnight. They haven't detailed the exact nature of the problem, but the reactor has been shut off, and there has been a leak or escape of some radioactive material from the reactor core into the outer containment shielding. They say they have it contained within the outer shell, but they are worried as hell about it getting out."

The president whistled again. "And you say the Russians haven't answered them?"

"It's pretty chaotic over there sir. Maybe the CIA can give you better information on what's going on in Moscow, but from what we can tell, they've basically been telling Castro that they have too many problems of their own right now. He's on his own."

"Er... Langley was not as well prepared for Y2K as the Pentagon, Colonel, so it may be a while before I get a report from the CIA. But tell me, what happens if the radiation gets out?"

"That's not really my expertise, sir, but I understand that it would depend on the exact nature of their problem. I'm told that, even in the case of a complete meltdown, it's only the Cubans who really need to worry about radioactive leaks. As far as the U.S. goes, I'm more worried about news leaks."

"News leaks?"

"Yes, sir. The Cubans aren't discussing the situation openly, but there's always the chance that civilian scientists with very sensitive equipment might pick up traces of unusual emissions from Cuba, if there are any. If word got out the wrong way, people would think of a Chernobyl accident happening right in their front yard. They might panic and an uncontrolled evacuation of southern Florida could follow. Many people would be hurt in the stampede."

"Jesus! Are you talking riots and stuff like that?"

"Yes, sir."

"Jesus! How do we stop it?"

Alexis savagely suppressed the impulse to tell the president that her name was not Jesus, and concentrated on answering the question. "We can't, really, sir. It's up to the Cubans. We might offer to help, but there's no guarantee they'd take our help. Still, that may be our best chance. Trying to put a lid on all the science labs that might be able to detect the Cuban problem might scare people as much as telling them the truth. With all the power failures and other problems we've been having, people are already frightened enough."

The president mumbled something distinctly unpresidential before speaking into the phone again. "Colonel Thomas, I want you to bring copies of everything you have on this over to the White House immediately. I'm calling an emergency cabinet meeting and I want you there to answer questions. As soon as we're done, I want you on the first plane to Guantanamo. Take your best people who know about the Cuban situation. And find whoever it was who was in charge of dealing with the Three Mile Island emergency... Would they still be around? Or take anyone else you can find who knows about dealing with nuclear disasters like this... Maybe someone who knows stuff about the Chernobyl accident. Or... Heck, you probably don't need me to tell you who to take—just put a team together and get ready to go."

"But sir, other Y2K problems are cropping up all the time. I'm not really qualified to deal with nuclear emergencies, and if I'm in Cuba, my team may not be as effective in responding to situations here. We won't really know how hard hit the civilian branches of the government are until Monday, and that could be pretty bad."

"One thing at a time, Colonel, and the civilian branches are coordinating through the Critical Infrastructure Assurance Office, so you don't have to worry about them. You don't have anything that's as clear and present a danger as this, do you? Anything that affects primarily the military?"

"No sir. There are the Los Angeles bombings, and the fact that massive difficulties are obviously transpiring in the former Soviet Union—difficulties they aren't talking about—but neither of those pose the same level of identified threat as the Cuban situation at this time. Sir." Before he could answer, she rushed ahead. "I recommend that you allow me to assemble a team with a few Y2K experts and some people from the Department of Energy and the Nuclear Regulatory Commission, as well as anyone I can find who's knowledgeable about the Chernobyl accident, as you suggested. I'll have them report directly to me and to the Secretary of Defense. That way we can keep you briefed and I can stay here, where I'm most likely to be needed."

"Well, I guess that sounds good. We'll do it that way." The president covered the mouthpiece of his phone, but Alexis could hear his muffled voice asking someone in his office a question.

"And by the way, good job keeping things together there at the Pentagon. We may need you to help some other folks out before this is over."

"Thank you, sir. I'll pull together my materials for the cabinet briefing and begin assembling the Cuba team."

"Thank *you* Colonel. We'll meet in an hour."

Alexis hung up the phone, grinding her teeth. Whose bright idea was it to put a civilian in charge of the military anyway? What kind of dimwit would even think of sending her off to Cuba at a time like this? She closed her eyes and rested her head on her arm. Things were not looking better.

*   *   *

1:19 p.m., EST

Click.

"Many people with late model luxury, sports, and other cars are finding that their vehicles aren't working right, or working at all today. Apparently, the Millennium Bug has infected the computer chips in many newer cars. Angry owners don't understand why their cars should care what the date is, and there is already talk of a class action lawsuit..."

Click.

"...said that the Beijing fire started when a computer-controlled smelting furnace malfunctioned, causing overheating that led to a melt-through..."

Click.

"...and now we have word from Mexico City that during the brief time power was restored, the computer that controlled the city's 'Circuito Interior' expressway system malfunctioned, causing hundreds of high-speed automobile accidents. Power is out again, and the death toll..."

Click.

"...well, I'll tell you Larry, my company fixed all its Y2K problems well ahead of the deadline. We've even tested our systems today and everything is working fine. But our suppliers—that's another question. There weren't enough Y2K certified suppliers before today, and after today, I think we'll have a harder time than ever getting raw materials and..."

Click.

"...reporting live from Washington, where rumors are flying that something major has the Oval Office gearing up for a large scale emergency. For the past several hours more pizzas have been delivered to the White House than since the night before Operation Desert Storm. Cabinet members have been seen coming and going, as well as Federal Emergency Management Administration, Nuclear Regulatory Commission, and military officials..."

Click.

"...oh Brad! I just knew you couldn't have been cheating on me with my best friend..."

Click.

"...not our fault! I can show you the certification on all the components we bought. All the chips were supposed to be Y2K-compliant. We were sold some bad chips, and there's no way we could have known..."

Click.

Beep-beep! Zooooooom! CLANG!!!

Click.

"...nel thirteen is temporarily off the air due to a computer malfunction. Please stand by..."

Click.

"...ext on the Geraldo show: computer programmers who say the Y2K problems were a carefully planned government conspiracy. We'll be right back, after these messa..."

CLICK.

"Merde!" Michel turned the set off and tossed the remote onto the sofa. He stretched, then rubbed his eyes. Nothing but shit on the tube. Shitty news, or shit for mindless people. He should have stayed in bed with Natalie. Getting up to look out of his apartment window, he observed that the city was unusually quiet for a Saturday afternoon.

Perhaps everyone was inside, numbing their minds on all the shit.

*   *   *

5:23 p.m., PST

"C'mon Trish, you've been watching that shit all day!" Prudence took the TV remote and switched the set off. "Let's get ready for work."

Trish didn't move. "Should we bothah? Ah mean, they've got the power back on here in Vegas, but there's so many problems around the world! Do you reckon people wanna go out and...and look at girls?"

"Are you kidding? Now more than ever! It'll help them get their minds off of bad news they can't do anything about anyway."

Trish made an unsure face.

"Men are stupid animals. We both know what they use instead of brains—they'll be there."

"Ah'm not so sure all men are like that. Ah s'pose a lot of them might wanna stay home with their families, or somethin'."

"I'll tell you what, I'll call Larry and make sure we're on for tonight. It is a Saturday night, after all!" Prudence picked up the phone, dialed the club's number, and hung up after a few seconds. "It's busy."

"Ah remember when Ah was, oh, about thirteen," Trish's expression took on a melancholy look, "and the government sent those tanks to smash up that church in Waco, with the little kids still inside. Ah remember watchin' it on TV. Ah didn't understand what was happenin', or why...and then it caught fire, and that big ball of flame went up over the building...and the folks weren't comin' out...and there was no fire engine... Ah felt so helpless—it was awful!" She gazed up at Prudence. "Ah feel like that now, only I feel it more."

Prudence didn't know what to say, so she took Trish's hand, pressed it to her lips, and held on to it tightly.

"Ah keep thinkin' about all those folks that died in those hospitals last night, when the electricity went out and the emergency power didn't come on right away! And the bombs in L.A., and the thousands of folks that died in the factory fire in China!" Trish couldn't get the images she'd seen on the news out of her head. "Ah just wanna git in bed and stay there, or maybe wake up and find that it was all a dream. Did you hear that newsman say that they figger more than 15,000 people have already been keeilt by this computer thang, and the first day ain't even over yet?"

"Trish, you *need* to dance tonight! Get your mind off all this stuff. I'll call again." Prudence punched the redial button, shaking her head. It rang this time. "Hi, this is Prudence, is Larry there? Yes, I'll hold on... Larry? Are we on for tonight?" She played with the phone cord while listening to his answer. "All right, we'll be there." She hung up.

"So, the club'll be open tonight?" Trish was still skeptical.

"Yup. You aren't the only one who wasn't sure. Larry says the phone's been ringing off the hook with all kinds of people wondering if we were on tonight." She laughed. "He says that even the club has Y2K problems: the cash registers are all printing the year 1900 on the register tapes! But he says he doesn't care what year they say—they're working well enough for him. And from the phone calls he's had, he thinks the place will be packed tonight." She pulled Trish up by her hand. "So we'd better go get ready!"

Trish stood slowly. "Prue, don't your wings evah git tired?"

"Sure they get tired Trish... Flying free is hard work! It's easy being a slave; you do what you're told and you don't have to make any decisions. But would you rather go back to how you were before?"

"Nevah!"

"Me neither. So let's get going!"

"Okay."

The two headed for the shower—it was going to be another long night.

* * *

10:47 p.m., PST

"¡Estupidos!" Angel and Cabron were riding in a battered old delivery van, with Cabron behind the wheel, by the same police station they had attacked at midnight. The street in front of the station was closed off with police barricades and yellow tape, all bleached of color by the sodium-arc streetlights. But the building was large, and had a parking entrance on the street behind, which was still open to traffic.

Angel jerked his thumb at a squad car and an armored vehicle parked in front of the parking entrance, and shook his head. The *pendejos* had not gotten the message. It didn't seem to penetrate their thick skulls that they were all going to end up being statistics if they insisted on pretending that nothing had changed. They thought that they could park their little toys in front of their wounded buildings and make people believe that they were still in charge. Well, Angel would teach them the lesson again, and again, if necessary. He had better toys and more money!

Still, he had to be careful; the cops would be on the lookout now. He'd have to outsmart them in order to surprise them, and the attack would have to be quicker. So, he and Cabron would both use RPGs simultaneously.

The lesson had to be taught and getaways made smoothly, before the cops could realize what was being done to them. It was important that the police not figure out—until it was too late—who their adversary was.

Cabron continued down the street and around the block, pulling over two blocks from the front of the police station. It was time to make their final check. He and Angel had to be careful clamber-

ing into the back of the van because part of the bottom had been
cut out, opening the floor to the street below. Behind the cut-out,
two RPGs and launchers were secured to the floor, in the same
suitcase they had used earlier.

"Prepara los," Angel ordered.

Cabron retrieved the tubular weapons and inserted the grenades, making sure they were ready to fire before setting them
down again in the open suitcase. Next, he took out a home-made
bomb with a trip-cord detonator and worked his way forward again
to duct-tape it to the back of the front passenger seat. When it was
taped up firmly, he put his ear plugs on and handed a pair to
Angel.

The gang leader accepted the plugs and leaned over to better
appreciate the simple beauty of the Soviet RPG-7s. He'd bought
them with the money from the bogus Y2K-compliant computer
chips. The alien-looking Cyrillic lettering stenciled on the metal
cylinders added to their deadly beauty in his mind. The missiles
themselves were sharply pointed—rocket-powered arrows with
explosive tips.

"Es tiempo." He flipped his wrist over to check his watch: the
glowing numbers showed it to be getting close to 11 p.m. As at
midnight the night before, two-man teams—this time in old vans—
were preparing all over the metro Los Angeles area. "¡Vamonos!"
The timing didn't need to be to-the-second; as long as all the
police stations were hit at about the same time, the message would
be delivered.

Cabron settled back into the driver's seat and pulled back out
onto the street. There was very little traffic so late at night, allowing him to drive slowly as he rounded the corner and headed back
up the street behind the police station. Angel carefully eyed the
pavement passing below the van, ready to give the signal. Not
directly behind the police station—but near enough—the manhole cover showed in Cabron's headlights and he slowed even more.
An irate motorist leaned on his horn as he sped around and past
the van, but the two ignored the distraction. When the manhole

cover emerged at the leading edge of the hole in the floor, Angel called for Cabron to stop.

Trying to give the appearance of having engine trouble, Cabron put his emergency flashers on and climbed in back again with Angel, who was already levering up the man-hole cover with a crow-bar. The two took hold of it as it came up and heaved it into the front of the van. They knew they had only a minute or two before someone from the police station came to investigate the stalled vehicle.

Handing one of the deadly rocket-powered lances to his lieutenant, Angel whispered, "¿Listo?" Cabron grinned and pulled the sliding door open—all the others were welded shut. The two leapt out onto the street and moved quickly to the ends of the van, to keep the backblasts from reflecting off its flat panels and burning them.

Angel lined up his sights on the armored personnel carrier and Cabron put his on the squad car. Both pulled their triggers as soon as they had their targets steady in their sights—no time for any countdowns. Even with ear protection, the roar of the rockets and the blast from the explosions were deafening. The exhaust fire blackened the ends of the van and scorched some trees behind it. But by then, the grenades had hit their targets, both of which erupted in flame.

They jumped back into the van, Cabron sliding the door shut while Angel attached the bomb's trip-cord to the door handle. As soon as the booby trap was set, the two crawled down through the hole in the floor, around the van's drive-shaft, and through the manhole into the sewer, clutching their empty launchers to their chests. Angel took off, running as fast as he could, crouched, in the direction previously decided upon. Even though his ears were still ringing, he could make out the splashing of Cabron's feet in the water behind him when he took off his ear plugs. They got to an intersection, turned right, and kept running. After going straight through another intersection and on for about two hundred meters, they came to a glow-stick they had dropped through the manhole cover above their heads, a half-hour earlier. Listening for passing people first, they pushed up on the iron disk and slid it aside.

Cabron was taller, so he peeked through the opening and then clambered up into the night air. He reached down to help his leader up, but Angel waved the hand aside and hoisted himself through the opening. Their getaway car was still there, waiting for them.

Hands trembling from the adrenaline rush, Angel pulled the keys from his pocket and the two were off, driving at a leisurely pace toward a condemned government housing project where they were to meet the other teams.

Cabron was grinning and laughing—a kid on Christmas morning. "Jefe, I can't believe it! The police won't have the people or the balls to stop us now!"

Angel accepted the praise without comment. He believed his soldiers were becoming fanatically loyal—better not to tell them that he had no idea how all this was going to end up.

*   *   *

11:59 p.m., MST

"There, you see, Merlyn?" Anna was kneading his neck muscles again, as he hunched over his keyboard. "I wasn't being paranoid!"

"Anna, I never said you were paranoid!"

"Oh yes you did!"

"Well, okay, but I was joking..." He held up a placating hand. "I admit that you were right about the need to be more cautious than I was being about our location. And it's a good thing you convinced me, too!"

"So, what are you up to now? A hundred inquiries from people wanting to know if they can come stay with us?"

"No, I passed that mark before lunch. We're over two-fifty now, and a good tenth of those are from people I've never even heard of!"

Anna smiled and gave a slight bow, as though just completing a performance for her audience of one. "Now, aren't you glad I insisted that we meet people away from the ranch?"

"Yes, Beloved, I am. And I'm glad you insisted on nyms and anonymous remailers for all our e-mail. You are wise and gracious and I am infinitely pleased and proud to be your partner."

"Flatterer!" She laughed and kissed him on the spot where his hair was beginning to thin. "So what are you going to do?"

"Well, for starters, I'm going to delete all the mail from strangers. Better that they never get any confirmation of whatever it is they think they've heard. As for people we know, but didn't invite... I hate to do it, but I'm going to pretend that the idea is new to me, and—without actually lying to them—encourage them to find some land somewhere and build a community on it. It's the ones we did invite that will be tough..."

Anna waited for him to finish.

"I'd forgotten how many people I'd discussed the idea with, people who declined to participate or never followed up. Now all of the sudden they are all interested, and we can't possibly fit them all. I'll make a list, and we can agree on which ones to give the remaining spaces to, and which ones to suggest they contact other people about forming a defensive community of their own. It's a sad thing to have to decide, and I'll need your help. Do you mind?"

"Of course not." She swiveled his chair around and sat in his lap. "We're partners, right?"

"As the captain said: Absa-fraggin-lutely!"

CHAPTER 25:
THURSDAY, JANUARY 6, 2000

"I'm learning to fly,
But I ain't got wings
Coming down,
Is the hardest thing."
—Tom Petty and the Heartbreakers, *Learning to Fly*

Trish couldn't understand it. Razor and Rapier were as popular as ever—business was booming!—but the patrons didn't seem as rapt as they did before. They were there in larger numbers, but they weren't really *there*.

She commented on it to Prudence. "Ah reckon somethin' weird's goin' on. It's like they only come to the club because they don't wanna be somewhere else...somewheres they might have to pay 'tention to what's goin' on."

"Who cares?" Prudence shrugged. "We're making more money than either of us thought we would. At this rate we'll have enough saved up for college a lot faster than we thought possible. I can't wait until we can afford to give up dancing!"

"Don't it worry you none that if thangs get really bad, your MBA won't be good for much?"

"No." Prudence shook her head. "The news *is* pretty scary, I'll give you that, but it seems that—except in Los Angeles—the worst is behind us. The government says most everything should be back to normal in a couple months."

"And you believe them?"

Prudence gaped at Trish in momentary surprise. "Since when

did you become a political analyst?"

"Now Prue, there ain't no cause to go takin' that tone with me. Ah may sound like a ditzy southern belle to you, but you know good n' well that Ah got more brains'n that! And as it happens, this whole Y2K thang's got me inter'sted in how people work together—or don't. Ah want to know why some companies survived with barely a scratch, and why others went belly-up. Ah wanna know why thangs look pertty normal around here in Vegas, but they git worse and worse every day in L.A. Don't you wanna know what makes thangs like that happen? Ah think Ah might just major in political science!"

"I'm sorry Trish." Prudence took her hand. "I didn't mean it that way. It's just that I hate politics, I guess. I can't imagine wanting to study it. Ugh!" She kissed her. "Let's not argue, okay?"

"Okay."

CHAPTER 26:
FRIDAY, JANUARY 14, 2000

"They're complicated people
Leading complicated lives,
And he complicates their problems
by telling complicated lies."
—Barenaked Ladies, *The Flag*

"Ninety-five thousand?" Jared was outraged. "Mr. Johnson, this house is worth at least twice as much!"

"Worth twice as much to whom?" The real estate agent was calm, but had obviously had many similar conversations in the recent past. "Look, Dr. Christensen, I'm not trying to insult your home, I'm simply trying to tell you that in these uncertain times, few people are moving and everyone is holding on to their cash."

"Yes, I understand that," Jared tried to calm himself, "but... I don't know. I can't accept an amount so much less than what I paid for the house—that won't even cover the mortgage!"

"You're lucky to get an offer on your house at all, let alone this quickly after putting it on the market, but it's up to you, of course."

"I'm sorry, I just can't accept that offer."

"Very well then, Doctor. May I make a suggestion?"

"Sure."

"If you can't accept this offer, I think you should take your house off the market. No one is buying right now, and you are simply not going to get what you want for it. If you wait for the market to recover, you'll do much better."

"And when do you think the market will recover?"

"I wish I could tell you! But the president said in his speech last night that Y2K has done its worst and that, now that the Critical Infrastructure Assurance Office knows where all the problems are, they can fix them and get everyone back in business. It shouldn't be too long."

"Well, thank you, Mr. Johnson. I accept your advice; please pull the listing."

"Will do, Dr. Christensen. Give me a call when you're ready to sell."

"I will, thank you."

He turned to Emily, who had brought him a glass of milk when the real estate agent called. "He thinks we should hold on to the house until the market gets better," he told her.

"Jared, the other women in our ward and I have never seen so much need for our relief society. How long do you think it will take for things to get better?"

"I don't know, Hon, I don't know." He rested his head in his palms for a few seconds, then looked up again. "Mr. Johnson seems to find reassurance in the president's speech, but I don't feel so confident, myself. The president has only a year left in office and would probably say anything to avoid looking bad. In fact, since his party could well lose the oval office over this, I'd think he'd do anything he could to make things look better than they are."

"I never trusted him!" Emily didn't usually show much vehemence, but she had very strong feelings about the president. "It's not so much his private life that the tabloids won't leave be, but the way he doesn't seem truthful. I can't stand it!"

"Well, I won't argue with you there, but you know what really scares me? I was talking to the bishop about the relief work you and the others are doing. It's not just that so many people need our help—you would expect that with all the bankruptcies and layoffs that started last year—it's the number of elderly we're seeing. They haven't been getting their social security checks since last October, when the federal government entered its fiscal year 2000. The government's had a few months and they haven't been able to do something as simple as printing checks, and that makes me very nervous about the president's claims that everything will be okay."

"Humph!" Emily snorted. "Well, that explains one thing."

"What?"

"One of the things we've been doing is to help folks look for jobs. You wouldn't believe how many ads there are for government work in the 'help wanted' section of the newspaper! The Social Security Administration is hiring all kinds of people, even without experience or special skills. And it's not only Social Security. It's also the Department of Housing and Urban Development, the Federal Emergency Management Administration, and even the Internal Revenue Service."

"FEMA and the IRS too?"

"Yes, and more!"

"That's bad, really bad."

"Why?"

"Because it means they didn't make it—Y2K compliance before the deadline, I mean. Every federal employee in the country must be under some kind of gag order not to talk about it, or we'd have heard about it in the press. Heck, I don't think they could keep it from leaking from so many people. They must have some kind of 'national emergency' power that is allowing them to censor the press. I ought to browse the web to see what's being reported outside the mainstream media."

"And what does it mean that those agencies didn't make the deadline?"

"I don't know for sure, Honey, but it means—at the very least—that a lot of people won't have any money to buy food with soon. As you know, it's already happened to folks who had no savings."

"Oh."

"'Oh no' is more like it!" Jared couldn't help but give a small chuckle. "You know, Hon, I'm thinking that maybe, instead of selling the house, we should get a second mortgage. My work with the Church will secure our family's income, so I'm sure we'd be able to pay it off, and if things get really bad we could use the money to prepare better for emergencies."

"Are you sure we would be able to pay it back if things got really bad?"

"Well, if they got *that* bad, there probably wouldn't be anyone at the bank to receive payment anyway. We wouldn't get a loan *in order* to not pay it back, and we would pay it back, if things hold together or get better. But if the bank we owed the money to ceased to exist, it couldn't be a sin not to pay it back."

"Jared, all of this frightens me." She sat on his lap and hugged him. "If you think it would be wise, it sure seems like a good idea to me to be as prepared as we can be!"

"Any sensible person would be scared, Honey—it frightens me too. But that's okay, as long as we do something about it. Don't you think our ancestors were frightened when Governor Boggs issued that extermination order against Latter Day Saints in Missouri? We'll prepare, as you say, and we'll make a journey to a safer place—Utah—as they did. Okay?"

"Okay." Emily breathed more easily. Whenever she was beset by difficulties, it always made her feel better to remember how much harder the Mormon pioneers had it. Many had trekked over a thousand miles across the plains and through the Rocky Mountains on foot, dragging their meager belongings behind them on hand-carts. Unmarked graves dotted the flanks of the trail the entire way. "At least our trip will be easier than theirs!"

CHAPTER 27:
MONDAY, JANUARY 24, 2000

"Would I lie to you?
Now why would I say something that wasn't true
I'm asking you, sugar, would I lie to you?"
—Eurythmics, *Would I Lie to You?*

"Colonel Thomas, how good to see you!"

"Thank you, Mr. President."

"Well done on that Cuban thing!"

"Excuse me, sir?"

"Could you brief us, please? I believe your team handled it quite well, but I want the others to hear it from you."

Alexis refrained from asking him if he was joking—barely. It was plain to see that the assembled cabinet was anything but amused, and she had already talked back enough to her Commander in Chief... But neither she nor her team had actually *done* anything! Oh well. "Yes sir."

This whole thing should have gone to someone else to handle—why had the president insisted that she stay involved? Who could know with *this* president? She shrugged inwardly and inclined her head at Captain Smith, who set up an easel stand with a number of enlarged photographs mounted on cardboard. He handed her a laser pointer.

"Ladies and gentlemen, this is a photo of the Cuban nuclear power facility before the accident. It was taken from a satellite that passes over the island daily, before Y2K hit and we lost contact with it." She circled an area on the first photograph with her pointer.

"This is the main reactor building—this circular structure here, beside the control center. Those are the cooling towers beside them." She checked some figures she had on a notepad. "The time-stamp on the plate shows that the photo was taken at fifteen thirty-nine, on December twenty-eight. The island was partially obscured by cloud cover through the remaining days of 1999, so this is the most recent clear picture we have of the facility before the accident."

No one moved. Every pair of eyes was focused on the photograph—except the president's. Was he looking at her breasts? "Ah... As you can see, uh..." Alexis was rattled for a moment, and then got back on track. "As you can see, things look fairly normal. Cars in the parking lot, maintenance crews working on some equipment in the northwest corner there. No signs of trouble. The amount of steam coming from the cooling towers suggests that, even though the plant was still relatively new, they had it working pretty hard."

The Secretary of Labor spoke up. "Colonel Thomas?"

"Yes, Ms. Secretary?"

"If the Cubans had a nuclear facility going right off our coast, why didn't we know about it?"

The Secretary had missed the first cabinet briefing on the Cuban situation, so Alexis tried to be patient as she explained. "The information was not classified, but few people were interested in it." She pointed to several people around the table. "Some other cabinet members knew about it before the accident, perhaps because it had more direct bearing on their areas than it does on the Department of Labor, Ms. Secretary." Alexis inspected the faces around the table, making brief eye contact with each person. "Generally speaking, the public is unaware of the facility. That's probably all for the better, because it helped to avoid mass panic and a disorganized evacuation of southern Florida—as might have happened if the problem had become public knowledge."

"There was that much danger of radiation?"

"No, but most people are not very informed about the true

dangers of radiation from nuclear power plants—or bombs, for that matter. How do you think the people of Florida would have reacted if someone told them there was a Chernobyl malfunctioning right off their coast?"

There were no more questions.

"When my team arrived in Guantanamo, they immediately contacted the Cubans who normally interface—such as they do—with our command staff down there. They denied knowing anything about a nuclear power plant and told us that if they did have one, it wouldn't malfunction. Mr. Bernard Colton, of the Department of Energy, has a great deal of knowledge concerning the Chernobyl accident. He tried telling them that the team was there to help, if they would let them. The Cubans wouldn't listen."

Alexis paced. Thinking about the time her team had wasted cooling their heels in Guantanamo, and her own frustration with having nothing to report day after day, was enough to make her angry—not to mention the slightly nauseated feeling she always got when she had to speak to the president. "That kept up for almost two weeks. I got more information from my overseas observation team up here, and the reconnaissance airplanes we had fly over the island."

On cue, Captain Smith flipped the next picture forward.

"Observe this second photograph, taken on January 7th." She pointed things out with the laser as she mentioned them. "Look at all the military vehicles—they have the whole facility cordoned off. See the way there are no personnel visible? No steam coming from the cooling towers either—it's been shut off." She paused. "We knew all this, but the Cubans were stonewalling us, even though they were asking the Russians for help at the same time... And the Russians were still telling them that they were on their own!"

The Secretary of Defense took advantage of a pause to interject. "And what, in your opinion, Colonel, could be keeping the Russians so busy? Why wouldn't they take the time to help their old buddy Castro keep his cigars from glowing in the dark—not to mention save themselves from having another one of their nuclear power plants blow a hole in whatever pride they have left?"

"That's the question that's been keeping me up nights, sir." Alexis held the secretary's gaze as calmly as she could. "Nothing my team has turned up yet gives any indication as to any one specific problem over there. Their telecom is still a shambles and no one is talking anyway. There are signs of fighting between military units, possibly even between military units and civilian mobs. It's hard to get anything straight about what's going on. Things really seem to be falling apart over there." She turned to face the president. "What about Langley? Is the CIA back in action yet?" She glanced back at the Secretary of Defense again. "Frankly, sir, I have no idea and no basis for guessing. But I'll tell you, it is *very* alarming."

The Secretary shook his head, frowning. "Langley's back in action, but they haven't uncovered anything you don't know."

No one moved. They hardly breathed. Even the president was paying attention to business again. "Finally," Alexis continued, "just yesterday, we got word from the Cubans. They admitted that they had a nuke and that it had malfunctioned, but insisted that they had taken care of it. They offered Mr. Colton and other members of my team an opportunity to fly in for an inspection, in one of their choppers."

She gestured and Captain Smith brought the next photograph forward. "This is what they found when they got there." A large gray oval shape occupied the same spot where the reactor building had been. A wave of muttered questions rolled around the room.

Alexis raised her voice and carried on explaining. "Apparently, after determining that there were no integrity problems with the cooling towers or the lines that connected them to the reactor, they brought in some prefabricated cement blocks—the kind they use for preventing beach erosion—and made a crude wall around the few structures actually holding the contamination. They then capped all lines to and from the reactor and poured cement into the enclosed area.

"Given that the area occupied by the cylinder is," she checked her notes quickly, "a little more than one hundred meters long and a little less than one hundred meters wide, that makes for a little under 400,000 cubic meters of cement. They told us they used rocks and boulders to fill in some of the space because, as the oval filled up, they were running out of available cement. However, they insisted that the problem was now safely contained in the one giant block.

"Mr. Colton was there. He witnessed their, uh, solution, first hand. I asked him if he thought the cement block would hold the contamination. His reply was that we would never have handled it that way in the U.S., but that it should work for a while. He said that since the block wasn't even reinforced with steel, even slight movements of the ground could crack it open.

"He also reported that he tried to explain to the Cubans that their solution would make the real clean-up job that would eventually have to be done more difficult, but they were insulted by his suggestions. That was the end of the tour." Alexis motioned Captain Smith forward. "Captain Smith reports on an interesting conversation he had on the way back from the tour. Captain?"

Captain Smith was clearly not comfortable speaking to the president and his cabinet, but he cleared his throat and did as he was asked. "I went up front to check out the cockpit. The pilot turned out to be kinda chatty. I guess he wasn't very excited about nuclear power in Cuba, or something. He told the me that he'd heard that some people had been trapped inside the reactor building when the emergency containment doors slammed shut. As far as he knew, they were still in there when the cement was poured." Having said his piece, he retreated to his easel-stand.

Most of the cabinet members sat back with shocked and horrified expressions on their faces—except the president, who straightened his papers and took out a pen. "So, Colonel, in your estimation, has the danger of radioactive contamination being detected in United States and setting off a panic in Florida been averted?"

"Well... Yes sir, but only temporarily. If anyone does measure something unusual, we can release photographs and say that the problem has been contained. However, it is a very crude fix, and it could fail at any time."

"Excellent, Colonel." The president beamed, as though at a television audience. "Now, as you told me before, radioactive material containment isn't really your specialty, so we'll have some others take over monitoring the Cuban situation. Right now, I want you to get back to work on digging us out of this Y2K mess."

The president made a point of closing his folder on Cuba and opening another on domestic Millennium Bug problems. "In fact, the measures you took at the Pentagon seem to have been highly successful—more successful than you yourself predicted they would be, if I recall correctly. If only NORAD and SAC had implemented your Y2K fixes instead of their own! And if CIAO had followed a methodology like yours, we'd have a lot fewer problems on the civilian side!"

Alexis thought it prudent not to comment on her opinions regarding the commanders at NORAD and SAC, nor the director of CIAO—it was all she could do not to laugh at the latter.

"So," the president continued, "what I want you to do now is to work with them on getting back on-line. I've already issued new orders; you won't find any foot-dragging this time, Colonel! Then I want you to help the next most vital installations, as defined by the joint chiefs. You will receive your orders from them and be acting under their direct authority—and mine. Also, during this emergency I'm placing the Coast Guard under the jurisdiction of the Navy, so they can benefit from what you're doing more quickly than they would under the Department of Transportation, where they are now. After that, we'll need to make the methods you've developed available to CIAO and the general public; that should help the civilian organizations that are in trouble. In fact, I want to hold a press conference tonight, announcing that during this emergency, the military will be placing its computer expertise at the disposal of CIAO and any civilian organization that needs help."

"Tonight, sir? I thought you wanted me to help with military installations first—that will take months—years, really—if we're talking about getting *everything* working!"

"Yes, the military and civilian government agencies come first, but the public needs reassurance! You're photogenic. Reassuring the public is as important at this point as actually fixing the problems, and you're just the one to reassure them."

"But..." That would be like lying to them!

"Do you have a question, Colonel?" The president's tone made it clear that he hoped she did not.

"No, sir. I understand my instructions, sir."

"Very well."

The president gabbled on for a while longer, addressing the cabinet members. After a few minutes, he stopped, as though remembering that Alexis and Captain Smith were still there, and dismissed them. What the cabinet turned to next, Alexis didn't even want to think about.

It did occur to her, as she drove back to the Pentagon, that the president's praise had just upset the plans of whoever had engineered her promotion—if, in fact, it had been designed to saddle her with the blame for Y2K failures within the armed services. Dealing with the situation, she mused, was similar to opening a Russian matroshka doll. You figure one layer out and think you've dealt with it, only to find that there's another within. How many problems would she solve before she got to the one she couldn't solve?

That wasn't an image she cared for. Bad metaphor. Maybe it was more like an onion; after peeling off enough layers of problems, there would be none left. Yes, that was a much better image!

But which one was more accurate?

CHAPTER 28:
MONDAY, JANUARY 24, 2000

"Go on, take the money and run!"
—The Steve Miller Band, *Take the Money and Run*

"Yes Max, I am fine." Michel leaned back in his chair and pressed the phone to his ear. The quality of telephone connections to Latin America had grown erratic. "How are ze beaches in Costa Rica?"

"Fine, Michel, though the humidity never goes away."

"Voila! You see, zere was no need to abandon ze ship so soon. Now you will 'ave to put up wis tropical wezer and insects."

"The storm isn't over yet, Michel, you've only reached the eye of the hurricane. So tell me, with the market in chaos and the Dow devastated, when are you going to pull out?"

"But Max, I am making more money zan I ever 'ave in my life! You would know zat if you had not pulled all your money out of stocks."

"Too risky, Michel. I couldn't take the chance that you'd be wrong about the companies you thought would survive Y2K."

"Well, I did get some wrong, but in ze majority of cases, I was able to predict which companies would be ze hardest hit. I 'ave lost some of my older customers, who 'ave cashed out even more of zeir commodities zan you, but Wall Street has its eye on Gerard Financial Management. I 'ave had to hire more people, and I still cannot keep up wis ze business!"

"That's great, Michel, that's great. But think about those customers who're pulling out and don't get cocky. Remember the euphoria before the crash!" Max' voice dropped to a whisper. "How's my present? Have you checked on it lately?"

"Ze truck?" Michel stammered. "Ah, no, I 'ave to be honest Max; I forgot it was zere, after ze world did not end on January first."

"Well, remember what I said about the eye of the storm, old friend, and don't forget my present when you need it."

"Okay Max, I promise. I will even go turn ze engine over myself, before I go home zis evening. Okay?"

"That's great. Look, I've got to go. Got a date on the beach. You take care of yourself, Inspector, you hear?"

"I will Max. Sanks for calling!" Michel hung up the phone and then stared at it in surprise. What had Max called him?

He sat forward in his chair and stabbed the intercom button. "Grace!"

CHAPTER 29:
SATURDAY, JANUARY 29, 2000

"I can count it on my fingers
I've got all my reasons not to feel
I'm numb as rigor mortis
Scared by monkey faces
Drowned in shark fins
But I don't feel like feeling
Feeling like you."
—Soundgarden, *Face Pollution*

"But... What are you building, Angel?" Rosalia had all but given up hope of reaching him. And yet... She had seen his defenses crack once, and it was worth trying again, even though trying meant risking more beatings. They were her punishment. She should have tried harder when she and Angel were younger. Well, she couldn't change the past, but she could try to fix things now! "Why do you tell me these things about the police quitting their jobs and the governor's declaration of a state of emergency? What good does any of this do? It seems to me that all you do is kill and destroy."

"I *am* building something! I'm building something there's never been before...a new...kind of city! That's what. I'm building a new city where rich white people don't call the shots and have the police arrest other people just because they look Latino. When I'm the boss, everything will be fair, and the killing of Latinos won't get ignored by the law. *I* will be the law!"

"That won't bring your parents back."

Angel was on her in an flash. He had a handful of shirt in one hand, and the other hand drawn back for a punch, as he would if he were going to punch a man. For a span of unmeasurable time, the world stopped and all he could feel was her heart beating beneath the fist he had balled in her blouse. Then he let go of her and pushed her away. "Why do you always do that to me? Nobody makes me mad the way you do... Are you trying to get hurt or something? You like pain now?"

"No Angel, I don't. And I don't make you mad—the anger is inside you because you never let it go." She stood her ground and kept her gaze fixed on his. "Why not let it go, Angel? It hurts me every time you hurt someone else, because another little piece of the good person you keep locked inside you dies. A little bit more of the boy I did once love is lost forever."

"Stop saying that!!" His fury returned double strength. "Por Dios! I can deal with the National Guard, why can't I make you see that I am creating something new here, something good?"

"Because no one can *make* anyone else see anything. You can lay the truth before them, but they may choose to close their eyes. My eyes are open, but what I see is that you create nothing. You weren't thinking about creation at all, until I mentioned it."

She tried to reach out to him, but he batted her hand away, in many ways still a petulant child. "You cannot make a community at gunpoint, Angel. All you are doing is destroying people's lives and what little community there was left in this city." She wasn't trying to overact. Her heart *did* ache for the hurt little boy Angel had been—the little boy who had lost his parents in a drug bust gone bad.

He seemed to be thinking it over. The muscles at the sides of his jaw worked as he wrestled with his feelings.

Sensing a ray of light shining from the crack in Angel's defenses, Rosalia tried to open it further. "Your parents were innocent victims of the war on drugs, Angel. The cops who butchered them aren't even around any more. None of your murdering will bring them back. None of this—not the cop killings, not the way you evade the National Guard, not the way you think you are gaining control of this city—impresses me. If you really want to impress me, then let me go. Let it all go. And find some way to rebuild some of the things you've destroyed."

Angel felt a pressure building in his skull as she spoke. When she stopped, it didn't get any better. Her gaze was a rack that held him tight, twisting in an anguish he didn't understand and couldn't escape. Screaming something wordless, he pulled out his gun. Both of them could see how it trembled in his hand.

The instant he lined up the sights on Rosalia's head, he realized that there was only one way the gun could change her mind, and it wouldn't result in her seeing things his way. For a second, he could almost see her point, but then his old habits of thinking returned, and slammed the door on the light she had glimpsed. "You're wrong! Jorge was wrong! Those people will never respect our rights unless we force them!" He pressed the gun against her forehead.

"Are you finally going to kill me?" She stood before him, refusing to flinch. The gun metal was warm, warm with the heat of Angel's own body. "Or are you just going to bash my eye again? It's started to heal...but I can see you don't want to let anything heal."

This time Angel wouldn't let himself be goaded. Somehow, that always put Rosalia in control of their conversations, and he wasn't going to give her the satisfaction. However, he couldn't think of an answer, so he tucked his gun back into his pants and stalked out of the room.

CHAPTER 30:
SUNDAY, JANUARY 30, 2000

"And give us these days
Our daily bread
Only you we praise
Almighty dollar."
—Extreme, *Money*

When Merlyn and Anna came in from their daily ride, Goya was grumbling under her breath, putting away groceries.

"¿Que pasa, Goya?" Merlyn asked, reaching to help her to put things away.

"No, you no help." Goya swatted him away. "I never find anyting!"

"Okay, but *is* there anything I can help you with?"

"No. You say dees was coming, but I no especk eet so soon!"

"What?" Both Anna and Merlyn asked at the same time.

"No *cilantro* een de store! Not many vegge tables eider. And fruit? Ees too expensive! Beeg waste of time—drive all dat way to empty store! A truck full of money ees not enough to buy my cilantro!"

Merlyn and Anna turned to each other before speaking simultaneously again: "No imports!"

"Don't worry, Goya," Merlyn tried to reassure her, "the greenhouses will be done soon. We'll be able to start growing our own fruit and vegetables in less than a week. It'll take a while before any are ready to eat, of course, but we'll have them before long. I'll ask The Optimist to plant some cilantro first thing, okay?"

Merlyn hugged Goya, who tolerated his affection with exaggerated patience, before heading down to the basement control center with Anna. The new control center, with its almost-completed tunnel to the mine redoubt, had replaced their study as the electronic nerve-center of the Dollar Ranch the week before. It was time to go down and see what news the Net had brought in.

As their footsteps receded, Goya heard Anna telling Merlyn that she was glad that The Optimist had proven so knowledgeable about greenhouses and hydroponics. Goya wasn't sure what hydroponics were, but she heartily agreed about the greenhouses. And The Optimist was rather handsome, now that she thought of it.

CHAPTER 31:
TUESDAY, FEBRUARY 15, 2000

"All the things I could do
If I had a little money."
—ABBA, *Money, Money, Money*

"Prue! It's Larry on the phone!"

Prudence picked up the extension in the bedroom. "I've got it!" She waited for the click. "What's up, Larry?"

"Ah... Prudence, we need to talk."

"Isn't that what we're doing?"

"Well, yes, but I'd rather do it in person."

"Not a chance. This is our day off."

"Uh... I really don't want to do this over the phone, but we really need to talk!"

Prudence let him stew a bit before answering. "So talk."

"Well, it's like this." Larry tried hard not to let his nervousness creep into his voice. "We need to renegotiate your contract."

"Are you nuts?! We're the only thing keeping your club going and now you want to gouge us?"

"Prudence, it's not like that." He was unable to keep a whining edge from creeping into his tone. "The customers are still coming in, but they're not buying drinks. I'm not even breaking even when the house is packed!"

"Aw, turn down the violins, Larry. We've got a contract, and you and I both know that you can't afford to lose us—our act is the only thing bringing the customers in at all!"

"You can't expect me to pay you more than I'm collecting at

the door!"

"Why not? You have been."

"But that was when I was making money selling drinks!"

Prudence didn't answer.

"Look, don't play hard-assed bitch with me! I love your act—you're right about how important it is to the club—but I can't do it at a loss. And it's not only me that's having problems. Nobody's even bothering to come in on the nights you two are off, and when they do come in, they just sit there. They don't pay for private dances any more than they buy drinks. You can play tough, but it won't do you any good if I have to shut the club down."

That got Prudence's attention. The plastic handset was suddenly slick under her fingers. She could hear his accelerated breathing. Could the old tightwad be telling the truth? She didn't want to alter the contract, because once they started down that road, there'd be no stopping it. But she wasn't ready to stop dancing yet! She and Trish still had about three semesters' worth of tuition money to save up.

"C'mon Prudence, you can't do this to me—you'd be doing it to both of us!"

"Keep your pants on Larry, I've got an idea." She waited for him to calm down and continued when she was sure he was listening. "We don't change our contract—we *never* touch the contract!—but Trish and I will work up some new variations on our number that will make the customers buy drinks and pay for private dances. How does that sound?"

"Like what?"

"Oh, I don't know yet. We'll think of something. Trish is really the one who thinks up the dance routines." Prudence could tell that Larry was eager for options. "Maybe we could set it up so that all the other girls are sex-slaves of some kind that we fight to free—hey, maybe we could make you an evil space sorcerer and kill you every night at the end of the act! Then we find some way to involve the customers in the rescue, a way that ends up with them buying at least one drink and one private dance. I'll talk to Trish about it, and we'll let you know what we come up with."

"That sounds great, Prudence! But don't even think about putting me in the act. I get stage fright. Just call me as soon as you work it out. I'll even spring for some new costumes for the other girls. Hell, at this point, I have nothing to lose!"

"All right, Larry, we'll call you in a couple hours, and we'll start rehearsals tomorrow. It might take a couple days to get it all together, since we'll be involving more people."

"All right. If that's the only way. Call me as soon as you—"

"Bye Larry!"

"Bye."

CHAPTER 32:
WEDNESDAY, FEBRUARY 16, 2000

"The way your heart sounds
Makes all the difference
It's what decides if you'll endure
the pain that we all feel
The way your heart beats
Makes all the difference
In learning to live."
—Dream Theater, *Learning to Live*

It was utterly unprecedented. The Church was recalling its missionaries—*all* of them!

It was an astounding thing... At any given time, the Church had tens of thousands of missionaries working in more than a hundred countries—not to mention within the United States. And now the missionaries were being called home and Church members around the world were being encouraged to move to Utah. Even the mission presidents were being recalled, and overseas facilities were being turned over to local Church members who wanted to stay in their countries.

The actions were among Jared's own recommendations, but it was shocking to see them actually taking place—to see it on CNN and in the papers.

"It's the right thing to do," Emily told him. Jared was taking the day off—the couple had slept in late and were now talking while cuddling in bed. "In times like these, we can't risk having those missionaries stranded, far from their families. And here at home, our relief efforts are bringing the gentiles to us faster than the missionaries ever were. It's better for the young people to be with their families and safer for all Church members to draw together."

"I know, Em," he answered, "but it's...painful...seeing all the missions shut down!" He got up and shuffled to the bedroom closet. Less than a minute's rummaging brought to light the bundle he was looking for: an old cloth and leather gun case. He brought it back to the bed. Setting the elongated bag down, he unzipped it and examined the rifle.

Emily sat up. "You think that old thing still works?"

"Your dad took good care of it, and it hasn't been fired since he passed away. I'm sure it'll work just fine, after we clean it up."

"What are you thinking?"

"I'm thinking that there's been a rising tide of crime since before January 1st, and it may not be safe to drive all the way to Utah without some protection."

"Will that be enough? It's only an old twenty-two."

"There are many places you can hit a body—almost anywhere on the head or neck—where a twenty-two will kill, or at least neutralize an attacker. I know; I've seen the results in the hospital. But no, I don't think this is enough. We can't count on one person in case we run into trouble, and we might need something with more power and accuracy."

"Well, we didn't get as much from the second mortgage as we wanted, but we did get enough to buy some practical equipment for self-reliance." Emily was fiercely protective of her children, and it was clearly audible in her tone. "We've already traded the Lexus and the Caravan for a Suburban—I'd say this counts as the next most important thing on the list!"

"I agree. So... I guess I'm going shopping today. Want to come?"

"No, we'd have to bring the younger kids. Too much hassle—you go ahead."

"All right, Hon." He zipped the gun case up and put it back in the closet.

An hour later, after a hasty breakfast and a search through the yellow pages, Jared Christensen entered a gun shop for the first time in his life.

The first thing he noticed was the smell.

The shop had an indoor range in the basement, and the combined smells of gunpowder, gun oil, and Hoppe's #9 cleaning solvent were thick in the air. Jared didn't know what it was that made the smell, but it was surprisingly pleasant. It wasn't a perfume, to be sure, but it was a heady aroma that spoke of power and well-cared-for tools.

And that was the next thing he noticed: the shop was neat, clean, and well lit—not at all the grubby place television had led him to expect.

He approached the counter hesitantly. The woman behind it greeted him in a friendly manner: "Welcome to Joe's Shootin' Sports, what can I do for you?" She was blonde, in her late forties, but slim and fit. Her face was lined with character, but attractive and unencumbered by makeup.

Perhaps it was from being out of his element, or something else, but whatever the reason, Jared vocalized the first thought that entered his mind: "You don't look like a Joe!"

The woman laughed. "No, I'm Mrs. Joe."

Jared blushed. "I'm sorry. Please excuse me. I didn't mean to be rude."

"Aw, that's okay. A lot of first time gun-buyers say funny things."

She *would* recognize his inexperience. One thing was clear: a time might come when it would be dangerous for him to make it so plain to people that he was inexperienced with guns. Whatever else he did, he would have to practice—and make sure the whole family practiced—if whatever he bought was to be more dangerous to would-be attackers than to his own family.

Mrs. Joe was waiting for Jared to say something, so he stammered, "I... Well, thanks." And meant it; he was already learning valuable lessons. "I'm going to be doing some traveling with my family, and we don't feel safe about it, so we want to buy some tools for protection. I'm thinking that we'd mostly want some pistols, but maybe one higher powered rifle would be a good idea too."

"'Tools for protection,' I like that!" Mrs. Joe nodded wisely. "And your thinking about travel safety is smart. Any of you have much experience shooting?"

Jared blushed again. "When my wife was a kid, she went shooting with her father sometimes." He'd never been self-conscious about his ignorance of guns before. For crying out loud, he was a doctor, not a policeman! Somehow, in spite of his defensive thoughts, he felt as though he had committed some horrible negligence in not learning how to use tools that could protect his family from harm.

"Okay, so how much time do you plan to spend practicing with your tools?"

"Time?" Jared ran a hand through his hair. "I'm not sure. We would want to all get as much practice as we could, but I'm a doctor. These unsettling times seem to be manifesting themselves in a rash of illnesses that my patients can feel, but don't show up on any tests. I've been very busy..."

"Well, If you could put some serious time and effort into it, a semiautomatic pistol would be the way to go. If you don't think you'll have the time to develop that kind of skill, a basic revolver would be a better choice."

"Why the difference?"

"An auto-loader offers you more shots, faster reloading and less recoil than a revolver. The tradeoff is that it's got more moving parts, so there's a slightly higher chance something can go wrong. If you're going to use an auto-loader for self defense, you have to learn how to deal with those problems instinctively. If you were planning on target shooting, a malfunction wouldn't matter that much, but with 'tools for protection' you have to consider it."

"Hmmm. I guess we should start with revolvers. What do you suggest?"

"Makes sense, going with revolvers. Besides, you can always get into an autoloader after you've had some experience."

"So, what kind would you suggest?"

Mrs. Joe didn't even bat an eye. "I would recommend a .357 Magnum. It's a powerful cartridge that would cause serious grief to any attackers not wearing body armor." She took him down the counter to where he could see a shiny .357 through the glass countertop. "That's a Smith and Wesson Model 66, four inch barrel."

"A .357 Magnum?" The doctor tried not to squeak. "That'd be quite a handful, wouldn't it?"

"Don't worry, a .357 isn't that hard to shoot after you've had some practice. But you wouldn't have to start off with that load anyway. You see, a .357 Magnum can also shoot .38 Special cartridges, which are much less powerful. The .357 gives you more flexibility—you can learn on the milder .38s and then move up to .357 when you're ready. It also gives you a broader choice of ammunition than you'd have if you bought a Model 10, for example, that shoots .38, but can't shoot .357."

"That sounds reasonable to me." Jared hesitated. "Uh... Can I see it?"

"Sure." She opened the counter from behind and took the weapon out. Before handing it to him, she made a show of opening the cylinder so he could see it was empty.

Jared took the gun with both hands. It was heavier than he expected. The grip settled comfortably into his right hand and the shiny metal was cool and hard against the fingers of his left. It weighed in his hands—nearly as heavy as the rifle he'd pulled from the closet at home. "Are they all this massive?"

"No, but heavy is better for beginners. You won't feel the recoil so much, and that one has a longer barrel to make it easier to aim."

Jared imitated her and was surprised to see how easily the latch released the cylinder. It rotated freely and without sound when he thumbed it, and then snapped shut with a click when he flipped his wrist over.

"Don't do that!"

Jared looked up in surprise. "Why?"

"Flipping the cylinder closed can bend the crane."

"Oh." The gun was obviously a precision-crafted tool, something with a design that had been refined over many years of production. "Sorry." He handed the weapon back. "What about the rifle?"

Mrs. Joe wiped the revolver off with a rag before setting it back in its place. "Another 'tool for protection?'"

Jared nodded once.

"Okay. Like the revolver, then, you'll need something easy to shoot and reliable in operation."

"Um-hm. What would you recommend?"

"Well, you have lots of choices there, but if what you want is high power and accuracy, you probably want something in chambered in 30.06." She pronounced it 'thirty-ought-six'.

"Why? What's thirty-ought-six?"

"That's the caliber. The number refers to the diameter of the bullet, though 30.06 bullets are actually three hundred and eight one-thousandths of an inch in diameter. The 30.06 is a high powered 'deer hunting' round. That's good, because the trajectory of the bullet is flat—very accurate—and the slug packs a punch. Another thing about the 30.06 is that it's a common cartridge, easy to find. That may be the one thing that matters more than anything else soon. .270 is good in that way also, and actually has a faster, flatter trajectory for the bullet, but it's more likely to go straight through your target and transfer less energy. And besides, I don't have any semi-autos in .270."

"I need a semi-auto?"

"Yup! You're not planning on deer-hunting. If some gang of hoods jumps you at a rest area, you want something that will fire many rounds in rapid succession."

"Oh. So what do you recommend?"

Mrs. Joe turned to survey the many gun racks—few of them full anymore—that lined the wall behind the counter. "Hmmm. You know, I'm having second thoughts about a 30.06 for you. We don't have any M1 Garands in stock right now and that's the only serious 'protection' rifle in 30.06 worth talking about. Here, have a look at this one." She handed him a menacing military-looking rifle.

"Is... Is it a machine gun?"

She chuckled. "No, it's not a 'machine gun.' It's an M1A, a civilian version of the old M14 rifle. It's an ideal rifle, even if you're not going to Camp Perry."

"Not going where?"

"Never mind."

"The alternative would be this Heckler and Koch 91 here." She placed a weapon with an even more menacing appearance on the counter. "They're both accurate enough, they both fire a .308 Winchester cartridge, which is also the same ammunition the military uses in their medium machine guns, though they call it 7.62 NATO. The cartridge is a little less powerful than the 30.06, but just as easy to find, and more fit in a smaller magazine. Both of these rifles have 20 round magazines and can easily be equipped with scopes."

"They're both the same kind of gun? They look so different!"

"Yes, they look very different, and that's something you should think about. The M1A, with its wood stock and a 5 round magazine, is not as intimidating. But that can be good, if you don't want to attract attention. The HK 91, on the other hand, looks downright mean, and that could be enough for you to stop a fight without having to shoot anyone."

"Well, if I ever need to use it, I don't think avoiding attention will be an option. And I like the idea of possibly not having to shoot anyone at all..." Jared examined the HK 91 more closely, prodding it as he might poke a patient's body. "What exactly does 'semiautomatic' mean, anyway?"

"Semiautomatic means that you don't have to do anything to

chamber the next round; you just keep pulling the trigger until it runs dry. The HK 91 is a great 'battle rifle': versatile, powerful, rugged, and dependable." She lifted it and held it out to him for his inspection. "And it's accurate too—even a beginner with a little practice could hold off a lot of bad guys at 200 yards with this gun."

Jared found that the rifle, contrary to his experience with the revolver, was much lighter than he'd expected. When he commented on it, she told him that the gun actually weighed about ten pounds, and that because of its weight the recoil wouldn't be too bad. Jared wasn't sure how much recoil he could handle, but she assured him that it would be manageable, with practice. Mrs. Joe explained its operation for a few more minutes, while Jared worked the action and learned how to insert and remove the magazine. Everything had a snug fit, everything worked perfectly—the rifle was another piece of precision engineering.

After talking a while longer about the merits and limitations of other rifles, Jared realized that he didn't know enough about guns to tell whether or not the woman was steering him truly, but the same would be the case at any other gun store. And he liked her. None of her actions gave him the impression that she was trying to hide anything—there were certainly more expensive rifles in the shop she could have tried to sell him. He thought he could trust her. "All right," he decided, "I'll take the HK, and I want six of the Model 66 revolvers."

"Six?"

"Yes, six."

"I don't think I have that many. A lot of people have been buying guns lately—I have very few pre-owned revolvers left. I'll sell you that used one you checked out before, and as many new ones as I have left, but I may not have six. You could either go somewhere else and get some more, or get one or two in another caliber."

"I don't want to go anywhere else."

"Well, if you're investing in that many tools, you might want to have two of them in .22 LR. That way you'd have a very inexpensive and very light recoiling cartridge available for practice. Even lighter recoiling than .38 wadcutters, the lightest cartridge we can get you for your Model 66s."

"Great—I'll take two of the .22s and four .357 Magnums. I want whatever you have in the Smith and Wesson, and then maybe the rest in some other brand."

"Now you're thinking!" Mrs. Joe smiled approvingly. The she counted out several forms from a stack she had by the register. "You start filling these out, and I'll round everything up for you. You realize, don't you, that you'll have to wait five days before you can take the handguns home?"

"Yes, I know." Jared's tone drooped as he took the forms. After looking them over in dismay, he dutifully took out his pen and began to comply. "But you know, there's something wrong about honest people needing to wait five days before they can protect themselves."

"Tell me about it!" Mrs. Joe made no attempt to disguise her indignation. "I had a customer last year who was raped and slaughtered by an ex-boyfriend while the gun she'd bought was still here, waiting for the five days to be up. It's supposed to be 'innocent until proven guilty' in this country, but that's not how they treat gun owners. It's treason, I tell you, unconstitutional!"

Jared believed her. They spoke a little more while he filled out the forms and she called his information to the police for his 'Instant Check' clearance. Then he paid for his purchases—and the 'Instant Check' fee—in cash. He left the store weighed down with two bricks of 500 rounds each of .22 cartridges, several boxes of .357 and .38 Special ammo, a half-dozen twenty-count boxes of .308 rifle cartridges, and the HK 91 slung over his shoulder. The bag with the ammunition also had a beat-up cardboard box that showed signs of having been mailed a dozen times, in which Mrs. Joe had put four twenty-round magazines for the rifle, eight "speed loaders" for the .357s and four for the .22s, and a variety of gun-cleaning tools and chemicals.

In spite of the weight, a strange sense of joy and lightness of heart came over him. It was a beautiful sunny day.

Jared thought about it as he drove home. The rising crime wave had really been preying upon his mind—the news reports portrayed an image of the police being totally swamped. There were no safe neighborhoods anymore. The whole world was going crazy! This was much better: having a chance to prevent a tragedy, rather than relying on the police to try to catch perpetrators after the fact. What a liberating experience!

He found himself whistling and smiling, as he drove. Yes, it was a beautiful day!

CHAPTER 33:
MONDAY, FEBRUARY 21, 2000

"Here comes the rain again
Raining in my head like a tragedy
I want to breathe in the open wind."
—Eurythmics, *Here Comes the Rain Again*

Brigadier General Thomas sat in her office, fuming, and thinking about the stack of reports she had just waded through. Idiots! What a hopeless mess!

She picked up the phone and punched an intercom button. "Mr. Allen?"

"Yes General, what can I do for you?"

"Oh, don't rub it in. I wish I was still good old Major Tom, and I wish I hadn't been handed this Life-forsaken mess to clean up!" Alexis sighed. "The president thinks he helped me by promoting me and giving me a medal, right there on TV, but he didn't. How could a draft-dodger understand the military mind? The brass at every installation we talk to knows that I got this promotion because the president wants to look good, not because I earned it. The star on my collar is an affront to their entire careers and they resent it. And rightly so! So, where I once had the problem of dealing with people who didn't like someone from Washington telling them how to run their show, now I have the problem of dealing with people who don't think that I—personally—should even be talking to them. Hell, with this president, they probably think I slept with him to get my promotion!"

"Well, they may think you don't deserve it, but I know how

hard you've been busting your butt for the last couple years trying to save theirs."

"And you know what his answer was, when I told him I didn't need or want the promotion?" Alexis was on a roll and didn't register Allen's comment. "He said, 'image is everything,' just like in that stupid TV commercial. He thinks the public will have more confidence in the government's efforts to fix Y2K problems if the new Computer Czar is a general and not some lowly colonel! If he'd spend as much time working on solving problems as he does trying to look like he's solving problems, the public would have a *reason* to feel better about the future!"

"Well, at least *I* didn't call you Czar."

Alexis groaned. "You know, that stupid press conference last week has pretty much stopped our progress dead in the water. Everyone is calling me that now! I hated press conferences enough to begin with—all a big waste of time—and now this!"

Allen cleared his throat. "Uh, did you call to blow off steam, or did you need something? 'Cause if you're gonna vent about the president, I'd just as soon provide you with a shoulder to cry on, rather than talk about it on the phone."

This was followed by a brief silence in which Allen wondered if he'd gone too far. He had admitted to himself some time before that he had a crush on Alexis, but he was too professional to let on, and he didn't think she felt the same way about him. He regretted letting the remark about the shoulder slip. He wasn't sure what he'd do if she ever found out about his feelings and their working relationship suffered as a result. A sense of vertigo welled up in him as the silence stretched out.

But Alexis wasn't thinking along those lines at all. Criticizing the Commander in Chief could be a punishable offense... When had she become so relaxed about speaking with John? For some time, Merlyn had been the only person in her life she could feel completely comfortable speaking her mind with. And now here she was carrying on, in a way most indecorous for someone of her rank, with a civilian she didn't really know that well—come to think of it! "Quite right, Mr. Allen." She paused to collect her thoughts. "I did have a reason for calling, and it wasn't to complain." And then, to soften the formality of her words: "But thanks for being my punching bag. I feel better now."

"Any time!" He wondered if she could hear the relief in his voice. "So, how can I help you, Alexis?"

"These reports are useless. NORAD says they have the primary power back on. Isn't that great? Now they can *see* that nothing is working! SAC says they have some limited radar coverage of the U.S., but it's pretty pitiful, from what I can tell. Their main detection systems are not back on-line. A lot of key bases have fallen back on World War II technology. It's helping them to answer my phone calls, but doing precious little else. The only thing saving us from invasion, assuming that anyone would be interested in this basket-case of a country, is that everyone else's militaries are in even worse shape than ours!

"And the civilian branches! It's a goddamned disgrace! I haven't even gotten a report from CIAO. The Social Security Administration's much-vaunted Y2K preparedness has turned out to be a sham—their people are *still* finding things they overlooked! HUD is worse off because some of their branches implemented different and incompatible fixes, and the results not only brought systems down, but scrambled datafiles that someone forgot to back up. And Treasury! They didn't even pretend to be ready and now their whole operation is a shambles, especially the IRS."

"I've been wondering about the Department of Treasury." Allen sounded intrigued, as though the situation were an interesting plot twist in a good movie. "I haven't been paid for a while, and neither has anyone I know here in the Pentagon. A lot of GIs living on bases or sailors on ships won't care too much—their pay is nothing compared to sitting in a heavily defended place with food in their stomachs and a roof over their heads. But most service members don't live on bases or boats. I hear the AWOL rate is way up and I bet you'll see a lot of those turn into genuine desertions, if Treasury doesn't get its act together soon. I think I've heard something about military vouchers, but with things as crazy as they're getting, I don't know how many people would accept them."

"Right. So, we knew when we started out that these folks were hurting. We knew it was urgent, right? Now—more than a month after Cuba—we finally get their reports and the fools don't even suggest courses of action! They've spent a month detailing the extent of the disasters caused by their lack of preparation, and have come up with nothing whatsoever on what to do about them."

She stopped short and tapped on a stack of reports. "Um, I take that back; the military installations all have action plans in their reports, but they'll take years to implement. The civilians are clueless. I understand that we are supposed to help them, but how can we do that if they won't even say what it is that needs to happen or where the help is needed? If we don't get things going again soon, we'll end up in the same kind of chaos that has taken over in Russia!"

"And so you want me to...?"

"I want you to go over there and shoot the idiots, but that's not in the procedure manual, so I guess we'll have to go talk to them. And not just the Washington crowd—they're too busy writing reports that make everything look like someone else's fault. We need to travel to various operation centers, get feedback from people who actually do things like print the damned social security checks and run the radar at SAC. We need to know what they need to get the essential things going again."

"So you want me to make some travel arrangements—"

Alexis cut in. "No, you can coordinate with Captain Smith and have him make those arrangements. Tell him I said so and give him a list of prioritized military destinations—you know which ones as well as I do."

"Okay. And me?"

"I want you to call each agency blockhead—I mean agency head—and get me a list of mission-critical sites that must be gotten going again in order to get the civilian agencies back in business. Then we'll go check 'em out ourselves, get a feel for what needs to happen. We'll meet with installation COs on the spot, and send instructions back to the agency heads. You don't mind traveling, do you John?"

"Not at all, Alexis." Actually, he hated flying, but he didn't want to get left behind. "It'll be nice to get out of this basement for a once!"

"Good."

"Okay. I get what you want to do; we'll take some key analysts with us into the field and coordinate with the ones back here, accelerating the implementation of change at the places we visit. I'll start building the list of civilian sites, but it's pretty late—after seven already. Most of those people—the agency blockheads—will be gone for the day. I'll start compiling the list first thing in the morning. If they cooperate, I should have the list by tomorrow afternoon."

"There is no 'if' about that, John. You tell them that the Computer Czar wants the information and she wants it now!" Alexis grinned savagely. "If that doesn't get their attention immediately, you find a way to suggest that my next report to the president will highlight their personal responsibility in this fiasco—that ought to get them moving."

"Yes, ma'am!"

"And please don't repeat that blockhead thing to anyone—a leak like that could really make what little cooperation we're getting evaporate..." The new general sighed heavily. "But you know, I will give the president this much: it's a damned good idea to keep those people in their jobs until they either fix the problems, or admit full responsibility and resign in disgrace. I've never seen so many bureaucrats work so hard!"

Allen laughed. "Yes, ma'am."

"Stop calling me that. It's Alexis for you, mister!"

"Yes, Alexis—ma'am!"

They both laughed. Life, it was good to have a civilian around! But it reminded her of what was going on in the civilian world around her and she sobered quickly. "John, have you seen Captain Smith's report?"

"No, Alexis, it was marked for your eyes only."

"Well, lots of people are starting to get desperate and angry, especially with the government. Some people have actually started taking pot-shots at passing government vehicles. Riots have broken out when the food's run out at soup kitchens, and the first people they lynch are the most recognizable government employees: anyone wearing a uniform. Uh, don't worry about Captain Smith—I really need to take care of that myself. Sometimes I forget that you're not in the chain of command. I'll get him to arrange for hardened transportation—maybe some of Gishesky's babies out at Fort Belvoir."

"Gishes—what?"

"Sorry," Alexis chuckled, "I was talking about Major Gishesky, an old fencing opponent of mine who flies Cobras out at Fort Belvoir. But I wasn't thinking straight; Cobras only seat two people. What we need are some Blackhawks."

"You know someone who would stand in front of you while you're holding a weapon?"

Now Alexis really laughed. "Yes! But don't worry, I trounced him."

"I'm sure you did!"

She flipped through her on-screen rolodex as she spoke. "You know, there is a bright side to this; I'll get more flight time than I have in ages. Do you fly, John?"

"Not me! You know I was in the Army once, a *looong* time ago, and I did get some training in choppers, but I didn't like it—I was strictly an infantry kind of guy!"

"Okay, John. Don't worry, I won't make you try to fly one! But I'm tired of trying to make things happen by remote control. We're taking our best people and we're going out there to kick some butts back into gear!"

"Yes ma'am!"

Alexis hung up the phone with a smile. She liked John Allen.

She liked his sense of humor. And she liked the way he had much of the discipline she admired in military officers, without having all the attitudes and neuroses she hated in her soldierly brethren. He was good to have around.

CHAPTER 34:
WEDNESDAY, FEBRUARY 23, 2000

"She takes care of herself
She's ahead of her time
She's always a woman to me."
—Billy Joel, *She's Always a Woman*

Perhaps Max was not so foolish after all... Somewhere out there among the buildings Michel could see from his office window, someone was committing suicide, someone else was being raped, and yet another was being murdered. Or perhaps it was not merely some*one*. He no longer imagined himself to be atop Mt. Olympus—the view now inspired thoughts of Barad-Dûr, the Dark Tower of the land of Mordor, in J.R.R. Tolkien's *Lord of the Rings*.

Natalie stood behind him, also looking out and thinking somber thoughts.

"It is all coming apart," he told her. "We do not 'ave ze same problems zey do in Los Angeles, but sings are still coming apart."

"I think Los Angeles may be part of our problem—everyone's problems." She leaned closer, wrapping her arms around him and leaning her head on his shoulder. "People see the breakdown of authority there and think that it could happen here, or anywhere, really. Our cute Computer Czar comes on TV and tells us that the Departments of Education and Commerce are back in business, but neglects to say how long it will be before the welfare or social security recipients get their checks. People are losing faith in the system. They're giving up on it. They are scared and starting to do whatever they think will save them, and that usually means abandoning the way things have always been done. That frightens them all the more and makes them resentful."

"Spoken like a true psychologist." Michel teased his lover sometimes, about needing her counselor's services. The truth was that he had picked up a lot of her way of drawing her clients out—more than either of them knew. She had a rare ability to get to the bottom of what was troubling people. His unconscious imitation of her questioning techniques had enabled him to do the same with his clients and ensured that they felt he was attending to their needs. Natalie was a big part of Michel's own success as an advisor.

She returned his teasing with a gentle poke in the ribs.

He laughed softly and then turned to face her. "So what is ze answer? How do we stop it?"

"I'm not sure we can. I'm not sure anyone can. If the Computer Czar appeared on TV tonight and announced that everything was fixed, and that all the starving people would be getting their checks in the mail soon, I don't think that would stop what has started. People are abandoning the systems they believe caused this mess, and I don't know what new ones they will seek out as replacements."

"I can not see anysing any more." He leaned his head against the glass. "I look into ze future, and I 'ave no idea what to tell my clients. Even ze companies zat were prepared for Y2K are taking a beating in ze market. Everyone is pulling zeir money out of stocks. For now, all zey want is cash, and I cannot say zat I blame zem... But where does it stop? If all ze money is taken out of Wall Street, ze economy will fall apart."

"It's one of those systems people have lost faith in." She took his hand. "Many brokers' clients pulled their money out a long time ago. Yours had more faith in the stock market because your skill saved them from the losses others suffered earlier on. But now it's beyond anything you can do—people are losing faith in that system entirely."

"And what do you see? What do you see when you look into ze

future, my dear Natalie?"

"I see either chaos, or some new order. But I can't say how such an order would come about, or what form it might take. The military still seems strong. Perhaps we are facing a military dictatorship. I don't know. But one thing I am sure of: things will get worse before they get better."

They were silent for a while. Finally, Michel sighed and turned from the window. "Well, at least I still have some work to do trading commodities."

"And I have plenty of clients!"

They smiled into each others' eyes.

"So, we 'ave work, and we 'ave money." Michel kissed her forehead. "Let us go out for dinner!"

"Oh Michel, the restaurants will be so empty!"

"Zen we will not 'ave any problems getting a table at ze best one in town! Where do you want to go? Your favorite? Pick whichever one you like, and zat is where we will go tonight." He kissed her again. "Is it psychologically unhealsy to want to 'ave some fun and get away from sinking about chaos?"

"Not at all!"

"Zen let us go!" He pulled her toward the door. "But we will take my new truck. Zere are too many gangs out zere and not enough police."

"You have a new truck? You haven't mentioned anything about getting a new car."

"Oh, you will love him!" He laughed. "He is ze 'eight of style and class... He was a present from Max!"

"Since when has anything of Max's been the height of style and class?"

"You will see!" Michel took her hand and guided her to the elevator, turning off the lights as they left.

In the elevator, Natalie clung to him, sensing that they were both falling into a dangerous future.

When the garage elevator doors opened, the scene was even gloomier than Michel remembered. More lights must have gone out. The dust-shrouded sedan was in the same place, still lying in state. He led the way around the elevator shaft, feeling in his pocket for the keys to the armored car.

When it was clear that the truck was their destination, Natalie stopped and laughed. "Oh, Michel, this is just...so...Max!" She laughed again.

"Is he not?" Michel joined her in a chuckle as he opened the back. "Would you like some ice cream?"

"I like drumsticks..." Natalie started to laugh and stopped short when she saw the inside of the truck. Michel handed her up into the back and she whistled appreciatively, inspecting the various cabinets and fixtures. "Good God, Max really was expecting the worst, wasn't he?"

"He only looks like an ice cream truck because of ze paint and ze bells. He is actually an old armored car wis a new engine." Michel grimaced. "I was hoping never to 'ave to use him."

She grinned. "Well then, let's use it for fun! Let's not go out for dinner, let's eat here. There's plenty of food in the cabinets— I'll cook you a nice dinner!"

"You? But you 'ate to cook!"

"Not exactly. I hate the drudgery of cooking every day. This will be more like camping out. It'll be fun. Please Michel, I don't want to go eat in an empty restaurant..."

"Okay, sweet Natalie. Can I 'elp wis somesing?"

"Why don't you drive us to your apartment building—that way we can go upstairs after dinner and have some dessert."

"Zere is a bed over zere..."

"More like a couch. I'm not that kind of psychologist!"

They both laughed.

"But... You will get bounced around while I drive, no?"

"A challenge! Go!" She pointed to the driver's seat, mock severity in her voice.

He laughed and held up his hands in surrender.

The engine turned over smoothly and the lights came on, illuminating the layer of dust on the windshield. Michel hunted briefly, activated the wipers, and put the truck in gear—thank goodness it was an automatic! He had to navigate carefully to get around the cement pillars of the parking deck.

Before starting up the ramp, he dropped the truck back into park and turned to watch Natalie over his shoulder. She was so beautiful—he loved the way her golden-brown hair flowed over her shoulders—and so...perfect for him. He knew it was cliché, but he often thought of her as a dream come true—the spirit of his longings made manifest in flesh and blood. He also knew he'd never find someone like her again. "Natalie, why 'ave we never spoken of marriage?"

She stopped pulling cans and boxes from the cabinets. Turning very slowly, she leaned back against the range. "I don't know, Michel. Why do you think we haven't spoken of marriage?"

"I love you."

"And I love you."

"And I like being wis you."

"And I with you."

"Natalie, will you marry me?"

"No."

"What? Why?! I..."

She came over and placed a finger on his lips. "Listen, you big lug, I love you, and I want to be with you more, but now is neither a good time nor place to start a new family. Maybe when this all settles out... When the time and place are right, I would be honored to be your wife."

"But zen, why not say yes now?"

"Shhhh. Just drive." She turned back toward the kitchenette.

He caught her hand and kissed it before returning to his own task.

Shifting the gear selector back to drive, Michel eased them out into the night.

CHAPTER 35:
FRIDAY, FEBRUARY 25, 2000

"If you listen to fools, the mob rules!"
—Black Sabbath, *The Mob Rules*

Milford, CT:

"What do you mean you won't take 'em?" The soldier leaned across the counter, radiating anger. "The President issued an executive order under his emergency powers. You have to take 'em. Everyone has to take FEMAscrip."

"But... Please!" The old man tried not to quake as he returned the soldier's unyielding gaze. "I have a box full of such scraps of paper back in my office. I don't wear a uniform, so no one will take them from me. I can't use them to pay my bills, I can't even use them to pay for more stock for my store."

"That's not my problem."

"My family depends on this convenience store, it's the only thing we have left. We're not like a big supermarket with lots of credit with suppliers. If you people keep shopping here and paying with papers I can't use for anything, I'll go out of business!"

"Life's tough, pal. I gotta eat too."

Resigning himself to the inevitable, the shopkeeper rang the scrip into his register and bagged the cigarettes and potato chips the soldier was 'buying'.

*   *   *

Tampa, FL:

Mrs. North wandered up and down the aisles of her favorite
supermarket in shock. Five dollars for a gallon of milk? Two-fifty
for a carton of eggs? How was a retiree to live?

In the first place, the FEMAscrip they had started sending out
was not as much money as her social security check had been. In
the second place, no one wanted to take the scrip. And now that
the National Guard had forced the issue, prices everywhere were
skyrocketing.

Mrs. North sighed and pushed her cart right past the coffee.
No bacon either. Nor jam. All she could afford was the milk, bread,
eggs, and rice she had in her shopping cart. She only had twenty
FEMAscrip dollars left, and it had to last her a whole month!

Well, maybe by then the Computer Czar would have the machines that print the social security checks fixed.

*   *   *

Amarillo, TX:

"We ain't takin' no more monopoly money!" The young clerk
in the hardware store was outright hostile. She looked at the navy
blue blazer with FEMA spelled in large block letters on the back
in the same way Jews had looked at black SS uniforms in Germany
in 1939.

The man from FEMA tried to appeal to patriotism. "That's a
fine way to treat the boys in uniform who put their lives on the
line every day, trying to hold the country together."

"Lives on the line? We ain't at war!"

"Aren't we?" He pointed out the door. "It's a madhouse out
there. Just the other day at St. Luke's homeless shelter, they had to
close the doors when they ran out of room. The crowd outside got

ugly, so my men and I moved in to calm things down. They turned on us, some with sticks, some with knives, and a few with guns. I lost several men!"

"Well, I'm real sorry, but we cain't take no more of that funny money. It's ruinin' us!"

"You have to. We need the supplies to fix up more shelters, and the executive order makes FEMAscrip redeemable at any retail outlet."

"Wassup with that? This FEMAscrap looks like play money to me. Why don't they use real money? Gummint's got tons of it!"

"It's not like that. The government doesn't have any money it doesn't take from people like you and me first—we don't just print more whenever we need it, like in third world countries. Besides, even if they could get the presses working again at the Department of Treasury, printing a bunch of money like that would set off hyperinflation."

"Hyperinflation, huh? Looks to me like prices are goin' up plenty fast as it is!"

"Well, you've got a point there, miss, but the law is the law..."

"Hey, if the presses ain't workin', how'd they print the FEMAscrap?"

"It was printed a long time ago. It's been in storage in case there ever was an emergency like this. But that doesn't matter! We've got homeless people to help, and you have to accept the scrip."

"I don't care what you say. It's still ruinin' us and the boss told me not to take any more FEMAscrap. He's runnin' out of real money to pay us with. If that happens, I'll be nothin' but another one of your homeless people!" The clerk leaned back and crossed her arms. "What you gonna do, shoot me?"

The man from FEMA lost his patience and opened his jacket, revealing a pistol in a hip holster. "I don't have time to argue with trailer park trash like you. We are the law now," he put his hand on the butt of the pistol and leaned forward, "and we will use force if we have to."

The blood drained from the cashier's face, and, with a sullen look and no more words, she rang up the sale.

Pocatello, ID:

The pawnbroker frowned when the FEMA agents came up to his counter. "Whatever you want," he announced, "it's not for sale."

"Waddaya mean not for sale?" At a nod from their leader, a woman in a FEMA jacket, the men fanned out through the store and prepared themselves for trouble. "That snow blower out front has a sign on it that says: For Sale, $625."

"It's not for sale." The pawnbroker was a burly man. He crossed his arms behind his back in a way that he hoped would conceal the fact that he was reaching for a pearl-handled Colt .45 he kept tucked into his pants.

"Look," the FEMA woman was getting tired of the constant crap people were giving her, "you don't want any trouble. We need the snow blower for the soup kitchen. The one they had broke down. Our commander authorized us to go out and buy one, so you're gonna sell us one!"

"Hah! You can't call giving me a bunch of scrap paper 'buying' something. No sale." He whipped his arm forward, holding the pistol with rock-steady aim at a point between the woman's breasts. He couldn't tell that the bulk under her jacket was a bullet-proof vest.

"You can't—" She broke off when the shopkeeper made his move and then resumed speaking very softly. "I wouldn't do that if I were you." She had obviously been in such situations before.

"Tell your gang of thieves to put their guns away and leave my store, or I'll shoot." The burly man kept his pistol trained on her heart. "I'm tired of you assholes thinking you can push everyone around 'cuz a bigger asshole in the White House says it's okay. We're all just tryin' to stay alive, and you parade around in your

FEMA jackets and army uniforms, pretending to help us, while you're really robbing us!" He clicked the safety off.

A man to the squad leader's right misinterpreted the pawnbroker's move and fired his weapon. The sharp report startled the other two FEMA men who had their guns on the shopkeeper, and the big man ended up with several holes in him before he hit the ground.

"Shit!" The squad leader glared at her fellows. "Waddya do that for?"

The man who fired first knew he was in trouble. "I thought he was going to pull the trigger!"

"He was only clicking the safety off!"

"Oh."

"Oh is right, now we're going to have to fill out all that paperwork twice today!"

The others groaned.

"All right. Let's load up the snow blower and see if we can find a cop to clean up this mess."

The FEMA squad trooped out of the pawnshop and back to their truck, pausing to cut the chain off the snow blower with a pair of bolt-cutters taken from the pawn shop.

*   *   *

New York City:

It wasn't a very large convoy. The three National Guard supply trucks were led and followed by a pair of V-150 armored cars—not nearly enough armor for this section of Harlem. Not only that, but the V-150s were not the turreted kind with the serious guns, and the guardsmen riding in them had the top hatches open.

The convoy was traveling through a canyon-like street that would eventually take them to the main Harlem shelter, but their way was blocked by a three-car wreck. All five vehicles came to a halt.

The V-150s were squat, angular, and powerful. Their 504 V-8 diesel engines enabled them to operate on a 70 degree incline and their large flat tires made them comfortable working on a 40 percent side slope. A hydraulic winch for self recovery was fitted to the front of each. Two guardsmen got out of the lead vehicle and started playing out the cable and hook from its winch. They were planning to drag one of the wrecked cars far enough out of the way to allow the convoy to pass.

Seconds after the two men affixed the hook to the bumper of one of the cars, they noticed the rushing shadows closing around them. There were too many to count. Some were old. Some were very young. Some were evidently street gang punks. They appeared tattered and disorganized, moving with the parsimonious motions of the starving.

And yet, the attack was not without method or purpose. A Molotov cocktail the size of a large pickle-jar was heaved into each of the armored vehicles, while the gang members gunned down the exposed guardsmen and sprayed the cabs of the trucks with flying lead. Soldiers who tried to escape the flames in the V-150s were shot or beaten senseless as soon as they emerged.

It was over almost as soon as it began, but things didn't go according to the gang's plans. Their hungry allies didn't wait for the loot from the trucks to be driven to a safe place and divided evenly; they began tearing at the boxes as soon as the fight was over. The clamor of the battle had also attracted other hungry hands.

There was no stopping the school of human piranhas, once they struck. The trucks were stripped bare in short order, and the one gang member stupid enough to try to interfere was promptly stabbed in the back. Even the bodies of the dead were stripped of anything that could be of value.

Chapter 36:
Monday, February 28, 2000

"With a few adjustments now
Living in the perfect system
the adjustment's simple there is really no pain
You'll hardly notice anything has changed."
—Oingo Boingo, *Perfect System*

Angel sat with Ejercito Dragon's lieutenants at the conference table and smiled. His expensive new suit and extra-wide tie were supposed to impress people with his wealth, but actually made him resemble a low-class pimp. Few of the lieutenants drew the comparison and none of them dared say anything, but they also did not imitate his mode of dress. "Hermanos," he glanced around, not entirely comfortable with their stares, "would you have believed this a year ago?"

There was laughter around the table, a large polished slab of mahogany roughly the size of an aircraft carrier's flight deck. The room was the boardroom of a defunct corporation. It was large, luxurious, and totally beyond what anyone present had thought they would attain.

"Of course not. But I knew it." Angel hoped that none of them could tell that he was flat out lying. "I brought us here." He thumped his chest to emphasize that it was because of him that they enjoyed the power and wealth they did. "Look at us. Ejercito now has *offices*! And not just any offices, but six floors on top of the tallest building in the city. We have power, and you have mansions, cars, and all the women you could want. All of this is ours, and the police—what few are left—don't dare bother us!"

More laughter swept around the table. Angel was right. Who cared if he did go a little overboard with his clothes, he also made them rich!

"Even the National Guard can't stop us. There are too many problems and not enough of them. Those weekend wimps only signed up for extra money. Now they are getting paid with paper no one will take, and they are getting shot at if they report for duty. I hear they are having as many second thoughts as the police. So instead of reporting in, they are staying home with their families, trying to figure out where to get the rent money. There is no power in California that can stop us!"

This time there were cheers and some whistling.

"But it's not enough!"

This got their attention.

"We are in control, but the people are afraid and they are leaving. It's okay for the police to be too scared to show up for work, but we need everything else to keep going. We need customers, yes?"

They all laughed again, but nervously, not sure where Angel was taking the discussion.

"So I have an idea about how to make them stay."

Everyone was listening.

"We announce that *we* are the new government of Los Angeles!"

No one moved, except Cabron, whose head snapped around in surprise, and no one said a word. A paper someone let go fluttered to the floor, its soft movement easily heard in the hush. Was this a joke?

"Think about it." Angel went on as though it were an everyday proposal he was discussing. "We put out the word that we have taken over—it's true anyway—and say that we are hiring! We take over empty apartments and houses, and give them to our employees. We pay people with real dollar bills—no need to launder our money any more. We tell the businesses that there won't be any taxes in the new city of Los Angeles! That will make them stay, and even attract some new ones. We make this a place where business people come to do business without having to pay taxes, and we continue making money the way we always have. With things falling apart all over the rest of the country, it won't be long before people actually start moving here!"

The group remained motionless, still too shocked to think of anything to say. This was no joke—Angel was serious! The idea made some kind of sense, but it was too big for them to absorb quickly. Become the government? Suddenly, the room burst into conversation.

Angel let them argue about it for a while, then called for silence and laid out a step-by-step plan he had worked out. He explained it twice, carefully emphasizing how much money it would make for each of them.

In they end, they accepted the plan. They were not sure it would work, but it certainly sounded good... And they knew that no one crossed Angel and lived. The motion passed unanimously.

What Angel didn't tell them was the reason he'd made his decision—and hence theirs. In truth he didn't understand it fully himself, and could not have articulated it. Somewhere in his mind, though, he knew he meant to prove to Rosalia that he *could* create something.

CHAPTER 37:
TUESDAY, FEBRUARY 29, 2000

"Riders on the storm
Into this house we're born
Into this world we're thrown."
—The Doors, *Riders on the Storm*

The Dollar Ranch appeared quite different on Merlyn and Anna's daily ride—or it would have if they could have seen much of the valley. The watchtowers were built and Jimmy had been busy with the bulldozer, clearing fifteen sites for the soon-to-be-built houses. Construction was proceeding in spite of the intense cold, but had stalled for a few days, while the Dollar Ranch awaited the passing of another storm system.

The clopping of the two horses' hooves was muffled by the falling snow, which danced down in huge white flakes—some more than an inch across. The horses stamped and snorted, their breath making clouds of steam that floated lazily to the right. If the storm kept up, there'd be more than two feet of fresh snow by morning.

Anna reined her horse to a stop and leaned against Merlyn when he pulled up next to her. "Are you sure about building the houses? The local governments haven't given up yet."

"Beloved, they are hollow trees. They may look strong, but they will be entirely swept away in the coming storm."

"I believe that, my dear partner, and I see the winds gathering force. But they don't know they are dead yet, and could cause us grief before they fall."

"I don't think so. The county government was hit pretty hard by Y2K. Sheriff Grant told me himself that few county employees are showing up for work—they haven't been paid for two months. Tax assessors, building inspectors, and other bureaucrats are all looking for more practical ways to survive, and everyone knows it. Look at all the construction going on in plain sight on the properties we passed last time we drove into town!"

"Yes, I agree—intellectually, at least. It's just hard to accept emotionally. The old world is going, I can see it, but it's going to take a while to sink in. It's frightening. It reminds me of..." She halted her horse and leaned over to take Merlyn's hand. "Well, it's more frightening than I expected. People are retreating into themselves, caring less about what their neighbors do—as long as those neighbors don't do anything threatening. The world isn't disappearing, it's fragmenting. Look at the disintegration in Los Angeles!"

Merlyn kissed her hand. "The scenes we see on TV certainly are frightening, and 'fragmenting' is a good word for what is happening, but it's not all bad. People are thinking more independently—they have to in order to survive—and are no longer subscribing to the corrupt authorities that once ruled them. What you're describing as caring less about neighbors could also be seen as greater self-reliance and respect for other people's privacy."

"That's not a very convincing argument."

He laughed. "You're right. And yes, people can get pretty savage and uncaring in chaotic times..." He pulled Anna closer, and his horse obliged by stepping closer to hers. "You know I don't know any better than anyone else how it will all turn out. But I think it's a good sign to see other ranches and farms building new buildings. It means that the Dollar Ranch is not the only place for refugees from the cities. It also means that local government authorities won't be able to do anything to stop us."

"Well," Anna pulled her scarf down for a moment and kissed him, before sitting up and kicking her horse back into motion, "that's good. I know the families are getting tired of camping in the barns. Building their houses will not only take care of that problem, but it will give them something to occupy their attention while everything is falling apart outside."

"I hope you're right. It's going to be *very* ugly."

"It probably already is, in those places around the world—Russia, for example—that have gone silent on the Web. There is nothing to do about it now but wait and see how the chips fall here in the U.S."

They rode on, silence settling on them like the snow.

CHAPTER 38:
WEDNESDAY, MARCH 22, 2000

"In Europe and America,
there's a growing feeling of hysteria
How can I save my little boy
from Oppenheimer's deadly toy
I hope the Russians love their children too!"
—Sting, *Russians*

4:47 p.m., EST

Howard Kistler, the National Security Advisor, reentered the cabinet room and interrupted the meeting he'd left ten minutes earlier. His complexion had gone pasty and his voice trembled as he murmured into the president's ear, "We have a situation!"

The president didn't bother whispering. "This whole last year has been one damned long 'situation', what is it now Howard?"

Kistler straightened and answered so that everyone could hear, his voice still quavering. "You'd better pick up the line there and find out for yourself. It's taken us a while to authenticate the call—it's being relayed from a radio signal being picked up by that German installation General Thomas' team got working again this morning. The sender is a Russian general no one's ever heard of. But from everything we've been able to check, he's legit, and he's got bad news."

The president let out a sigh of martyrdom and picked up the phone. A man with a very slight Russian accent was arguing with whomever had been holding the line while Kistler had checked out the call. Clearing his throat first, the president broke in. "This is the president speaking."

"Ah, Mr. President, at last! Listen, we don't have much time, you have an ICBM headed your way, with six 25-megaton warheads—"

"What!?! Who is this?"

"My name, as I've said many times, is Pavel Petrov. I am the commander of a secret last-resort nuclear missile facility that was built immediately prior to the end of the Soviet era. You don't have time for all my credentials, I'm telling you, you have a missile headed your way—in fact, it has taken so long to get through that the missile should be MIRVing now. You should be safe where you are in Washington, but by the time..."

Another line began buzzing urgently and Kistler picked it up. He listened briefly and then covered the mouth piece and hissed at the president, "It's SAC, they've picked up the Multiple Reentry Vehicles!"

The cabinet members sitting around the table sat up. They'd understood that whatever had interrupted their meeting was not good, but it had not occurred to them that the problem could involve nuclear weapons.

"General Petrov, I've just received confirmation of what you're saying. Are you sure Washington is safe?"

"I think so, yes. The system was designed to respond to a preemptive attack on your part. It was supposed to fire off a wave of missiles at your capital and key military installations, as well as similar targets in Europe and China—it has malfunctioned and has decided that Moscow has been attacked. When we discovered what was happening, we were able to take measures to stop most of the missiles, but not all of them. One is headed your way, but my information tells me that its warheads are all targeted on key military installations, such as your SAC and NORAD. Mr. President, you must warn them!"

"That's already being taken care of. But tell me general, why are you warning us?"

"Because this is an accident, a result of the year 2000 problem! I have no desire to see any Americans killed, and I must beg you, please, not to retaliate. I know many will die, but the Russian people who will die if you retaliate had nothing to do with this! If you have any satellites still working—I tell you honestly that we do not—you should be able to see that I am telling the truth. There have just been a large number of explosions across Russia, because we blocked some of the silos and shot down several of the departing missiles. You must believe me; this is an accident! Your CIA will be able to tell you that we are in no shape to try to invade America, and if we were launching a first strike, there would be hundreds of missiles headed your way, not one." Petrov could hear the silence as the president thought about it. He stopped talking to give the American time to think it over.

"Howard," the president turned to the National Security Advisor, "how many missiles is SAC tracking?"

"MIRVs, sir. They're tracking six. They think they all came from a single SS-24, or similar large missile."

"Okay, General Petrov, it looks like your story checks out, hold on a minute." He put the Russian on hold. "Howard, tell SAC that we have information that the launch was accidental—a Y2K glitch. Tell them not to retaliate, unless we can determine that the action was, in fact, deliberate and that we need to defend ourselves. Tell them to button up right away, if they haven't done it already. Go to DEFCON1, or whatever they call it. From what our Russian friend is saying, they are likely to be hit. Get NORAD on another line and tell them the same thing. And tell them to put out the word to all our submarine captains and other strike commanders that they are not to attack unless they can determine that the United States is in danger of being invaded. Got it?"

"Yes, sir!" Kistler began sending out the instructions.

The president turned to the cabinet members and actually grinned. "Don't worry," he told them, "none of the warheads are headed this way."

"And a good thing too!" The Secretary of Defense spoke first. "With the emergency session of Congress going full-tilt and all of us here, the country would be completely leaderless if Washington were to be hit..." His sunken eyes and pallid complexion spoke of the degree to which he was still in shock.

Then the Secretary of Labor spoke up. "Mr. President, how could this happen?" She was dazed and spoke dreamily. "How could they fire missiles at us without us knowing?"

It was the Secretary of Defense who answered. "Without our satellites, we're virtually blind. SAC is only partly operational; what they have working wouldn't pick anything up until the warheads were inbound."

"All those people!" She struggled with tears. "Do we know where the bombs are going to fall, Mr. President?"

"No..." The president picked up the phone again. "But Petrov does." When he hit the button for Petrov's line, the Russian was apparently talking to an underling of his own, in Russian. "Uh, General Petrov?"

"Nye kooltoorney— What? Oh, excuse me, Mr. President. Yes?"

"Ah, can you tell me where those MIRVs will be hitting?" He gestured for the National Security Advisor to drop what he was doing and pick up on the line so he could take notes.

Kistler held up a hand. "NORAD wants to hear it from you anyway. Let's switch lines."

The president raised his eyebrows, smirked, and then took the line to confirm NORAD's orders.

Kistler picked up on Petrov. "General Petrov, this is Mr. Kistler again, could you repeat that list of targets?" He spoke aloud as he wrote down the list. "NORAD... Fort Huachuca in Arizona... SAC... The missile fields in North Dakota... Fort Leavenworth— Jesus! That's right by Kansas City!" He mopped his brow on his sleeve. "I know you're sorry General. We'll just have to see what happens. It's too late to even warn the cities—the warheads will be hitting any time now. But we can begin issuing orders to move emergency supplies... What? Yes, that's near the city of Omaha. And the last one is bound for Fort Meade—*did you say Fort Meade?*"

Everyone in the room froze, except the president, who bolted for the door.

"But... Fort Meade is right outside the beltw—"

The warhead was programmed to detonate 13.5 miles away, in the air over Fort Meade, Maryland, where the National Security Agency was headquartered. It missed, exploding over the border between the District of Columbia and the state of Maryland, about six miles away. Unstable isotopes formed by the ripping asunder of oxygen and nitrogen in the air, and of the material in the bomb itself, decayed at a very high rate. The decay emitted intense levels of gamma radiation in the most lethal concentrations the weapon would produce. Searing radiation flashed out at the speed of light, and in less than a second, the shock wave from the blast slammed into the earth. It rebounded and the reflected wave combined with the original wave to form a circular Mach Front. This expanding circle of destruction flattened every building, tree, bridge, lamp post, and even fire hydrant within ten miles.

In Russia, General Pavel Petrov heard the line go dead.

As the fireball formed, the heat from the thermonuclear reactions taking place set everything flammable within seven miles on fire. Smaller fireballs erupted wherever fuel tanks were ignited, little brothers to the bigger one rising into the stratosphere at 300 miles per hour. Afterwinds, attaining speeds over two hundred miles per hour, began sucking dirt, dust, and lighter debris into the sky beneath the rising ball of cooling gases.

Towering miles over the ruins of Washington, the mushroom cloud rose into the sky. It, and the others like it across the U.S., were the only tombstones most of the dead would ever get.

CHAPTER 39:
THURSDAY, MARCH 23, 2000

"And a wind came across Europe
That would twist and turn our fate
For as well as bringing freedom
It had let loose men of hate."
—Savatage, *This Is The Time*

7:01 a.m., PST

"Prue! Come quick, it's on TV!"

"...word is now coming in from our Brussels correspondent Leon Forgette, who survived the Brussels blast and verifies that NATO headquarters and most buildings in that city have been destroyed. This bombing was apparently an air blast, as was the one over Washington D.C."

A computer map of Europe appeared behind the newswoman, with blinking dots marking the sites bombed by the Russian missile that had MIRVed over the continent. "The warheads targeted on Paris, Bonn, Athens, and Ankara also exploded in the air, devastating those cities. The one bound for London appears to have missed its target, falling into the North Sea instead, where it detonated very near the surface of the water, at the mouth of the river Thames."

The inset screen now showed images of London buildings protruding from dirty water. "The blast created a huge wave more than two hundred feet high at the mouth of the river. The wave then surged up the river valley, losing altitude as it advanced, but

still swamping many municipalities along the way and inundat-
ing London itself in a matter of minutes. Effects from the same
blast were experienced across the North Sea, where many ships
have capsized."

The map switched to show blinking dots over locations in
China. "Worst hit was China, which apparently received warheads
from two missiles, two of which fell on Beijing, and the remainder
of which fell on several military installations near the cities of Xining,
Urumqui, Lanzhou, Chongquing, Wuhan, and Shanghai. With
the exception of the Beijing explosions, all of the warheads detonated on or in the ground, creating a much larger radioactive fallout problem in China."

The inset map now changed to show the United States, with
red dots showing the strikes on the American mainland and yellow ovals showing the areas where radioactivity was estimated to
be lethal. "There is no assessment yet of the death toll in Europe
and China, but the situation is hardly better back here in the
United States, where the death toll is now projected to come to no
less than three million people and could go more than twice as
high." The image on the inset screen changed to an archived clip
of a nuclear fireball transforming into a mushroom cloud. "No
cameras in a position to record any of the blasts in the United
States have survived those events, but this footage is of a weapon
with the same destructive power as those that fell on the United
States."

The inset screen zoomed in to show the western strikes and
their associated fallout regions. "There is nothing fortunate about
this terrible tragedy, but we were lucky that only three of the
warheads were ground bursts: the one that fell on the North American Defense Command, under Cheyenne Mountain, in Colorado;
the warhead that fell on a silo field in North Dakota, and; the one
that fell on Strategic Air Command, outside of Omaha, Nebraska.
Dangerous fallout is expected to come down over one hundred
miles east of those explosions, but the other blasts were in the air
and carried most of the radioactive debris they produced high into

the atmosphere, where military experts say it will disperse to close to background levels of radioactivity."

Aerial shots, taken at a very long range, were shown of various craters and their encircling layers of destruction. "The cities of Omaha, Nebraska, Atchison, Kansas, and Washington, D.C. have essentially been destroyed. Apparently the Atchison warhead was intended for Fort Leavenworth. Also destroyed was Fort Huachuca in southern Arizona."

The image switched to the NORAD emblem. "For those of you just joining us, the latest breaking news is that this horrible worldwide catastrophe is apparently the result of an accident—an accident set off by a long chain of Y2K problems. Less than an hour ago, we received word that the North American Defense Command under Cheyenne Mountain, NORAD, survived the attack. The installation had its own Y2K problems before the attack—which is why we didn't have any early warning of the missiles—and is apparently a shambles now.

"The survivors can't come out because of the intense radiation above ground, but they were able to reestablish contact through their hardened underground communication system. Air Force General John McLeod, the commander at NORAD, says that he spoke to the president immediately prior to the explosions and that the president told him that the missile that carried the nuclear warheads to America had been launched by mistake. He was given specific orders not to retaliate, unless it could be determined that the United States was in danger of being invaded."

A map of Russia came on screen, with a flashing red dot roughly in the middle. "Confirmation of this has come directly from the source, if the following transmission is genuine. This recording was forwarded to us by our Brussels correspondent, Leon Forgette, who says that the broadcast is easily received on the frequency utilized by Radio Moscow, before it went off the air several months ago. Anyone with a working radio in Europe can hear the message."

The newswoman stopped talking and a rich tenor voice-over

was played. "Lyoodee meera..." Only a portion of the Russian message was played before the recording skipped to the same voice giving the message in English. Other than the Spanish-sounding rolled Rs, the speaker had an excellent command of American English. The news network broadcast the message in its entirety:

"People of the world, this is General Pavel Petrov. It is my great regret to inform you that, as great as this tragedy that has befallen us is, a still greater one may yet come. During the cold war, the government of the United Soviet Socialist Republics constructed a last-resort defensive system—what you might call a Doomsday Device.

"The system was designed to have override control of all Soviet inter-continental ballistic missiles—ICBMs. In the case of escalating hostilities, the source of the threat was to have been informed of the secret installation—but not its location—and more missiles were to be targeted on the aggressor's country. In the event that Moscow was bombed, the system would strike back immediately, hitting key military and strategic targets.

"This is why so many of your countries have been attacked; there was a series of system failures, starting on New Year's Day, that finally culminated in the system deciding that Moscow had been destroyed yesterday. It attacked immediately and would have sent forth hundreds of missiles back in the days of the Soviet Union, but many of those silos were no longer in service. Others malfunctioned, and yet others I was able to have blocked. We even managed to shoot down most of the missiles we didn't block, as they were taking off... But obviously, not all of them.

"We sent out messages, warning foreign leaders of where the rockets were likely to drop their warheads, and tried to explain the nature of the accident. Unfortunately, the Chinese either didn't believe us or didn't understand us, because they launched a limited strike before the two missiles that were targeted on the Chinese mainland dropped sixteen warheads on their country. Moscow was already in ruins from fighting between military factions, rioting, and looting, but what was left of it was destroyed by a number of thermonuclear explosions, not long after Beijing and Washington were destroyed. St. Petersburg was also destroyed, as were a number of military installations across our country.

"This may not seem like bad news to families, lovers, and friends of casualties in your countries, but it is. The last-resort machine was programmed to retaliate for an attack on the Soviet Union with a first wave of missiles, after which time it was to give foreign aggressors two weeks in which to surrender to the Soviet leadership—which was supposed to have survived in deep bunkers. If they did not surrender, or the Soviet leadership did not survive, the machine was programmed to respond with a second wave of missiles—everything left in the arsenal—which would include many missiles targeted on civilian targets.

"Unless something is done, there will be another attack.

"But whatever is done, it should not include any more attacks on any targets within the former USSR. The machine is programmed to retaliate immediately, if it determines that more attacks are being made. It has data gathering stations scattered around Russia, though I don't know how many are still working.

"The machine was also programmed with a countermand password, but everyone who knew the password was still in Moscow when the Chinese struck—we were as blind to incoming missiles as you were. There is now no one left alive with the knowledge necessary to order the machine to stand down.

"The Doomsday Device is fully automated and self-contained, with its own nuclear power plant. Its bunkers are sealed and wired with sensors that will trigger an immediate response if any attempt is made to enter them before the countermand password is given.

"The missiles themselves are scattered all over the former republics of the Soviet Union, and I no longer have the means to coordinate their destruction or blockage. I have a few men left at my disposal, but we do not have the resources to travel to each possible missile site and ensure that no more rockets leave Russia.

"I have given top priority to reestablishing communication

with the machine. Unfortunately, I do not have the countermand password, and the machine will assume a hostile takeover within Russia if it receives too many incorrect passwords.

"People of the world, I regret to inform you that the machine is preparing another nuclear attack on targets around the world, and there is nothing we can do to stop it before time runs out. I'm afraid I cannot even tell you the exact locations that will be bombed, now that the records that were in Moscow have been destroyed and the Russian military chain of command has disintegrated. I can say that every large city is a potential target. At this point, all I can give you is the location of the machine's local control center, and encourage the governments of the world to send their best people to help our experts dismantle it.

"The machine is modular, dispersed in a series of sealed bunkers lined with sensors. As I said, it is programmed to attack immediately in the event of any attempt to enter or bomb the sites. Even a preemptive nuclear strike would not eliminate the problem, as the controlling computers have a triple redundancy and are dispersed over thousands of square kilometers. The bunkers are very deep and hardened.

"The entrance to the control center is located near 89° 41' 07" east, 58° 52' 30" north. We encourage all governments able to respond to send a team of their best experts to meet with ours at the control center, as soon as possible. This is a distress call: we need help, and it is in your own interest to help us. We have until April 5th, at latest, to find a way to deactivate this machine. Do not let your anger at this monster built by the Soviets make your decisions. Do not attack, or the consequences will be most unpleasant for everyone. Thank you!"

The recording ended and another voice took over, presumably that of the Brussels correspondent. "According to the message, the so-called Doomsday Device is located in a remote area on the southern edge of western Siberia, northeast of the city of Novosibirsk. Back to you, Linda."

The newswoman took her cue and fixed her eyes on the camera. "With the President, his cabinet, and the joint chiefs of staff all dead, and even the vice president and the Congress dead as well, there seems to be little more than confusion about who is in charge, or what to do about the possibility of a second attack. Confusion is definitely the watchword of the day, and confused people everywhere are not waiting for authorities to issue instructions, as correspondent Cindy Levin tells us in this special report from New York City. Cindy?"

"That's right, Joyce. People here are assuming that, whatever other targets there might be, the Big Apple will be definitely be one of them. Families are piling their belongings into their cars and heading out of town. Many of them have no particular destination in mind, but don't want to take any chances on how soon the Russian machine may attack. The Hudson River bridges are all clogged and there are signs of collisions or fires in two of the tunnels. Traffic everywhere is backed up for miles. We'll keep the story covered for you, Joyce."

"Thank you, Cindy." Joyce turned back to the camera. "We are receiving word now that soldiers on military bases are now abandoning their posts in large numbers. For more on this story, we go now to Roger Jacobs at Fort Bragg, in North Carolina. We apologize for not being able to bring you any video, but we are having some technical difficulties of our own. What can you tell us, Roger?" A file image of soldiers marching in parade showed on the screen beside Joyce's head as she listened with the viewers.

"It doesn't look good, Joyce. Officers are not commenting, but, if our satellite TV truck was working, you'd be able to actually see the exodus. I spoke with one soldier who asked not to be named, and he said—"

Another recording was played. The voice was young, and shaky. "Ah know Ah sworn an oath, but Ah haven't been paid money Ah ken use in a long time, and that wasn't part o' the bargain! Ah'm tired of civilians takin' shots at me because they're mad at the gummint! God gave me a higher duty to protect mah family, and

Ah sure as hell ain't goin' to stick around some fool base and wait for a nuke to fall on mah head!"

Roger's voice returned. "He also told me, off the record, that there weren't enough MPs to chase down all the soldiers who are now AWOL, and that the officers know it. They're trying to hold on to enough people to move assets off base to places that might not be bombed. Some are just hoping to secure vital components of tanks and other weapons so that unauthorized personnel can't use them. Things are really starting to collapse out here, Joyce."

Joyce frowned into the camera. As the day progressed, she found herself using that word—collapse—more and more frequently.

Trish stared at the screen with wide eyes, and even the normally unflappable Prudence could think of nothing to say.

*   *   *

10:58 a.m., EST

Michel made the mistake of sleeping in late, thinking that there was little point in rushing in to the office—he hadn't gone in yesterday and would probably close it down soon anyway. After wandering into the kitchen and staring into space for a few minutes, his stomach growled and he jerked as though waking from a deep sleep. Apparently, he had started the espresso machine, but he couldn't remember doing it. Shaking his head, he put a croissant in the toaster-oven and refused to turn on the television or radio, as he had done the day before, because he was tired of bad news.

It was almost noon before he decided to go to work and see if anyone besides Grace had bothered to come in.

When he finally switched on the radio for a traffic report, all he heard was some nonsense about a Russian Doomsday Device. "...fear of the possibility of another nuclear strike by the malfunctioning Russian machine has led to rioting and spontaneous evacuations of many major urban areas, including Atlanta, Chicago, New York City, Philadelphia, and Boston…"

Nuclear strike? New York City?! Michel rushed to the nearest window. Twenty-three floors below, the street was deserted, except for a family tying some belongings onto the back of an overloaded pickup truck, and a few of the abandoned late-model cars that had stopped working after New Year's Day. Farther away, he could see a slice of expressway between buildings. It was packed with bumper-to-bumper traffic. Overhead, the sky was a solid sheet of dismal gray, hanging low.

"Merde alors!" He quickly finished dressing, gulped down his espresso, and tried calling Natalie. No dial tone. That was probably why she hadn't called… He dashed for the door.

Halfway down the hall, he thought better of it and dashed back to his apartment. Du calm… Qu'est-ce que jai besoin? *Calm down. What do I need?*

He pulled out a large suitcase he had stashed under his bed and threw in all of his underwear, tube socks, wool socks, and undershirts. Looking through his closet, he picked out the warmer and more durable clothes: jeans, khaki pants, denim shirts, turtle-necks, sweaters… No suits, no ties. Might as well use the Armani for a dish rag now!

The suitcase was buried in a pile of clothes by the time he'd gone through the closet and drawers. One hour and twenty-five 'merdes' later, he had scrounged everything he thought would be useful in an uncivilized world and packed it into three large suit-cases and a number of small bags, including a backpack.

First shouldering the backpack, he picked up one of the suit-cases in either hand and headed back down the hallway. It oc-curred to him—after he mashed the call button with the corner of a suitcase—that if there happened to be a mugger in the elevator, his hands would be full. And there probably wouldn't be anyone monitoring the security cameras!

Michel had imitated Max's trick of parking the truck on the bottom parking level so that it would go unnoticed. The elevator ride had never been so long! But when it was over and the doors opened, the armored car was parked exactly where he had left it. Breathing a sigh of relief, he carried the bags over and put them down so he could snag the keys from his pocket.

Inside, he shoved the suitcases under the table and searched in one of the drawers under the driver-side gun rack. As he'd thought, it held a handgun and what he assumed was ammunition for it. He pocketed a handful of ammunition and stuffed the gun into his belt before turning to go for his other belongings. Halfway to the elevator, he again thought better of what he was doing and returned to the truck.

Inside again, he sat down at the table to find out how to work the gun and to see if it was loaded. The gun was black and had several buttons and levers, in addition to the trigger. On the side of the weapon his thumb would be on—if he held it in his right hand—the words SIG SAUER were stamped into the metal, slightly off-set. Beside that, smaller letters read, SIGARMS INC., EXETER - NH. Not very helpful.

He flipped the Sig over. This side had the words P220, and MADE IN GERMANY stamped in the metal. .45 AUTO was stamped in tiny letters in a slightly recessed part, closer to the back of the gun, and there was something that suggested a serial number. Merde! Why hadn't he followed Max's advice and learned how to use one of these things?

Aiming the gun out the door of the truck, Michel pushed the button on the handle by the back of the trigger. It resembled what he thought a safety catch might look like. To his surprise, a flattened metal tube fell out of the handle and clattered to the floor between his feet. Picking it up and turning it over in his hands, he determined that it was the magazine. Six circular holes in the metal showed that it was loaded with five fat cartridges.

Relieved to know that it was not loaded, Michel put the gun on the table and tried the first lever. It wouldn't budge. The second one swung down and back, moving the hammer slightly, but didn't do anything else. The third one only moved slightly, also producing no visible effect.

Not sure what else to do, Michel pointed the gun out the back of the armored car again, aiming at the cinder-block wall behind the truck, and pulled the trigger. It was a little stiff, but it pulled the hammer back and released it. The pistol discharged with an unbelievably ferocious BOOM that left his ears ringing. The recoil twisted the weapon out of his unprepared hand.

But... He'd taken the bullets out!

Michel stared at the gun on the floor and felt something he did not often experience: self contempt. How could he let himself remain so ignorant of something that could be so important?

He picked up the gun again and examined it more carefully. Its shape had changed. A larger and a smaller tube were exposed in the front, the metal part with the words stamped in it having slid back. The larger tube must be the actual barrel. The sliding part had remained back, after firing the shot, and he could see inside the gun, down to where the magazine would fit.

The magazine!

There had only been brass visible in five of the six holes—one of the bullets must have been loaded into the shooting part of the gun.

Michel rummaged in the drawer and found that Max had left him the gun's owner's manual. He spent another quarter of an hour making sure he knew how to load and shoot the gun before putting the magazine back in. Chambering a round, he tucked the gun into his pants again. He still had no idea what the third lever did, and he hadn't figured out where the safety was (he didn't know that his P220 didn't have one), but he didn't want to spend any more time on it. He was getting more and more worried about Natalie and he wanted to check on Grace as well. The gun was uncomfortably tight in his belt. When had he gained so much weight?

Feeling much humbler and a little safer, Michel returned for the rest of his things, locking his apartment behind him as he left.

Leaving the parking garage, his intention was to go for Natalie immediately. He wished she had not gone back to her place the night before. Why hadn't she come over? She always got up earlier than he did. She must have missed the news as he had...or maybe she was making preparations of her own. But...she lived in a townhouse; she could scarcely have missed the commotion out-side her window—she was a much lighter sleeper than he was! And she'd have been done getting ready hours ago! Well, too late now. He'd have to go over and find out.

A cold drizzle that would soon turn to icy rain began to fall. Perhaps it was the city's way of cursing at the ingrates who were abandoning it, an attempt to reward their disloyalty with misery. Soon the roads would be slick and dangerous, and people's be-longings on luggage racks and in pickup trucks would be soaked.

With everyone in a panic, it would probably be wise to go by the bank first. They'd need lots of cash for their escape. Escape to where? Maybe out west, he'd always wanted to see the American west, but he'd worry about that later. Right now, he must get to a bank, quickly!

The branch office nearest his apartment was closed, even though it was a weekday afternoon. The next branch he tried was open, in the sense that the doors were open, but there was no one there. Michel drove right up on the sidewalk to look inside; a giant might have taken the building and shaken it upside down and not pro-duced as great a mess! The vault was open and papers were scat-tered everywhere.

There was one more branch office between his location and Natalie's house. He decided to make a last try.

This time, he found someone. Perhaps he was the manager—he was wearing a crumpled suit and a loose tie. Whoever he was, he was nearly delirious.

"What 'appened?" Michel asked him.

"I don't know," the man answered. "There was a mob outside when we opened. They poured in... God, it was like a flood! They all wanted to withdraw their money. *All* of them! All of their money, all at once! We tried to offer them cashier's checks, but they just laughed. When we tried to limit how much cash we would give each depositor, they went crazy. I've never seen anything like it... I don't know what got into them—they tore the place apart! They took everything..."

"So," Michel knew the answer, but asked anyway, "you do not 'ave any money locked away in a safe somewhere? I am a depositor—I should be able to wisdraw some of my money."

The man laughed at him. After a bout of increasingly spasmodic heaving that grew closer to sobbing than laughing, he shook his head. "There was a cash safe behind the counter. When I wouldn't open it, they took the whole safe! There might be some valuables in some of the safe deposit boxes that haven't been emptied, but I don't have the keys."

He began his sobbing laughter again.

Michel decided he was wasting his time and left the man where he sat on an overturned bench. His consciousness of how long he was taking was mounting a urgency that pressed on him.

Back in the truck, he decided to go back to the first branch—his own. Even though it was getting late and the doors were closed, there might be a chance he could get at the gold and silver coins he had left in his safe deposit box, along with a bag of cut diamonds and a few other valuable items.

What was it Max had said... Something about not needing to go looking for a war because the war would come to him? The city did indeed give the appearance of having been stricken by a war!

When he got to the bank, it was as he had left it. The feeling that he had wasted entirely too much time already was growing to intolerable levels, so he decided not to bother with trying to fool with the locks. Instead, he drove the truck right through the front of the bank. There were bumps going over the curb and the steps, but the doors disintegrated with barely a discernible thump. He was in luck; the bank had evidently suffered the same treatment the others had, and the vault was open. He wondered who had bothered to lock the doors on his or her way out, then chuckled; he had done the same thing at his apartment!

Leaving the engine running, Michel jumped out of the armored car and stepped self-consciously over the scattered papers and broken glass. It was not every day he made use of this kind of drive-through service! Most of the safe deposit boxes were open. A few even showed signs of having been forced, but his was closed and undamaged. After finding the bank's vault keys in another box, he was able to open his own without any problems. The gold, silver, and diamonds were exactly as he had left them.

Almost as relieved as when he'd found the armored car where he'd left it, he quickly transferred the contents of the box to a Nordstrom's shopping bag and returned to the truck. Not being able to see to the right or left, he barely missed a stray dog when he backed out through the demolished doorway. On the street again, he gunned the engine and headed for Natalie's house as fast as he dared go on the wet streets. Fat icy raindrops spattered on his windshield as he drove.

Arriving at the two-story sandstone building, Michel knew right away that something was wrong; the day had darkened considerably and there were no lights on inside.

And the front door was wide open.

Instant panic gripped him, and he would have forgotten to lock the truck if he hadn't made a habit of locking the door as he got out of his car. With a sinking heart, he raced up the stairs to the door, hoping now only to find the place empty.

He did not get his wish.

There was no one in the living room, so he dashed up the stairs to the top floor. Nobody in the bedroom, nor in the guest room—though he did find the shower curtain ripped halfway off the rod, and some mud on the still-wet floor. Mud? Someone with dirty shoes had stood where Michel was, while water had fallen outside the bathtub. Maybe someone had broken into the house when Natalie was in the shower! But where was she now?

Dreading the answer to that question, Michel stumbled down

the stairs and began searching the ground floor. Please, please—not Natalie! Don't let anything happen to Natalie! When he got to the kitchen, he noticed that the back door was open. On his way to investigate, he slipped on a sticky mess that had spread over the floor, catching himself on the edge of the counter as he started to fall.

It was Natalie.

Footprints—red, turning brown—led out the door and down the back steps.

From the looks of things, she had taken some time to die. And whoever had slain her had taken as much pleasure from watching her die as from whatever else he had done to her.

Michel didn't make it to the bathroom before losing his breakfast. When he did manage to kneel over the toilet, he was able to flush away the remaining bile, but he could not wash away the images. Natalie's smooth skin...marred with burns and lacerations...her long honey-colored hair...matted with coagulated blood. Her blood! So much blood...

If he had come right away...

If he had not bothered with the banks...

Oh, mon Dieu!

If he had only gotten up earlier, or turned on the radio sooner, or not spent so much time picking the right clothes...

*   *   *

1:00 p.m., PST

"Trish! It's starting again!"

Trish rushed back from the bathroom in time to see aerial shots of freeways clogged with huge numbers of cars, none of them moving. A male voice-over was saying, "A disorganized evacuation is happening in many major metropolitan areas, including New York, Atlanta, Chicago, Miami-Fort Lauderdale, Dallas-Fort Worth, San Francisco, Seattle, Minneapolis-St. Paul, Indianapolis, Philadelphia, Boston, and many smaller cities near military installations. Something particularly strange is happening in Los Angeles, where the so-called government of Angel Jesus Ramos Ortega appears to have set up roadblocks on major highways, in an attempt to *prevent* people from leaving. Our helicopter crews are reporting several incidents of vehicles attempting to run the blockades and being shot at by Ortega's 'security' forces. In at least one instance, a roadblock has been forcibly removed from the roadway."

The scene switched to a talking-head shot, with the words 'Martial Law' on an inset screen beside the newsman. "In another late-breaking development, Air Force General John McLeod, the commander at NORAD, has declared himself Commander in Chief Pro-tem and has also declared martial law. Our military experts are not sure whether or not command should fall to NORAD, as the Pacific Fleet Command and a few other military authorities are still functioning, after a fashion, and it is possible that some civilian authorities survived outside the Washington area.

"However, even without the desertion problems the military has been having, martial law would be difficult to maintain over the entire country. This combined with the fact that the NORAD command staff can't actually leave what's left of Cheyenne Mountain, or interact in a useful way with those outside, has rendered the declarations virtually meaningless."

The scene now switched to a National Guard depot full of trucks and other vehicles. There were no people in sight. "The National Guard has been all but demobilized by the extremely high rate of failure to report for duty."

The next image was of Alexis, taken at Hill Air Force Base in Utah, two hours previously. "Army Brigadier General Alexis Thomas, the late president's so-called Computer Czar, announced that she would be taking her team of Y2K experts and other volunteers to the site of the Russian Doomsday Device, even though she had no orders to do so." The image of Alexis was replaced by one of General Jace Weber, USAF, the commanding officer of Hill Air Force Base. His deep baritone blared out of the television's speakers: "General Thomas has demonstrated an extraordinary ability to solve tough problems. She knows more about Russian computers *and* Y2K problems than anyone else in the country—probably in the world. As there is no one with the clear authority to assign her the task of leading the U.S. mission to Russia, and no time to wait for the chain of command to reestablish itself, I am lending her what assistance I can. We have word from some of our NATO allies that they will also be sending teams to Russia, and I have every confidence that their combined forces will solve the Russian Riddle..."

*   *   *

3:39 p.m., MST

Merlyn, this is so stupid!

Alexis was using a borrowed computer and an unencrypted chat program. She wasn't worried about security any more—she'd be out of the military soon enough—but was annoyed with having to type at Merlyn when she was so close to the Dollar Ranch's actual location. How frustrating to find out how close she was, and not be able to go see him!

Oh, I don't know. There are lots of places those missiles might come down, but the place you'll be is not one of them.

Alexis laughed.

Well, there is that—unless some idiot decides to try to nuke the machine while I'm trying to defuse it... But what about you...and Anna?

I think we'll be okay. There are no significant military installations nearby, so I don't expect anything to come down on us. But even if something were to come down nearby, we'd still be as well off as anyone could be.

How so?

Merlyn waggled his eyebrows, knowing Alexis couldn't see him, but enjoying it anyway.

Did I neglect to mention that one reason we bought this property is because it has an abandoned lead mine on it?

Now Alexis really laughed.

You old rascal! I should have known that you'd have thought of every possibility!

Actually, it was Anna's idea. We were looking at a property in Utah that had an abandoned coal mine on it. We didn't like that piece of land—not as easy to defend as this one— and the coal mine was very dusty. But it reminded her that many Colorado mountains had been mined for silver and other things. The lead in these rocks doesn't really matter— simply being underground is protection enough—but the tunnels are nice and dry, and deep enough to protect us from anything short of a direct hit... And I don't think the Soviets knew about us when they built their machine. Anna also had the idea of using it for the redoubt you suggested. I can't wait until you get to meet her. I think you'll really like her!

Alexis didn't know what to say, so she changed the subject.

I really don't want to go to Russia. I'd much rather drop everything and come join you! :(

Well, we'd like that too, but if there is anyone who can make a difference over there, it's you.

Thanks Merlyn, you're sweet. But really, I don't know anything about getting inside booby-trapped Russian bunkers, or disarming nuclear missiles. I'll try to find some volunteers who know about such things to join my team, but I wish I didn't have to go. I'm only doing it because there is no one else.

My dear warrior princess, you are under no obligation to sacrifice yourself.

Hah! I have no intention of sacrificing myself. But, from what you just told me about the Dollar Ranch's location, you are straight east of here—exactly where the wind would blow the fallout if Hill or Salt Lake City were hit. Consider this my payment for admission; I want to make it safe for us to live there!

I don't tell anyone our location, not until we've met in person elsewhere. I guess my trust in you is paying off... But seriously Alexis, you don't have to do this. Even if they take out Hill and Salt Lake, we'll be all right. :-)

Humph! That may be, but I don't want you—or me—to have to deal with it. I want to live in a world where this thing doesn't escalate, so I'm going to see to it that it doesn't!

Well, I know there is no point in arguing...if you've made up your mind.

I have.

Okay, then we'll honor you for your decision and love you in our hearts until you return.

Alexis was glad that the internet link lacked audio and video—she was blushing furiously.

So, when do you leave?

Tonight. I'm almost done assembling my team, but it's taking more time than I had expected. I have some people in Germany we'll try to meet up with, and there are some specialists here at Hill who have volunteered to join us. My NORAD crew was on their way here when Cheyenne Mountain was hit, so they're okay, but my Washington crew is probably dead. There might be some survivors in the bottom floors of the Pentagon where we had our offices, but they'll stay underground for some time if they want to keep their hair.

I'm sorry if you lost any friends there.

By my Life, Merlyn, it's hard to believe what's happening! Everything seems so peaceful here in Utah, like nothing special had happened beyond the Y2K paralysis of the federal government. Everywhere else, we hear about people heading for the hills, including the police and civil authorities. There are pile-ups of cars left right on the highways where they happened. Little country towns across the country are filling with refugees and there are even reports of whole cities of tents springing up in the national forests and parks in the mountains back east.

It does seem like something from one of those 'End of the World' science fiction novels... So, what do you do next?

I'm about to go brief my team. The folks here at Hill are being kind enough to give us a ride; they're loading our choppers—we've got three of our Blackhawks here—into the belly of a C-5 Galaxy right now. After we've checked out our equipment and supplies—we can't count on anyone sending us more!—it will all be palletted up and stuffed into the back of the Galaxy behind our choppers. We'll leave as soon as we're ready, stopping at Elmendorf Air Force Base to refuel, and then heading on in to Russia. There's a military air strip long enough for the Galaxy near Novosibirsk. We'll unload the Blackhawks, extra fuel, ordnance, and stuff there and then fly northeast to the coordinates General Petrov gave in his radio broadcast. Hopefully we won't find any angry Russians ready to shoot us, or hungry ones ready to try and steal our supplies! We'll have to make a few trips to ferry the stuff. Lucky for me that these Blackhawks I inherited can lift a 9000 pound pallet!

Wow, sounds like you've—

There was no click, but the connection was broken.

"Shit!" Alexis tried to reestablish contact, but got only error messages. She disengaged her modem and picked up the phone. Wait a minute...she didn't know Merlyn's phone number! They'd always communicated through the internet, so all she knew were his addresses on-line. Hmmm... She dialed 970—she thought she remembered that to be a Colorado area code—and then 555-1212 for information.

"We're sorry, all circuits are busy. Please try your call again later."

"Shit," she muttered again, slamming the phone down, "I hate that recording!"

Still grumbling, she straightened her uniform and tried not to slam the door as she left the office she had borrowed. What really bothered her was that she had not been able to say good-bye.

John Allen and Ensign Beck were out at the C-5, with the other members of Alexis' recently expanded team, going over the equipment. Six pallets with 600-gallon containers of avgas were ready to go and being rolled up the rear ramp and into the cavernous cargo hold of the Galaxy. Once in Russia, the containers would be attached to trailers so that they could be moved from chopper to chopper by the HUMVEE they were taking. It would make refueling much easier.

Alexis craned her neck, looking up at the top of the gargantuan airplane's tail, 65 feet over her head. 'Galaxy' was a good name for such a ship! She could stand in the air intake of one of the four General Electric TF39-GE-1C turbofan engines and not touch the inside top without jumping—real high. Together, the four engines put out 164,000 pounds of thrust, enough to push the plane and over 200,000 pounds of cargo to .72 Mach.

Allen mounted the ramp into the cargo bay and raised his voice. "Echo?" He didn't hear one, but gave a boyish grin anyway.

Chuckling, Alexis joined him. "This is going to be one hell of a trip!"

He grinned, and the two ambled forward to inspect the neatly packed Blackhawks. Hill personnel had helped them to install four External Stores Support System pylons to each of the helicopters. These frameworks could hold machine guns, external fuel tanks, and up to sixteen Hellfire missiles—a laser-guided weapon powerful enough to destroy any known armored vehicle. Everything was neatly in place. "I've been looking at some maps. Where we're going is over 3500 miles from Elmendorf—this plane couldn't make it there and back, even without any cargo. How are going to get back home?"

"You are unusually knowledgeable about military aircraft for a civilian, John... But then, I didn't pick you for my team because you were a dunce!" She smiled ruefully. "The truth is that there may not be an easy way to get back. Hell, we may not even get there, if there are Russian commanders left who don't take kindly to seeing American military cargo transports in Russian airspace! We don't know much about what's going on over there, but it looks like their chain of command is in even worse shape than ours. Remember that they've been nuked too; commanders operating on their own could decide they don't like us, or not even know that Petrov invited us!"

"So, that's why this is an all-volunteer mission?"

"Yes. We'll go over it in detail when we're done checking the equipment. I want everyone who comes along to do so with their eyes wide open—we can't afford to have anyone trying to change their minds later."

The two moved forward into the crew compartment in silence. It was different—it smelled different from the cargo section...no longer an odor of machine oil and diesel fuel, but the 'airplane smell' so familiar to travelers on commercial airlines. After looking over the food stores in the second galley, Alexis picked up where she had left off: "The CO here is hoping that we find some friendly Russians at Novosibirsk. They're trying to establish radio contact with Petrov to get him to help, but haven't been able to yet."

"Can't they send another plane alongside us—one loaded with nothing but fuel?"

"With our logistical structure smashed, the desertion problems in all branches of the military, and the civil governments collapsing, the CO doesn't know when he'll be getting any more fuel—and I don't think McDonnell-Douglas will be making any more planes for a while—so he wants to conserve as many resources as possible. Another plane loaded with fuel could get there, but then there'd only be enough fuel for one of the planes to come back. Either way, he loses a plane, and that way he'd risk losing two. So, this C-5 is all we get. We'll either find a way to refuel it, or have to leave it in Novosibirsk and come back in our choppers."

"If we can."

"Right."

"Besides, there might not be anyone to even attempt a rescue if we fail in our mission."

"Okay then, we'll just have to make sure we help the Russians and then charge them for our services in jet fuel!"

Alexis chuckled again—John could always make her laugh. "Damned straight! No checks, no credit cards!"

*   *   *

5:05 p.m., PST

The television was spewing misery again. This time it was an image of scores of bodies lying in a street. A mob of thousands had attacked a food truck protected by a force of fifty policemen and Army infantrymen. Hundreds of people in the mob had been shot, but every one of the men in uniform had been all but torn apart. Trish turned the set off before it could bring more death into the apartment.

They were showing fewer and fewer new images anyway, as they lost contact with more and more correspondents and news bureaus. "Ain't this whole thang just horrible, Prue? I cain't believe all this is happenin'!"

Prudence scooted closer to Trish on the sofa and held her in a long tight hug. "I can't say that I saw this Russian thing coming, but I knew things were getting bad. It's all because of stupid men and their stupid wars! Women would never have built a 'Doomsday Device'!"

"You may be right Prue, Ah don't know... But what do we *do* about it?"

"I don't know, Trish, but let me show you something." Prudence rushed to the bedroom and returned with a large package. She opened it and drew out a sword and another package. "It's a real rapier for you. You've learned how to use one, so you might as well have one that can actually cut, in case anyone tries anything on you. These are for me."

She opened the smaller package, which had a set of razor gaunt-lets. They weren't as shiny as the props Prudence wore on stage, but they were much sturdier—not props at all. "I've learned how to move in these, so I figured I might as well get some real ones, in case we get into trouble. I had them specially made for me."

"You really reckon we're fixin' t'have that kind of trouble?"

"I wish I didn't! Look at all those people leaving the big cities, Trish, where are they going to go? Even Las Vegas might be a target, and there's no food on the shelves in the stores as it is, how are people going to feed themselves? *We* need to worry about how we're going to feed ourselves! It's a mess out there and men are going to get mean. We need to be able to defend ourselves."

Trish tried not to, but she couldn't keep herself from crying. "Oh, this is just *awful!* And now that you mention it, Ah don't feel safe heah at all. Ah wish we had some nice quiet place out in the country—maybe a farm where we could grow our own food—somewheres people wouldn't find us."

Prudence sat up straight. "Now that's something I hadn't thought of! I have a cousin who has a ranch in Montana—well, she and her husband do. Why don't we give her a call and see if she could use a few extra hands around the place? It's been a long time, but I think I still have her number somewhere." Prudence got up to search for the number and came back with a small bur-gundy address book a few minutes later.

"It's no use Prue." Trish had her tears under control for the moment, but they were threatening to spill over. "Ah tried the phone and it ain't workin'!"

Prudence refused to be defeated. "Trish, remember how hope-less you felt when I found you?"

Trish nodded. "It's just that... Sometimes Ah think we'll nevah reach that clear blue sky!"

"Trish, I don't know when we'll get to places where the sky is clear and calm, but can't you see that the important thing is that we're flying?" Prudence took Trish's hands in her own. "Think about it. You've been in control of your own life since you hitched a ride with me; you've been calling the shots and deciding which way to go. Getting there will be great, but it's also great to be making the trip—our trip!"

Trish nodded again.

"We'll solve this problem. I've got the address, and we've got maps. We'll pack everything that's either valuable or useful and go. All we need is the guts, and I know you've got 'em. I *believe* in you. We'll be fine, you'll see!"

"Ah know you're right... And Ah do enjoy flying with you, even in the stormy weathah. Ah'll try not to let it git me anymore." Trish dabbed at her eyes. "Look at me, what a mess Ah've made o' mahself! Give me a bit to pull mahself togethah and Ah'll help you get ready."

"Take your time. I'll make us a bite to eat first, and then we can pack. Okay?"

"Okay. But no more instant soup. Ah'm gettin' sick of instant soup every day!"

Prudence laughed. "All right. I'll splurge and open a can of real Campbell's Chicken & Stars soup!"

* * *

7:11 p.m., PST

"Jefe, no los podemos parar."

"¡Lo se!" *I know...* "¡Vayanse!"

Angel stared out the window of his skyscraper—his skyscraper!—without seeing, and slammed his fist against the glass.

The messengers retreated and left him alone in his office.

The roadblocks weren't working! People were finding other ways out of the city, on smaller streets. All of the coastal region of southern California was really one non-stop city. It was easy to get around roadblocks set up on the highways—or anywhere else. He had done it himself enough times when avoiding the police! He didn't have enough men to block every street—what was he supposed to do, build another Great Wall of China? The people were slipping through his fingers and there was nothing he could do to stop them.

They had laughed at his proclamation of a new, fairer, freer government, and now they were laughing at his roadblocks—when they weren't shooting at them. His men were used to terrified victims who didn't fight back. They were completely unprepared for desperate and armed people fleeing in a panic. Several of the roadblocks had even been rammed off the roads, the men manning them overwhelmed.

Angel surveyed his sumptuous office. How could he have risen to such power, only to lose it so quickly? No! He still had his army. He looked down at the Pierre Cardin suit he'd taken to wearing after he'd declared himself mayor, and then at the new uniform that had been delivered that morning—he'd designed it himself and he was sure it had enough brass and ribbons to impress his troopers and his enemies.

The people were leaving, and he couldn't stop them. Rosalia's voice came back to him: "*Tell me Angel, what will you do when there is nothing left in the bag to take? How will you feed your appetite when there is no one left to steal from?*" Her voice echoed in his head, taunting him, deriding him, causing him more pain that he had ever inflicted upon her. It was as though her words were etched more deeply in his mind than anyone else's... He couldn't get rid of them. "*You cannot make a community at gunpoint, Angel.*" Her accusing voice echoed in his head. "*All you are doing is destroying people's lives and what little community there was left in this city.*"

Por Dios, if he couldn't make a community, he'd find those who could, and make them... What? Make them refill the bag of gold! By God, if they wouldn't obey him as mayor, they would fear him as leader of the most powerful fighting force in California! It was time to take his best lieutenants and make them Captains in a real fighting force!

There had always been plenty of human sheep, willing to be

led to the slaughter. Angel simply could not imagine a world in which there were none.

He turned to call for Cabron, but the electricity died again. Without power, the intercom would not work, and Angel had to go look for him himself.

*   *   *

10:45 p.m., MST

The heads of the fifteen families, and a few others, were all crowded into the basement command center for the 'Official Perimeter Defense System Activation' celebration. It was a subdued celebration, to be sure, with the Russian threat hanging overhead... But now that law and order had completely broken down in the country, the activation of the Dollar Ranch perimeter defense system—on which many of those present had worked very hard— was certainly worth celebrating.

The people were packed closely together. Jimmy and Ed didn't seem to mind—the two had become all but inseparable anyway— but everyone else jostled and craned their necks to get a good look at Anna's computer screen.

Dreamer had persuaded The Owner of the Dollar Ranch that a small electric fence below the tops of the encircling hills would not be easily seen, unless attackers already knew it was there and were close at hand. So, the perimeter status screen now showed more status lights than Merlyn and Anna had at first envisioned. There were lights for the motion detectors and heat sensors, automatic guns, electric fence, observation cameras, PA system, remote controlled land mines and Fougasses, and a system status light for the backup command center in the redoubt.

"Okay, okay," Anna did not raise her voice, but the room quieted anyway. "Everybody settle down, please." After a little last-minute jostling, everyone was ready. "Okay, see how the master systems status lights are all burning green? The letters inside—for

those of you in back—say 'Inactive.' Now watch." Anna clicked
on a button labeled 'Arm Perimeter Defense System.'

Each system cycled through a test and calibration routine. As
each systems check was completed, the corresponding status light
changed to amber. When all the lights were amber, everyone
clapped and cheered.

"We're secure now. Nothing comes in or out of this valley
without our knowing about it!" More cheers. "Thanks for all the
hard work, everybody!" Anna pointed at one of the amber lights
with a long, delicate finger. "The letters inside the amber lights
say, 'Stand-By.' In the event of an intruder who does not withdraw
when warned off, the system will automatically go to 'Active' and
these lights will flash red. You don't want to be outside our perimeter when those lights are blinking red! Gray would indicate a
malfunction in a system."

"What happens if a deer wanders by?" Ed asked. "They're about
man-sized and warm."

"Well, the PA system would probably scare it off, but if it
didn't, the system would open fire after thirty seconds, unless we
stopped it. When the motion detectors and thermal sensors are
triggered, an alarm goes off here, and in the mine. It's a bit like
having a certain number of rings on the phone before the answering machine takes over. If whoever is here in the control room sees
from the cameras that it's a deer or some other non-hostile situation, we can click on a button like this," she put the mouse pointer
over a white rectangle labeled 'Manual Stand-by', "and that section of the weapons system will stand down. Otherwise, we can
have venison for dinner." This answer was the largest set of words
anyone could remember Anna speaking before a gathering of
people.

"Geez," The Optimist chuckled, "that's one hell of an answering machine!" He was a tall, burly, dark-haired man, with a thick
black beard and a barrel chest that boomed out laughter that could
be heard halfway across the valley.

"So, ees on now?" Goya didn't pretend to understand how it

all worked, but was glad to see that people she trusted thought that they were all safer now. "De ranch ees safe now?" She worked her way over to where The Optimist was standing while she spoke.

It was hard to see who spoke in the crowded room, but Anna could discern Goya's accent in any crowd. "To be honest, no. I don't think we'll be able to say that we are safe until the global crisis is over and some kind of peaceful order reestablishes itself. But our perimeter is secure from anything we're likely to have to deal with—it would take a full fledged military attack to get in here now."

This sobering thought quieted the room down again.

"Now that the system is up and running, we'll need fewer sentries. But the watchtower guards will need to make sure no one goes near the perimeter who has no business there—like life-guards at a swimming pool before The Collapse. The area around our valley has just become a kill-zone. The electric fence alone could kill someone, and Life forbid a stray child should go beyond the perimeter when the person on watch in the command center happens to be in the bathroom!"

There was an appreciative silence.

"So," Anna continued, "after everyone has a sip of the champagne Merlyn has waiting for you upstairs, make sure you tell everyone in your groups to stay away from the perimeter and only go in and out through the main gate. We are no longer *the* Dollar Ranch, but *the town of* Dollar Ranch and we will defend ourselves. Everyone understand?"

Everyone mumbled or made some other gesture of assent, filed out of the room, and tromped up the stairs. By the time they reached the champagne on the dining room table, the more festive mood had returned. Most of the houses were done, their defenses were in place and working, and life in the little town of Dollar Ranch was exciting!

CHAPTER 40:
FRIDAY, MARCH 24, 2000

"Oh Oh people of the earth
Listen to the warning the prophet he said
For soon the cold of night will fall
Summoned by your own hand."
—Queen, *The Prophet's Song*

Jared eyed the 'Rest Area, 1 Mile' sign suspiciously as he drove by.
Several of the girls were saying that they needed to go to the bathroom. They wouldn't do it by the roadside, of course, but the next
town on the map was still quite a distance ahead. Kansas was such
a huge state, and so empty!

The Christensens had taken a long detour around the part of
I-70 that was closest to the city in eastern Kansas that had been
bombed—Atchison. Jared was eager to make up for lost time, but
he decided that it wouldn't hurt to pull into the rest area and see
if there were any indications of danger. He was a little self-conscious about being so suspicious, but he remembered Mrs. Joe's
comment about a rest area. The appallingly rapid collapse of law
and order since the Russian announcement certainly made it seem
that a bit of paranoia could be a good thing these days.

Pulling the Suburban off the highway at the rest area exit,
Jared could see nothing suspicious. In fact, there were no other
cars or vehicles in the parking lot at all. The place gave every sign
of being deserted. Sighing with relief, he parked the Suburban
angled toward the curb, as close to the bathrooms as he could get.

The kids made an immediate break for the doors.

"WAIT!" He shouted the command at the top of his lungs—coming from a man who rarely raised his voice, it had an immediate effect. "Everyone wait here until I check the place out." He took the old .22 rifle from under the front bench seat, checked to make sure there was a round in the chamber, and took out the Heckler and Koch. He handed the higher powered rifle to Emily—she had turned out to be a better shot with it.

"Everyone stay in the car until I wave," he ordered, and then got out. It was strange to walk the clean sidewalk to the tidy rest room building and see no one. The afternoon sunshine warmed the grass, which rippled in a gentle breeze. It was unearthly quiet, the stillness broken only by the soft whisper of the Suburban's idling engine. It was peaceful. Spooky. Jared kept half-expecting a ghostly mini-van full of children to pull up and disgorge its load of passengers.

He crept all the way around the building, feeling a little silly, but hearing and seeing nothing out of place.

"All clear!" He waved toward the car. All five girls immediately piled out. Val seized the opportunity to climb over into the front seat with his mother and inspect the various instruments and dials along the dash board. Their old car had not had a 4x4 control lever, nor nearly as many buttons!

The doctor stood watch with the .22, as four of the girls trooped by and into the women's room. The second youngest, Debbie, ran about on the grass. Of the five, only Kathy, the oldest, had brought one of the family revolvers with her—she had it in her purse.

Jared watched Debbie celebrating her freedom of movement, smiling as the girl cavorted on the grass—until a chorus of screams erupted from the women's room. The other girls all came running back out—all except Jenny, the youngest. The reason was clear in less than two seconds, when a skinhead in his early twenties emerged from the rest room, holding a spike-handled knife with a black blade under Jenny's chin.

He caught sight of Jared the instant he cleared the door and shouted for him to drop his gun. Jared cursed himself for not checking inside the rest rooms, while making a show of slowly placing his rifle on the ground. He wasn't sure he could aim it and hit the punk before the latter could cut Jenny's throat.

While her father was the center of attention, Kathy drew her gun out of her purse—but the skinhead spotted it as she turned. "Drop the iron little bitch, or I'll slit your sister's throat!" Then he shouted at Emily, who was getting out of the Suburban with the HK 91. "You too, mama-bitch! You all drop your guns or she gets it!"

They had no choice. Emily and Kathy complied, placing their guns carefully on the ground where the young man could see them. "What do you want?" Emily demanded.

"Oh, nothing much—just your guns, your car, and maybe one of your daughters... Ran out of gas a couple miles back and I've been waitin' for a ride to show up." The skinhead laughed without mirth. "Now, one at a time, I want each of you to pick up your gun by the barrel, and then throw it into the car without getting too close. Then back away from the car! You! Mama-bitch, you're closest, so you pick up that rifle by the barrel and throw it in the car, and then back away!"

Emily reached down slowly to comply. Now that he mentioned it, she did remember seeing a motorcycle on the side of the road a few miles back. She picked the HK up by the barrel and turned toward the car. To her horror, she saw that Val had retrieved one of the Smith and Wessons from under the front seat and had the tip of the barrel wedged in the cleft between the open driver-side door and the frame of the car. He was so small that the skinhead had not seen him.

Emily wanted to shout at Val to stop. It was clever of him to realize that he had been missed—the top of his head barely came to the level of the dashboard—but she didn't think Val could hit the man. He had tried hard during the family's shooting practices, but had not come anywhere close to mastering the skill of shoot-

ing consistently straight. The guns were so heavy in his little
hands...he could barely pull their triggers!

But she dared not say anything for fear of prompting the
skinhead to hurt Jenny.

For his part, Val had never acted with such confidence in his
short life. He had been struck motionless by the horror of seeing a
real Bad Guy grab his sister, but then he'd realized that the man
couldn't see him. That made him feel a whole lot better! The next
thing he realized was that the bad man would hurt Jenny if anyone else tried to stop him. So, if Jenny was going to be saved, he
would have to save her. He had felt very small and helpless at first,
but then he had remembered his father's 'tools for self-defense'
under the front seat. His older sisters all had their own guns, but
he and Jenny were told they were too young. Sure enough, the
two .22s were right there on the floorboards, next to Jared's .357
Magnum.

He knew that he wasn't supposed to touch them without permission, but he thought his parents would forgive him under the
circumstances. Sliding one of the .22s out of its hiding place should
have scared him, but he found the weight reassuring. He caught a
whiff of cleaning solvent and checked the revolver to see if it had
been loaded again after being cleaned. It had. He loved the way
the cylinder swung shut and clicked exactly into place. Sticking
the front of the barrel between the car and the door was a great
idea, he told himself. It made the big gun sit still without wiggling, and it also made it less heavy, which had always been his
main problem with it.

While his mother was throwing her gun onto the front seat,
Val was so concentrated on what he was doing, that he didn't see
her expression, or he would have stopped. Instead, he was trying
to remember everything she had ever told him about shooting: the
little stick on the front of the barrel should line up evenly with the
square-shaped notch on the back; the target should look like a
lollipop candy sitting on the little stick at the front; you have to
hold the gun real still when you pull the trigger, or you'll miss.

Val knew that what he was doing was not like homework he would get a chance to fix, or a test where he could get some wrong and still get a hundred because of extra credit. If he missed, the bad guy might hurt Jenny, or—worse—he himself might hurt Jenny. But it was clear to him that no one else could stop this awful thing from happening. It was up to him!

Taking his time, he aligned the sights the way his mother had told him to and started to pull the trigger, then his father got in the way, carrying his rifle by the barrel. When his father was no longer blocking his shot, he tried pulling the trigger all the way back, but it was wiggling the weapon too much. So he pulled the hammer back with his thumb until it clicked and stayed back. He had to help his thumb with a few more fingers, but he got the hammer back and ready to fall with only a slight pressure on the trigger.

Again, he aligned the sights as carefully as he could—with the ugly man's bald head looking like a gross lollipop candy on top of his front gun-sight—and slowly squeezed the trigger. Without realizing it, he was holding his breath. His concentration was complete. He didn't even feel the thump on the seat when his father tossed his rifle into the car.

The Smith and Wesson went off with a loud BANG and Val dropped it in surprise. Of course! He hadn't put any ear plugs in!

When he thought to look up, the bad man had fallen down and Jenny was still standing. Mom was rushing over to Jenny, and Dad was rushing over to him. All of a sudden everyone was screaming or laughing.

Jared picked up his son and hugged him fiercely. "Val, I am so proud of you! What a great shot! You saved your sister! I am *sooo* proud of you!"

Jenny, who had stood frozen since being grabbed by the man and forced outside the bathroom, now began to bawl. The gunshot had startled her and she had wet herself. She was tremendously embarrassed, but was otherwise unhurt.

The family quickly took care of their business—giving wide

berth to the dead skinhead—and prepared to leave.

Inside the car, Jared turned to Val and held out the weapon with which the boy had saved his sister's life. "Here, son, you keep this now. You've shown that you know how to use it properly, and that you can be trusted with it."

"But Daddy, isn't it a sin to kill?" Debbie knew that her brother had done a brave thing, but it also seemed to be a horrible thing.

Jared regarded his daughter soberly before answering. "It is a sin to *murder*. Val only did what he had to do to save Jenny."

It was Val's turn to cry now. He did feel horrible about what he'd done, in a way, but he was also proud. The feelings were so strong, he thought he'd burst! Trying to hold feelings inside must be what squeezes tears out, he thought to himself.

CHAPTER 41:
SATURDAY, MARCH 25, 2000

"Liberty or death, what we so proudly hail
Once you provoke her, rattling of her tail
Never begins it, never, but once engaged
Never surrenders, showing the fangs of rage
Don't tread on me."
—Metallica, *Don't Tread on Me*

8:37 a.m., Novosibirsk Time

"Still no response from the control tower, General."

"Radiation levels?"

"Slightly elevated, but not dangerous. Novosibirsk must not have been hit."

"Good! With that headwind, and all the flying around radio-active areas we've done, we probably don't have enough fuel left to go looking for another airstrip...do we?" Alexis raised an eyebrow at the Galaxy's captain and he shook his head. "Take us over the city before lining up for landing. We need more information."

"Yes, ma'am." It was not long before the ruins came into view. "God, this one's still burning!" The captain had noted and re-ported to Alexis that many of the cities they had flown over before nightfall showed signs of having burned. It was not yet light and blotches of glowing red were clearly visible below, raw wounds on the darkened face of the earth.

"A lot of these Siberian towns were started as prison camps. Some of them were still mostly labor compounds. I guess the peasants rose up against their lords." Alexis' expression grew grim. "Captain, there probably won't be any runway lights."

"Well, it'd be better if our GPS system was working, but at least there's no cloud cover. Between what we can see, and what our instruments tell us, we should be able to land without any problems."

"Will we have enough runway, if we don't touch down right at the beginning?"

"Not to worry, General. A C-5 Galaxy has surprisingly short runway needs, for a plane her size: only a little over 12,000 feet for take off—fully loaded—and less than 5,000 feet for landing. This strip is almost 15,000 feet long. We'll be fine."

The captain was right, and in less than twenty minutes, the C-5's two loadmasters were busy with the unloading process. Up in the cockpit, Alexis was surveying the Russian air base through the windows with the flight crew. The unloading would take some time, and she was in no hurry to get out into the cold Siberian pre-dawn air.

The co-pilot was the first to comment. "It looks deserted."

"Looks can be deceiving, Lieutenant, but you may be right." It was hard to see around the flight crew, but Alexis couldn't make out any signs of life. There wasn't a working electric light anywhere within view. "It's hard to imagine a Russian air base with any personnel simply ignoring the landing of a United States Air Force jet."

"Well," the captain added, "that answers one question; we're not likely to find any fuel here. Look over there, those were storage tanks—that must have been some fire!"

"Yes... I see it." Alexis wanted to say something a little more colorful, but decided it wouldn't be good for morale. "Captain, have Lieutenant Daniels radio back to Hill and let them know that we're not going to get any help refueling here. Tell them we're proceeding to the Doomsday Device bunker immediately. And ask them to put their thinking caps on about extraction—when we're done here, we're going to need help."

"Yes, ma'am. I'll have him get right on it."

"And, Captain?"

"Yes, ma'am?"

"You and your flight crew will stay here. We'll need someone to guard the C-5, and to service it so it'll be ready if we need to load and take off in a hurry. We don't have much fuel, but maybe your boys can scrounge up enough around here to get us as far as Irkutsk, where there's an airport. Give it your best shot, at any rate."

"Yes, ma'am!"

*   *   *

1:07 a.m., MST

"It looks like a roadblock."

Trish sighed and slowed the car. They had suffered many delays leaving Las Vegas—not the least of which was a difficulty finding gasoline—and were only now entering Utah, traveling north on I-15.

The roadblock was made up of cement construction barrier units, blocking all northbound lanes and even the shoulders. A police cruiser stood by, lights flashing. All traffic coming into Utah was being forced off the road and into a rest area, where two more cruisers were parked and a uniformed state trooper was talking to the driver of the first in a line of vehicles. As Trish pulled up, the foremost car was let through and the whole line rolled twelve feet forward.

The officer was tired, sagging visibly when Trish and Prudence finally made it to the front of the line—but not as arrogant and bossy as they had expected. "May I see your driver's license and registration please, ma'am?"

"Sure thang officah... What's goin' on?"

"These are troubled times, ma'am." He took her papers. "We're checking every car that comes in, to make as sure as we can that vehicles entering our state are not stolen, or carrying people against their will." He flashed his flashlight toward Prudence. He could see that there was no tension between the women and so did not have them get out of the car and interrogate them separately. "Are you traveling together of your own free will?"

They both nodded. "Are theah really that many kidnappers on the road tonight?"

"As I said, these are troubled times, ma'am." The officer didn't seem to want to discuss it much, but his tone gave the impression that he had seen many ugly things in the last few days. "Are the two of you coming to stay in Utah, or going on elsewhere?"

Prudence had had enough of this dressed-up *man* poking into their business. "We don't have to answer any..."

Trish placed a placating hand on her thigh, willing her to be silent.

"We're goin' to Montana, officah, to stay with family."

"That might be a good idea." He handed Trish her license back. "This registration is in the name of Prudence Olsen, not Patricia McFadden. Would that be you, ma'am?" He pointed his flashlight in Prudence's direction again.

"Yes."

"May I see your driver's license please, ma'am?"

"I'm not even driving—I don't have to show you anything!"

"No, you don't," the officer agreed calmly, "but I don't have to let you into Utah, either. We are in a state of emergency, ma'am. We only want to make sure that we keep dangerous people out— people who could hurt you while you're here—if we can."

"Prue, jus' show it to him, so we can git out of heah!"

Prudence wanted to tell this *man* what she thought of his precious Utah, but knew that Trish was tired and gave in, pulling her license out of her purse sullenly. The officer inspected it, and her, and then handed it back, along with the car's registration. "Thank you ma'am." He made some notations on his clipboard and removed something reminiscent of a fluorescent green ticket— a really *big* ticket—from the clip. Large block letters, black on green, spelled out: TRANSIENT. "I'm going to put this sticker on your antenna. It'll be easy to take off when you leave Utah, but it must remain in place as long as you are in our state. Okay?"

"Okay," Trish didn't like it, but didn't see any point in arguing.

"Now, if you don't mind pulling ahead, I need to get to the next car. You're free to get back on the highway, but I recommend that you stop and rest for a while. It's late, the rest rooms are clean, and the Church has set up some complimentary refreshments and snacks inside the building. Good evening, ladies." He pulled up his clipboard, waiting for the next car.

Trish pulled forward. "You know, Ah could use some coffee. Want to pull in?"

"You know what church he means, don't you?"

"Who cares what church it is? It's nice to see some folks actin' civilized for a change."

"It's the Mormons."

"Ah don't care if it's the Hare Krishnas! Ah've got to pee!" Trish had to park some distance from the welcome center building, because of the number of cars. On what had previously been a plain field of grass, there were now two rows of temporary buildings. Her grumbling notwithstanding, Prudence got out with Trish, and the two headed toward the main building.

Inside, there were several folding tables set up. One had two coffee urns, stacks of cups, a bowl of assorted herbal tea bags, and some dispensers with sugar, cream, napkins, and spoons. There were also several pitchers with a variety of fruit juices. Another table had doughnuts, some fresh fruit, and some vegetable snacks. A third table had a number of pamphlets and a large stack of copies of the Book of Mormon. The scene resembled a church picnic more than a refugee relief setup.

The two dancers hurried straight to the bathrooms, and then wandered over to the drink table. Trish took a styrofoam cup and poured from the first urn. It was hot water. She tried the second one, and it too only had water. "Hey! Wheah's the coffee?"

The girl behind the food table smiled pleasantly and answered in calm voice: "The body is a temple. We have provided healthier refreshments."

"Is theah a Coke machine around heah?"

"Yes, but it ran out of sodas a long time ago."

Trish counted to ten in her head. "Wayell, is theah one of these teas that won't put me to sleep while Ah'm drivin'?"

"Sure! The peppermint has a little zing and tastes great."

Trish filled her cup with hot water and put a peppermint tea bag in it. While it was steeping, she wandered over to grab an apple. She addressed the young woman a little sheepishly, "Are y'all sure you don't want us to pay somethin' for this?"

"These are troubled times," the Mormon girl answered, echoing the policeman outside. "We are all children of the same Heavenly Father. It is our privilege to be able to serve our brothers and sisters in their time of need."

"Oh," was all Trish could manage. Prudence waited for Trish to finish, refusing to accept any gift from the Mormons.

"After you fortify your bodies with these refreshments, you might want to fortify your spirits with some of the things from Brother Olsen's table."

"Hey Prue, didja heah that? That fella over theah is called Olsen too!"

Prudence winced, wishing that Trish wouldn't talk to these people. They were just out to brainwash her.

But Trish had gone over to the literature table. "And what would you recommend," she was asking the Mormon behind the table, "to fortifah mah spirit, Brothah Olsen?"

The man didn't hesitate. He picked up a copy of the Book of Mormon and placed it in her hands. "I always find a great deal of comfort in the Word of God, Miss. You may have that copy, if you'd like. If you tell me what troubles you most, I could recommend some passages."

"What bothers me," Prudence cut in, "is why your cops are

still out there working, when the ones in other places ran for the hills days ago, just like everyone else."

If Brother Olsen was bothered by Prudence's open hostility, he didn't show it. "The state and county governments weren't able to pay the police here, as happened in other states, but the Church stepped in with some emergency support to keep things going. From what I understand—though it's hard to tell for sure now that the TV networks and long distance telephone companies have gone down—Utah may have the only functioning government left in the United States. I don't know how, but apparently someone in the Church knew this was coming and the Church was prepared to step in and help hold things together."

"That's wonderful!" Trish exclaimed.

"That's great," Prudence added, less enthusiastically. "So now the Mormon church has taken over the state government?"

"No, Miss," Brother Olsen replied calmly, "The Church of Jesus Christ of the Latter Day Saints is only helping. The state government is still secular. But there is much work to be done, many things to be rebuilt. So, many Latter Day Saints are returning to Utah, and others who are not Church members are choosing to come here and join us. We are welcoming everyone who is honest, hard-working, and who wants to help."

"Those temporary buildings outside!" Prudence understood the strategy in a flash. "You offer folks a safe place to stay and the chance to earn a living, and you'll have converts by the truckload!"

"We are not here to force our beliefs on anyone, Miss. We are only here to share the Word of God and hope that people will let Jesus into their hearts. When He is there, it is He who speaks to them, He who tells them which beliefs are correct. But it is true that Utah will be a safer place for honest, hard-working people than most other places soon. Will you two be staying? I know many men and—"

"Polygamous pig!" Prudence spat at Brother Olsen and grabbed Trish by the arm. "C'mon Trish, let's go."

"No, wait! That's not what I was going to say!"

"Save your breath! C'mon Trish!" Prudence dragged Trish out.

Back at the car, Prudence decided to take a turn driving and got in on the driver's side. Trish hesitated and then got in on the passenger side, still holding the Book of Mormon Brother Olsen had given her.

"Don't tell me you're going to keep that thing," Prudence scoffed as she backed the car out of the parking space.

"If Ah do, it's mah business!"

Prudence gaped at Trish in surprise. There was genuine anger in her voice.

"Don't you evah," Trish continued, "*evah*, drag me out of anywhere like some kind of child!"

Prudence stopped the car. "I'm sorry Trish..." She was temporarily at a loss for what to say. She had only been thinking about the Mormons and hadn't considered how Trish might feel about her actions. "I guess I kind of went ballistic—that Jesus freak trying to get us to join his harem..."

"He was doin' no such thang! He was sharing his religion, the same way his people have decided to share their whole state with anyone who wants it. Ah don't know what he was goin' to say before you cut him off, but Ah know it had nothing to do with polygamy. You jus' went and reckoned you knew what he was after, because you *always* reckon you know what men are after!"

Now Prudence was starting to get angry. "How can you stand up for that religious nut? I thought you were on my side!"

"Ah'm a bettah friend than Ah think you'll evah know, but that's not the point. Man or woman, it doesn't matter; you can't go treatin' people like sheeit when they haven't done nothin' to you!"

"I don't know what's gotten into you," Prudence was more than a little shocked by Trish's arguing back, and didn't quite know how to handle it. She didn't want to fight, but she didn't want to give in, either. "But I tell you one thing; I've made up my mind that I don't want to go through Salt Lake. These Mormons give me the creeps. We'll turn east on I-70 and head north again in Colorado. The ranch is in eastern Montana, so we were going to have to turn east again sometime anyway."

"Whatevah." Trish didn't want to argue either.

They drove on into the night, Trish napping, and Prudence wondering about the significance of this, the first angry exchange of words the two had had. Neither remembered that Cheyenne Mountain and NORAD were in Colorado. If they had, they might have avoided the whole state for fear of radiation. They might also have avoided a lot of grief.

*   *   *

1:23 p.m., Novosibirsk Time

Dawn came late to the headwater region of the river Ob, even in late March, and it was not only past dawn, but past noon when General Pavel Petrov heard the three Blackhawk helicopters approaching. It was still cold as hell, a high cloud cover having moved in with the sunrise and stalled overhead. He mounted the mound of earth that covered the entrance to the 'DDCC' (Doomsday Device Control Center, as the British had taken to calling the installation), trying not to show how cold he felt, and watching the precise helicopter movements with eager anticipation.

All three American helicopters were carrying payloads; two had pallets and one had some kind of vehicle suspended beneath. The three hovered over the clearing briefly, then headed toward the side farthest from the Harrier jet the British had come in and the Russian Hind helicopter that was Petrov's own means of transportation.

All three choppers set their burdens down in a straight line, released them, and slid backward to alight. The machines reminded him of dragonflies, the way the could hover an maneuver so precisely. He'd been fascinated by some dragonflies he'd discovered in a bog when he'd been a child and his family had taken a trip down to the Crimean coast. How they darted and dipped, and held as still in the air as he could sit on a chair! That fascination had never faded and probably had a lot to do with his on-going interest in helicopters. The three before him now kissed the ground lightly with their landing gear and a squad of soldiers sprang from each. When the men were clear, two of the Blackhawks lifted again and headed southwest. There must be more supplies on the way!

The French had sent two Mirage jets with a pilot and an 'expert' each, whom Petrov had had to go all the way to Novosibirsk to fetch in the Hind. The Germans had told the French that they were sending a convoy over land, but Petrov didn't expect them to show up. There was also word from the English that they thought the Japanese had dispatched a team but that their plane had gone down somewhere over Mongolia. He didn't think anyone else would come.

Petrov had become increasingly depressed by the pitiful resources being sent and had begun to suspect that the leaders of other countries had decided to bomb the Doomsday installation. He had been careful not to give away the precise location of the bunkers as a precaution against just such a possibility, but they might try it anyway—if they were desperate enough.

Now, seeing the large American task force, his spirits lifted again. At least *someone* was taking the problem seriously. He could see at least twenty men securing the vehicle—it turned out to be a HUMVEE—and unloading the pallets. One of the men left the group and headed toward the bunker. Three Blackhawks and more supplies on the way! Dark and deadly, strong and swift, tough and flexible—the American helicopters were beautiful. Petrov had always admired the Blackhawk design, even though his Hind was equally deadly and more heavily armored.

The American soldier noticed Petrov as he approached and, recognizing his rank from his uniform, scrambled up the mound and saluted, his breath puffing like cigarette smoke. "General Thomas' greetings, sir," he mumbled in hesitant Russian, "may we have permission to set up camp on that side of the clearing where our equipment is?" As he spoke, the remaining helicopter lifted off and headed southwest—probably bound for Novosibirsk.

"Da," Petrov returned the salute and the American turned back to rejoin his companions, who immediately began opening crates and stretching out a large expanse of canvas for some kind of pavilion.

The HUMVEE now became the center of activity in the American camp, obviously where the American commander was giving orders. Impressed all over again with the efficiency and discipline the Americans displayed, Petrov decided not to await their commander in the control bunker, but to go meet him instead. Clambering down the mound, he stepped briskly along what was soon to become a well worn path between the American command pavilion and the Russian control center, where the other teams were housed.

Approaching the HUMVEE, he came upon a young woman with her back to him, watching the erection of the pavilion. He cleared his throat when he was a few feet behind her. "Excuse me..." Petrov had been about to ask her if she could direct him to the American commander when he noted the star on her collar and stopped mid-sentence.

"General Petrov, I presume?" Alexis turned, smiling, and saluted. Her bearing telegraphed energy, competence, and no recognition of the freezing temperature whatsoever.

Petrov knew it was rude, but he couldn't keep his jaw from dropping; this *was* the American commander! He was doubly befuddled because this strange woman—who had to be much older than her youthful countenance intimated—knew him by name, whereas he had no idea who she was. Finally, he found the presence of mind to mutter, "da," return the salute, and take off his fur hat.

Rather than getting offended—much to the Russian general's relief—Alexis laughed. "Preevyet, General!" She laughed again. "Oh, don't look so pained. After all, I heard your voice on the radio and you gave your name, whereas I doubt you've been watching enough American TV to have had a chance to see the 'Computer Czar.'"

"No. No television. Things have been so..." He didn't want to tell her that the disintegration of the Russian chain of command had gotten so bad that he hadn't even received a decent intel report for some months before the accident. And the newspapers had ceased operations even before then. Then the implications of Alexis' comment sunk in and it was Petrov's turn to laugh, "So, the tsars return to Russia, after ninety years. Your name wouldn't happen to be Anastasia, would it?"

"No, it's Alexis. Alexis Thomas."

"Well, General Thomaseva, I commend you. Your pilots executed a beautiful maneuver—especially whoever was flying the one with the vehicle underneath—and your soldiers have shown great efficiency in setting up camp! It is good to see someone taking this problem seriously."

Alexis smiled again, but was thinking as fast as she could. Your typical Russian general had the ego of a football star and the friendly cooperative disposition of a sphinx. It was good that she had caught this one off guard; it might make it easier to get him to drop the posturing and bullshit and just play it straight with her.

She decided to give him another nudge. "I flew the chopper with the HUMVEE underneath. I don't get to fly as much as I like anymore, so the chance to log hours on her was too good to pass up! So thank you... We try." She suppressed another laugh when his jaw dropped open again. Generals do not normally do their own flying, doubly so for Russian generals. Watching his countenance change as he forced himself to regain his composure, she decided to ease up on him. "Look, General, we've got a lot of work to do and no superiors looking over our shoulders, so let's not get all hung up on formalities. Okay?"

He nodded.

"This Doomsday Device of yours *is* a serious problem, and we should concentrate our efforts on solving it, not fussing over trivialities. Since I am here on my own authority and since I doubt you have an authority to report to—or you would never have been allowed to ask for help—let's put matters of rank and branch of service aside for now. Let's be partners in solving this problem, okay? May I call you Pavel?"

Petrov had seen plenty of boldness and bravado in his day, but rarely such frankness. She was here without orders? Simply acting on her own? The idea was more shocking than the notion of her doing her own flying... But had he not, having no other choice, gone outside the normal bounds of military protocols in asking for help in the first place? Did anything matter besides stopping the second launch? He found himself agreeing without thinking it through.

"Great, Pavel. Well, I would be pleased if you would call me Alexis. And with that out of the way, we can get down to business." She moved to lean against the HUMVEE, and the Russian followed suit.

"Of course." Petrov was drawn by this brash woman. He liked her style. "Allow me to brief you. The English have sent—"

Alexis cut him off with a chopping gesture of her hand. "Never mind that now. You can start by telling me the truth about the Doomsday Device."

"What?"

"The truth, Pavel—we can't start solving the problem until we know exactly what we're dealing with. It's clear that you were not completely forthcoming in your mayday broadcast. You and I both know that nobody would design a doomsday machine that would sit around quietly while its weapons were decommissioned. The machine may be a Soviet relic, but your government must have been maintaining it, or it would have interpreted silo deactivation as hostile action. Right?"

Petrov felt suddenly too warm under his coat. It was making him dizzy. He unbuttoned the coat and flapped it a few times. He had seriously underestimated this woman three times in as many minutes. He must get his mental feet back under him and *think!*

Alexis could see that she had blind-sided the Russian and jolted him hard enough to make him drop his guard. As any trained fencer would, she pressed in immediately. "I thought so. Russia has been maintaining the facility and keeping a lot of the rockets flight-ready, at least until recently."

Pavel Petrov was reeling. No one was supposed to know! But obviously, she already knew... Still, he didn't have to confirm it. Moscow would have him shot! But Moscow wasn't there anymore... There was no one left, really, no one that mattered but he himself—and the American. He sighed and decided there was no point in pretending. "It is as you say."

"Life! Do you have any idea how many treaties that violates?"

He threw up his hands, discomfort written all over his face. The decisions had not been his... Was it a mistake to bring these foreigners onto Russian soil? He was certainly breaking most of the rules and military conventions he had lived by for so long—hardly even acting as befitted an officer of the Russian army—but it was all for the Rodina, for the homeland.

The homeland!

He fought back a surge of emotion, as he had been doing with increasing frequency of late. Everything had been falling apart for so long! Month after month of things getting worse and worse, and him powerless to stop it—he was so exhausted... And now Moscow had been obliterated by missiles. No more! It had to be stopped!

But was he doing what had to be done—or was this treason? The American's unauthorized actions implied that her country would be unable to invade, even if all of Russia's defenses were down, but what if that wasn't true? He searched the frank and unguarded expression on Alexis' face and wanted to trust her, wanted to believe that she was there to help him. But trust does not come easily to anyone who rises in the Russian military hierarchy. It was too late to back out, though, and he did need the help...

"Da, but you have to understand," Petrov finally explained, "Russia has been invaded so many times!" Under stress, his English came out more accented. "Military command believed secret of last-resort installation had been kept. So, even after fall of Soviet Union, Russian government kept it alive as last defense against possible aggression. They were maintaining computers that sent constant 'stand by' signal—interruption of signal was to be machine's main indication Moscow has been destroyed—and dragging feet complying with disarmament treaties."

"Oh, I understand it well enough Pavel, but that doesn't make it right, or even good strategy. If this had been found out before Y2K hobbled the world's militaries, it might even have prompted a confrontation like the Cuban missile crisis."

The old general shrugged and made an effort to calm himself, to remind himself to say 'the' and 'a' again. "I know. I told them much the same thing." He shook his head sadly. "Paranoia lives deep in the heart, Alexa. It is hard to root out once it sets in! There was a strong fear that Russia's enemies would strike her while she was down, weakened... I was placed in charge of the small maintenance crew that kept the retaliation system's computers, power supply, and other equipment at the ready. Perhaps it is because I objected to the maintenance of the last-resort facility that I was stationed here. It is a punishment—I was sent to Siberia!"

"I'm sorry to hear that, Pavel." Either the man wasn't like other Russians—or generals—Alexis had met or he'd been shaken up by what he'd been through more than she'd realized. Whatever the reason he was being so talkative, she wanted to keep him going, and prompted him further. "But at least it put a man of good conscience in a place where he has been able to do some good." He might not be so forthcoming if the conversation stopped and he regained his composure. "So how did this happen? What set the machine off?"

"The power failed in Moscow in the first seconds of New Year's Day, as it did elsewhere in the world. Our Moscow headquarters had backup power, but in the increasing chaos, fighting broke out between different military factions. The building eventually fell to forces that didn't know what it was. They took the stores and fuel, and let the countermand and stand-by machine fail."

Alexis leaned forward eagerly. "Is the countermand machine still there, in Moscow? Could it have survived the Chinese attack?"

"Nyet." He ground his teeth together angrily for a moment before explaining. "When the Moscow machine ceased transmitting, the bunkers here automatically sealed themselves off. That was my first warning of serious trouble. The system was preparing its first strike, so I tried to get word from Moscow, but got no answer. The telephone lines went down on New Year's day, and have stayed down ever since then, but I had radio contact with my superiors up until that point. With things collapsing all around us, I was trying to get them to turn the machine off, but they wouldn't listen—probably wanted to use it as a bargaining chip in the power games they played..."

The man paused to think, but was talking freely now, as though having passed a decision point beyond which there was no return. Alexis waited for him to continue.

After a deep sigh, he did. "I was getting no reply, and did not have much time to try to stop the attack, so I got on the radio and contacted as many commanders as I could. I explained what was about to happen and ordered everyone of lower rank to stop the missiles by any means necessary. The rest I pleaded with. Many wouldn't listen, but then I told them that there was a good chance they could be hit by retaliating rounds, and that there would be no warning. Many changed their minds. Of those, some ordered silo commanders to disregard orders coming from the device. Others couldn't stop the countdowns, so they used whatever they had at hand to stop the missiles themselves. The commander of a mechanized division told me he'd have tank commanders block silo portals with their tanks and then run—some brave men probably lost their lives trying to do just that. Another general ordered his men to shoot down departing rockets with portable surface to air missiles."

He sighed again. "Still, I have to admit that many wouldn't

listen to me; they didn't care what happened to a bunch of foreigners, or wouldn't take orders from me because I was not following the chain of command... So—well, you know what happened after that." He stared off into the distance, as though wondering why this burden had befallen him. "And now, I can't even raise them on the radio any more, so we'll have no help stopping the second wave, and no information on the targets the missiles are programmed to hit."

"I see... But you were going to tell me about the countermand computer?"

Petrov chuckled dryly. "So I was. Well, I can't see how it could hurt, so I might as well tell you that soldiers and even commanders had been abandoning their posts, even before the end of last year. It has become a headlong flight since the Chinese bombed us. Every hour, I could raise fewer and fewer people on military frequencies. However, not too long after Moscow was struck, I raised an Army captain who was on one of the roads leading out of Moscow."

The Russian closed his eyes. "His men had been posted at a checkpoint situated on a rise that, while nearly fifty kilometers from the center of Moscow, was high enough to overlook much of the city. He told me he'd been lucky; he'd been inside an armored personnel carrier on the far side of the hill from Moscow when the bombs hit. That sheltered him from the heat and radiation, and also lessened the effects of the shockwave. When I got him on the radio, he told me that he knew he'd be dead soon anyway, so he might was well go have a look."

Alexis could hear the sorrow in Petrov's voice. How many friends and loved ones had he lost?

"He came back about twenty minutes later. He reported that the air was not clear, but that he thought he could make out four or five craters, each about a kilometer across. I asked him to describe where the craters were with respect to the city center, and he told me. Rest assured Gen—Alexa, the countermand computers no longer exist." The Russian looked haunted.

Alexis sat on the HUMVEE's bumper so the Russian could do the same without having to ask for a seat. "There's more to that story, isn't there?"

Petrov's erect military bearing slumped, graven lines of sorrow deepening on his face. "The captain had helped me and he was dying. I decided to stay with him on the radio—be at his side for as long as he could tell I was there. It didn't take long. He narrated it to me as it happened. A crowd of civilians, many of them cut, burnt, and bleeding, came up over the hill on the road. They too probably knew that they were dead men and women, but they were trying to get away from Moscow's ruins anyway. The captain's men had been outside when the warheads detonated. They had been burned by the radiation and then suffered more damage when the shock wave hit. The ones who were not killed right away were leaning against his vehicle, waiting to die."

Petrov grimaced at the bitter memory.

"When the civilians saw the soldiers' uniforms, they became enraged—berserk. They attacked with their bare hands. One of the soldiers opened fire with his Kalashnikov. I could hear it clearly over the radio—it was one of the newer ones that shoots the lighter round. But they charged anyway. I could hear the people snarling like animals when they got closer, and the screaming of the men as they were ripped apart. The people were cursing the men, cursing their uniforms, and cursing the military—blaming them for the fighting in Moscow and for the bombing. The radio went silent not long after that."

Alexis let out a long breath. "I lost men and women under my command, Pavel. I had a team in Washington when it was hit...but I wasn't talking to anyone when they passed away."

Petrov closed his eyes and massaged them with the fingers of one hand. He didn't want to mention—didn't want to remember—the fact that he'd misunderstood Fort Meade's proximity to Washington and might have been able to save more lives if he'd had a better knowledge of American geography.

"So, what have you done since then?" It was clear that Petrov had been deeply disturbed by what he had experienced since the activation of the Doomsday Device. Alexis wanted to keep him talking.

"Not much that's been useful." He smiled ruefully. "I've been trying to find a way to get into the bunkers without triggering the system—trying to figure out a way to order the system to stand down. I even considered giving more precise targeting information to Western powers; if the installation could be destroyed completely enough to render it incapable of retaliating, it might be worth having a little more radiation to deal with here in Russia. I've tried many things, Alexa—but can't think of anything I am sure will work."

"You decided to ask for help pretty quick."

"Yes, well, I knew from the start that I'd need help. I'm a soldier, not an engineer nor computer expert. My experience is with helicopters and logistics, not computer systems."

"Then we have something in common, my friend—the choppers, at least. Speaking of which, we wasted a lot of fuel flying around looking for this place!"

"I'm sure you understand that I didn't want to risk someone bombing it while we were still trying to solve the problem. So, I gave coordinates that were close enough for anyone who actually came here to help and didn't answer radio calls that could enable a missile commander to pinpoint my location."

Alexis held up a placating hand. "I might have done the same thing, if our positions had been reversed."

Petrov smiled apologetically. "I want to stop this machine, and I can't do that if someone kills me first. Since I no longer have a high command giving me orders, I decided to ask for help. The Rodina has always been more important than the occupants of the Kremlin, to a real soldier anyway. Getting the Radio Moscow transmitters working again was difficult, especially since I couldn't go there myself, but at least they aren't actually *in* Moscow and survived the bombing. One of the few strokes of luck I've had since this began was finding a commander—an old friend of mine—

who was close enough to get fuel and generators out to the broadcast facility. He patched me through…" His voice faded and then he fixed Alexis with an imploringly earnest gaze. He needed her to understand, needed her to approve of his decisions, though he couldn't admit that to himself. "It had to be done, you understand, I needed to make sure people knew it was an accident, and that attacking Russia again would only make matters worse."

"It must have been a tough decision, but it makes sense to me," Alexis agreed. The poor man was haggard, his mental discipline weakened—these last months, weeks, and days must have been hell for him. She wanted to reassure him more, but needed to get all the information she could in case he decided to clam up later. "So, how many missiles do you think there are left? And if we can't get the machine to stand down, are you sure we won't get any help deactivating them?"

"No, there is no way. Even my friend who helped me with Radio Moscow is off the air now. The handful of men I have left here might even have deserted if they weren't kept fed and warm here, or if there was any place to go on foot. Everywhere else, things have fallen completely into chaos." Petrov shook his head firmly for emphasis. "No. We won't get any help intercepting the second volley."

He stood, pulled a map out of his pocket, and spread it out on the hood of the HUMVEE. "The 'good news' about the desertions, as you pointed out, is that a lot of those rockets need crews to keep them flight ready. We probably don't have to worry about any of the truck-borne missiles. And the ones that need liquid oxygen aren't going to have any. Even the ones with solid rocket engines won't be able to launch if the silos have lost power. There are only a few possible sites that would have weapons with solid fuel and the power to launch." He pointed out their locations on the map. "Here, here, here, and here. I'm pretty sure of those. We might also find some here, here, and here. And, there might be others that I don't know about."

Alexis, standing now as well, whistled softly. "Shit! That's still a lot of sites! And even if we had enough fuel and men to cover each site, that wouldn't help us with the ones we don't know about... And what about subs? Can this thing issue orders to a nuclear missile submarine?"

"I'm not sure—I think it needed the satellites to communicate with the submarines. The captains could keep the missiles from firing... But they'd have to know that the order was to be disobeyed, and I never got through to anyone in the admiralty who wasn't in Moscow when it was bombed. I'm not sure how to appraise that threat. It is hard to tell how to assess any of this logically..." The Russian gave hints of being close to tears. He had been carrying the weight of the problem alone, and it showed. He might not even have called for help if the accident had happened a few months earlier, before his energy and discipline had been worn low.

Reacting more out of compassion than out of any tactical desire to get more information from the man, Alexis placed both her hands on his forearm and leaned forward. "You have done well, General Pavel Petrov—as well as anyone could, in your circumstances. Don't blame yourself for the folly of others, and don't fall to despair. You have called for help, and I am here to help you."

Gratitude welled up in the man and, for a second, she thought he might lean over and kiss her. But he collected himself and saluted her. "General Thomaseva, on behalf of the people of Russia, I accept your offer of assistance!"

Alexis returned the salute, helping the Russian to preserve his dignity. "Thank you, General. Why don't you invite the leaders of the other teams over and bring whatever blueprints and schematics you may have of this installation? By that time, my men should be done setting up my pavilion. In fact, so as not to waste any time, tell everyone that dinner's on me. Okay?"

"Da. Or, as you say in America, 'roger'!" The Russian bent his waist in a slight bow, put his hat back on, and turned to go. After he had stopped by the rooms the English and French contingents were using, located underground in the residential part of the bunker, he stopped by one of the sealed doors the led to the DDCC section of the bunker. He placed a hand against the frigid metal, thinking that his long months of frustration would come to an end soon—one way or another. Then he realized that he had somehow ended up following the American woman's lead. How had that happened?

*   *   *

4:16 a.m., MST

Trish awoke to find Prudence pulling the car into a gas station. "Where are we?"

"Salina, Utah."

"Wow, look at yonder gas station! They've got their lights on, everythin' clean and ready for business, jus' like befoah!"

Prudence didn't answer, getting out to pump the gas instead. There was a neatly printed cardboard sign that read: "No Credit Cards, No Checks" and underneath, "Price = $10/gallon Cash, $5.00/gallon trade. Pay Cashier First."

Ten dollars a gallon! Prudence went inside to make sure the sign was right. "Kinda steep prices for gas, aren't they?"

The man behind the counter was unperturbed. "Not at all, ma'am. No one knows when we'll get any more gas."

"So, what do you mean by trade?"

"Oh, anything valuable. Gold and silver coins are okay. Tools in good shape work—ammo is great."

Prudence didn't want to part with her tools, and didn't have either of the other things mentioned, or anything else she could think of to trade... And in this state, she might not even be able to trade sex for what she wanted! She peeled off $150 from the wad she carried in her purse. Judging from what they'd seen in downtown Las Vegas, it was a lucky thing that she'd never trusted banks; college was out of the picture now, but at least they had cash!

Returning to the car, Prudence found that Trish had already

cleaned the windshield and was working on the other windows with a squeegee. After finishing, she roamed around for a bit to stretch her legs and made a pit stop in the restroom, while Prudence topped off the tank. Then Prudence trotted in for her change—the little Saturn had a small tank, and it had not been empty—and to use the restroom herself. When the man started counting bills back to her, she held up her hand. "Could I have that in trading stuff? Maybe a Coke from the cooler over there and some bullets?"

"Well, you're paying with cash...but if you don't mind the exchange rate, I guess that'd be okay."

Prudence nodded curtly.

"All right, I owe you thirty-six dollars. I could give you half a box of twenty .44 magnums for thirty bucks, two-fifty for the Coke, and a box of fifty .22s for the rest. How would that be?"

"Fine." Prudence fetched the Coke and put it in the plastic shopping bag the man gave her with the cartridges.

Back in the car, Trish was behind the wheel. "Whatcha git?"

Prudence almost giggled. "Bullets."

"Bullets? We ain't got a gun!"

"I know. But I figured if he was willing to take them in trade—offered better terms for bullets than cash, actually—we might find other people who'd take them in trade as well."

"You're probably right!" Trish pulled out of the gas station. "You know, it's amazin' how normal thangs look here in Utah."

"It's normal to pay ten bucks a gallon for gas?"

"Well, it's bettah than Vegas, at least. Heah, thangs are still open for business. People don't point guns at you if you git too neah."

"It *is* amazing that we found enough gas to get out of Vegas...and I still feel bad about breaking into those garages when we were looking for jerry cans."

"Them houses was empty. The people weren't goin' to be usin' that gas anyway. But that's exactly what Ah mean. Once everyone figgered that theah might be Russian missiles instead of tourists and gamblers comin' to town, the whole place fell apart. We had to collect itty bits of gas from people's lawnmowers just to git out of town. Heah, we pull up to a clean gas station with clean bathrooms and pay for gas like we used to."

"We're going to Montana, Trish."

"Ah know, Ah know!" Anger flared again. "Ah'm just sayin' that you may be judgin' these people wrong, Prue. You should give people—even men—a chance before you decide you know what they're like. These ones sure are doin' somethin' right."

"You know I can't stand religion, least of all from a bunch of hypocritical *men* who put women down. Fucking polygamists—"

"They don't do that no more, Prue."

"Maybe, maybe not, but they still put women down!"

"In what way?" Trish was digging in heels Prudence didn't know she even had. "Did you know that the guvnah heah is a woman?"

Prudence didn't know it, but was in no mood to admit her ignorance. "Look, let's not talk about it anymore, okay?"

"Okay."

The black was giving way to electric blue before them, as they drove eastward without speaking. Dawn in the desert is a uniquely beautiful thing. The clear dry air kept the stars visible overhead, even as fire lined the ridges and mesas before them, a ruddy overture to Helios' coming ride across the sky.

At Green River they rested for a while, stretched their legs with a brisk jog, and took turns napping. In spite of her feelings about Mormons, it was obvious that even Prudence felt safer in Utah, and the two wanted to take advantage of the feeling before they left the state.

Before heading back to the highway, they topped off the gas tank again and filled up some of the larger jerry cans they had kept in the trunk. By then, it was lunch time, so they went to a McDonald's drive through. Afternoon sunshine warmed them as they waited for their order. Other than the high prices and willingness of people to barter, everything was amazingly normal.

All of that changed when they left Utah and entered Colorado, about an hour later.

*   *   *

12:53 p.m., MST

Jared was glad to see the roadblock when the family arrived at the Wyoming-Utah border. Although they had not been attacked again, it was a relief to finally be nearing their destination. None of the family had felt safe since leaving Florida, but ever since the incident in Kansas, everyone had been very nervous. Burned-out wrecks of cars with bullet holes in them had been appearing with increasing frequency along the roadside until they reached the desolate stretches of Wyoming. It was enough to cause nightmares, and not only in the children!

The family had been traveling west on I-70, but when they stopped at a place in eastern Colorado called Burlington, they had heard of trouble in Denver, and rumors of other trouble farther west. Burlington was an agrarian town with a truck-stop. The gas stations had stopped accepting paper money, but were open for business; they were turning their supply of gas into ammunition, non-perishable foods, and other valuables.

So, after filling up, the family had turned north, taking US 385 until it hit I-76 at Julesburg, Colorado. From there they had driven four miles east and doubled west again on I-80 in Nebraska. This suited the Christensens fine, as it would keep them from getting too close to the Colorado Springs area, where Cheyenne Mountain was—a distance of 100 miles was about as close as they wanted to risk, and Burlington was 120 miles from NORAD. The I-80 junction was on the opposite end of Nebraska from Omaha, where SAC had been hit, and the prevailing winds blew eastward, so Emily and Jared thought their route would be as free of dangerous radiation as they could hope for.

From the 76-80 junction, they had traveled west on I-80,

through Cheyenne, and stopped to refuel again in Laramie, Wyoming. This turned out to be fortunate, as most of the other towns they passed in Wyoming had been abandoned. Rawlins, Rock Springs, Green River—a town on the river that gave the town in Utah the same name—all showed no signs of life. It was a land of high deserts—not an easy place to live when the grocery stores ran out of food.

There were places where the sands blew red, and Debbie, sitting all the way in back, asked if this was what Mars looked like. Along another stretch, where not even the hardy western sagebrush was able to take root, dry washes revealed layers of earth that showed innumerable shades and textures of white, gray, black, red, pink, and even an odd pastel green. The wrinkled wilderness was so hypnotically alien that, for once, no one had anything to say for more than an hour...until Kathy remembered a book she had read for a geography report. The book stated that the green color could be caused by copper ores in the earth—it could also indicate the presence of uranium.

Now, a few miles west of the last town in Wyoming, they came to a truck-weighing facility that had been a 'Port of Entry' to Utah. Jared was pleased to see that it had been converted to a welcome center and security checkpoint. When they got to the front of the cars lined up to enter Utah, the trooper asked to see Jared's driver's license and registration.

"Here you go, officer. We're from the Tallahassee ward, on our way to Salt Lake City."

The trooper smiled. "Brother Christensen, is it? If you wouldn't mind waiting a minute, please, sir." He checked something off on a clipboard and then jogged over to his cruiser. When he returned, he had a narrow scroll of thermal fax print-out. "I have this message for you, Brother Christensen. Apparently the folks in Salt Lake are very eager to see you."

Jared read:

Brother Christensen,

My office is sending this message out to all eastern and
southern entry check-points. It would seem that you were
more visionary than any of us had dreamed. Please proceed
to the Church office building at once. The house we had for
your family is too near to Hill Air Force Base and we are
evacuating that area. We have secured a large apartment for
you, right across the street from the Church office building,
and would like you to help us with further implementation
of your contingency plans at the earliest possible time. We
will brief you upon arrival and help your family settle in.

Warmest regards,

Richard Young

Jared put the fax down and turned to his family. "Well, it
looks like we'll be going straight to Salt Lake."

The trooper appeared about ready to salute. "I was told that
that message was very urgent sir, and it came in on my fax machine
two days ago." He affixed a large orange 'new resident' sticker to
the Suburban's antenna. "If you'll go on through, please ?"

Jared tipped an imaginary hat at the border guard and began
pulling forward.

"And sir? Don't mind the speed limit. We're only concerned
with people who are harming others these days. Just drive carefully, and get there as fast as you can."

"Thank you, officer. I will!"

*   *   *

2:01 p.m., MST

The mesas, buttes, and flat expanses of eastern Utah's deserts were giving way to more mountainous terrain when they reached the border. The incoming side of the freeway had the now-familiar cement barriers, police cruisers, lined up cars, and welcome center surrounded by makeshift shelters. There was also a roadblock on the outgoing side, leaving only one lane open.

No vehicles lined the outgoing lanes of the interstate, waiting to leave Utah.

"Afternoon, ma'am," the trooper greeted Prudence when she rolled down her window. He took the big green sticker from the antenna and checked something off on his clipboard. "You're welcome to leave now, if you want, but I should warn you that we've heard some pretty bad things from over the border."

"Like what?"

"Gangs and violence, ma'am." He tisked. "Don't let anyone force you off the road; they'll take everything you have, and hurt you too."

"Thanks." She began rolling her window up.

"Prue, we could go back. We could go no'th through Salt Lake and into Idaho. There are a lot of Mormons up there too."

"We could, and that might be exactly what they want us to do." Prudence set her jaw. "I don't trust these Mormons the way you do. There are more important things in life than clean gas stations." Stomping on the accelerator to punctuate her statement, Prudence took them into Colorado.

Trish stared out the window, not wanting to even look at Prudence, for fear of starting another argument. At first, there was nothing particularly strange or alarming. Then, after they had passed Grand Junction, she began to see burned out wrecks and an increasing number of skid marks on the road. They passed a town called Parachute, and Trish thought about trying again to get Prudence to turn around, but one look told her that it was useless.

It wasn't until they reached the town of Rifle that Trish got really scared by the number of wrecks, mostly on the other side of the road. She turned to say something to Prudence, but it was too late.

"Look at that!" Prudence was pointing through the windshield at a car parked across the road with the words 'PULL OVER!' painted in red drippy letters on the side. There were several vehicles and people milling around on the side of the road, immediately beyond the blockade. "Remember what that cop said about not letting anyone force us off the road? We'd pretty much have to stop in order to turn around and I don't think we should risk it!"

Instead of slowing down, Prudence stepped on the gas and slipped by the blockade, using the inside shoulder. She had the Saturn floored, but the loaded car had trouble getting over ninety miles per hour on a downhill. Through the back window, Trish watched a car kick up a cloud of dust as it accelerated out of the parking area and onto the road after them. "Prue, they're coming after us!"

Prudence gritted her teeth and kept the pedal to the floor, guiding the protesting car around the curves.

What happened next wasn't exactly clear to Prudence, but they flashed under the overpass in the center of Rifle and there was a gut-wrenching crash. Metal teeth of some kind stabbed through the roof of the car on Trish's side, all but ripping the car in half and dragging it to a violent stop. Prudence's head slammed against the driver-side window as the car slewed around. Trish's Book of Mormon and assorted junk that had been in the back seat came flying forward.

In the sudden silence, Prudence heard the ticking of cooling metal, sharper and clearer than it had ever been before.

Still in a mental fog, she wondered why the airbags hadn't deployed. Then she remembered that they hadn't actually hit anything. Instead, something had... She sat up straighter, shaking off her grogginess.

"Trish?"

No answer.

"Trish, are you all right?"

Still no response.

Prudence's head cleared a little more and she released her seat belt and turned to see if she could help Trish. Trish wasn't there. That whole side of the car was gone, ripped away by the metal teeth. She could see the steel thing on the road behind her, at the end of a ruddy smear of mangled flesh, metal, and plastic. It was as though a giant shark had taken a huge bite out of the passenger side of the car, chewed it up, and spat it out on the road.

The sight froze Prudence in place.

No more thoughts entered her mind until a car came screeching around her and skidded to a halt in front of the remains of the Saturn. Another squealed to a stop behind her. And then another.

Prudence could see armed people swarming out of the cars. Her razor gauntlets had been on the rear seat, behind her, but were now near her side, having bounced off the dashboard when everything got thrown around. Reacting to the threat without conscious thought, she pulled the metal gloves on. She barely had time to fasten the snaps before her door was opened.

A man reached in to grab her and she swung at his face. Her outside left razor sliced through his nose and buried itself in bone. She jerked it free and the man fell to the ground screaming.

Now the initiative was hers. She leapt from the car, swinging and spinning through the crowd of attackers—who had assumed she would be dazed or unconscious. She danced with an uninhibited joy she had not experienced for years, slicing muscle from arm here, slitting open a belly there, and aiming for the eyes as often as she could. As the miller's daughter had spun gold from her loom in Rumplestiltskin, Prudence spun death from her dance.

She never saw the gun, or who shot her, but she heard the

crack of the report and felt the sudden pain in her left shoulder. Still whirling, she crumpled to the ground.

Her vision began to blur, but she fought to retain consciousness. "Assholes!" She screamed at the faces gathered above her. "Fucking bastards! You murdered her! Fucking *men*!!" She began sobbing. "*You murdered her!!!*"

Two of them grabbed her by the arms and forced her to a kneeling position in the middle of the roadway. The pain from her shoulder was incredible. When her eyes cleared, the obvious leader of the gang was standing before her: a middle-aged woman with the build of a pro-wrestling champion. She was giving orders to others to clear the bodies and treat the wounded.

A woman? Prudence suffered a blow more powerful than the one the bullet had delivered. *A woman?*

The woman pulled a gun from her belt and strode up to Prudence, grabbing a fistful of her hair. "You slashed six of my men!" She put the muzzle of her gun on Prudence's forehead. "Say your prayers, bitch!"

Prudence could feel the cool metal circle of the end of the gun barrel on her forehead.

A woman?

Reality was swimming away from her.

*   *   *

3:04 p.m., MST

Michel was tired. He'd been a driving maniac, discovering that Max had been right about how fast the truck would go. He sped at almost one hundred miles an hour, well-nigh flying over the land when the highways were flat and straight—which they were, most of the way through the middle section of the country. The truck could handle it, but it was crazy to go so fast, he thought, when he had no idea of where he was going.

When he'd regained consciousness on Natalie's bathroom floor, he'd simply fled. His only thought had been to get away from New York, away from...her. Mercifully, the truck was undisturbed where he'd left it, locked tight as a bank vault.

He recalled how other-worldly Manhattan had been, deserted. The traffic he had seen earlier had dissipated and gone who-knew-where. Both the Holland and Lincoln tunnels had been clogged with the debris of burned-out cars, so, he'd ended up taking the George Washington Bridge. The traffic on the bridge had been heavy again, but most of it had headed south for I-95, so he had opted for I-80, westbound.

He had driven west on I-80 all the way through Pennsylvania before he'd begun giving any thought to a destination. He was still wondering where to go when he'd crossed into Ohio, and had somehow ended up on I-70, heading west from Columbus. He wasn't sure how the interstates had changed on him—he didn't remember turning south—but remembered being confused by some signs and assumed he'd made a wrong turn.

Gas had been something of a challenge to obtain, so he had taken to looking for a place to refill when the needle showed half a tank. When he did find a gas station open for business, there were usually two or more armed people on duty. They were mostly interested in trading for food, but would take silver and gold. A few expressed disappointment that Michel did not have stores of ice cream to trade. None would take paper money, even at the exorbitant rates Michel offered.

It was at a gas station that he noticed posters in the windows advertising cigarettes or beer—he couldn't remember which—that featured images of snow-capped mountains. He had always loved the French Alps, and thought that he might find some solace in the Rockies. It wasn't a precise destination, but it was a goal, and he'd continued west as fast as he could go—still fleeing memories he could not escape.

In the St. Louis area, he'd been warned not to go farther west; one of the nuclear bombs had exploded north of Kansas City. From what he remembered, the blast had taken place a good fifty miles or more north of the highway he was on, and he had the protection of the truck's armor, thanks to Max! He drove all the way across Missouri and past Kansas City with the windows rolled up and the vent closed to outside air. He'd been told that the wind was carrying the fallout east and north of Kansas City and he thought he'd be all right.

Fearing that rest areas would not be safe, he had pulled off to the side of a side road the night before—making sure he couldn't be seen from the highway—to sleep. Other than that, and stops for gas, he had been driving the whole time.

Michel had refueled in Burlington, not noticing the large family in the Suburban that was pulling out as he arrived. He was also unaware that continuing west on I-70 would bring him to within 60 miles east northeast of NORAD, at the town of Limon, Colorado, and had not shut the armored car's vents or windows.

His first real encounter with trouble had been in Denver, where some young hoods in two beat up cars had tried to force him off the road. The imbeciles had not stood a chance against the armored truck. Michel had crushed one of the cars against a cement side-wall, after which it had ceased to be a problem. He had shoved the second one off the inside of the roadway, where it ran headlong into the pylon of a bridge. It had crumpled like an accordion.

Having passed Denver, Michel still had no idea where he was going, but the mountains were an uplifting sight. Tall, snow-clad, and beautiful, they beckoned to him. He remembered reading *Lost Horizon* and wondered if he had, perhaps subconsciously, set out to find his own Shangri-La.

He didn't know. But he did know that, as he wound his way through the Colorado Rockies, he began to feel the first easing in the pain that had been driving him for two days. The deep-blue of the afternoon sky was a stunning contrast against the jagged sun-drenched rocks of the mountains. He could see places where layers of rock that had once been the floor of an ancient ocean had been twisted around by titanic forces until they thrust straight into the sky. All that power, leaping for a goal it could never reach! He slowed considerably, taking in the beauty as he drove on.

Rounding a corner, he came upon a roadblock: an old beige station wagon with the words, 'PULL OVER!!' sloppily painted on the side with red paint. After his experience in Denver, he had no intention of pulling over, so he drove right by, using the outside shoulder. A few gutted cars rotted on the side of the road, just past the station wagon, but there were no people, and no signs of pursuit.

A town appeared on his right when he rounded another corner. A large group of cars were parked on and off the road on both sides of the highway, on his side of an approaching overpass. Without thinking about it, he slowed to take a look.

The scene was complex, but he understood what was happening in an instant. Some heavy farm implement with large downcurved metal blades had been chained to the pylons of the overpass and dropped on a car that had passed beneath. He supposed that that was what happened to cars that declined to pull over at the roadblocks...

But something had gone wrong. The roadblock he had passed had been unmanned.

Chiding himself for rubbernecking, he slowed more. People were standing around in a circle on the eastbound pavement of the interstate. A large individual, he couldn't tell what gender from his angle, had a gun to the forehead of a woman kneeling on the roadway. The woman's long honey-colored hair reminded him of—

"Mon Dieu! Pas encore!" Michel dropped the armored car into a lower gear and—leaning on the truck's horn—headed straight for the circle of people.

The ring scattered at the sudden sight of an ice cream truck, bells jingling, bursting through the metal guard rail that divided the highway. Michel veered to the right and slammed on the brakes, skidding to a stop beside the inert form on the pavement. Before the circle could regroup, he leapt from the cab, scooped up the unconscious woman, and heaved her through the door, over the driver's seat. She rebounded off the passenger seat and landed on the floor, half-sprawled into the back section of the truck.

Michel didn't have time to see to her comfort. He barely had time to jump in and slam the door before hearing the loud *CRACK-ZIIING* of a bullet ricocheting off the armor plating behind his head. This prompted him to make another round of silent prayers of thanks to Max—a habit he'd been getting into since leaving New York. With each passing minute, the Frenchman was more and more grateful for his friend's foresight.

Pulling around in a tight circle, he headed over the median again and back the way he'd come. There were now two cars coming from that direction—perhaps the roadblock had not been completely unmanned after all? Slamming on the brakes again, he screeched around and changed directions.

Then he remembered the farm implement that had been dropped on the car of the woman he had just rescued. There was a pretty good chance that the same setup existed to stop cars coming from his direction. Michel wasn't sure what damage such a trap would do to an armored car, but he didn't want to chance it. He made a quick decision to exit the highway, running over an exit sign that read 'Rifle' as he did so.

There was no traffic in the town, and the traffic lights were not working, but he would not have slowed or stopped if they had been. He was heading north on a small two-lane road not far out of Rifle—Colorado 13, less than a mile past the Colorado 325 turn-off—when his pursuers overtook him.

One of the cars shot past him and tried to get him to stop by slowing down. Michel bared his teeth and stomped on the gas. There was a satisfying crunch as the truck's thick bumper turned the car's trunk into wadded-up tinfoil. The jolt sent the car careening off the road as it went straight and the pavement curved left. Someone in the car behind him was shooting at the armored truck, perhaps not realizing that it was armor he was shooting at. Michel leaned on the brakes, causing the pursuing car to run into him before its driver could stop. With the front end crushed in, that car also dropped out of the chase—thanks to Max!

Michel was sure that there would be more cars joining the chase soon, but there were no branches in the road, no places to try to lose his pursuers. He pushed the old armored car as fast as it would handle the curves, trying to put as much distance between himself and those behind him as he could. Before he could recognize it for what it was, he streaked past a small collection of houses with a road sign that proclaimed them to be the town of Rio Blanco.

Merde! He'd have to be more careful about the next town— maybe he could find some help. The woman on the floor moaned. Merde, *merde!* He would definitely have to get help. He could see that she was wounded—her shoulder was a bloody mess. She needed to be seen by a doctor.

Michel came to a junction before hitting another town. Good! Some of the pursuers might take the wrong road. He decided to try something he'd read about in a book; he skidded around the corner onto the left branch of the T-shaped intersection, then backed carefully and turned to head in the opposite direction. The truck was no sports car, and it tipped alarmingly as he rounded the corner, but, to his satisfaction, the double rear tires left wide black skid-marks, pointing in the wrong direction.

Not long after that, he came to a small town called Meeker. Someone ducked into a house when he came into view, so he stopped to ask for help. The man came to the door, but wouldn't open it.

"Please, you must 'elp us!" Michel pleaded. "We were attacked on ze highway. My friend is hurt, I need to get her to a doctor!"

The man in the house wouldn't open the door. "You been messin' with the Rifle Gang? I don't want no part of it. I'm sorry about your friend, but I can't help you. Helping you would be as dumb as inviting Ms. Abel over to play a computer game—they'd kill me!"

"Well, if you cannot 'elp me, who can?" Michel didn't understand what computer games had to do with anything, but didn't want to take the time to find out. "Is zere not a Sheriff around 'ere somewhere, or somesing?"

"Sheriff? Hah!" The man made a noise that was more of a bark than a laugh. "Ms. Abel done in the Sheriff straight off! There ain't nobody around that could protect you from the Rifle Gang, 'cept maybe the folks up at the Dollar Ranch."

"Dollar Ranch? What is zat? Where is it?"

"Dollar Ranch don't let nobody in."

"Please, my friend may die! Just tell me where ze Dollar Ranch is, I will talk to zem... I must try, just tell me!"

"Well, it won't do me no good for you to be standing on my doorway when Ms. Abel comes by, so okay. You go north, toward Craig. Right out of town there are two roads leading off on the right—take the second one and keep on it for a while. It'll turn into a gravel road and about fifteen miles from there, you'll come to a burnt ranch house on the right side—that's what happened to the last family that tried to say 'no' to Ms. Abel and the Rifle Gang. You can't miss it. You pass that and go for about a mile and a half, and then you come to a dirt road, also on the right. It's not marked, so you have to be careful, or you'll miss that one."

The man in the house fell silent, trying to remember what he knew.

"I'm not really sure how far it is down that road. I've never been all the way there. But that's the road that will take you to the Dollar Ranch. You'll pass some other ranches along the way, but they won't be able to help you. You keep going on that road, and I'm told you'll know you're there because it will look like you've come to a dead end against some hills. But it's not a dead end. You just keep going, and when you think you're about to run out of road, you'll turn a corner and there will be a guarded gate. They never let anyone in, but I sure don't want you here when Ms. Abel shows up, so get goin'!"

"Sank you!" Michel did not wait for a reply, but ran back to the truck and jumped in. Seeing no immediate sign of pursuit, he straightened the woman out on the floor, accidentally catching and tearing his shirtsleeve on one of the bloody ax-like gloves she was wearing. He did not know much about medicine, but thought he remembered that it could be dangerous to move an injured person too much, so he left her on the floor. The wound was not very large, and it didn't seem to be bleeding too profusely—must've missed the major arteries and veins in the area. Not wanting to risk having his pursuers catch up with him while he was stopped, Michel quickly got out some large adhesive bandages. He ripped the woman's shirt open and placed one on the entry wound and, after a moment's indecision, lifted her shoulder and put another one over the exit wound.

That would have to do. He wiped his hands on a towel from the kitchenette dispenser and climbed behind the wheel again.

It was north of the burned ranch house that the Rifle Gang caught up with him. He had missed the dirt road and was back-tracking to look for it when he spotted three cars headed his way. Three cars together driving faster than was safe on the gravel road; it had to be them! At the same time, he found the dirt road.

Knowing that he would need some time to convince the people at the Dollar Ranch to let him in, he decided to try to... inconvenience... the oncoming cars. Leaning on the horn again, he headed straight for them. They must have known that he didn't want to crash any more than they did, but the sight of the heavy truck headed straight for them, horn blaring, was too much. One after the other, they swerved and careened off the road.

Michel swerved to a stop, spraying gravel, and labored to bring the armored car around as fast as he could. With a savage grin, he side-swiped two of the three cars before getting back on the road. This time he didn't miss the dirt road and was pleased to see a huge cloud of dust go up as he veered off the packed gravel. With luck, one of his pursuers might drive off the road from not being able to see in the dust!

Stomping on the accelerator again, he took the corners as fast as he dared. The truck leaned ominously outward with each turn. There were several branches off the road, tempting him to make a few turns to try to lose the cars chasing him, but he remembered the fear of the man who'd given him directions. There simply wasn't any point in going anywhere, unless the people there could stand up to the Rifle Gang.

The left side-mirror revealed that the lead chase car had stalled for some reason. The two behind it were having to negotiate a steep bank off the side of the dirt road to get by. That ought to buy him some time! He pushed the truck faster.

It was late in the afternoon by the time he came to a stop, dust billowing, outside the gate of what could only be the Dollar Ranch. Michel was certain he had the right place, not only because of the four heavily armed individuals he could see behind the steel bars of the gate, but because the gate itself was built in a style reminiscent of the cement block-houses the Germans had built along the coast of his native Normandy during World War Two. The sturdy fortifications gave him hope that *this* ranch could stand up to any gang!

Michel jumped out of the truck and approached the gate with his arms wide and his hands open. "Please," he spoke as loudly as he could without yelling, "you must 'elp me! We were attacked on ze highway by ze Rifle Gang, and my friend is hurt. She is bleeding and unconscious. Ze gang is right behind me, and zey will surely kill us bos, if zey catch us!"

One of the guards answered him. "Why 'must' we help you? You are not one of us."

Desperation rose in Michel, a thought-obliterating tide of bile, but he fought it back and kept control of his mind and tongue. He was so tired! He wanted to go to sleep, but that was simply not a choice. "We may not be one of you, but we are not your enemies eizer. Please, my friend must see a doctor or she will die, and...we were attacked for no reason... And I could pay for your doctor's services; I have gold and diamonds!" The guard who had spoken was a girl with long blonde hair and blue eyes. Surely someone so young could not have lost all her compassion?

But the girl's eyes narrowed in suspicion. "How do I know

you're not with the Rifle gang? That truck could have ten guys in back with rifles. If we open this gate to let you in, you could stop the truck halfway through, which'd make things easier when your reinforcements showed up, wouldn't it?"

"No! I am not wis zem! They..." Michel stopped mid sentence when the first chase car came tearing around the corner. He'd been warned that the Dollar Ranch never let anyone in... Could they really be so cold-hearted? Without another word, he returned to the armored car, and made sure his gun was ready to fire.

The pursuing car came to an abrupt stop, producing an even bigger cloud of dust than Michel had made, and a tall man got out. "You there, in the truck!" He suddenly realized how foolish it was to expect the driver of the truck to listen to him and changed tactics. "Dollar Ranch! That truck is being driven by a fugitive from the law! Those people refused to pay the highway toll, have assassinated five officers, and destroyed four cars. We demand that you turn them over to our custody immediately!" The second surviving chase car hurtled around the corner and screeched to a stop, barely missing the first.

There was no response from behind the barricade.

The man waited for some time before getting the message that the people behind the gate would not interfere—then he smiled. Turning back to the truck, he walking around the side so he could see into the driver's window. "You in the truck, surrender in the name of the law!"

Inside, Michel was getting the two spare magazines for his Sig Sauer out of the drawer it had come from. The he remembered that there was another drawer and retrieved a duplicate Sig and its backup magazines. He gave the rifles a thoughtful look, but he'd not yet taught himself how to shoot with them, so he decided to stick with the hand guns and chambered a round in the one he'd just pulled from its drawer.

Outside, the man was losing his patience, or his nerve, standing in plain view of the unfriendly watchers in the Dollar Ranch. He raised his gun and aimed at the driver's window of what he could now tell was not an ice cream truck at all. "I'll give you until the count of three to come out with your hands up, and then my men will open fire!" There were only four gangsters—two from each car—but their quarry was run to ground and they surrounded it confidently.

Michel stood behind the driver's side firing port, but didn't push the muzzle of his gun through, not wanting to warn his attacker. He tried to line the gun up on the man as carefully as he could so that he could shoot back if he had to.

"Three! Two! One!" The man fired what he intended to be a warning shot.

Seeing no choice, Michel decided to shoot back. He stuck the gun through the gun port and pulled the trigger. The gun roared again, the blast reverberating in the enclosed vehicle and causing Michel to flinch, his ears ringing. Ignoring the ringing and seeing his target still standing, Michel pulled the trigger until the gun ran out of ammunition and its slide stayed back, waiting for a fresh magazine. The man dropped. Jerking the gun out of the port and tossing it on the table, Michel turned, grabbed the backup gun, thrust it out the opposite port, and began shooting again. He swiveled the gun, trying to shoot both men he could see, one after the other, but the gun was empty before he could hit either of them.

The men Michel was firing at realized that they were exposed and dashed back toward their car so as to be able to shoot from behind cover. On the other side of the truck, the man Michel had seen go down was not actually hit, but had simply thrown himself flat when he'd made the same realization. He too ran back to his car with his partner, cursing himself for having stood out in the open like a fool.

For his part, Michel was dismayed that the man he'd thought he'd hit wasn't even wounded. He threw the Sig beside its twin in disgust—what was the point? He'd need a lot more practice before he could hope to hit anything with it! Instead, he slid behind the

wheel of the truck again and dropped the gear selector into reverse.

The men from the Rifle Gang had taken up positions behind
their cars, when the truck started rushing back toward them. The
second set of pursuers could only turn and run as the heavily armored vehicle, with steel bumpers specially reinforced by Max's
mechanics, rammed straight back into their car. *CRUNCH!!* Even
to the watchers behind the gate, the impact was loud.

The pair of gangsters from the first car stared, shocked motionless. Then the truck pulled away from the twisted remains of
the other car with no visible damage and turned—the ice cream
cone painted on its hood a spearhead aimed right at them. In a
mad scramble, the tall man managed to get behind the wheel of
his car, slam it into gear, and peel out, just before the armored car
roared through the spot he'd been standing on. He spun the wheel,
trying to see where the damned ice cream truck had gotten to, and
thinking that if it came down to a demolition derby, he'd lose.

Michel was pleased to see that his new choice of weapon was
working better than his first— all praise to Max!—and struggled
to get the armored car turned around for another charge. As he
backed and turned, the car he'd missed stopped and the three
men on foot jumped in. Wheels churning up gravel, the car shot
back down the road, surely gone to seek reinforcements. With a
sigh, Michel eased the armored car back up to the gate and got out
again.

"Perhaps now you can see zat I am telling ze trus!" Michel
struggled to keep tears of frustration and fear under control, not
entirely succeeding. "We are honest people, willing to pay or trade
for what we need. We would not bozer you if zere were any ozer
way, but my friend will die before I can get her anywhere else! Will
you please help us?"

"Well," a female voice of indeterminate age replied at once,
"that was an impressive show, but still, you didn't hit anyone—It
could all be an elaborate trick."

Michel was breathing hard and gave up on trying to control

his tears.

"But we've got reinforcements now," the voice continued, "and can check out your story. Step farther away from the truck, put your hands up in the air, and don't make any sudden moves. There are five AR-15s pointed right at your head. Understand?"

Michel had no idea what an AR-15 was, but he did as he was asked, holding his empty hands out wide to show that he understood. The gate slid back a few feet, and a group of ten to fifteen men and women poured out, surrounding the back of the truck. One scowling young man covered Michel with a rifle. The blonde girl who had first answered Michel was among those behind the truck.

"Okay," the young man gestured with his rifle while the female voice continued, apparently from a loudspeaker in one of the guardhouses, "now, I want you to open the back of the truck, very slowly, and without saying a word. There are more folks and more firepower watching you from behind the gate than you might think, so don't try anything. Understand?"

Michel nodded and turned toward the back of the truck as slowly as he could force himself to. His impatience was the only thing keeping him moving, but it could also be the thing that got him shot. When the door swung open, it was the blonde who spoke first. "Look, there really is a wounded woman in here! That much, at least, is true."

She trotted a few steps toward the left gatehouse and spoke to it as though it were a person. "Anna, there really is a wounded person in the back of this truck, warn the Doc. Ed and I'll bring them up. Meanwhile, we'd better get some more reinforcements down here. It may not be for days, and it won't be less than a couple hours, but we're going to have company."

A male voice with a slight island accent answered from the loudspeaker. "We were both watching, Jimmy, and we agree. Take them on up to Doc's and then bring the man back to the gate as fast as you can. Keep an eye on him. I'll be right down myself."

The girl—Jimmy?— returned to the back of the truck and

addressed Michel. "Well, whoever you are, we don't let many people in, but you're in luck today. We're having a two-for-one special." She grinned. "Let Ed get in first and then follow his directions."

The young man climbed in Michel's still-open door and settled into the passenger seat, making sure that he could keep his rifle pointed at the Frenchman as he pulled himself into the driver's seat. Jimmy climbed in the back to have a look at the wounded woman and closed the doors from the inside.

At a grunt and a gesture from Ed, Michel shifted to drive and pulled through the now fully-open gate. Looking over his shoulder, he could see Jimmy sizing up the situation and trying to decide what to do about the wounded woman. Neither was saying much, so he tried to start a conversation and find out more about these strange ranchers. "So you believe me now, yes?"

Ed scowled. "I don't believe you now, no. This doesn't look like a wooden horse, but it sure as heck isn't an ice cream truck!"

Jimmy turned and smiled. "Actually, I do." She was surprised to find that she did feel she could trust this stranger with the funny accent. He had the guts to stand up to the Rifle Gang and the decency to try to pay for the help he needed. Either that, or he was a very good actor, and the Rifle Gang was willing to lose some of their vehicles to plant a spy inside the town of Dollar Ranch... "But I probably shouldn't." Most of the Rifle Gang members she'd seen were local people gone bad, and Jimmy had never heard of anyone in the area with a strong French accent. That was one piece of evidence, at least...but they'd still need to watch him until they were sure they could trust him.

"Sank you! I do not know how I can prove myself to you, but I will try!"

Ed said nothing and kept his gun at the ready. Jimmy had the woman's legs straightened out and was looking her over.

"I hope ze law will not come down on ze Dollar Ranch too hard!" Michel tried again.

"Ms. Abel is not the law; she's nothing but a thug!" Jimmy snorted with undisguised indignation. "We wouldn't have anything to do with her when she came around here trying to extort a tithe, so we were eventually going to have trouble with her anyway..." Jimmy laughed. "Well, I didn't care much for Ms. Abel anyway. She takes herself and her eco-babble a little too seriously!"

"Who is zis Ms. Abel?"

"I'll tell you later. Right now, I need to see if I have to do anything immediate for your friend." She struck her chest with her thumb. "Name's Jimmy." She waved at Ed. "That's Ed."

Ed grunted again and pointed at the left branch of a fork they were approaching in the road.

Michel took the turn. "My name is Michel Gerard and I 'ave never been so pleased to meet anyone in my life!"

"Geez, what a mess!" Jimmy lifted the injured woman's torn shirt, taking care not to disturb the blood-soaked bandage, and checking for other wounds. She pointed at the pair of razor-sharp gauntlets the woman was wearing. "What're these?"

"Uh..." Michel stammered. "Er... Well, ze Rifle Gang 'as been chasing me since I found her, and I 'ave barely had a second to see to her wounds, or even make sure she was still alive..."

Ed rolled his eyes.

Jimmy pouted at Ed. "It's okay, Michel. She's alive now. If she continues living, it will be because of what you did for her... Found her, you say? I thought you said she was your friend."

Her compassion was a great relief to the Frenchman. "Uh, well, I sink of her as a friend. She reminds me of...someone. When I found her, ze Rifle Gang had crushed her car and had her out on ze road. Zey were going to kill her, so I had to do somesing..." Michel gripped the steering wheel tightly. "But no, I guess it would not really be true to say zat I am her friend. I do not even know her name."

Jimmy put her hand on his shoulder and squeezed, eliciting an angry glare from Ed. "Well, she may not know you, but I'm sure she couldn't have asked for a better friend! From what I can tell, she's been shot in the shoulder, but is otherwise okay. She's lost a lot of blood, but if we get her to the Doc quick enough, she should live."

*   *   *

8:31 p.m., PST

"It was the Y2K thing! And the Russians! I would have built the new city of El Angel, if it hadn't been for them!"

Rosalia shook her head, a raven lock falling across her eyes as she did so. "No Angel, without the Y2K problem, you never would have had a chance, and without the Russians, the police and National Guard would have eventually crushed your pitiful gang. You need to admit that you set out to do something that isn't possible."

"That's a lie!" Angel knew she was doing it to him again—making him angry so that he would make mistakes—but he couldn't help himself. If there was one thing he couldn't stand, it was to be told he was wrong. "What do you know about it?"

Rosalia combed her hair back with one hand and turned to the bookshelf. Once it had become clear to her that Angel was never going to let her go, she had asked for the books back. She didn't care about any of the other things she had broken, and didn't miss the large room with the big bed, but she'd go crazy without books. The bookcases and the books had been brought to her new cell, with no comment from her guards.

She found what she was looking for. "You don't think I know what I'm talking about?" She held up the book so he could see the title: *Tao Te Ching*. "This is very old, full of very wise observations distilled from many centuries of keen observation." She leafed through it.

"Verse fifty-eight reads:

> "When the will to power is in charge,
> the higher the ideals, the lower the results.

Try to make people happy,
and you lay the groundwork for misery.
Try to make people moral,
and you lay the groundwork for vice."

"Old philosophers! What could they know about California in
the year 2000?"

"A lot," she answered quietly, but Angel wasn't listening.

"You're wrong, Rosalia. I'm going to take over some of the
gated communities that have survived. I'll unite them and rebuild
Los Angeles into El Angel, just like I told you I would. You'll see!
Tonight, we march on Beverly Hills!" He laughed a joyless laugh.
"Those rich people sit behind their guard houses and gates, thinking that the problems the rest of us have out here don't concern
them... Well, we'll show them! We'll put some of those movie stars
to work rebuilding the city!"

He left her with that, not bothering to listen to her reply.

*   *   *

7:49 p.m., MST

The evening gloom was deepening as the people of Dollar
Ranch prepared for war.

Merlyn thought the Rifle Gang would attack the front gate.
They might try something else, but they hadn't shown much intelligence as they went about their marauding business, so he concentrated his forces near the front gate. If the defenders kept enough
4x4 vehicles handy, they should be able to get to any other part of
the perimeter before anyone could break through. Since they were
on alert, all sixteen watchtowers were manned, and there should
be plenty of warning.

Jimmy and Michel, after carrying the wounded woman into
Doc's place on a stretcher, had offered to help, as Ed stood by,
frowning.

"She'll be all right!" The doctor, whom Jimmy knew only as 'Doc,' had reassured them. "It looks messy, but she hasn't lost as much blood as it might seem; you did a good job slowing the bleeding, Mr. Gerard, and it was only a .22. The patient's young and healthy, I'm sure she'll be fine, and I don't need any help. You three go take care of this business with the Rifle Gang, and leave her to me."

On the way back to the gate, Ed sat in the passenger seat again, still keeping his rifle aimed at Michel. Jimmy scrubbed at the still-drying blood on the floorboards with some paper towels and water from the kitchenette.

Michel tried to smile at the young man, but he only stared back with unconcealed hostility. But why? The Frenchman couldn't remember doing anything that might have offended him. "So," he tried to start a conversation in the friendliest tone he could manage, "I was told by a man in Meeker zat ze Dollar Ranch never lets anyone in. I am 'onored to be ze exception!"

"That's not true!" Ed reacted as though Michel had made a personal accusation. "We just don't take very kindly to demands and threats from people who wouldn't listen to us when we warned 'em to get ready for Y2K. And them as we knew were honest and willing to pull their weight didn't need to come in, until the Rifle Gang started attacking everyone! And it's not 'ze Dollar Ranch', we're our own town now, so it's just 'Dollar Ranch'."

A silence bristling with animosity and bewilderment settled in the front of the truck, until Jimmy came forward and crouched between the two front seats. She was looking at Michel and holding the razor-ax gauntlets she had taken off Prudence before putting her on the stretcher. "What do you know about these?"

"Not much." Michel kept his eyes on the road while driving. Night was falling and he was not good at remembering directions. "Zey had her on her knees, and were about to shoot her in ze 'ead, when I showed up. I guess I interrupted..." He muttered something in French Jimmy couldn't make out. "I scared zem by smashing srough ze metal wall between ze sides of ze road, jumped out and picked her up. She was already unconscious, maybe from ze blood she lost. She never woke up ze whole time zey were chasing us."

Jimmy was bright-eyed. She could imagine the daring rescue, see it in her mind—and all for the sake of a stranger! "They're unusual weapons." She turned the gauntlets over in her hands, not in the least bit squeamish about the blood dried on them. "From the looks of them, I'd say she took a few of Ms. Abel's thugs out before they shot her. Hah! Wouldn't it be great if she got Ms. Abel herself!"

"Well, I do not remember killing anyone, so, unless one of zose imbeciles in ze cars chasing me massacred zemselves, she must 'ave killed ze people ze man at ze gate mentioned."

"Wow!" The girl's voice was full of admiration. "She must be something else with these!"

Michel grunted and pulled to a stop in a parking area behind the gate.

Jimmy rummaged in back and then handed the Frenchman one of his rifles, while pocketing several of the magazines that belonged to it. Then she handed him some of the yellow foam cylinders Michel had seen in the drawers with the hand guns. They were about one centimeter in diameter and about one and a half in length.

"What are zese?" He asked.

Jimmy giggled and Ed snorted. Then the girl held them up to her ears. "They're earplugs, silly! It must have really hurt to fire those shots cooped up in here without any ear protection!"

Michel grimaced. "I can still 'ear ze ringing!"

She showed him how to use them. "You know, we wouldn't have let you in if you'd tried to tell us that we had some kind of duty or obligation to save you. People who think their needs are more important than other people's needs are dangerous. But because you offered to trade, you showed that you might be trustworthy. Instead of trying to make us do what you wanted, you tried to find a way to give us something in exchange for what you wanted. That was a very moral approach to take."

Michel did an abrupt reassessment of Jimmy in his mind. "'Ow old are you?" Then he put up his hand. "Never mind. Zat was rude of me to even ask. You are obviously an extraordinary young woman—kind of like Grace, but younger. I should treat you as I would any ozer competent adult."

Jimmy positively glowed at the praise. "Who's Grace?"

"She is—was... My secretary back in ze Big Apple. I do not know if she is still alive."

"You came all the way from New York?"

"Yes." Michel hoped the ranchers liked New Yorkers! "So, what can I offer ze Dollar Ranch in exchange for your 'ospitality? I do not know zat anysing I 'ave is wors as much as ze lives you 'ave saved."

"Aw, a few bandages up at Doc's, and maybe a few rounds of ammo later tonight, it's not that big a deal. But I'll tell you what to offer The Owner if you decide to stay."

"Ze Owner?"

"Merlyn."

"Merlyn?"

Jimmy giggled again. Ed was clearly unhappy about the conversation, but the young woman ignored him. "Not the magician! Though sometimes you'd think he was one, the way he always knows what's going to happen next. No... Merlyn is just a wonderful man—the owner of our town—Dollar Ranch—the one who provided us all a place to stay while the world goes crazy."

"I would like to meet zis Merlyn!"

"You will. Soon. It's Anna's turn to run things from the command center up at the Big House, so he's probably already down here at the gate, getting everyone ready to deal with the Rifle Gang. Anyway, if you think you want to stay, offer him the use of your armored car in exchange for an apartment at the Big House. We have lots of 4x4s, fast cars, and even a bulldozer, but nothing as armored as your truck. We could use it when we have to go out for things. I'm sure that if you offer to maintain it and drive it for our mutual benefit, that'd be worth one of the apartments they have left up there."

"I will remember zat. Sanks!"

They got out of the truck and headed for the gate, where a substantial force was already assembled. A black man of medium height and build was going over defensive plans with the group. His skin was very dark, and his hair was in a thick afro cut. His English was fluid and sounded highly educated, with a trace of island flavor. It was the second voice Michel had heard on the loudspeaker after his fight with the Rifle Gang.

Jimmy shouldered her way through the crowd and spoke up. "Merlyn, this is Michel Gerard." She pointed to Michel, who was suddenly wishing Jimmy were a little less exuberant. "He's the one that's brought us this little tiff with the Rifle Gang, sooner than we'd anticipated, but he's also brought an honest to goodness armored car that we could really use. It looks like an ice cream truck, but he smashed up five of their cars with it, and it's only got a few dents and scratches in its paint!"

Jimmy had everyone's attention and hammed up the rest of her introduction. "The lady we just left up at Doc's place is some kind of martial artist. From what Ms. Abel's goon said, that woman took out several of her men single-handed—well, she used both hands—but she didn't even have a gun! Now she's been hurt and Michel here rescued her. He wants to help defend Dollar Ranch."

The crowd drew back from Michel, sizing him up. He felt acutely embarrassed, suspecting that Jimmy's introduction might give some of them an exaggerated idea of his own prowess. He was no Buck Rogers—he didn't even know how to shoot straight!

But Merlyn was already extending his hand. "Welcome to Dollar Ranch, Monsieur Gerard! Any idea why the Rifle Gang chased you all the way to my doorstep?"

"I am sure zat revenge has somesing to do wis it, but it could be zat zey are mad at me for not paying zeir toll."

There were a few scattered chuckles and Merlyn inclined his

head, grinning. "You'll forgive me if I ask you to stand aside while we finish going over our defensive plan? You seem like a good fellow, but we don't really know you yet. Jimmy, you already know your stuff, so you and Ed keep an eye on him."

Michel agreed and accompanied Ed and Jimmy to the gate.

The defenders had waited for more than two hours before a warning from one of the sentries made a quick end of all conversation. "You all know what to do—let's go!" Merlyn only raised his voice slightly, but it had the effect of a barked command. The gathered townsfolk quickly assumed pre-assigned positions.

Soon, everyone could hear the unmistakable rumble of a large diesel engine, and not long after, the rattle and clank of caterpillar treads. Michel imitated Jimmy when she put her ear plugs in. She handed him a magazine, which he waited to fit into his rifle until he thought no one was watching.

As Michel assumed Merlyn had ordered, the defenders waited until the clanking had advanced quite close—maybe fifty meters— before turning on a battery of flood lights. A brilliant crescent of light bathed the area in front of the gate. The light revealed a rusty old bulldozer with some slitted iron plates welded over the front of the cab, leading a column of pickup trucks full of armed men.

When the lights switched on, a megaphone boomed Merlyn's voice out at the attackers. "You are engaged in an act of aggression. We have you in our gun sights. Withdraw at once, or we will defend ourselves with whatever force is necessary!"

The bulldozer continued its steady advance, but Merlyn's warning evidently angered the others. Several of the pickups fanned out and the men in them started firing.

"Nimrods," Jimmy muttered, "they won't be able to aim well with the trucks bouncing over rocks and stuff, and now they've exposed themselves!" She shouldered her rifle while Ed kept his aimed in Michel's general direction.

Michel shrugged and imitated Jimmy. He was surprised at how well he could hear with the ear plugs and wondered what good they would do.

The next thing he heard was a thunderous whoomp-whoomp-whoooomp, and was glad for the ear protection. The explosions missed the bulldozer, but hurled two of the pickups still behind it into the air. A third swerved violently to avoid one of the craters that had suddenly appeared in the road and tipped over, spilling its passengers before rolling over several of them.

There was no order to fire and the defenders did not all try to fire at once. It started gradually and grew to a torrent of fire that filled the air with so much gunsmoke that Michel could taste it. Jimmy took her time aiming carefully and squeezed her trigger when she was good and ready to. The din was unbelievable. Michel pulled one of his earplugs part way out and pushed it back in hastily; it was painful! And that was before the big guns kicked in—there was one atop each guardhouse, large and black, firing faster than Michel thought a person should be able to.

Unseen by Michel, Anna watched the scene on the monitors in the command center. If the attackers fanned out enough, the TJC-30s in the gun emplacements to either side of the gate would kick in, firing at almost machine gun speed. That would help the defenders, but the bulldozer could be real trouble! The big guns in the guardhouses were Barretts, not TJC-30s, but also equipped with belts of ammunition—one of them should take care of the problem. She put the left gun on automatic and switched one of her screens over to show what the cross-haired gun-camera of the right-hand Barrett was seeing.

Using a joystick to swivel the gun, she lined up the crosshairs on the advancing bulldozer. Since the computerized mechanism would be pulling the trigger, she didn't have to worry about steadying her wiggle. All she had to do was cover the spot where she estimated the driver's head would be—at this range, the bullet would not drop significantly—and click the fire button.

On screen, a hole appeared in the iron plate and the bulldozer veered left. It began carving a tight circle in the dirt road, its operator slumped over the controls. Anna patted the computer console and swiveled the ugly black .50 caliber weapon back and forth again, in search of another target.

For Michel, posted between the two big .50s, the thundering of the continuous fire around him was beyond anything he had ever imagined. The two big ones discharged at different rates, the one on the left much faster than the one on the right. Each time they went off, they spat a lance of flame—visible even in the flood-lights—behind each bullet. Wherever they shot, an attacker was knocked flat and didn't get up again. In addition to the deep-throated boom of the guardhouse guns, there was the steady chatter of machine guns coming from either side of the gate.

Jimmy's rifle going off right beside him was subdued in comparison, but its firing did remind him to try to do something useful himself. He leaned his rifle—he had no idea what kind it was—on one of the gate bars and sought a target. He made out someone running for the bulldozer, aimed as carefully as he could at the moving target, and pulled the trigger. Nothing happened! While he wondered what was wrong with his gun, someone else dropped the man before he could get to the still-circling machine.

Then Michel realized that he had never taken the safety off. Imbecile! He cursed himself and tried not to let anyone see him flicking the safety off. At least he had known enough to chamber a round before trying to shoot! Hoping no one had noticed, he tried to find another target. They were all running away! He lined one up, but couldn't shoot a man in the back, even though that man might have been the one who had hurt the woman who resembled Natalie. The battle was over—it had lasted less than five minutes. They had won!

The abrupt silence was much louder to the advisor than the gunfire that had preceded it.

A quick check showed that one defender had been shot in the arm, and two had been grazed. The one with the wounded arm was a woman Michel had not yet been introduced to, who spoke broken English with a heavy Spanish accent. "Nex time, I stay een de keetchin!"

The release of tension was palpable as everyone laughed.

When they ventured out to check on the attackers, under the watchful eyes of guards manning the Barretts and scouts sent ahead with radios, they found twenty-seven dead and five wounded. They treated the wounds on the least hurt of the five, and told him to take his four comrades in one of the remaining pickup trucks and go, on condition that he swear never to attack Dollar Ranch again. The man agreed readily enough, and drove off. The seventeen dead were dumped unceremoniously into the craters left in the road by the mines and then bulldozed under.

By the final tally, Dollar Ranch had suffered one bullet wound, two scratches, and spent about two hundred rounds of ammunition. They had gained another bulldozer, two slightly perforated pickups, and—most important of all—greater confidence that their defenses would work against real enemies.

They had also gained a Frenchman who swore he would sleep for the next two days, and then work out a deal with Merlyn.

CHAPTER 42:
SATURDAY, APRIL 1, 2000

"She don't take no prisoners
She gonna give me the business
Got a dragon on my back
It's a dragon attack."
—Queen, *Dragon Attack*

¡Mierda! Angel knew he needed to concentrate, but he couldn't get his mind off of Rosalia. He had thought of killing her so many times that he'd lost count, but to kill her would be to admit defeat. And now it had become a focus in his life to prove her wrong.

But oh, how angry she made him!

The last time they'd spoken, she'd shouted, "Ein Volk, Ein Reich!" as he was leaving. He wasn't sure what it meant, but he knew that the words were Adolph Hitler's, and the comparison burned in his heart—all the more so because he knew there was truth in it.

Shaking his head, as though he could physically thrust Rosalia from his mind, he tried to concentrate on the task at hand. His lucky 9mm was securely tucked in his belt, his body armor was strapped on tight—one of many gifts some careless cops had left for him in an abandoned police station—and his autoloader shotgun was loaded for bear.

A light blinked three times from a gate in the fence.

He turned to Cabron. "Get on the radio and tell the diversionary force to start the attack on the front gate in exactly five minutes from..." he checked his watch, "now!"

Cabron relayed the order.

"Now, tell the captains that the back gate has been unlocked and it's time to move in. Remind them to wait outside their assigned targets for exactly sixty seconds after the commotion starts up at the front gate, and that we need prisoners for the work teams. Anyone who kills unnecessarily will answer to me! Make sure they remember that anyone who disobeys my orders will be court-martialed."

"¡Si, General!" Cabron relayed the instructions and stowed the radio.

Seeing that he was ready, Angel signaled to him to follow. They sprinted for the gate, slipping in between two other teams, and then headed for the house that was their target. It was the house of a particular television star Angel had wanted for years, and his intelligence reports told him that she was still living in this gated community, as well as a few other starlets he would give to his captains—the ones who followed orders and kept their troops under control.

It was an uphill run, and Angel was slightly winded when he and Cabron reached the house and hid themselves in the bushes outside the front door. The house was part of a neighborhood that had a formidable wall encircling an entire hilltop. Apparently, someone had acquired enough backup generators and fuel to keep the entire hilltop lit at night. This had attracted desperate people from the surrounding area, people who had now become a kind of serf population, living in a school building near the bottom of the hill. It was these people who had been making armed scavenging forays for their masters in their castles on high.

After Angel's raids on other gated communities the previous week, this one had started hiring drifters with military or police experience to beef up their security forces. Word was spreading about Ejercito Dragon, and the castle-dwellers had more than a hundred armed men in their security force now.

This was not a serious threat to Angel's force, now boasting 10,000 men, but it would provide some trained scavenger teams and set an example for other pockets of armed resistance. It would also provide some...rewards...for his captains who succeeded in enforcing discipline on their troops.

In his mind, he imagined his army in triumph, like the Greeks in that boring history book Rosalia had so loved. Angel remembered well a series of plates that depicted Achilles' defeat of Hector, the wooden horse, and the really great one of the ensuing slaughter of the Trojans. He'd let his captains enjoy the rewards of sacking Troy all right, if they followed his orders! And he'd get to have Helen.

The little citadel would present no serious problem to Ejercito Dragon, but it was good that the movie stars and rich people didn't know much about security. They had hired several of Angel's men, who had garroted the watchmen at the back gate moments earlier. This would enable Angel to take the hill with little bloodshed, which was important for both taking over the scavenger teams and for setting an example.

It was strange how some communities like this hung on, even when everyone else had abandoned the city. What made them stay?

Angel did not have long to wonder about it; an alarm shattered the stillness of the night. The sharp reports coming from the gun battle at the front gate were easy to discern in the calm night air, and they could even make out the bellowing diesel engine of the armored personnel carrier—one of the few police vehicles that had escaped the RPG attacks.

As Angel had predicted, a security contingent ran from the house as soon as the alarm rang out. The same was happening all over the hill.

Waiting the allotted minute, and seeing no other movement in the house, Angel and Cabron moved carefully from the bushes to the door. The fools hadn't even closed it on their way out! The two entered the house silently, guns at the ready, and quickly scouted out the front rooms: no one. The gang leader motioned Cabron—who was all but drooling with anticipation, thinking of the flesh he'd be savoring after the raid was over—toward the stairs to the upper floor. Angel himself took the rest of the first floor and stole back toward the kitchen.

He found what he was looking for quickly enough: the stairs to the basement. Getting closer now! He could almost smell her, and had to shift his pants around to make room for his growing erection.

The stairs were made of cement and did not creak as he descended. Reaching the bottom, he peeked carefully around the corner of the stairwell—the whole basement had been made into a recreation room. There was a hot tub, a pool table, a music system as expensive as the one Rosalia had trashed, a battery of arcade-style video games, and a large round bed with red satin sheets.

Angel smirked and advanced into the room. Suddenly, a woman—it was her!—ducked up from behind the hot tub and shot at him. Clearly, she had no experience with guns, because she was unprepared for the recoil and nearly dropped her pistol into the tub before ducking back down. But beginner's luck was with her; she managed to hit Angel squarely in the chest.

He barely registered the impact. There were a lot of dead cops who'd still be alive if they had worn their vests more often! The woman peeked over the spa and stared at him in shock, utterly frozen by the sight of him still standing. Angel leveled his shotgun at her as Cabron's voice came from somewhere above in the house. "¡Jefe!" Then more clearly at the top of the basement stairs. "¿Estas bien?"

"¡Si, Cabron!" He switched to English, to make sure the woman would understand how completely hopeless her situation was. "No problems here. They should be done rounding up any of the security guards left alive at the gate. Go outside and radio the captains, tell them to bring their prisoners to the park by the school. I'll be there in a while, and I'll want to see the prisoners alive when I get there!" Blood pounded in his erection, demanding release.

"¡Si, General!"

Angel could hear Cabron's footsteps as the latter headed for the door. That must have been how the woman had heard him coming! He motioned to her with his shotgun. "Leave the gun on the floor and get up."

"I... I'm not dressed!"

Angel sent a blast of pellets over her head. "Lesson number one: if you want to stay alive, you will never, *ever*, argue with me. Now get up!"

She threw the gun out on the floor where he could see it and stood slowly, looking down.

Angel frowned. Her breasts were exactly as he had seen them so many times through flimsy negligées and negligible bikinis. Maybe they had no choice about looking as they did, as full of silicon as they were...but the rest of her! She was much dumpier that he had expected. It wasn't so much that she was fatter, exactly, but she was not as curvaceous and fit as she appeared on screen.

"Look up," he ordered.

She complied, slowly. Her face was blotchy and streaked with tears, but it was definitely the one he'd seen so many times on television.

Angel felt cheated. Angry. He would have hit her, had she been standing right in front of him. Instead, he snarled, "Do you want to live?"

She was trembling so badly she could hardly mouth the word, "yes."

"Then, you will crawl over here on your hands and knees and beg for your life." He unfastened his vest and unzipped his pants, even though the pressure there was subsiding. "You will beg me for the chance to allow you to serve me."

The woman dropped to all fours without hesitation and began crawling across the floor.

Angel scowled. Rosalia would never submit like this!

He should have been enjoying this—had dreamed about it for years—but all he could think of was how hollow a victory it was to dominate someone with no will of her own and little else in her mind. He was completely shriveled by the time *his* TV star reached him and began pleading.

She told him she would do anything, told him how much she *wanted* him in her mouth, and began reaching for his trousers.

Suddenly Angel snapped his attention back from thoughts of Rosalia and gaped at the woman before him. She had her hand inside his pants and was fondling him, to no avail—but right above and to the side of where her wrist disappeared into his zipper, was his 9mm! She could have easily taken the gun and shot him while he was distracted! But she had no spirit. She had accepted defeat and was doing exactly as she'd been told, unlike Rosalia, who still fought him after so many months!

Utter contempt and disgust for the repulsive creature fawning before him was all Angel could feel. He couldn't bear the sight of her any more and jumped back, leveling the shotgun at her head.

She didn't try to duck, or back away. She just cringed and cried. Before Angel's disbelieving eyes, she lost control of her bladder, and a pungent pool of amber liquid began spreading beneath her. Furious, Angel was about to pull the trigger, and then he remembered his orders to his captains.

He had to set an example.

Cursing in Spanish, he reversed the shotgun and clubbed the woman on the head. He suppressed an urge to vomit, seeing her lying in the pool of her own making, and retreated up the stairs. He'd send Cabron back for her—Angel never wanted to see the woman again and Cabron's toys never survived his games.

As he jogged down the hill to join his forces, it suddenly occurred to him that it was April Fool's Day.

CHAPTER 43:
SUNDAY, APRIL 2, 2000

"If you need me,
Let me know,
Gonna be around,
Take a chance on me."
—ABBA, *Take a Chance on Me*

Michel sat across a table from Merlyn in the dining hall. Several people were gathered around, making Michel slightly self-conscious, but they were all happy that he had decided to join their community, so he welcomed their company. He was comfortable with all sorts of people—he couldn't have been a successful advisor without that trait—but didn't care to be the center of attention in a crowd. Unlike Jimmy, he did not enjoy a spotlight.

He'd been at the town of Dollar Ranch for a week now, but was still getting to know people. A tall blond man known only as Dreamer turned out to be Jimmy's father. He was sitting beside another man: an individual with a basso profundo voice people referred to as The Optimist. The middle-aged woman with the thick Spanish accent turned out to be named after two painters: Goya and Siqueiros. Jimmy was there, of course, with Ed—her ever-present, if not exactly friendly, companion.

Most striking of all was a stunning oriental woman named Anna. Her beauty was not girlish, but ageless; she could have been 25 or 250. She was something like a wife to Merlyn—they were often together and were constantly using a variety of terms of endearment for each other—though they were not married and had different last names. Both names were difficult to pronounce correctly; Merlyn's was something African and Anna's was something like 'woo' or 'hoo.'

While people tended to call Merlyn 'The Owner', everyone referred to Anna as simply 'Anna'. When she spoke, which was not very often in large groups, everyone listened. She had some kind of internal power. It projected invisibly and made Michel want to bow to her, not in submission or servility, but in reverence.

It was Anna who produced a written version of the agreement Michel had reached with Merlyn. It was this kind of wordless coordinated action, and the frequency with which they would speak at the same time—saying the exact same words—that had many Dollar Ranch residents half-joking and half-believing that there was telepathy between The Owner and his partner.

To his surprise, the contract didn't simply outline the exchange of armored scout and courier services for an efficiency studio. It spelled those considerations out as a small part of the details regarding the mutual obligations being agreed to by Michel Gerard and The Owner—apparently that title was no mere nickname.

Large cursive letters atop the first sheet proclaimed: *SOCIAL CONTRACT.*

"What is zis?"

Merlyn and Anna answered at once: "This is a purely voluntary community; everyone signs this contract if they wish to live here."

"But what is all of zis stuff in 'ere?"

Jimmy suppressed a giggle and Merlyn took over the explanation. "You've heard of social contracts, haven't you? They are hypothetical agreements between people in a society. According to the theory, governments were supposed to derive their authority from social contracts. The problem always was that—even with documents like the United States Constitution—the social contract was never more than a theory. No one ever signed one, and it was impossible to use one to control the government."

Several of the other Dollar Ranch residents were making noises of assent.

"So," Merlyn continued, "here in this valley, we decided that the only way to avoid all the problems people had with governments run amok in the twentieth century was to get rid of the ambiguities—by having a real social contract. Every adult resident and property owner has signed one, including Anna. I, of course, am party to all the contracts and have signed them all. It spells out our agreements, obligations, duties, rights, and dispute resolution mechanisms. This way we don't have government of some people by other people—no tyranny of the majority or dictatorship of the minority. What we have here in Dollar Ranch, to the extent that you can say we have government at all, is government by *universal* consent of the governed. No one has to be here and no one has to stay, but everyone who does stay agrees to abide by this contract."

"Zat is...remarkable!"

This got a good laugh from everyone in the room—everyone except Ed.

Anna leaned forward and everyone fell silent. "Michel, read it carefully. It is important that everyone understand the nature of our community. That way they join with fully informed consent, and understand how things work. You will find that, other than the sections that deal with your specific exchange with Merlyn for your apartment, everything else deals with your freedom and your rights—and how they are guaranteed. A governance system serves no purpose at all, if it does not guarantee those things. Read it, and sign it only when and if you are ready."

Michel did read it carefully, and was very impressed by what he read. The document had no fine print, and was exactly as they had described it: an agreement made by all residents of Dollar Ranch, aimed at guaranteeing the freedom and rights of each.

He noted, with considerable relief, that all of the rights enumerated were related to self-control of one's life, liberty, and property. There were none of the so-called rights such as those to food and shelter—which necessarily obligated others to provide such goods—that had been the norm in the socialist European countries he had fled.

Michel was satisfying himself on a few final details, discussing them with Merlyn, when one of the town's innumerable children came running in, looking for him. "Monsieur Gerard! Monsieur Gerard!"

"Yes?"

"Doc says the lady is asking to see you!"

"Zat is wonderful! Tell him I will be right zere!" The child scampered off and Michel turned to his new friends, all of whom had stayed to witness the signing of the contract. "Does anybody 'ave a pen?"

Several were produced. Michel was rewarded with a soul-warming smile from Jimmy when he chose hers and signed the contract with a Hancock-like flourish. There were cheers all around—except from Ed—and Michel stood to go.

Merlyn signed below Michel's signature and scooped up the contract. "Michel, welcome to Dollar Ranch! I'll make a copy of this and slip it under your door, okay?"

"Yes, fine. I must go now, yes?"

The little gathering broke up and Michel hurried to the doctor's clinic. When he got there, the doctor told him that the woman had been awake for several days, but had been grief-stricken and depressed, and had asked not to be disturbed. She was better now, and had asked to see the man who had saved her life.

Michel knocked gingerly at the door.

"Come in."

He swallowed his heart and opened the door slowly. There she was; propped up in bed, awake, alert... So much like Natalie, and yet not the same. She was younger, but that wasn't it; there was something about her face that was shaped in the way Natalie's had been...but...still different. Perhaps it was the greater prominence of her cheekbones? Michel wished he had a hat or something to occupy his hands with.

"Allo," was all he could think of to say.

She gazed at him intently—probing, measuring, looking for...what?

Michel squirmed until he simply had to do something to break the ice. "Ze doctor, he said you asked to see me?"

She dipped her head slightly, her eyes still searching.

"My name is Michel Gerard. What is yours?"

She stared out the window a while before replying. Clouds were scurrying by, changing shapes as they went. "You can call me Razor. Who I was died back on that road where you found me."

The voice was not at all what Michel had been expecting. It was sharp, powerful, assertive—not at all the voice of a grief-stricken woman recovering in a hospital. "Well, Miss Razor..." He stumbled over the odd name. The whole valley was full of people with strange names! And why was she looking at him with such an inscrutable expression?

With a start, he realized that he had drifted off in mid-sentence. "Ah..." Merde! "I am very glad to see you alive and well! I was much afraid zat I was too late when we finally brought you in to see ze doctor."

"Please, just call me Razor, not Miss."

"Yes, Razor."

"The doctor says you came in and held a sort of vigil over me while I was unconscious."

"I did, yes, for a time. But zen he told me to stop so I would not disturb you."

"I needed to be alone." Her attention shifted back to the clouds sailing by her window. She managed to convey a combination of doubt and self-confidence when she brought her focus back to Michel. "Why did you do it?"

"I... I do not know, really. I wanted to make sure you were okay, I guess. It made me feel better to see you breazing."

Breazing? She covered her mouth with her hands and tried not to laugh, but she couldn't help it. "Forgive me Michel, but..." She let it out. "Do me a favor and say, 'does your dog bite?'"

That laughter—what musical tones! Michel smiled; he knew

this game. He laid on his best Clouseau accent. "Deuz yeur deug beht?" Seeing her respond, he added Grace's favorite Clouseauism for good measure: "Neht now Cato! Eh em trying to defuze zis behm!!"

Razor laughed and laughed, until the pain in her shoulder brought her up short. "Oh God, that's funny!" She wiped a tear from her eye. "I'd ask you to ask for a room with a phone, but I think it'd hurt too much!"

They both chuckled, Michel with relief at the reduced tension.

"Ze doctor warned me zat you need your rest and zat I should not stay too long, so please tell me, what can I do for you?"

She eyed him sharply, then relaxed. "For starters, you can accept my thanks for saving my life. I'm not accustomed to feeling helpless, and I was sure I'd had it when that *woman* put her gun to my head."

There was something very odd about the way she stressed the word: *woman*. Michel was sure there was a story behind the emphasis. "It was a very bad sing, what zey were doing to you."

Razor held his gaze without responding.

"It was only a reflex. I am sure you would 'ave done ze same for me..." Michel was no schoolboy, but her direct probing look had him blushing. What was she searching for?

In shame, she let her head sag. "No, I wouldn't have. Not then." She raised her head. "But I've had a lot to think about this last week, and I've decided to 'mend my ways,' as they say."

Michel fidgeted, unsure of what to say.

"Until recently, I hated all men," she explained, "because of the way I thought they oppressed women." Razor felt bitter acid rising again, but it was directed at herself this time, not at any man or men. She shook her head and continued. "So, I can't say that I would have stopped to help you... But I can say that I've learned that women can be as oppressive as men. In the way that matters most, there aren't any such things as Men and Women, there are only Individuals—individuals who do good or bad things."

That was what Trish had been trying to tell her, if she'd only been listening. "In my own way, I was being as much a chauvinist and bigot as the men I accused, because I was judging men as a group, and not on their individual merits." Trish had been right about a lot of things.

Michel still didn't know what to say, so he waited her out.

Razor smiled ruefully. "I'm sorry, I didn't mean to lecture. It's just that I've been cooped up in this bed, and I've been doing a lot of thinking."

Michel's heart melted when she shook her flowing hair—Natalie had done that. And that smile! But he thought once again that someone might be praising him more than he deserved. "To tell you ze trus, you look very much like someone I loved. I am not sure I would 'ave stopped for just anyone eizer, but someone..." He suddenly had trouble breathing and slumped into the arm-chair across from Razor's bed. "Someone like zose who were hurting you..." Tears came unbidden to his eyes. "Someone tortured her—butchered my Natalie!"

The grief in his voice and face seemed genuine, but Razor had years of suspicion to overcome. Intending to test Michel, she got out of bed and—ignoring the pain in her left side—put her right arm around him. She held his head to her chest. He was mumbling something about his Natalie, about the phones all being out, about being too late, about her blood, *so* much blood, slippery on the floor...

He made no move to grope her, or even to respond to her presence. This was no act, no ploy to get at her; he was lost in his own pain. Without realizing that she had started crying as well, she took his chin in her hand and brought his gaze up to meet her own. "Michel, we all make mistakes... I was not alone when they attacked me."

This brought Michel's thoughts back from wandering the paths of guilt to focus on the pain etched on the face above him. Her tears were falling, falling on his face, falling on his lips, falling...

"Her name was Trish." Razor was unaware of the salty flow.

"She was my partner...my lover...my best friend..." Her words faded away, and it was her turn to lose herself in memory. Suddenly, her breath caught. "'*I'm a better friend than I think you'll ever know*,' Trish said. Well, I know it now..." Now that she's gone!

Razor's thoughts ebbed and surged repeatedly over the same rocky shoreline. "You know, she tried to get me to go another route." In more than one way! "We were even warned about trouble on the highway in Colorado. Right before...before it happened...she was going to try to get me to turn around, but I killed that conversation with a look before it got started. If only I had known what else would die with it! They—those people who attacked us— they dropped something off the bridge. It had metal teeth that came through the roof of the car like it was made of paper. She died instantly—I hope."

Michel stood and held her close. "It was some kind of farm machine, maybe somesing for breaking up clods of dirt. I saw it. It had smashed your car. But I did not know it had fallen on anyone!" He wiped the tears from her eyes. "It was not your fault! Zose evil people, ze Rifle Gang, zey are responsible—all you were doing was driving your car and minding your own business."

She smiled and wiped the tears from his eyes. "And you were doing whatever you needed to be doing when...whatever happened to Natalie happened."

"But ze blood was so fresh, if I had—"

"If you had gotten there earlier, you might have been attacked as well, or only have given yourself the opportunity to feel rage and helplessness while she died in your arms. From the way you've described it, she was beyond saving a long time before you got there."

For the first time since that horrible afternoon when he had discovered Natalie's body, Michel forced his mind to go back and look at the scene carefully. The fact that there were no police or ambulances to call upon, the number of deep cuts, the rope around her neck and ankles... "But I didn't even bury her!"

"As I understand it, New York City is as empty of living people as a cemetery. The place she lived is as good a tomb as any hole you could have dug in the dirt."

Michel trembled, thinking back... Each memory was a glass shard, shredding his mental peace as he dragged it up for examination. In the painful light he could see that Razor was right; even if he'd gone straight to Natalie when he'd gotten up, he probably would not have been able to save her. There was nothing he would have, could have, or should have done—nothing that would have mattered. In a convulsion of agony and release, he clung to Razor and wept, and wept...

...and she was weeping too, cutting her mental hands as she turned over her own sharp memories, examining them anew...

Suddenly, they both became conscious of their closeness. Razor tensed. This was it; she had placed her wounded body and soul into this man's hands. If Prudence had been right about men, Michel would make a move on her, try to hit on her while she was vulnerable. The heat of emotion and the dampness of tears made her sensitive to every place where they were touching; she had not been so intimate with a man since Kat had pulled her off the street.

Michel stepped back. "I would like to ask you somesing."

"What?" Here it comes!

"I..." He cleared his throat. "I want you to let me 'elp you." He stopped and thought about it. "No, zat is not what I meant to say—I do not sink you need any 'elp." He couldn't find the right word. "I want to... It would mean a lot to me...if you would let me...*serve* you." Michel winced at the word. It wasn't exactly what he wanted to say, but it had worked for Don Quixote in *Man of La Mancha*...

Reality started spinning around Razor again. "You..." She stumbled and he caught her uninjured shoulder, steadying her. "You don't want anything from me?"

He let go of her. "No. It is enough to know...to know zat you exist."

Razor sniffed. He hadn't made a pass at her. Even now, as he helped her back to her bed, he didn't try to hold her closer than was necessary. A word entered her mind that she had never thought of using without sarcasm before: gentleman. He was being a gentleman. "I never expected to be rescued by a knight in shining armor, let alone one in a shining ice cream truck!"

Michel chuckled and stepped back from the bed. "And I never expected a patient in a 'ospital to 'elp me ease my mind... Natalie would sank you for 'elping me if she were 'ere." He refused to let himself start crying again.

"Oh, I'm good at kicking people in the butt." She winced and tried not to move her wounded shoulder. "That reminds me, where are my gauntlets?"

Michel shrugged. "I am not sure." He crossed over to the closet. "Maybe in 'ere?" Her clothes, mended and clean, were there, but not the gauntlets.

"I guess that's not the kind of thing they leave lying around a hospital," she sighed.

"You are joking, yes? Everyone in zis place walks around wis a gun, or some ozer weapon!" He tried a chest of drawers next. "But you know, I never felt zis safe in New York City, where only ze police and ze criminals had guns." He found the gauntlets in the top drawer and offered them to her.

"Ah-hah!" She took them from him, and checked them over. "Someone must have cleaned them up for me."

"Zat was probably Jimmy. She is a remarkable young woman who seems very impressed wis what you did wis zose."

"Yeah, well, I didn't have a gun... I hope I'll still be able to use them! The doctor tells me that the bullet managed to go through without causing too much damage..." Razor chuckled. "They don't look very practical, do they? But I guess the Rifle Gang learned a thing or two about underestimating bladed weapons!"

"And ze people of Dollar Ranch!" Michel agreed.

"I understand that you fought them off at the gate and then, after dropping me off, went back to fight them again."

Michel snorted. "For all ze good I did! I forgot to take ze safety

DON L. TIGGRE

off my rifle and did not even fire a single shot! But zese people—
zese Dollar Ranchers—you should 'ave seen zem! Zey taught ze
Rifle Gang a lesson zey will never forget."

"Well, I thank you anyway."

There was an awkward silence. Michel again wished for something purposeful to do with his hands and began edging toward
the door. "I need to go. You should get your rest, and I need to
take care of some errands before ze meeting tonight."

"Meeting? What meeting?"

"I am not sure what it is about. Ze Rifle Gang has wisdrawn,
for now, at least, but zey could be stupid enough to attack again.
Perhaps zat is what Merlyn wishes to discuss."

"Who's Merlyn?"

"Ze Owner." Michel laughed. "Now I will probably get in
trouble for disturbing your rest wis news your doctor has not decided to share wis you."

"To hell with that; this rest is killing me! Maybe I'll sneak out
of here tonight and find out what's going on... I want to know
more about this place I've landed in."

"Well zen, if you are going to be sneaking tonight, I should let
you get your rest zis afternoon. Yes?" He stepped through the
door, but, before closing it, he poked his head in for a last word.
"Sanks again for ze kick in ze butt, and please sink about my request!" He closed the door.

It was crowded that night, when Michel entered the dining
hall of the Big House. The fifteen families had sent more than one
person each. The room was large for a house that had not been
originally designed to hold as many people as it now did—the
boarders ate in rotation—but it was almost full, and people were
still coming in.

He spotted an open space and slid onto a bench beside Dreamer
and near Ed. The younger man ignored him and the older one
waved in greeting.

Merlyn was calling the meeting to order when Jimmy showed
up and managed to insinuate herself between Michel and Dreamer.

Ed had been saving a space by his side, obviously in hopes that Jimmy would take it. Without a word, he gave Michel a murderous look, and stalked off.

Jimmy pretended not to notice. "Dad, did I introduce you to Michel Gerard this morning? He's our new armored cavalry division."

The blond man smiled at Michel and held out his hand. "My friends call me Dreamer."

Michel shook with Dreamer. "I remember. You are ze builder, yes?" The iron grip was definitely that of a man who did hard work with his hands.

"Yep." He turned to his daughter and asked about Ed.

Jimmy made a rather un-tomboyish pout. "I don't know what's gotten into him lately. He acts like he owns me, and I don't like it. He's got a temper, and he gets really mean when he's mad." She leaned against her father. "Can't a girl want to sit next to her father?"

Dreamer was about to answer that he was not the only person she had sat beside when Anna welcomed everyone—the room calmed immediately.

"Thank you, Anna." Merlyn kept his voice low so everyone would remain quiet. "Our scouts, including our new armored division..." He stopped while everyone laughed and Michel simulated the color of a ripe tomato with his cheeks. They had all heard about Michel's rescue of the mysterious woman who called herself Razor—whose reputed prowess with her unusual weapons had grown with each telling of the story. "Our scouts have returned with some interesting news. We had only found out about the Rifle Gang ourselves a few days before they attacked, so we didn't have a very good idea of their size, but we seem to have dealt them a very serious blow."

The crowd cheered, not thunderously, but enthusiastically. Jimmy jumped up and gave a loud whoop. In the first real test of Dollar Ranch's defenses, none of the defenders had been seriously hurt—definitely something to feel good about!

"From what we can tell, the gang is pretty much out of business. The armored division reports that they have abandoned the overpass and the roadblocks on the highway. Others are reporting that they are no longer holed up in the Rusty Cannon Motel. We don't know how many of them are left, or where they went, but it seems likely that they won't be bothering us anymore!"

There was more cheering. In the commotion, Michel didn't notice Razor enter the room, until she put her hand on his shoulder and sat in the place Ed had vacated. The two smiled, but made no other greeting. Jimmy was acutely aware that Razor sat closer to Michel than the press of the crowd actually required.

"But that's not why I called this meeting!" Merlyn raised his voice a little and the crowd settled down. "Does everyone know Randy from Winnipeg? Stand up, Randy." A shy-looking teenage boy who had been sitting beside Merlyn blushed bright red, stood for a second, and then sat back down. "Randy here knows ten times more about ham radio than I ever will. He's helped us so that we can broadcast and receive from farther than I imagined possible." Merlyn took a cassette recorder he had in front of him and slid it over to Randy.

"Since the phone system stopped working, we haven't been able to get news over the internet. We've been in the dark about what's been going on elsewhere for over a week, except for the news Michel brought with him. Now we're starting to pick up some interesting things on the radio, and I wanted you all to hear some of them for yourselves."

He waved a hand at Randy, who pressed the play button on the recorder. A loud and boisterously cheerful male voice filled the room:

"Hiya folks! This is Beethoven Bill, playin' my favorite Beethoven hits, because you can't call me and tell me what you really want to hear. And this is Radio Bill, broadcasting on—aw heck, who cares about all that stuff anyway! There's no FCC anymore, so I don't have to waste your time reading all kinds of crap you don't want to hear anyway. Hey,

that means you don't have to put up with any of those annoying emergency broadcast system screeching tests! Isn't that great? Anyway, if you can hear me, just mark the dial and listen in from time to time. We'll be readin' the news at the top of every hour and playing classical music to smooth your day on its way, every day.

"Yes, you heard right, every day! That's this hour's news: Radio Bill has its first sponsor, and they're payin' me enough for me to keep bouncing my broadcast off the moon and back again twenty-four hours a day. Isn't that great?

"And how are they payin' me, you want to know? With gold! Not just any gold, but freshly minted gold coins in different denominations—and get this—these coins aren't just pretty; they are redeemable for ammunition! That's right folks, pretty soon, you'll be seeing coinage in use all across America, coins that have the value of precious metals, and are redeemable for one of the most useful commodities on the market these days.

"Ain't that great folks?! That means that folks like me, who couldn't grow anything if their life depended on it—in fact, I haven't been able to grow anything even though my life has depended on it! I'm sayin' that folks like me can now go about doing other things that we can do better, and trade our work for something that will feed our families. And I think that's great!

"So where can you get some of these coins? The coins are available at all First Freehold Bank of America locations—formerly Big Bob's Army/Navy Surplus locations. It just so happens that Big Bob is a gun nut and a gold bug. What a great combination that turned out to be, huh? So, Bob knew that people didn't trust paper money anymore, but they still need money. Right? Everybody can't grow and make everything they need for their whole lives, right? So he got to thinkin' that gold all by itself is nice, but who knows how much it'll be worth when people have more important things on their minds than jewelry? Bullets are more practical. So he decided to combine the two: gold makes great money—rare and easily divisible and all that stuff—and ammunition is a valuable commodity that is useful to all kinds of people.

My favorites are the 30.06 pennies. These little cuties are guaran-

teed 99.9 percent pure and are redeemable at any First Freehold Bank of America location for a box of twenty rounds of premium 30.06 rifle ammunition. There are also some bigger silver coins for making change. Isn't that great? I think that's just great!!

"So folks, when you're buying, selling, or trading, remember to ask for First Freehold Bank of America gold coins! For any of you who don't remember Big Bob's Army/Navy Surplus, every state west of the Mississippi has at least one. Look for a phone book in the nearest big city. I know this sounds kinda amazing, but every Big Bob's had its own generator, and Big Bob uses ham radio to talk to all his managers, so he's been able to keep 'em up an' runnin. Right?

So, the First Freehold Bank of America is open for business! If you have ammo for guns you don't have, or neighbors who won't trade for ammo, bring 'em on in to the bank! Uh, that's the ammo, not the neighbors! Anyway, Big Bob's boys'll turn 'em into gold that people will take. Food and other valuables are also being accepted for trade, on an as-needed basis. And Big Bob'll take gold jewelry and bullion in trade as well! I just think that's great!

"Now, I'm in the mood to celebrate. I'm so glad I don't have to go out and try to grow my own food, I just can't tell ya! But Beethoven can, with his music. So, in celebration of this great news, this hour of the Beethoven Bill show is going to feature the master's masterpiece: the choral symphony No. 9, Ode to Joy."

"Y'all enjoy this now!"

The opening notes of Beethoven's Ninth Symphony swelled into the room, but were cut off sharply by the end of the recording. Everyone started to talk at once. Merlyn had to call them to order by banging on the table. "Folks! Beethoven Bill may sound like a corn-ball, but he made an excellent point: without a medium of exchange, people are on their own, to survive or die, based on whatever they can grow and build on their own. With a medium of exchange—money—they can concentrate on whatever they do best and trade for things made by other people doing what they do best. This *is* great news!"

The crowd started off again, but he reined them in before they could really get going. "That's not all, folks!"

As everyone was settling down again, Razor found herself pondering some new experiences. Michel still made no attempt to touch her—his respect for her space was complete. And the only thing he had asked of her since saving her life was...to *serve* her! What a strange choice of words... He was what Kat would have called 'good people'; honest and brave, like Trish. She could feel his warmth as he sat beside her—it was oddly comforting. Without consciously intending to, she began leaning against him. He wasn't overly muscular, but he was a big man. His solidity was reassuring.

Razor may not have fully noticed what she was doing, but Michel did. And so did Jimmy.

"People!" Merlyn pounded an imaginary gavel on the table. "People, that's not all the news!" Calm slowly returned. "Randy also rigged up a better antenna for our AM receiver, and we got a new signal in, loud and clear, from what was once Utah."

Razor sat up straighter, as did most of the others in the room. Word had spread about Utah, about their border guard, about they way they still had a government.

"Randy, put that other tape in please."

Randy put the tape in and pressed the play button. The voice that filled the room now was a tired one, but unwavering. It was the voice of a woman who had endured much, but had the strength to do so.

She was reading a statement:

People of America,
This is Arlene Waller, governor of the late state of Utah, broadcasting this message on Beehive Radio, 1160 AM. As I speak, it is 9:00 p.m., mountain time, on Saturday, the first of April, in the year of our Lord, two thousand. This message will be repeated every hour for the next 48 hours, and then daily at noon for the next month. Everyone must know what has happened, that we may move forward.

We in Utah have been as shocked and devastated as the rest of you by the nuclear attack on our country and the disintegration of law and order across the land. You may have heard the same rumors we have: rumors of lynchings of former government officials. Rumors about the disintegration of the United State's military structure, which was well under way, even before the attack.

We have sent out scouts and found evidence of many killings of former government officials, and no evidence of any substantial segment of the armed services still functioning as a cohesive whole. Apparently the anti-government sentiments that had been growing throughout the nineteen nineties fully blossomed with the advent of the year 2000. Particularly singled out have been federal employees and Congresspersons who were not in Washington at the time of that city's destruction. Some of you may have heard that the Secretary of State survived the attack on Washington, having been hundreds of miles away on an airplane at the time. This is true, and he did go to Philadelphia to try to pull the remnants of the chain of command together, but he was lynched by a mob as soon as he made his intentions public.

I guess people were mad about many things, but simply could not forgive anyone in the federal government for letting the country fall apart.

There are many indications of the complete collapse of our economy and society as a country, but I won't get into them. What is obvious is that the government of the United States of America has ceased to exist. It may even be accurate to say that the people themselves rose to abolish it, as Thomas Jefferson said they might, two hundred and twenty-four years ago. I do not believe that things would be as they are now, if our governments had not failed their people so completely with regard to the so-called Millennium Bug.

Therefore, seeing that the union the state of Deseret joined in eighteen ninety-six—becoming the state of Utah—no longer exists, I hereby declare the state of Deseret to be reestablished.

The state of Deseret will occupy the same geographic borders previously occupied by the state of Utah, and will expand to include outlying communities only upon petition for admission to the state by those communities. The state of Deseret will obey the laws established for it before its admission to that union which no longer exists, until a constitutional convention can be convened, no later than six months from today. The state of Deseret desires only peace with all its neighbors, be they individual farms or whole cities, but we will defend our borders with whatever force is necessary and will not tolerate the gang-land chaos we see around us.

Honest, hard-working people who hear this message and do not feel safe where they are now living may wish to emigrate to the state of Deseret. There is much work to be done and we could use the help.

While it is true that most of those living in the state of Deseret are and shall be members of the Church of Jesus Christ of the Latter Day Saints—Mormons—it is also true that the government of the state of Deseret is and shall be prohibited from establishing a state religion.

Hill Air Force base has recognized me as the highest ranking public official still in office and formally placed their forces into the service of the state of Utah yesterday. With this declaration, I hereby give the base a new name as it enters into the service of Deseret: the Deseret Air Force Base. The General of the Deseret Air Force tells us that the 'Computer Czar', General Alexis Thomas, has several plans in play in Russia and believes that no further launches will be made from there.

Brothers, sisters, Americans, we have endured many black days, and may yet endure more, but we must begin getting on with the task of rebuilding America and the world. I welcome those who would join us, and caution any who would hinder us.

Thank you, and may God be with you.

The room went briefly silent, then broke into conversation again. Some were alarmed, some regarded the news as good. Razor, having misjudged the Mormons once, kept her thoughts to herself.

This time, Merlyn let the conversation go for a while—there was no stemming the tide—before calling for quiet. "Ladies and Gentlemen! Whatever you may think about Mormons, or Big Bob the Banker, I want to point out that both of these things show

how incredibly adaptable people can be, even in the face of world-shaking catastrophes. Whatever else it means, it means that we are not the only ones organized to survive and to build something new from the rubble."

He stood up. "You are all welcome to stay here and discuss matters, but try to keep it down; I'm going to bed. Good night!"

Jimmy elbowed Michel and tipped her head at Razor.

"Oh, excuse me." Michel made the introduction. "Razor, zis is Jimmy, ze one I 'ave told you about. Jimmy, zis is Razor."

Jimmy giggled. "Don't you just love that accent?"

Razor chuckled in response. "Yes, it's fun... And by the way, do I thank you for cleaning and returning my gauntlets?"

The girl beamed. "Could you show me how to use them?" Jimmy had been very impressed by the bladed weapons and had even taken to carrying a short dirk in her right boot, in case an emergency arose and she didn't have her rifle handy.

Razor laughed harder, then winced. "Maybe. It's not that hard, actually. It's like dancing. Do you like to dance?"

"I haven't done much of it..." Jimmy pulled on her father's hand. "Daddy, can they come over for a drink and some talk? I'd love to hear their stories!"

Dreamer glimpsed the shadow of pain that his daughter, in her excitement, missed on Razor's face. "I think Miss Razor needs to get back to bed before Doc finds her, and I think Michel has to get the truck ready for his next foray."

"Ah, yes," Michel smiled at Dreamer gratefully. "And I too am tired. But I would be 'onored to be your guest Jimmy, and Dreamer. Perhaps we could share dinner some ozer time, yes?"

Jimmy agreed, and Dreamer knew better than to try to argue with her.

Razor asked Michel to walk her back to the infirmary and they all bade each other good night.

On the way, Razor took his hand and whispered, "Yes."

Michel's heart leapt. "Zat is—"

"But there's a condition."

"What?" He wasn't sure whether this was a good or bad thing.

"You may...serve me," she stumbled over the antiquated use of the word, "but you must let me do the same for you."

Michel started to protest. "I did not ask for zat. I do not want you to feel obligated..."

She squeezed his hand. "I know you didn't ask for it—that's one reason I offered. And I don't feel obligated—or I wouldn't even be talking to you. But fair is fair, I *will* feel awkward or obligated if you don't let me return the favor. So that's my condition. Take it or leave it."

"Well, what did you 'ave in mind?"

She shrugged. "I'm not sure yet... You haven't exactly said anything specific either. But I understand that everyone here works or provides something of value to the town, so I need to think of something to do, something to trade for room and board. You're supposed to be an advisor, maybe you can help me think of some businesses to start up. And, in exchange, I could help you with your armored courier and scouting services—could you use someone to ride shotgun?"

Michel guffawed. "Hah! Ze way I shoot? Zere is nosing I could use more!"

"All right then. That's an example. We'll think of more. Deal?"

"Deal!"

He left her at the door to Doc's place, and, instead of trying to kiss her goodnight, bowed deeply and returned to the Big House, practically skipping as he went.

CHAPTER 44:
TUESDAY, APRIL 4, 2000

"Don't ask for help
You're all alone
Pressure
You'll have to answer
To your own
Pressure!"
—Billy Joel, *Pressure*

"Ma'am, we can't raise the C-5."

Alexis broke off her conversation with John Allen and studied the soldier, standing at attention beside the meeting table in the pavilion. His bearing communicated genuine alarm. "Say again, Private?"

"Lieutenant Daniels asked me to tell you that he can't raise the crew of the transport, ma'am. He says he's been trying for ten minutes."

"Thank you, Private." She gestured at Allen. "Let's go."

The civilian sighed and got to his feet. Together they hurried out of the pavilion and to the radio tent. Lieutenant Daniels was an Air Force communications officer who had volunteered to join the team back in Deseret. He wasn't technically part of the C-5's flight crew, though he had helped handle communications on their way in, so he had not stayed with the plane. He was waiting for them when they arrived and repeated his news.

Alexis had worried about something like this since the day they'd arrived and she had ordered the Air Force captain and his crew to stay with the transport plane. She tried not to let her voice betray her feelings as she spoke. "Understood, Lieutenant. Try raising Hill—I mean Deseret, and see if they can raise the C-5, or have heard anything from them."

"Yes, ma'am." The lieutenant got busy.

"Maybe they have a radio malfunction," Allen suggested, "or took it off line to service it?"

"They wouldn't do that without telling us... No. I hope it is a malfunction!"

"You hope that?"

"The alternative is that they can't answer the radio, and I can't think of any reasons for that that I like."

"Deseret says they haven't heard from them since this morning." The Lieutenant listened to his earphones before speaking again. "They say they have not received any distress calls and that their last report was routine. They'll try raising them, ma'am, but they don't think they will be able to, if we can't."

"Okay, thanks Daniels." The radioman shrugged apologetically and Alexis turned to Allen. "John, do me a favor. Round up the Mirage pilots. We're going to go check on the C-5, so we might as well go ahead and take them to their planes—we'd need to be doing that soon anyway."

"You got it, Alexis!" He trotted off toward the DDCC bunker.

Lieutenant Daniels caught Alexis' attention with a half-wave of his hand. "Deseret isn't getting any response from the Galaxy, ma'am, but they say they'll keep trying."

A cold feeling of dread came over the general. "If they get anything, let me know in my chopper."

"Yes, ma'am."

A little over three hours later, they were in the air approaching the Novosibirsk military air strip. Alexis was flying. Her men had been scandalized by their general's insistence upon flying herself, at first, but it soon became evident to everyone that she liked it that way, and they certainly were not going to argue with her.

On this flight, as had been the case increasingly of late, she had John Allen in the co-pilot's seat. She was using the flight time to familiarize him with the Blackhawk's weapons systems. It had surprised her when he'd asked to be shown—as much as he disliked flying—but she figured that it wouldn't hurt to have him expand his range of skills. She could always use another good gunner. Actually, as much as he disliked flying, it was surprising that he had come on the mission to Russia at all, unless...

Alexis slowed their approach and one of the Mirage pilots came forward to look out the front windows with them.

There was something wrong about the way the C-5 was sitting on the tarmac. It wasn't sitting straight on its twenty-eight wheels. As they got closer, the reason became clear; most of the nose section, including the cockpit and the crew compartments, were no longer there. From the looks of the twisted wreckage, some high powered explosives had hit the front of the big plane from the side facing a hangar with its doors halfway open.

"Hey!" Alexis spoke into her helmet mic and gestured at the Frenchman. "Isn't that the hangar where you two stashed your Mirages?"

The pilot nodded.

"Damn!" Allen was looking at the twisted aluminum shards around the gaping hole in the front of the transport. "We definitely won't be refueling that baby, or taking most of our stuff home—shit!"

The pilot nodded again and pointed. "Oui! Merde! I won't be taking my plane home eizer!"

Following his gesture, Alexis brought them down to hover a few yards above the ground, close to the hangar doors. There was nothing inside. "Let's go look for survivors!" She turned the chopper and slid it sideways a few yards above the ground, then set it down a short distance from the damaged front section of the Galaxy. "I'll stay here with the chopper. John, go with the Mirage pilots and see if you can find any survivors!"

The civilian unfastened his harness and saluted playfully before climbing into the aft compartment with the Frenchman. As soon as the Blackhawk was firmly sitting on its landing gear, the three men leapt from the helicopter and ran to the C-5. Clambering carefully over the sharp metal fringe of the fuselage, where it rested on the pavement, they disappeared inside.

A few long minutes later, five figures emerged, one leaning heavily on another, and two more carrying the fifth. As soon as they were on board, Alexis lifted the helicopter and headed back to base—the men obviously needed medical attention on the double!

After they had been airborne for some time, Allen returned to his seat in front and plugged his helmet in so he could speak to Alexis over the intercom. He had fresh blood on his clothes.

"Welcome back, John. Who are the two men?"

"The loadmasters. They were in the back of the forward compartments when the Galaxy was hit. There was one other crew member that survived the blast, but he bled to death before we got here."

Alexis gritted her teeth and resisted the urge to go looking for the stolen jets. They couldn't have gotten far, not without refueling, but she couldn't let the bastards distract her from her real target. Someone had murdered men under her command, but today was the day: W-Day!

"The one who's conscious says they had no warning, didn't see anyone sneak into the hangar where the Mirages were, let alone refuel them. His buddy's hurt pretty bad—took a lot of shrapnel—may not make it. He's pretty sure it was the Mirages that fired on them, because after the explosion, he heard them taxi away, and then take off. As quiet as things are around there, he couldn't miss it." Allen peeked out the window at the terrain passing below, then hastily focused on the console in front of him.

Things might be quiet, but that didn't make them safe. The whole world had become a more dangerous place... Or did it just seem that way? Whoever had fired on the C-5 had been the kind of person he or she was since before Y2K. After thinking about it another moment, Allen expressed his main question aloud: "What

I don't get is why they attacked. There's no way the Galaxy could have chased them, or even kept up with them, and it doesn't have any weapons!"

"Maybe they were afraid the crew would radio someone who could give the Mirages a better chase. Or, maybe they are just the type of people who don't like to leave any witnesses."

There was little more conversation during their flight back to base. Alexis radioed ahead so that their medic would be standing by when they arrived.

On the ground again, Alexis called for a meeting of all key personnel, as well as anyone else who wanted to attend. The French pilots sat by glumly, not sure what their role would be now that they had no planes to fly.

"Okay, everyone, listen up. I ordered those men to stay with the C-5 in Novosibirsk—no one is more upset about this than I am, but it doesn't really change our plans. We can grieve later. For now, if things go bad, we'll have fewer assets with which to try to shoot down departing missiles, but we were hoping not to have to do that anyway. Maybe we can take another look at using the Blackhawks or the Hind for deploying more ground teams—Captain Jones, can you and Captain Stewart look into that when we break?"

"Yes mayum!" Captains Jones and Stewart were the two Blackhawk pilots who had flown with Alexis on her Y2K repair missions stateside, before The Collapse. Captain Erickson had been with the team in Germany. Erickson had told her that he would try to meet up with her in Siberia, but hadn't shown—something must have happened to him. Captain Leighton had been in Washington with the fifth helicopter in her team, when the city had been hit.

Stewart and Jones, the two pilots she had left—besides herself—were a pair of matched opposites. Captain Stewart was a serene, efficient man, but Captain Jones was loud and obnoxious. He was from Oklahoma and made damn sure everyone could tell. Whenever he could get away with it, he even wore a cowboy hat.

As irritating as he could be, Jones was a fine pilot and knew more about Army helicopters than anyone else Alexis had ever met.

Alexis refrained from rolling her eyes at his exaggerated accent and resumed where she'd left off. "Great. So, for those of you who haven't heard it all before, let's review our thinking. We racked our brains for different ways to disable the bunkers—to break in without setting the system off—but couldn't think of any way that would work fast enough to prevent the Wh—the Doomsday Device from ordering the second attack. Then we thought about trying to crack the password, until General Petrov told us that he'd already tried a couple times and that the next incorrect password would trigger the device. Right General?"

"Yes. I didn't want to say so in my radio announcement, because I was trying to avoid saying anything that might prompt a government to decide to send a missile instead of help, but I've known from the beginning that the machine was programmed to attack immediately if three incorrect passwords were entered."

"Okay," Alexis wanted to make sure everyone understood that all options had been explored, "so then we considered giving the folks back home the precise coordinates of the three bunkers that house the device's CPUs, power supply, and so on. The idea was to see if they could take them all out simultaneously, but General Petrov told us that two of the three were so deep that there was no way it would work."

Alexis paused to make sure everyone was following her. "Besides, we called back to Hill—I mean Deseret—and they said that there wasn't anyone left who could reprogram ICBM fire-control computers. Apparently, the folks at NORAD are still alive under Cheyenne Mountain, but we all knew that their computers were on the blink before we came out here... And you," she turned to the French and British contingents, "have lost contact with the people who sent you, so there is no way to give anyone any targeting information in your countries, right?"

George Allistair, the English pilot, spoke for all of them. "Yes, we've been working with Lieutenant Daniels and have been able to raise some ham radio operators in Great Britain and France, but no civil or military authorities. We think that, as has happened in your country, people back home have blamed the authorities for The Collapse and attacked government employees, especially national government employees. Our armed services were also suffering desertion problems, as yours were, when we left. I bet those Krauts who were supposed to be on their way never even made it out of Germany!"

The Frenchmen held their silence in reluctant agreement.

"Right." Alexis looked into the eyes of each of her key players. "So, that's when we decided to try John Allen's idea of forcing the machine to give us the password." She tipped her head at the civilian, indicating that he should summarize for those who'd not heard the idea explained.

Allen cleared his throat. "Well, from the time we trigger the machine, it will take the rockets a while to lift off. They have a pre-ignition sequence to work through, gantries to be retracted, silo portals to be blown, and so on. After talking it over with General Petrov, we decided that we had between five and ten minutes after tripping the machine to give it the countermand password and stop the process."

"What I nevah got was how we were goin' to git the password." Captain Jones again.

"Well, to tell you the truth, we're not sure we can get it, but we have a way to try. The machine's CPUs use a first generation hard drive system for memory. The disks only hold about one megabyte of data. General Petrov's got all kinds of maintenance equipment here, including a machine that can read those disks and conduct surface scans. The idea is to break in to one of the other bunkers with a reader and a radio right there with us, go straight to the CPU, and tear the hard drive out as fast as we can. Then we'll scan the disk for the password with the maintenance reader, and radio it back here for Petrov to enter into the interface terminal in the bunker. There's one downstairs, right outside the control center bulkhead. If we do it fast enough, we can order it to cancel before any missiles get off."

"That's a bloody big 'if'," the Englishman chimed in.

"Yes Mr. Allistair, it is." Alexis took the conversation back over. "But it's been the best shot we've had. Our folks back stateside couldn't think of anything better, so that's been the plan for the last 36 hours. You and the French pilots were going to recon three of the missile fields within reach, and try to shoot down any departing missiles you could, if the plan didn't work. We were going to take ground crews to the only site we could reach in the helicopters, and do the same. It's certainly a risky plan, but 'improbable' is better than 'impossible,' and the folks back home have found it reassuring to tell people that we have a plan that might work."

Everyone was silent for a few heartbeats, thinking about the implications of the word 'might'.

"But I have a new idea." Those six words got Alexis their absolute undivided attention. "On the way back from Novosibirsk, I was feeling pretty bad about the men I ordered to stay there—in harm's way, as it turned out. Never mind that they would have wanted to stay with their plane anyway; I gave the order, and now they're dead. I was cursing the Y2K bug and all the destruction it's caused. It's brought the entire world to a stand-still, ruined almost everything... And that's when it hit me; we're up against a *computer!*"

She spread her hands and let the point sink in. "General Petrov, did you ever perform any upgrades on the machine's CPUs that would make them Y2K-compliant?"

"No..." Petrov's face took on a dreamy expression, as he reviewed his actions in his mind. "In fact, when I became aware of the Y2K problem, I ran a check of the software to see if it was vulnerable. We...didn't use as many microchips in our peripheral equipment, so the system was not vulnerable to the 'embedded system' problems you've told me you had in your country. The fire-control and decision-making software don't use date fields, so they're not susceptible. And it certainly worked well enough when it lost contact with Moscow!"

"Yes, I thought something like that must be the case, or it wouldn't have been able to launch the first strike. But what about other software on the system? Did your diagnostics have any scheduling features? Did you store maintenance logs with dates in the system?"

The Russian shook his head. "That was done with separate diagnostic computers. They are newer and are Y2K-compliant. I have one here in the DDCC bunker residential section—I can show it to you if you wish."

"I've seen it already." John Allen could see what Alexis was getting at and couldn't refrain from interrupting. "I know what you're thinking—it's a *great* idea!" He actually bounded out of his chair, unable to contain his excitement. None of the others had caught on yet. Alexis sat back with a smile and let him take it. "General, those systems are compatible, hell, not only that, they're designed to talk to each other! And we wouldn't be trying to give it a password, or access any of the mission-critical software. We could just hook up the diagnostic computer and have it install the maintenance scheduling software on all the Doomsday Device's CPUs. Then we could schedule some maintenance..."

Petrov got the picture. "The older machines might not be able to handle a date in the year 2000 and they'd crash—all of them!"

"Right!"

The crew got excited and started talking it over. Alexis waited a while before calling for order. "I'm glad to see you so enthusiastic, but it's only an idea. It might work, and it might not. We still need to be ready to try Mr. Allen's idea, in case this one doesn't work—and we shouldn't try either until we have all the anti-missile teams in place, in case we trigger the machine accidentally."

There was a chorus of "yes ma'am" around the room and the group sobered up, but the atmosphere was definitely less somber.

"All right. Jones, I want you to coordinate with the quartermaster and General Petrov on how we can get the most people and the most weapons that can take out a departing ICBM, to the largest number of possible launch sites."

"Yes mayum!"

"Mr. Allen, I want you to coordinate with General Petrov and his maintenance people—sorry Pavel, I'm afraid we're going to be keeping you pretty busy over the next twenty-four hours..."

"That's why I'm here, Alexa."

"Right. So, I'm going to need you two to prepare to implement both plans, the forcible password recovery plan and the Y2K system crash plan."

"Roger that!" For the first time since Alexis had met the Russian, he was excited, more purposeful: confident.

"Jacques and Jean-Paul," Alexis turned to the French pilots, "maybe you two could work something out and see if one of you could co-pilot for George?"

They both saluted. "Oui, madame!"

"Okay everybody, you have your orders!" These words were the cue ball hitting the pack. Everyone scattered in different directions, hope speeding each on his way for the first time since their arrival in Siberia.

The four-country task-force had a very busy night. Every person in the vicinity of the DDCC bunker felt that they had more preparations to make than they could get to. They pushed themselves harder. At 'W minus 30', everything critical was ready. Other things would have to be taken care of in-flight or during deployment. It was time to start moving out for 'Operation Wopperstop'.

The American soldiers had come up with the name. They had thought of calling it 'Operation 007', because James Bond was always saving the world from some doomsday device, but had decided against it because he was also always shooting up Russians. Besides, there weren't any voluptuous women tied to the missiles. Alexis had not been present, but someone from her team had remembered a movie made in the 1980s called *War Games*. In the film, it was the Americans who had placed their ICBMs under the control of a computer that had decided to figure out how to win a

338   DON L. TIGGRE

nuclear war by starting one. The computer's name in the movie was an acronym: WOPR. Once the idea had been suggested, it had spread like a virus, or a song that got stuck in the head.

Alexis took a two hour cat-nap before the scheduled beginning of Operation Wopperstop, after first assuring herself that everything was on schedule. Allistair and one of the French pilots took their naps earlier, because they had farther to fly.

Alexis' part would be to take John Allen's team to the nearest of the secondary Doomsday Device bunkers, the one they would be breaking into if the Y2K crash solution didn't work. She would remain with the team to bring them back, and to relay their signal from underground back to base, where it would be relayed to Petrov's team, also underground in the control bunker. They would be using special intercoms rigged with long wires to be able to relay information to the subterranean teams immediately.

"Mr. Allen, you're with me."

"Yes ma'am!" He accompanied Alexis to 'her' chopper—the one she had picked as her personal favorite—and ran through a final systems check with her. He had already loaded his equipment into the back.

Five minutes before Operation Wopperstop was scheduled to commence, all the team leaders reported to Alexis that they were ready to go. Stewart's and Jones' Blackhawks stood by, waiting to take a ground crew of Russians and Americans to the missile field within their reach. Lieutenant Daniels had all the commo channels worked out and tested. General Petrov had a diagnostic computer down at the control terminal and was ready to connect it and begin loading the scheduling software.

Alexis had Captain Jones call everyone over to her chopper for a last briefing—sometimes having a loud-mouth around could be useful!

Standing on one of the External Stores Support System pylons of her Blackhawk, Alexis scanned the upturned faces of the men, trying to memorize each tense, but eager expression as they were at that moment. It never even crossed her mind to feel insecure about being the only woman among so many men, nor to worry that they would not obey her orders. They were all soldiers, true soldiers in the best meaning of the word, and though they weren't all her men, each was loyal to the last.

"Well men, it's time. The Harrier is already on its way to the silos to the north, and the ground crews will take the closer silos to the southeast. I'll take Mr. Allen's team to the closest WOPR bunker, and everyone else will stay here and work with General Petrov and Lieutenant Daniels. Any questions?" Alexis winced when the word 'WOPR' slipped out. It had a way of insinuating itself into one's thoughts. It didn't seem very professional to use the nickname, but it was hard not to.

One of the Russians put up his hand and asked a question in Russian. Petrov was about to translate, but Alexis beat him to it. "Will we be bombed? I don't think so." As Alexis spoke, the Russian general translated for his men who did not understand English. "In the first place, we've had the folks at Deseret spreading the word to anyone who can hear that we've got a plan. In the second place, I doubt that there's a government left on earth that could get an ICBM off the ground right now. We know the U.S. can't—there is no United States any more—and China is in even worse shape. Reports from ham radio operators in western Europe are pretty definite: the civil governments of those countries no longer exist. I can't see anyone bombing us before we implement Operation Wopperstop." Ouch! There was that word again!

"If we fail, however, I can see one possible source of danger to us here: it is conceivable that a nuclear missile submarine captain could have orders to retaliate if more rockets fly. So, we must not fail."

Ensign Beck put up his hand. "Beg your pardon, ma'am, but what if a boomer is running silent and deep and already has orders to try to nuke this spot?"

"Fair question Ensign, but think about it. I can't say I had a very high opinion of the late Commander in Chief, but I can't imagine that he would have issued anything other than a *retalia-*

tion order. And, if a submarine captain does have orders to fire if
we don't report success, then he'd have to come up to check on our
progress and make sure we hadn't made it. Also, the folks at Deseret
say they've been able to reach someone at Pacific Fleet Command
in Hawaii—it looks like someone is still there, if not exactly in the
saddle."

The ensign nodded.

"Besides, the only known order the president issued before
Washington was destroyed was not to strike back unless it could
be determined that the United States was in danger of being invaded. That isn't happening and isn't going to happen. So, the
only risk I can see would be if we don't stop the machine from
making another attack. In that case, a boomer captain might decide to retaliate on his own, or based on some previous command—
if he didn't get the president's last order. And all of that assumes
their fire-control computers are even working." Alexis waited to let
Petrov catch up. The faces before her were still tense, but not quite
as nervous as before. "Any more questions?"

There were none.

"Good. We need to go. Concentrate! It's easy to get distracted
when you've got one eye scanning the sky for incoming warheads
and another scanning the ground for possible lift-offs! Besides,
you can't see an incoming MIRV, and it's bad for your eyes to look
in two directions at once."

There were a few wry chuckles.

"So stay sharp. Try not to worry about possible incoming bo-
geys. Remember that, thanks to General Petrov, any missile commanders who haven't heard from us also don't have the correct
coordinates for our location. And remember that the folks back
home are counting on us!"

The men were clearly determined, but still dispirited.

"Men, I can't tell you how proud I am to have served with you
here. I have never been privileged to work with a finer and more
dedicated group of soldiers. Your sacrifice, if that's what this turns
out to be, will be the price for an incalculable amount of good. I

am deeply honored to have been your leader," she gave a sidelong look at Petrov, "and your companion. Now, let's go kick some WOPR butt—I'll meet you back here for a beer when it's over!"

The men cheered—the Okie's rebel yell loudest of all—and the group broke. The two Blackhawks destined for the missile field to the southeast revved their engines and were away with their crews. It had turned out that they didn't have enough surface-to-air missiles, or men, to bother sending the Hind along with the two Blackhawks—better to save the fuel. John Allen's team climbed into the back of Alexis' Blackhawk, while the civilian himself climbed into the co-pilot's seat. A few helpers joined Lieutenant Daniels at the radio tent, and the remaining soldiers joined the Russian general in the underground terminal room outside the sealed bulkheads of the control center.

Alexis made a quick tour of the camp to reassure herself that nothing had been forgotten before sliding into the pilot's seat. Throttling the rotor up, she lifted the chopper smoothly, a black shadow sliding into the night. Of all the teams being flown out, Allen's was the one with the closest destination, so she set her speed to a leisurely fuel-conserving pace.

Once in the air and away from the camp, she unplugged her intercom and motioned to Allen to do the same so they could speak in private. "What do you think, John, are they ready?"

He regarded her soberly. "They're scared, Alexis, but I think everyone will do his part."

"Good."

"I think that if we have any problems it will be with the Russians, but old Petrov seems to have them pretty well in hand—and I think your talk helped."

"How so?"

"If our positions were reversed, most of them think their government—or surviving military command—would bomb the site, so they think ours will do the same."

"But we're here! Doesn't that show that at least our military is counting on us to solve the problem?"

342 DON L. TIGGRE

"Not to them." He sighed heavily. "Word spread from our team that we volunteered to come. Somehow, it's a liability in their eyes that we volunteered—it makes our actions look unsanctioned, renegade. They also think this whole expedition could be nothing but PR, an effort made so others can look like they tried peaceful solutions before being forced to resort to a pre-emptive strike, even though that's what's been planned all along. Hearing you actually admit that there could be commanders out there with orders to blast us made sense to them. It's the way they see things."

"Life, what a cynical bunch!" Alexis started to say more, but thought better of it. When she was younger, she would have denied vehemently the very idea that American officials would bomb their own personnel. It would be cold-blooded murder! But she had seen the American flag flying over a tank smashing down a church known to have children inside. Granted, those were FBI agents in the tanks, but it showed that Americans in uniform could be just as cold about killing the innocent as anyone else.

They flew in silence until Allen spoke up again. "Anyway, like I said, I think Petrov's got a pretty good grip on 'em. I heard him giving his own pep-talk last night, reminding them of how many Russians were vaporized in the last exchange. Lots of them have family out there, and they don't want to see more incoming warheads any more than we want to see outgoing ones."

"Good old Petrov. I really like him."

Allen agreed and then fell silent.

At 2:07 a.m., local time, Alexis set down outside the #2 bunker. General Petrov had reported that the countermand computer in Moscow had gone off-line at 3:54 a.m. local time, two weeks before, so the machine shouldn't order the second offensive in less than an hour and forty-five minutes, if it was going to do so at all.

Allen handed Alexis her end of their intercom and jumped out to join his team—half Russian and half American—as they carted their equipment over to the bunker entrance. According to Petrov, the door in the mound was not rigged to the WOPR's sensors; its designers had not wanted the weather or a stray animal to set it off. One of the Russians, a stout fellow with light brown hair, had been on the last team to service this bunker. He pulled out a set of keys and unlocked the door, while one of the Americans set up a portable light on a stand.

Alexis scanned the clear night sky. The stars blazed in a spectacular display undimmed by clouds. "Commo check. John, can you hear me?" Through her window, she could see him fumble at his belt for his end of the wired intercom.

"Roger that, Alexis. Loud and clear!"

She switched to the chopper's radio. "Daniels, commo check. You read?"

The lieutenant's voice came back immediately: "Roger that, General Thomas. Loud and clear!"

"Is Petrov in position?"

"Yes, ma'am. He's got his maintenance computer hooked up to the external terminal and has already typed in the command to copy the software onto the WOPR CPUs. He says he's ready to go, as soon as Mr. Allen's team is ready with the explosives and the other teams are in position."

"Roger. How about Allistair, and the other two choppers?"

"They are still en route, ma'am. I can patch their signals through, if you'd like to talk to them."

"Yes, please do, Lieutenant."

There was a pause. "Okay General, everyone's linked up. The ground crews will be linked in too, once they are dropped off. I can't patch Allen through your console from here, but you'll be able to talk to General Petrov."

"All right men, I want to be able to talk to everyone without changing channels or having Lieutenant Daniels relay, so keep the chatter down. If we have to fall back to Mr. Allen's plan, every second will count. Understood?"

There was a chorus of responses. "That's a good example of what I want to avoid, so no transmissions unless you are respond-

344 DON L. TIGGRE

ing to remarks directed at you, specifically. Allistair, what's your ETA on patrol?"

"One hour, fifteen minutes, General."

"Petrov, are you ready?"

"Yes, Alexa. We will play chess here until the rest of you are ready."

Alexis suppressed a chuckle. "Hawk One, your ETA?"

"We'll be in position to drop off the first ground crew in about twenty minutes, General."

"Hawk Two?

"Ditto, mayum!"

"Excellent. Let me know when you are in position—especially you, Allistair; everything else should be ready when you arrive on patrol."

"Yes, ma'am!"

Alexis switched to the intercom. She could see that some of Allen's team was inside, on the stairs that led down to the sealed door at the bottom. "John, how's it going?" As she asked, the rest of the team passed through the door and started descending.

"All right, I guess. This is one *looong* stairwell! I wonder how they built this place without anyone stateside catching on..." He stopped talking while the bobbing light disappeared down into the earth. It seemed that he was silent longer than it should take to reach the bottom, but his voice eventually squawked back over the intercom: "Okay, we've got everything we need down here— Petrov's boys are just a little skittish about putting the charges on the door."

"He said he didn't think they would trigger the system."

"*Think* being the operative word there..."

"Well, tell them to take it slow. Allistair won't be on station for more than an hour."

"Do you think it's worth the fuel, Alexis? Even if he sees one, his chances of shooting an ICBM down can't be very good, and that would only be one out of dozens in his patrol area."

"If there is a second wave, John, every single rocket we stop could mean tens of thousands of lives saved back home. It's worth it."

"I know, I guess... It just seems like such a long shot. And I can't even begin to guess what the probabilities are on what I'll be doing. Be right back." He clicked off for another time that felt longer than it was, reemerging with the other soldiers after Alexis had seen the dancing glow of the lamp return to the top of the stairwell. "All set, Alexis. They held 'em against the metal and then switched on the magnets, just like Petrov told them to. We've got the reader here, as close as we can get it without exposing it to the blast, so we're set." The men headed back toward the Blackhawk. "It's cold out here. We'll wait in the chopper with you."

The men climbed back into the helicopter, Allen dropping heavily back into the co-pilot's seat. They waited in silence, each wrapped in his or her own thoughts.

Some time later, Alexis caught Allen looking at her across the dark cockpit. The contrast between his coal black hair and fair skin was softened by the glow coming off the instrumentation. Though she had never seen him exercise, he was as fit as ever—not bulked out like a body builder or a football player, but broad-chested and wiry, more like a prize fighter. He was a beautiful person, in a masculine way. Funny, how such a physically impressive person earned his living thinking about computer problems...and was afraid of flying! He tried to hide it, but the evidence kept on piling up; it wasn't mere dislike, but real fear. Alexis had seen him gripping hand-rests and shifting in his seat during every flight—he even did it in airliners! She wondered again why he had volunteered to come.

For his part, Allen saw Alexis returning his gaze in the dim light and his heart did a somersault. He had been fighting various apprehensions since leaving Utah, not the least of which was all the flying around, but now found that he was no longer frightened. His feelings for Alexis had been a counterbalance to his fear, keeping it from paralyzing him. Now, watching her move, watching her think, watching her act, his love ballooned in his chest, leaving no room for apprehension. Whatever happened next, right at that moment, he was with the one woman he respected, admired, and desired above all others—he couldn't imagine wanting to be anywhere else. He knew that she didn't share his feeling of love, it was clear in the way she spoke to him, but that didn't matter to him. What mattered as that they were together, working on something that was important. Could life get any better than that?

After several more minutes of quiet introspection, Allen cleared his throat. "Alexis, why do you say 'Life' all the time?"

"Say what?"

"'Life.' You know, like, 'Life, what a cynical bunch!'"

The general cocked her head to one side and thought about it. "You know, I don't think I ever really thought about it, but... I don't believe in God, and we have all these expressions, like 'God knows why!'" She thought about it a little longer. "I guess I got into the habit because it didn't seem right to go around saying 'God' all the time when I'm not a believer, and if there's one thing I come close to worshipping, it's Life itself. I think all Life is precious, human Life especially so."

"That's... A remarkable thing for a soldier to say." The civilian leaned back against his window—every time he thought he knew her, Alexis showed an interesting new side of herself he hadn't yet seen. And every time it happened, he loved what he discovered!

"I'm not in the Army to kill, John, but to defend. The two can be the same, sometimes, but as motivations, they are entirely different."

"Oh, I didn't mean it that way—I meant... I just meant that your mind is a remarkable thing..."

She chuckled and the conversation died out again.

He checked his watch. Less than a half-hour had passed since the shaped charges had been affixed to the below-ground portal to the bunker. The reader was ready, to one side of the above-ground door. Everything was set. There was nothing to do but wait.

The radio squawked. "Hawk One to Hawk leader, all ground

forces deployed. I'm setting down in the center of my patrol area, until it's time to tango."

Allen jumped at the sudden interruption of his thoughts, but Alexis responded with absolute calm. "Roger that, Hawk One. Good idea, Captain Stewart; we need to save all the fuel we can."

"Thank you, General. Hawk One out."

A short while later, Hawk Two made the same announcement. As the Harrier continued north, the crews of all the teams counted the remaining minutes down. Time had flown by that afternoon, when they were trying to get everything ready, but now that things were in place, it dragged at a snail's pace. The seconds clicking off on their console readouts felt as long as minutes, or hours.

Finally, Alexis turned to Allen. "He'll be there soon. Time to get out and get ready to blow that door, if the machine doesn't like what Petrov does."

"Right." He crawled aft and exited the chopper with his team.

"General Petrov," Alexis keyed her microphone, "Mr. Allen's team has the charges in place and is ready to blow the door. Allistair should be on patrol soon. Standing by?"

"Yes, General Thomaseva, we are standing by. A single keystroke, and we will see what we will see!"

"Roger that." She switched off her mic and noted the time on her watch: 3:33 a.m. C'mon Allistair, where are you, dammit!

As if in answer to her thoughts, the Englishman's voice cackled over the radio. "Royal Air Force on station, General Thomas."

"Glad to hear it, Major Allistair!" Alexis checked the time again. No point in waiting; the machine would go off on its own soon enough, if they didn't stop it. "Hawk One and Two. In the air! Ground crews, ready your rocket launchers! Mr. Allen, stand by on that detonator switch! General Petrov, stand by!"

"Hawk One, on station!"

"Hawk Two, on station!"

"All right Pavel, load that software!"

For a few tense heartbeats, there was nothing but static, then the Russian General's tightly controlled voice came over the airwaves. "The system is not responding, General Thomas. Repeat, the system is not responding! It is ignoring the commands from the diagnostic computer—I've tried several!"

"Roger that." Alexis was the hub, she had to stay calm and cool, or the others wouldn't perform at peak efficiency. "Mr. Allen, you are clear to blow the door. Repeat, blow the—"

She didn't feel a tremor in the ground—too deep for that—but the fire and smoke that belched out of the stairwell could not be missed. The Russian who knew the interior lay-out of the bunker was the first in, followed by two men carrying the disk reader, and John Allen bringing up the rear. Smoke was still billowing out the upper doorway as their light dimmed and then disappeared down into the earth.

"General Petrov, the door is blown. Mr. Allen's team is on its way down. Do you see any sign of a response from the machine?"

"Negative. The system is completely frozen; we are locked out." There was a pause, after which Petrov's agitated voice returned. "General Thomaseva, we are locked out. Even if Mr. Allen does recover password, I do not think I will be able to enter it!" He was forgetting his articles again.

"One thing at a time, General Petrov. Allistair, any signs of portals opening?"

"Negative, Hawk Leader. All quiet up here."

"Hawk One?"

"Negative."

"Hawk Two?"

"No, mayum!!"

Alexis thumbed the intercom. "John, talk to me. What's going on?"

"We're at the CPU Alexis, and they're cutting the drive out right now... But the system looks frozen—which is funny because it's really hot and stuffy in here. It smells like ozone and burnt insulation, and I don't think it's all because of what we did to the door. My Russian friend here says he's never seen it like this. There are several malfunction lights burning and error messages on the screens that show anything at all. Okay, we've got the drive out and I'm putting it in the reader... Stand by for the password!"

Alexis switched back to the radio and relayed Allen's report to Petrov. "What gives, General? Did the system here freeze up as a response to the unauthorized entry?"

"I'm not sure, Alexis, I... No, it should be flashing warnings—there should even be an audible siren!"

"Allistair, still no sign?"

"Negative."

"Hawk One?"

"Negative."

"Hawk Two?"

"Hawk Two, negative. That's a big N-O! Yeeee-haw!"

Alexis rolled her eyes. "Can the chatter, Hawk Two. Ground crews, report if you see anything."

Silence.

"Petrov, what's going on?"

"I don't know... Is definitely something wrong."

Allen chimed in over the intercom. "Alexis, this disk is empty. There's no password here, that I can see. The diagnostic reader says the file structure is messed up. There are empty files being reported as having many kilobytes of data and other allocation problems. I repeat: the disk has been scrambled!"

Alexis relayed the news to Petrov, who was unaware of the history of the words when he voiced into the mic: "Obviously a major malfunction."

Chatter, laughter, and curses took over the bandwidth.

"Everyone pipe down and stay sharp!" Alexis bellowed. "We could be dealing with some kind of launch delay. Everyone stay off the air for the next five minutes, unless you have something new to report!"

The five minutes passed very slowly, but silently; no hostile activity was reported. "Everyone stand by. General Petrov, what's the word from control?"

"We're blowing the door here, stand by." Petrov's voice was

calmer and his articles were back. When he came back on the air, his voice was trembling slightly, but it was still under control. "The system is completely frozen up here too! I suggest we verify at the third bunker—it could still be active and firing from sites other than the ones our surveillance teams are monitoring—but it would seem that the whole system is inoperative."

"Roger that, General Petrov. I'll take Mr. Allen and his team to the third bunker to verify, but it looks like the show's been canceled!"

All of the units remained silent, absorbing the implications.

Petrov's voice was now completely under control again. "Agreed. Everyone else should return to base, you need to conserve fuel. Something has gone very wrong—or right."

"Roger that. Back to base everyone." Alexis couldn't keep herself from laughing. "Lieutenant Daniels, get on the horn and tell Deseret that Frankenstein's monster didn't work, and make sure they spread the word!"

"Yes, ma'am!" More laughter and cheers spread over the airwaves. This time she let them shout and laugh all they wanted—she knew all too well the powerful relief they were feeling.

When there was a break in the chatter, Alexis called for silence again. "Daniels, let's drop this conference call here... When you get Deseret on the air, I want to talk to them on a clear channel."

"Yes, General."

Allen had time to round up his equipment and get it stowed before the response came back from Deseret. He had his team on board and Alexis was lifting off when Daniels reported the connection.

A familiar baritone voice came over her helmet speakers. "Brigadier General Thomas, this is *the* General of Deseret Air Force here. I hear you have some good news for me?"

"Yes, General. We have just determined that at least two out of the three CPUs of the WOPR are off-line and will not be launching any more missiles."

"Of the *what*, General?"

"Of the...Doomsday Device, sir. We are en route to the third bunker to verify that the entire system is down, but had teams monitoring two of the missile fields the machine would have ordered to strike. There has been no hostile activity—no activity at all—and both of the CPUs we have already accessed are completely inoperative."

"That's great news, General. What do you think happened?"

"We're not sure yet, sir, but, given what I know about Y2K problems, I think the system may have been bitten by the Millennium Bug!"

"Y2K? But the system fired well after the new year began..."

"Yes, sir, it did, but it was dormant up until that time. My guess is that when it came on-line, it performed the first instructions it had, and then fell to a Y2K malfunction some time after that. We were actually planning on introducing a Y2K problem into the system ourselves, but found that it was already frozen up when we made the attempt."

"Terrific! When will you have confirmation on the third CPU?"

"Within the hour, General."

"Excellent! Regardless of how it happened, your team is to be commended for its efforts, General."

"Thank you, sir." Alexis hesitated. "Will it be possible for you to send an extraction team, sir?"

"Things are very tense here, General, as I'm sure you can understand. The country has collapsed into complete chaos, except here in Deseret. We have only a finite amount of fuel and aircraft, and we must husband them wisely. The loss of the C-5 was most unfortunate, and we don't want to lose any more aircraft."

Alexis couldn't say what she really wanted to tell him, so she simply replied, "I understand."

"But we don't want to abandon you either!" He added hastily. "Here's what I want you to do: you have several heavily armed aircraft and extra fuel. See if you can make it back on your own, or, at least, see if you can make it back to Alaska. We've lost contact with Elmendorf, but it's bound to be safer than Novosibirsk proved to be."

"Sir, that's over 3,500 miles, even with the extra fuel, there's no way..."

"I know how far it is General! I'm only asking you to try. You're not in any immediate danger, are you?"

"No, sir."

"Very well then: *try.* Bring your force as far back as you can. Perhaps you can even find some airfields along the way where you can secure more fuel. If you get stuck somewhere, whatever distance you've covered will increase the odds that anything we send out for you will have enough fuel to turn around and get you all back to friendlier airspace."

"Understood. We'll do our best, sir!"

"I'm sure you will. Thank you, General. Deseret out."

"Thomas out."

For a while, the only things that could be heard in the cabin were the howl of the engines and the rushing of the air.

"You know," Allen was the one who broke the stillness, "I was thinking they'd pull a stunt like that."

"We all knew this could be a one-way ticket when we came out here, Mr. Allen." Alexis' voice betrayed no emotion. "It was more than they had to do to lend us the C-5."

"I know, but...it just...seems a little ungrateful. We came over here to save their butts too!"

"Gratitude is irrelevant. He has millions of civilians to protect, and has to make the best tactical decision he can. I'd do the same thing, if I were in his position."

He searched her face, then passed a hand over his eyes. "Yeah, I understand... But that doesn't mean I have to like it."

"I never said I liked it either!"

Allen grinned. "So, how far do you think we'll get? Even with the external fuel tanks, these choppers will only go about eleven hundred nautical miles—that's not even halfway to Alaska."

Alexis was impressed all over again by his knowledge of military aircraft. He may not like to fly, but he was a professional and he knew his stuff! "I've been thinking about that. We'll have to play hopscotch, as General Weber suggested."

"Hopscotch?"

"Yes, hopscotch. We'll load up the extra tanks, and pack as much fuel as we can into the choppers themselves. It'll be a tight fit, with the Frenchmen not having a ride home, but it's our only choice. Then we'll head east, stopping at every airfield we can find to refill or top off our fuel tanks. Petrov can probably show us some that aren't even on the maps. I remember talking to the captain of the C-5 about a city a little over a thousand miles east of here called Irkutsk, it's got an airport. That might be a place to start."

Allen suddenly realized the implications of what she was saying. "Five thousand miles in a helicopter! Maybe I'll stay here instead!"

They both laughed, but had different reasons for believing his comment was a joke.

CHAPTER 45:
WEDNESDAY, APRIL 26, 2000

"No one knows what it's like to be hated
To be fated, To telling only lies
But my dreams, They aren't as empty
As my conscience seems to be."
—The Who, *Behind Blue Eyes*

Angel looked down with disgust at another crawling actress. This time it was Holly Hills, possibly the most famous porn star of the late nineties, celebrated for her fiery red hair and equally fiery performances. She was groveling now, as all the others had before her. None of these stupid whores had half the strength of character Rosalia had! Ah Rosa, if only you could see things my way...

Still, at least the conquest of the gated communities was establishing an effective foraging force. Ejercito Dragon was well fed, and now that he had turned his attention to abandoned National Guard depots, they were increasingly well armed, clothed, and provisioned. Now, if he could only figure out some way to get the electricity turned back on...

Click!

His gun was in the actress' hands. She had pulled the trigger. He would be sexless now, if the pistol had been loaded.

¡Por Dios!

He held out his hand, but instead of turning it over to him, she brought it to her temple and pulled the trigger again. Click.

"Good try!" Angel laughed. "Now give me the gun."

She snarled and threw it across the room.

He slapped her across the face. "You pass the test, but don't ever do that to *my* gun!"

"Test?"

"Yes, at last! I was almost out of movie stars... You're good, you know; you had me believing you were as stupid as the rest. You wouldn't believe how many women in your position reached right past the gun and into my pants. I'm not dumb enough to leave a loaded gun where you could get at it, but I've been looking for a woman with enough guts and brains to seize opportunities."

"You're not going to kill me?"

"Not now, not if you cooperate." He held out his hand to help her up. She ignored it and stood on her own. "I've been looking for someone who can understand what I'm doing, someone worth having at my side. If you play your cards right, I will make you Queen of all California."

"Hah! I'd rather die!"

"That can be arranged," Angel chuckled. "But not yet. You're too valuable as a reward for one of my captains." He paused and tried to look thoughtful. In fact, he had no idea what he was doing, or how to get what he wanted. And what did he want? He wanted to find someone like Rosalia, but who wouldn't make him angry all the time. "Still, this is a better beginning."

Thinking of Rosalia had given him an idea.

He retrieved his pistol, slapped in a magazine, and chambered a round. "Now, let's go."

She obeyed, desperately looking for a break—some opportunity to make a run for it. She didn't get one. She was packed into a truck with other prisoners, former neighbors and employees of Newport Beach Villas, the fenced mini-town that had fallen to Ejercito Dragon that night. Some were crying. Most sat despondent, showing few signs of life. The truck reeked of human fear and excrement.

She had some thought of trying to get everyone to rush the guards when they opened the doors, but her former fellow citizens were too afraid. Their terror and misery were so thick around her, she thought she might feel it with her fingers if she stretched out her hand. When they arrived at their destination and the doors were opened, it was obvious that rushing the guards wouldn't have worked anyway. There were at least twenty of them visible, all with their rifles pointing at the prisoners. She started to shuffle along with the others. Where would they be taken?

One of the guards stepped up and pulled her aside. She was blindfolded and pressed into the back seat of a car. The car drove for a long time—how long, she couldn't tell—taking many turns before it stopped and she was ordered to get out. She could feel herself being led across a parking lot, up some stairs, and into a building. She lost track of the twists of the hallways and thought she might have ridden an elevator, but she hadn't felt it move. Finally, she was shoved through a doorway.

Hearing the door slammed behind her, she decided it was safe to take the blindfold off. It made no difference—for all she could see, she was at the bottom of a coal mine. Groping back toward where she'd heard the door thump shut, she found the edge of the door frame and then a light switch.

She flipped the switch and the room was flooded with bright fluorescent light. It was a large room, all decorated in white. Lavishly furnished, the room had a thick white rug, white chairs, an enormous entertainment center, and an entire wall taken up by floor-to-ceiling bookcases. There was also a huge four-poster bed, in which a young woman was sitting up, blinking. She had a scar over her right eye.

"¿Angel?" The woman blinked in the light. "¿A que hora me levantas ahora?"

The actress had her own questions. She'd expected some kind of torture chamber—maybe a room full of those horny captains her kidnapper had referred to. Whoever this Hispanic woman with the long dark hair was, she didn't look like a rapist or an inquisitor. "Are you the Queen?"

"Queen?" Rosalia eyed the newcomer oddly. What was Angel up to?

"Sorry, it was something that man said when he kidnapped me. Who are you?"

"My name is Rosalia. I was a childhood friend of Angel Jesus Ramos Ortega, and now I am his prisoner. Who are you?"

Whoever she was, this Rosalia had obviously not seen any porno flicks recently. Judging from the number of books present, maybe that wasn't surprising. "I'm Holly Hills." The name obviously meant nothing to her, so Holly added, "I'm an actress. I guess it was this Anhel of yours who kidnapped me. He attacked the little town my neighbors and I had made out of our neighborhood. Who is he? Do you know what he wants?"

Rosalia inclined her head to one side. "Angel calls himself the general of Ejercito Dragon, the Dragon Army. He was a gang leader in Central Los Angeles before The Collapse, and now he seems to be building a real army. As to what he wants... Well, he doesn't tell me what is in his heart, though sometimes he comes to argue with me about what is in his mind. Whatever else he wants, he wants my love, and that he'll never have."

"Is that why you're here? But then... Why did he kidnap me?" Holly came over and stood by the bed. "He tried to scare me with something about 'giving me to his captains.' Why would he put me in here, with you, instead of with them?"

Rosalia glanced briefly at the mirror on the wall opposite the bed. "I don't know, but it probably has something to do with why his goons woke me up in the middle of the night and moved me back into this room."

"Back?"

"Yes, I woke up here when he first kidnapped me. I went a little crazy and trashed the place. I've been in a smaller room with only a cot and the books since then. *Do you like books?*"

There was something peculiarly intense about the way Rosalia locked eyes with Holly that made her understand that the question was very important. "Uh, yeah. Books are great." She wasn't sure what she was supposed to say, or do.

"Wonderful!" Rosalia bounced up and sauntered over to the

bookcase. She pulled out a copy of George Orwell's *1984* and thumbed through it. "I find that books like these help me through hard times." She motioned for Holly to join her and held her slender index finger under the passage that read:

> 'Now we can see you,' said the voice. Stand out in the
> middle of the room. Stand back to back. Clasp your hands
> behind your heads. Do not touch one another.

"I've read this one many times." Rosalia flipped to another page and pointed to the word 'he' and then the word 'listening.' She shifted her eyes to the left, indicating the mirror without moving her head.

"Yes," Holly agreed, "I understand. Books make me feel better when I'm upset too."

Blue eyes gazed into black, and both knew that they did understand one another.

CHAPTER 46:
MONDAY, MAY 1, 2000

"You say you got a real solution
Well you know
We'd all love to see the plan."
—The Beatles, *Revolution*

In a medium-sized meeting room on the thirty-third floor of the world headquarters office building of the LDS Church, an unusual discussion was getting underway.

The view of the Great Salt Lake and of the towering peaks of the Wasatch Front was breathtaking. Nature's grandeur was at its height, with the emerald tide of spring filling the valley, splashing up against the gray stone and glistening snow-caps of the mountains. It had to be admitted, however, that the beauty was not all nature's doing; years of back-breaking toil by Mormon pioneers in the late 1840s had gone into building the irrigation ditches that made the desert bloom in the Salt Lake valley.

Meaning no disrespect to nature or their ancestors, those gathered in the room that day were more appreciative of the electricity and other amenities they enjoyed.

Elder Jared Christensen, now of the First Quorum of 70, called the group to order. "Ladies and gentlemen, we are here to discuss the growth of Deseret."

Governor Waller and Kirsten Bytheway were the only women in the gathering of about fifteen Church, business, and government leaders assembled for the meeting. The governor's role was obvious, but Mrs. Bytheway's role—as the matriarch of an old

Utah family that had come through Y2K with an enormous quantity of functioning business assets—might well prove more important. The men in the group, including Elder Young, who was there on behalf of the President of the Church, all headed up business concerns or other powerful factions.

Conspicuously absent were any state legislators; people had lost confidence in the political process—it was only because of her enormous personal prestige that the governor had any clout left at all.

It was the kind of meeting that could not have happened since the time of kings: a gathering of minds that could decide upon things for a whole nation and set them in motion, without discussion or permission from anyone else.

"Ladies and gentlemen," Jared repeated, a little louder, "we are here to listen, to learn, and to make strategic decisions—decisions that will determine the fate of Deseret, and possibly of all of America, and hence the world."

All heads turned toward the doctor and an appreciative silence settled over the assembly.

"Before going over the reports and maps, I would like remind everyone that all the rules have changed." He made eye contact with each of the government people, particularly the head of the Department of Transportation. "Utah no longer exists. We are again settlers of Deseret, facing an uncertain future. When the pioneers got here a hundred and fifty-three years ago, they knew they were taking their lives in their own hands. There were no guaranteed happy endings, nor even guarantees of survival. We must embrace that spirit and make decisions as best we can—and we must take action. For perhaps a brief time, politics don't matter. If we decide wisely, our decisions will be ratified in the future. If we decide unwisely, Deseret will fall and chaos will take our people."

There were some odd expressions around the table, but most of those present had already reached essentially the same conclusions.

Jared, the only one standing, unfurled a large map of the western region of the former United States, on which Deseret had been shaded green. There were towns and cities to the north and south shaded with yellow circles. Some, in southeastern Idaho, were so closely packed that most of that area was shaded yellow.

"As you've probably seen in the report the Governor circulated yesterday, we have already received many responses to the proclamation of the re-establishment of Deseret. The yellow shading indicates communities that have voted to ask for admission. Most of them are towns in which the Latter Day Saint majority followed the Church's lead in preparing for Y2K and hence had enough cohesion left to be able to hold town meetings and vote. There are probably more LDS communities out there that haven't heard the proclamation yet, as well as others where the people have been so devastated that they haven't been able to respond."

"What about people and places that get surrounded by Deseret territory? Won't they make it difficult to enforce our laws?"

Jared didn't catch who asked the question, but it was one he was prepared for. "That's already happened, with the Blackfoot Indian Reservation. The Indians are right between Pocatello and Idaho Falls, both of which have asked for admission to Deseret. They were worried about it too, until we reassured them that we would not hinder their business, religion, or passage through Deseret. In some ways, it's as though nothing has changed. Before The Collapse, it was the state of Idaho that surrounded them, and they had a separate jurisdiction back then as well. Cars, people, produce, everything went right through the border as though it wasn't there, but the tribe administered its own laws within that area."

"Are you saying that we should have completely open borders, and not worry about pockets of heathen or gentile law in the middle of our own territory?" It was Lane Smith, an elderly businessman from southern Utah.

"It was never a problem before; I don't see why we should make it one now." Jared leaned forward and placed both of his hands on the map for emphasis. "Actually, your question touches on two issues. The most basic issue is that, right now, there is a power vacuum and no organized opposition to our activities. If we start annexing reservations, cities, or even just land, by force, we will give every pocket of civilization around us a reason to fear us. If we are seen as predatory—and make no mistake, that's how everyone but Latter Day Saints would view such actions—opposition will organize overnight."

"But we have border guards now!"

"Yes, but they're not really stopping anyone from going about their business, except for obvious criminals. If we had done it any other way, resentment and hatred would be brewing all around us, even as we speak. And that task alone has taxed our resources sorely. We simply cannot go around conquering people who do not threaten us and who only wish to be left alone. It would be wrong, even if it were not clearly a tactical blunder to do so. No. Persuasion is a far better route."

"What do you mean by persuasion?" This from Mrs. Bytheway. "Are you going to try to argue the Ute out of being Ute?"

"Not at all." Jared counted to ten mentally. He was a doctor, not a...a politician! He wished, not for the last time, that someone else more suited to the task had been chosen to serve in this role. "But consider the Native American and non-LDS communities that could end up finding themselves surrounded by Deseret territory. Think about what would happen over time. Either our ways would prove to be better, in which case most people would choose to join us, or their ways would prove to be better, in which case we could learn from what they are doing. If things are the same, but done differently, why should we aggress upon them or they upon us?"

He gave everyone a sharp look and thumped the map with his fingers. "Remember that we are only looking at a piece of paper here. Any attempt to move a border on this paper must either be done by force or by consent in the real world—and I'm telling you, force is not the right path. Coercing gentiles is not a path our Heavenly Father would approve of, and it is also the path guaranteed to cause outsiders to attack us. Either way, it would seal our doom, because we would have strayed from the path of righteousness."

"But still," Smith could not seem to come to grips with the concept, "I'm told that our border guards aren't even searching incoming cars for guns or drugs." He sat forward and waved his gnarled hands as he spoke, decidedly unhappy with the policy. "Open borders and autonomous pockets could lead to a situation wherein evil-minded men set up camps right in our midst and then prey upon us!"

Jared did not care for the way the conversation was going. This was worse than herding cats! "Look," he took a deep breath to calm himself, "if we can't agree on this basic principle, there is no point in any further discussion, because the state of Deseret will tear itself apart before any of the rest matters! It's simple, really, you can see the facts and figures in the reports yourselves. Either we concentrate on building something new, or we revert to barbarism, fighting to hold on to that which cannot be saved.

"You say you are worried about people bringing drugs into Deseret? I say that in these times, any people stupid enough to waste resources dulling their minds will be dead long before they can be a problem to us!

"You say you are worried about people bringing guns into Deseret? I say that we should welcome everyone with the intestinal fortitude to defend him or herself and their families! We can't possibly stop every crime that is happening in the world today, so if the people do not assume responsibility for preventing crimes themselves, crimes will not be stopped at all, and the land will run red with blood!"

That got their attention.

"Our ancestors carried guns, and that's the only reason they made it out of Missouri and then Illinois alive. When we were an oppressed minority, the authorities tried to disarm us. When they arrested Joseph Smith, the governor of Illinois told our forefathers: 'I know there is prejudice against you on account of your peculiar

religion, but you ought to be praying Saints, not military Saints.'
Are we now going to fill his shoes and look with suspicion at anyone with the means to defend him or herself?"

No one moved.

"And did the Prophet not defend himself from the mob with a
gun?"

No one breathed a word.

"Take a look at Brigham Young's statue: he went around with
a positively huge gun strapped to his leg! I tell you that if my
family and I had been stripped of our weapons on our way here
last month, we would be dead and I would not be standing here
right now!"

Jared had the momentum and he took full advantage of it.

"The Prophet said that the Constitution—and that includes
the right to keep and bear arms and the rest of the rights guaranteed by the Bill of Rights—was a divinely inspired document.
Those words are carved in stone, right across the street in Temple
Square." He pointed out the window, toward the temple. "That's
clear enough instruction for me. Is there anyone here for whom it
is not?"

Silence.

"Very well then. We will proceed in a manner befitting a free
people. We will allow people the free agency that God requires
they have in order for them to be able to *choose* to follow Him, and
not presume to judge in His place. We will lead by example, and
not by force. We will not allow the exigencies of the day to become
a temptation to fall into the trap of the police state. If the twentieth century taught us nothing else, it surely taught us that the
scourge of totalitarianism is not only evil—whatever pretexts are
given for it—but that it just doesn't work!!"

Into the shocked silence that followed came the crackling rustle
of a chair being rolled back from the table. Elder Young stood and
began clapping. Most of the others joined in and Jared blushed.
"Well said, Elder Christensen! It is the opinion of the Quorum of
the Twelve that we should, as you suggest, honor our pioneer an-

cestors by taking this crisis and turning it into an opportunity to do the work of God. The president also agrees with former president Ezra Taft Benson that the proper role of government it to protect rights, and thinks it should be limited to that function. The Church, he reminded me, is not the government—we are a voluntary association. Our resources should be channeled to supporting the family values we believe in and to building a new Deseret, even greater than the original. Neither the Church nor the state should squander resources on needless conflict." He sat down.

Well, that pretty much settles it, Jared thought.

There was no further argument.

Jared cleared his throat and started up again. "Since we seem to have reached consensus on that matter, let me share with you some details not in the governor's report. There are a few places, particularly around Silicon Valley and Indianapolis, where larger, more organized communities seem to be coalescing, but nothing nearby. You've got to understand how many terrified people there are all around us, people who believe they are all alone in the night. When they see a place that's safe from gangs and criminals, and is actually growing—causing the desert to bloom—they often want to join us. It's happening already: fully seventy-five percent of the people arriving at our borders say they are coming here to live and work. Of the remaining twenty-five percent, by the time they pass through Deseret, only five percent opt to continue to their original destination. That means that ninety-five percent of those who come here find that *this is the place!*"

He fixed Mrs. Bytheway with a gentle, but unwavering gaze. "This is what I mean by persuasion and leading by example. People see what we are doing here and decide that we must be on to something. The welcome centers report that most of the gentiles arriving express a genuine interest in learning more about our faith. Every stake president and most ward bishops are reporting a large increase in new Church members. Some are Saints newly arrived to Deseret from elsewhere, but more are converts." He transferred his gaze to Lane Smith. "All of this is happening simply by allowing people the opportunity to choose to join us."

He traced an outline on the map with his fingers. "The original Deseret included what became Utah, but also about half of Arizona, Colorado, Wyoming, and Idaho, as well as parts of New Mexico and California—not to mention *all* of Nevada. If we continue growing as we are now, we may well end up covering more territory with the new state of Deseret!"

"How will we manage all that growth, pay for all the construction and repairs that need to be done?"

"Excellent questions... Mr. Skousen, isn't it?" Jared got a nod and continued. "Especially since the Church put out the word early on, encouraging all Latter Day Saints to continue accepting those meaningless little pieces of paper with 'Federal Reserve Note' and 'FEMAscrip' printed on them. I'll let Mr. Huntsman explain his idea now, and then I'll say a few more things when he is done. Mr. Huntsman?"

Mr. Huntsman was a youngish looking man with straight brown hair parted neatly on one side. He stood when Jared sat down. "I was a vice president in operations at U.S. West, before The Collapse. With the Church's help—I would not have had work crews without the Church's help—I am the one who has kept the phones working here in Deseret."

He fell silent, allowing some time for everyone to reflect upon what a great blessing it was for them to still have telephone service—as well as the many other things still working because of that service.

"Between the phone service and the surplus power generation capacity here in the state of Deseret, we are more than lucky to be living in greater comfort than most people; we are actually sitting on some very valuable assets. And not just any assets, but assets to which access can be sold in small, transferable quantities." He stopped to grin and scratch his head. "Actually, I can't take full credit for the idea; I got it from Big Bob and his First Freehold Bank of America."

There were a few laughs around the table.

"Old Bob is a little nutty—I've met him—but there's no denying he came up with a great idea. How many of you haven't seen his coins?"

"They're everywhere!" Mrs. Bytheway's enthusiasm for the discussion increased markedly. "All our family businesses prefer them, and wouldn't take Federal Reserve Notes or FEMAscrip at all, if we had our druthers." She carefully avoided looking at Elder Young. "I had no idea Big Bob had so much gold!"

"He didn't." Huntsman seized the cue. "He had enough to get the thing going, and he had a *lot* of bullets, which suddenly became worth more than gold to most people. He started trading bullets for gold, melting the gold down and minting his coins. He has been able to make an enormous profit—you should see the size of the garrison he has at each bank location!—and put a new currency into circulation. Overnight he became one of the most powerful men in America, and not just because he could pay people in gold, but because he could feed, clothe, and house his people too. But more importantly, he single-handedly rebooted the national economy—which had come to a complete halt."

"So, are you suggesting that we should get into the business of bullets and gold?"

"No ma'am, I'm not. We can do better, and do more to get America going than even Bob has been able to do. He's got it started again—we want to get it *running* again!"

"How?" Several people asked this at once.

"Do you remember how popular pre-paid phone cards had become before The Collapse? Well, some people were actually using them like money, trading them with other people, exchanging them for things they wanted, and so on. It was basically the same thing Big Bob has people doing now, except that the cards didn't have the intrinsic value his coins do. We are not sitting on as much gold as Big Bob, but we are sitting on a lot of unused phone service and electric power. We can replace all the piles of greenbacks we've caused people to accumulate with phone cards and power cards that will be as cheap to make as paper money—cheaper if we make them with magnetic strips so they can be recycled back to us and issued again—and will be redeemable by anyone for valuable commodities."

"Yes!" Bytheway was getting excited. "The people will be very glad to get rid of useless paper money, and businesses within Deseret will be back on a sound basis!"

"And," someone else chipped in, "we could send out expeditions to reestablish phone service in other places. Deseret Phone Dollars—or whatever we call them—could become a national currency, like Bob's gold coins!"

"And that would fund the repair and maintenance of telecommunications across America, maybe even internationally!"

"And that would give us more work to give all the immigrants we're getting!"

"And something to pay them with! This is fantastic!"

"*WAIT a minute!*" It was Smith again. "Flying J and Sinclair Oil, I gather, still have most of their facilities intact. Once they hear what we're doing with the phone system, they'll do the same with gasoline, since it too has become a precious commodity. How do we stop them from flooding the market with pre-paid gas cards? Or anyone else sitting on anything scarce from doing the same?"

What a wet blanket, Jared thought to himself. Better let Huntsman answer—he didn't trust himself not to get cross and say something out of line.

"We don't stop them." Huntsman took it calmly. "If they want to jump in, so much the better! It's the same as with the borders; we don't have time or resources to stop other people from doing anything. We have to concentrate on building things ourselves. So some other folks introduce another currency, who cares? The value of our cards may fluctuate a lot while things are starting back up again, but they'll settle out. We would be putting out easy to use and easy to exchange units that would be redeemable for valuable commodities. Whatever anyone else does won't affect that. Value other people create won't take away from the value of what we're doing. Once the currencies are widely accepted, banks could even get back in business—though I think the practice of fractional reserve banking should be prohibited!"

Huntsman remembered a way of looking at things he had learned from Dr. Gardner at Brigham Young University and gave it a try: "It's not as though we are all fighting over the last pie, seeing who can get the biggest piece. Remember that Big Bob started this by baking a fresh pie. Now we are going to add two more pies to the feast—telecom and power pies. Others may bring more currencies to the table, but that will only make the feast bigger. All Americans will have more access to more commodities and more ways of exchanging their work for the things they need. We leave everyone be, free to produce whatever value they can, and we all win!"

The dam broke. For the first time in months, everyone in the room, even Lane Smith, could actually see a future in which things got better, instead of a never-ending slide into chaos. They all had ideas to share and all wanted to be the first to do so. Huntsman sat down and let them talk it over.

Someone—was it Skousen?—observed that if America got going again with multiple currencies and no central banking system, there could never be a similar currency collapse in the future. There could be fluctuations in the value of currencies, but people could avoid harm by diversifying their currency holdings, and the units would always be worth some amount of a valuable commodity—not just empty promises written on scraps of paper.

Someone else pointed out that there were public power and telephone utilities lying idle in all the formerly united states, and that they were basically available for salvage.

The possibilities were endless.

Jared let the conversation run on for several minutes. It was good to see everyone taken with Huntsman's idea, excited about building instead of fighting or conquering.

"Ladies and gentlemen!" Jared stood again and raised his voice to call the meeting back to order. The group quieted. "I'm glad to see you all so enthused, because we will need your support. You can begin to see the possibilities for us that will come if we focus on freedom, hard work, and growth—growth exclusively through consent and free exchange. None of this will happen if we attempt to achieve our ends by force."

He pointed to the former Air Force bombing range in the Great Salt Lake Desert on the map. "Deseret Air Force Base is at our disposal."

The room fell completely silent.

"I remind you of this because I want you to remember that we have the strength to fight back against any enemies who would make war upon us, be they within our borders or without. When I say that we must persuade and lead by example, that is exactly what I mean. I do not mean that we should simply sit by while others aggress upon us. We have the strength to be a free and open people. We do not need to revert to barbarism."

Jared's forceful words locked everyone's attention on him. Good. "We will need your support for our program of growth through freedom when we begin admitting outlying cities into the State of Deseret. We will need you to explain what we are doing and why it is right to those who listen to you. But we also want you to know that we have the means to respond, should anyone try to take advantage of our openness. Does everyone understand this?"

Everyone muttered some kind of agreement, or—at least—refrained from asking questions.

"Excellent!" He smiled. "Please think about these things. Remember that we'll be having a Constitutional Convention in five months. We will probably have to revisit all of these issues again at that time and we will need your support then as well. Thank you for coming!"

Chapter 47:
Friday, May 12, 2000

"Well life has a funny way of sneaking up on you
When you think everything's okay and everything's going right
And life has a funny way of helping you out when
You think everything's gone wrong and everything blows up in your face."
—Alanis Morisette, *Ironic*

"Uh-oh."

"More like, 'oh shit'!" John Allen was experiencing the same sickening feeling in his stomach that he'd felt the last time he'd come over a hill on I-95 and seen a cop pointing a radar gun right at his stomach.

"Well, we knew there was a reason why Elmendorf stopped responding to radio calls." Alexis' hopes had risen at first, when they came in site of the former Air Force base. Unlike the rest of the city of Anchorage, which was still smoldering, things at Elmendorf had given the appearance of orderliness, almost tidiness. But then she noticed that there were no people. And now they could see that the fuel tanks had been blown up, as they had been at Novosibirsk.

She activated her radio transmitter. "Hawks One and Two, Hind One, this is Hawk Leader, see that open hangar by the end of that row of transport planes? I think it's big enough for all of us. Let's set 'em down out front and taxi in. We might need to camp here for a while—Ayan all over again."

She was referring to a town on the edge of the Sea of Okhotsk, where the squadron of helicopters had alighted, practically out of fuel. They had found avgas at some of the abandoned military air strips Petrov had helped them find as they crossed Siberia, and even a little at the small strip near Ayan, but not enough. They had yet to get to the Bering Sea, skirt its edge, and cross the Bering Strait.

Several expeditions over land had turned up no more fuel, but had eventually led to the discovery of an abandoned old cargo ship, big enough to carry all of their helicopters and equipment on its decks. A second wave of expeditions had then ensued, in search of diesel fuel for the ship's engines. Fortunately, they had located several sources of diesel, and had even turned up a few fishermen in a local village—two of whom who had experience working on Russian sea vessels—who were willing to ferry the helicopters across the Bering Sea, in exchange for ownership of the vessel, help in securing fuel, and help effecting repairs. The fishermen would acquire of a ship of their own, and Alexis' slightly expanded team would get a ride home. It was a good deal for all concerned. To Petrov's obvious pleasure and Alexis' mild embarrassment, the fishermen found some paint with which they brushed a new name onto the ship: *Alexa Petrova*.

"You don't s'pose Deseret will come git us, now that we're back on American soil, Gen'l?"

Alexis smiled. She'd bet that Okie was wearing his damned cowboy hat, even as he flew. "We'll ask, Captain Jones, but I wouldn't bet on it. This may be American soil, but that doesn't necessarily make it friendly territory anymore... In fact, General Petrov, could you please radio back to the cargo ship and tell them that we might be needing another ride? Maybe we can make another deal with them; more fuel and supplies, if we can find them, in exchange for a ride down to Seattle, or San Francisco. Tell them this could be the beginning of a new line of business for them!"

"Roger that, Alexa. Your man Daniels is already on it. And please, remember to call me Pavel. My command no longer exists, there is no longer a Russian military, and I am no longer in what was once my country. I'm not a general any more, and don't want to be known by any titles. America is supposed to be the land of individualism; I only want to be me, Pavel Petrov, the individual."

"Right you are, Pavel!" Alexis laughed. "I've got similar thoughts for myself, once I get these volunteers back to Deseret." By this time, Alexis had her chopper over the hangar. She descended slowly, until the HUMVEE she was carrying settled firmly on the ground. Then she released the hook, eased downward, and slid into the hangar. There was enough room for all four helicopters to park side by side, without getting dangerously close. It must have been meant for something huge—maybe it was a C-5 hangar?

As Alexis pivoted her Blackhawk, Captain Stewart brought his chopper in low and deposited a 600-gallon fuel trailer neatly beside the HUMVEE. Rotating the helicopter further, so that the nose of her ship would point toward the hangar entrance, Alexis caught a glimpse of something angular and inky off to her right. It was hiding in the shadows, as far inside the hangar as it could be pushed. She set her Blackhawk on its landing gear and switched off.

Without a word, she released her harness and jumped out of the machine—rotors still turning. Ducking around the nose, she advanced about thirty feet before she was sure: it was an Apache. Not something typically found on an Air Force base! Maybe it had been low or out of fuel and someone had stashed it in the hangar for safekeeping?

John Allen joined her before the menacing lean shape. "AH-64 Apache. Two-seater. Faster and more maneuverable than our Blackhawks, but can't carry troops and isn't good for lifting much—an attack chopper. The nose gun is a chain-fed 30mm cannon. The four rocket pods on the articulated wing pylons contain 19 rockets each—probably with the M261 high explosive Multi-Purpose Sub-Munition warhead. The MPSM delivers nine M73 armor-penetrating submunitions, which are scored internally to maximize fragmentation and anti-personnel effectiveness. That gives the Area Rocket Control System a maximum payload of 684 submunitions. The rockets themselves have a range of seven and a

half kilometers and the launchers are fully integrated with the
Target Acquisition and Designation System, the Integrated Helmet and Sight Subsystems, and the Fire-control Computer. Two of
the rocket pods can also be replaced with Hellfire missile racks like
the ones we have on the Blackhawks." He turned to Alexis. "That
is one wicked killing machine!"

Again, Alexis was impressed with how much Allen knew about
military aircraft. She wondered briefly what else she might not
know about him, but then her attention was drawn back to the
Apache. Unobserved behind them, Captain Stewart had set his
helicopter down beside Alexis' and the Okie was releasing his fuel
trailer on the other side of the HUMVEE. "I suppose you know,"
she told the civilian, "that they didn't let women fly combat helicopters?"

His face split with a broad grin. "If we can find fuel for it,
there won't be anyone to stop you now, Alexis."

Her eyes glowed at the thought and her expression grew distant. Then she drew a deep sigh. "First things first, John. I've got
to get these volunteers from Utah—Deseret—home. If we can find
enough fuel, I'll see about taking the Apache with us. Otherwise,
I'll just remember where it is and hope no one else does."

"Right."

"Right." She took a deep breath and turned her back on the
agile black machine. "Let's see about setting up camp and contact-
ing Deseret." Denying herself a wistful look back at the Apache,
Alexis marched off to look for Lieutenant Daniels, Allen trailing
after her.

Petrov had set the Hind down, and was taxiing it into the
hangar.

It was late in the Alaskan night before John Allen had a chance
to speak with Alexis in private again, though it was not yet dark.
She was slumped over the desk in the hangar office she had appro-
priated, staring without seeing at the pages of a book. "Better get
some rest, Major Tom, it's going to be a long one tomorrow!"

The book was the base commander's diary—Captain Jones

had found it earlier in the evening. It turned out that the CO had set fire to the fuel tanks himself, in order to prevent their misuse. He had also had certain critical components pulled from the planes and hidden... It had occurred to Alexis that the Apache was probably not on his inventory of craft to ground and she had begun daydreaming.

She gave the civilian a tired grin. "I know, John, I know. I wish I had ten more of me to take care of everything that needs taking care of!" Lowering her head and resting it on the desktop, she mumbled at the wooden surface: "You know, I think Petrov's on to something. I can't wait to discharge my last duty and ditch this uniform!"

Looking first to see that no one else was in line of sight of the office's window, Allen moved behind her. "I know what you mean." He began rubbing her shoulders. "Alexis, the men are tired, but dedicated. They want to get home as bad as you want to get them there. You've just got to trust them. You can't solve every problem and locate every lost fuel supply yourself. You've been pushing yourself too hard!"

"Oh Life, that feels good!" She rolled her head from side to side to let his fingers work her exhausted neck muscles. "I know you're right, John, but there is so much to do! The choppers need maintenance, and we've only got one mechanic with us. We're running low on food, and we either need diesel for the ship, or avgas for the choppers. We've also got to keep our perimeter secure, in case whoever attacked Elmendorf—the diary says that a gang of marauders tried to steal some jets, that's why the CO grounded the planes—comes back for us. We've already lost one man because we didn't have the medical facilities to get all the shrapnel out of him...and can't risk getting anyone else wounded. We simply can not afford to make any mistakes."

"In that case, General," he walked his fingers down her back and ran them up her spine, "I suggest you get some R&R. You won't do yourself or the men any good if you're not at peak performance."

She swiveled in her chair, causing one of his hands to brush her cheek and the other to brush one of her breasts as she turned. "What did you have in mind, Mr. Allen?"

He dropped his hands to his sides and tried to swallow with a mouth suddenly gone dry. "Uh..." He tried to swallow again. "I..." He wanted to deny that he had meant anything sexual, but she had obviously taken it that way and didn't look offended. He was caught, suspended perfectly between fear and desire.

Alexis understood his dilemma at once and laughed softly. "An excellent suggestion, John, but I won't be able to relax or rest around here. Get our chopper ready—we've got enough fuel to scout out the area for possible hostile forces, and it's something I'd sure like to know more about! Besides, you could use some practice on the infrared equipment, if it ever gets dark enough. I'll fix us a picnic basket." She placed a reassuring hand on his arm.

Allen stiffened his spine and saluted. "Yes, ma'am!" He turned sharply on his heel and marched out of the office. That touch of her hand on his arm! He had to concentrate to walk straight.

Alexis chuckled, picked up a backpack, and grabbed a few small packages from her duffel bag before heading for the area of the hangar that was serving as a mess tent.

Was this wise? A general shouldn't fraternize with soldiers under her command... But John wasn't a soldier. And, one way or another, her mission would be over soon. She knew where she was going and it wasn't Deseret! So, that wasn't really the issue. The real concern was that she knew she did not love John Allen, and had seen signs of puppy-like adoration in his eyes.

She was still thinking about it when she met him at the Blackhawk. Allen had a map with him, which he unfolded after he climbed into the co-pilot's seat. Alexis made a walk-around inspection and then motioned to one of the two Russians who had decided to come see America with Petrov. He began rolling the hangar door open as the American general settled into her pilot's seat. She had ordered everything brought inside the Hangar—fortunately, there were offices and shops in the back corners, so their departure shouldn't be too rough on those trying to get some sack-time. Her hope was that if there were any hostiles in the area, and they hadn't seen the task-force's arrival, they might never know anyone had been there.

After clearing the hangar, they did actually scout the area. It was a clear Alaskan night in late spring, which meant that the sun shone as though it were late afternoon, and they were able to see quite well without using the night-vision gear. Alexis hovered over possible sources of fuel and Allen made notations on his map. They found several abandoned specialized vehicles for servicing aircraft, but no fuel trucks. The base's garage had a tanker truck in it, but there was no way to know if it contained fuel—and what kind—without going in on foot. Alexis hoped that its contents— if any—had been overlooked because the truck was obviously not serviceable. Flying in a wide loop around the base, they also located a small commercial air strip that might have something useful, but no signs of people, hostile or otherwise.

When they finished scouting, Alexis pushed the throttles forward to their stops. The turbine engines mounted on either side of the cabin pushed her back into her seat, and the Blackhawk shot forward. Alexis became a kid on a roller coaster, laughing wildly as she put the machine through a series of aerobatics. She had always experienced a mildly erotic thrill from the ever-present vibrations in helicopters—that night it added a whole new level of exhilaration to playing with the powerful machine. It would be more fun in the Apache, and it was wasting some fuel, but what the heck; they weren't going anywhere without a whole lot more fuel anyway.

Ooo, that felt good!

Alexis checked to see that they were well away from the end of the abandoned base with the hangar her team occupied, took the chopper up as far as it would go, and engaged the autopilot. Her mind was filled with images of washboard abdominal muscles as she wriggled out of her harness and helmet.

When she turned to Allen, his face was looking slightly green and his knuckles were white from the death-grip he had on his harness. Seeing her look, he smiled weakly, relaxed a little, and pulled off his own helmet.

She couldn't help but laugh again. "It's on autopilot." She had to raise her voice to be heard without the helmet intercom units. "We'll hover here. Don't worry—it'll be fine!"

"Oh, I feel much better already. At least the machine is sane when *it* flies!"

"You don't like my flying?" She made an exaggerated pout, poking out her lower lip a full half inch.

"Let's just say I'm glad I haven't eaten anything since this afternoon!"

They both laughed.

"Actually, I should apologize. I've been aware for some time that you don't like flying. I shouldn't have done that with you on board... I just can't resist sometimes; it feels so good!"

He rolled his eyes, as if to say that it was beyond him how anyone could think that having their guts yanked left and right, up and down, and out through the mouth was enjoyable.

"So, if you hate flying so much, why did you volunteer to become a backup gunner?"

"Because it's important. You... We might need me to know how."

"You already seem to know plenty about how!"

"That's only book knowledge. It's been good to learn how to do it for real!" What he didn't say was that it had also given him an excuse to be alone with her more often. He hadn't known anything about helicopters two years ago, but he'd seen how Alexis loved the machines, and how she lit up whenever they came into a conversation. After that, he'd read everything he could on Army helicopters, especially the ones he thought she would find more exciting, like the Cobras and Apaches.

"Okay, it's your business... Now Mr. Allen, what were you saying about R&R?"

"I was saying, General, that you need to rest and relax so you can achieve peak performance."

"Uh-huh." She was now halfway into the rear compartment, releasing his harness and pulling him after her. "I know what will relax me, if you're up to the task!"

"I'm always up for you, Major Tom!"

"Is that book knowledge you're talking about, Mister, or do you know how to do it for real?"

They laughed again and kissed—tumbling to the deck in the aft compartment. Alexis kissed with a hunger pent up longer than she cared to think about, Allen returned her kisses with an almost religious rapture. When they broke apart for air she unbuttoned his shirt and pulled his undershirt up. His chest was every bit as muscular as she had imagined it would be. She ran her hands over his body and breathed in his musky scent.

He was initially hesitant, feeling as though he were trespassing on sacred ground when he reached for her.

He'd known how active she was, but was nonetheless surprised by how muscular she turned out to be. Something else he had suspected was confirmed: her breasts were larger than the bulges in her uniform had suggested, confined as they were by a sport-style bra. His hands were walking up the steps to the temple, his mind spinning with euphoria. He caught her hands and kissed them. "Alexis, I love you!"

Suddenly the temple doors boomed shut.

She pulled back, not coldly, but looking stricken. "I thought you might."

"What's wrong?" Some guys gushed such words as a line to get laid. He said them and actually meant them, and now she was pulling back?

"John, I..." She bit her lip.

"It's okay, Alexis, I love you! Completely! Without reservation! You can tell me anything."

"John, I really like you..."

Oh shit!

"I enjoy your company. And I respect you. You're a fine man

and a good friend..." She couldn't look into his eyes. "But I don't love you. I'm not sure why... I just don't feel that way."

"I know that! I've known it for more than a year!" He kissed her hand again. "It doesn't matter. Maybe you love someone else, maybe it's the military environment, maybe it's something about me. I don't know and it doesn't matter—I still love you. It's not something I can decide not to feel, not something I can turn off like a light!"

"Oh John!"

"I don't care what the reason is, Alexis. You are the most intelligent, creative, honorable, and beautiful woman I've ever met. I love you and I can't change it—don't want to change it!"

"John, you're sweet, and I can't tell you how much I appreciate it, but I'm not sure that making love to you is a good idea. It might make it hard for you to live without some things you might never have."

"Alexis, I'm not some starry-eyed teenager. Even if you did love me, there might still be some things I could never have. Geez, nothing in the world is certain right now—we could both be dead by this time tomorrow! My heart is *my* responsibility, not yours. I've wanted you for so long, but never dared to hope..." It took all the self control he could muster to keep his voice from cracking. "You might love me some day, or you might not. What's the worst that can happen? I have a long-standing fantasy fulfilled and have to live the rest of my life—for however long that is—with only that wonderful memory. It's a chance I'm willing to take!"

By way of answer, she dove into his arms.

Allen couldn't contain his relief—didn't want to! The temple doors swung open again, and the acolytes bid him to enter.

Some people are beautiful to look at, Alexis was beautiful to feel. Her body was a joy to explore. The curves. The warmth. The softness. The firmness. The tactile fire of vitality. He did find her attractive to look at, but that was nothing compared to the ecstasy of his fingertips on her skin.

For her part, she had wondered for some time what the vibrations of a helicopter in flight would add to lovemaking, and was eager to find out. She liked his shape. She liked his smell. She liked the energy of excitement she could feel in him when he touched her. Alexis deftly undid his belt buckle and unzipped his pants. "Well done! You're not even a soldier, but you know how I like to be saluted!"

While Allen wiggled farther out of his pants, Alexis reached behind her, into the backpack she had tossed into the back of the chopper before taking off, and pulled out a condom. In answer to his raised eyebrow, she explained, "No, I wasn't expecting this, but I try to be prepared for everything. These are the kind that don't taste too bad, so, if you'll give me a back rub, I'll help you put it on!"

John Allen had never seen anyone open a condom package with one hand before. Alexis stroked him with her left hand while opening the disk-shaped package with her right—all with a practiced motion that shocked him. He'd watched her closely for roughly two years, and, as near as he could tell, she had no social life at all. When—and why—had she learned to do that? How many more surprises did she hold?

Alexis was about to show him a few of those surprises. She winked at him, popped the condom into her mouth, and bent further down, straight onto him. She barely had the condom halfway on when he couldn't take it any longer. He tried to lift her head but couldn't do it without using too much force. His frantic motions only made the moment more explosive.

Alexis slithered up and backwards, folding her arms under her breasts and grinning into his forlorn face. "Don't worry, John, I planned against that contingency; I brought another one." She retrieved a second package from the backpack and kissed him. "This time, you'll last longer—a win-win situation, don't you think?"

If sexual energy and release were visible light—and if it had been dark outside—the sky over Elmendorf would have glowed and pulsed that night, a dazzling display that would have outshone the aurora borealis.

When Alexis and Allen returned to the hangar, they called a meeting of the officers and anyone else who wanted to attend. The general let the civilian go over the map and show the others the spots where they might look in the morning for fuel and other useful supplies. After a few questions about possible hostilities, Alexis assigned tasks and the group broke up.

Alone again with John Allen, Alexis winked. "It doesn't look like anyone picked up on anything unusual. Is my uniform straight?"

"Your hair's a little messy," he grinned, "but the helmet always does that."

"Well, I'm relaxed now—thanks to your peak performance— so I think I'm going to catch some sack-time."

"Now I know why you couldn't relax here in the hangar. The way you scream when you 'relax', you'd probably scare the bejesus out of the men!"

She gave him her best 'Ms. Demure' look and refused to answer his jibe. "I recommend you get some rest too. We've got a busy day tomorrow."

"Yes ma'am!" He saluted her.

"You know that's not the kind of salute I like!" She slapped him on the butt on her way toward the door.

"Alexis, wait."

She stopped.

"What happens when we get back to Deseret?"

"Well, you know how I feel about my responsibility to my men. I'll need to come up with a way to see to it that the ones who didn't join us in Deseret get to wherever they want to go. I plan to release everyone under my command from their duty as soon as we get there."

"And then what?"

"And then we go home!"

He was silent for a few minutes before following up on that thought. "Home... I wonder where that would be now?"

Alexis considered her next words carefully before answering.

"We'll have to see what we see when we get back, but if things are as bad as I think they are, there won't be much of anything to return to outside of Deseret, except for a few small pockets of civilization. Since the chain of command above me no longer exists, I know where I'm going..."

He didn't say anything.

"If you want to, you can come with me."

This was obviously what he had wanted to hear, but hadn't dared to ask. "You're not just leading me on because I'm good in bed and made the mistake of falling in love with you?"

"Well, I don't know how good you are in bed, but you sure do make the cockpit live up to its name!"

They both laughed and were glad for the warmth of each other's company.

"Seriously John, even though I don't feel exactly the same way about you as you do about me, I do care a lot about you, and even love you, in a different kind of way... It may not have been such a mistake—to fall in love with me—we'll see what happens. Okay?"

"Okay." He let out a deep breath. "I'll try not to get my hopes up, but the gamble is certainly worth it. Count me in."

"Great! I can't think of a better companion for the trip. You know it's going to be a mess when we get there, don't you?"

"Yeah, but after tonight, I don't think I'll be afraid of flying any more!"

CHAPTER 48:
WEDNESDAY, MAY 17, 2000

"Foreclosure of a dream,
Those visions never seen,
Until all is lost,
Personal Holocaust,
Foreclosure of a dream."
—Megadeth, *Foreclosure of a Dream*

Angel stared at the reports, no longer quite seeing them, not quite sure whether to be pleased or afraid. The target in Anaheim was bigger and richer than the gated communities he had plundered, and he was confident that Ejercito Dragon could take it easily, but he wasn't sure where to go next.

He knew that now that his army had grown far beyond the number of people he could have personal contact with, his soldiers followed him only in part out of fear—the tool he was most familiar with. The fact that he kept them fed had a lot more to do with it, and personal respect for him had precious little to do with it. Word had spread of Ejercito Dragon's effectiveness at feeding itself, and of the perks that came with promotion. Many of them were desperate wretches, but Angel now had more than 100,000 men under his command, and they all expected the food, female slaves, and other booty to keep on coming.

He had to find more and richer targets. But where? He'd heard some intriguing things about Silicon Valley, but that was a long way off. Still, there might be some interesting targets to hit along the way...

Sighing, he closed the file on the reports and called to Cabron. "Busca El Gringo."

Cabron saluted and left to fetch the Gringo—an Army sergeant who had actually led troops during the Gulf War. Angel had been using the soldier as a consultant because he had never led a force as large as he commanded now, and needed to know how other armies—he wouldn't let himself think 'real armies'—organized things, coordinated deployments of thousands of men at once, and generally conducted their business.

When the man came in, he was dressed in battle fatigues, and appeared every bit the tough soldier that Angel wished his men would see in him.

The gang leader motioned the sergeant to a chair in front of his desk and showed him some maps, explaining different options he was considering for taking their target that afternoon. He had never consulted with the soldier on battle tactics before, but thought it wouldn't hurt. The target was important, a special place, a very wealthy place. "What do you say, Gringo? I think that if we do this right, we can do it without any casualties."

The veteran snorted. "You're dreaming! They'll never surrender. They know what'll happen to them and their women. They'll fight."

Angel was incredulous. "With 100,000 men and heavy armor surrounding them?"

"Sure. It could be 200,000 and they'd still fight. The worst thing that can happen to them is that they lose, which is what happens if they surrender. They might as well fight."

"Well, if they do, we'll just roll forward and crush them." No one spoke to Angel in this manner—except Rosalia—and he didn't care for the insolence one bit.

"Don't get overconfident. They could prepare countermeasures. Mine the field in front of the fence, or have some artillery stashed away that we haven't heard about yet."

"So, what are you saying? Don't attack?" Angel had been having an increasingly hard time controlling his temper of late. Under the desk, he pulled out his 9mm and toyed with it.

"No, of course we attack, but we do it smart. This plan is not smart. Massing your troops all together like that only makes it easier for the defenders to shoot them. It's idiotic. You give those orders, and your troops with military backgrounds will instantly know that their CO has no soldiering experience whatsoever. They'll desert at the first sign of trouble. What you need to do is—"

Angel face darkened dangerously and he cut the man off. "Thank you, Gringo, I see we don't agree. I will show you that we can take this enemy without a fight. You can go now."

"Suit yourself!" The man snorted and turned to leave.

As soon as the sergeant turned, Angel pulled his pistol and shot him in the back. The veteran crumpled and fell halfway through the door. "Hah! So much for your great military experience!"

Cabron came running into the room, gun drawn, but he relaxed when he realized that there was no threat to Angel. "¿Que paso?"

The great leader shrugged. "He disobeyed an order. Have someone clean up the mess, and then bring the Hummer around. It's time to go to the command post in the field and supervise the attack."

Cabron left to do as he was told, and Angel collected the maps and reports from his desk. What the reports didn't mention was the hulking gray form of a large warship, hove to off Sunset Beach. Had any of Ejercito Dragon's scouts spied it, or any of the support vessels that flitted about like worker bees serving their queen, they would not have thought it had anything to do with their immediate objective, more than eleven miles from the shore.

On his way to the command post, an office suite on the top floor of a tall building on Katella Avenue, Angel had an idea. The old Pomona base was nearly on his way, and today would mark Ejercito Dragon's greatest victory yet! It wouldn't impress Rosalia, but it might make an impression on Holly. He pulled up next to the heap of junked cars that camouflaged the garage where he had two emergency Jeeps stashed outside the old base, and ordered Cabron to bring Holly. Cabron was not long in returning with the blindfolded redhead.

Angel smiled approvingly—it was good not to have to tell Cabron exactly what to do. Anyone else would probably not have thought of the blindfold, if Angel had not included it in his orders. To an outside observer, Cabron may have seemed to be nothing more than a simple-minded minion, but Angel knew he was far more clever and dangerous than he let on—it was lucky for him that Cabron was completely loyal.

After they were well away from Pomona, Angel took the blindfold off Holly—he wanted to see if she would guess their destination. The roads they were taking were a dead giveaway. Would she figure it out?

But she didn't say anything. She hadn't seen much of the city since The Collapse and was finding it eerie... Empty streets. Burned out buildings. Signs of looting everywhere—but no signs of people. It reminded her of H.G. Well's description of London at the end of *War of the Worlds*. She hadn't actually read the book, but she and Rosalia had conversed through it, pointing to the words they wanted to say. Over the weeks, the actress had picked up most of the story line. She even remembered some of the more haunting words:

> 'Why was I wandering in this city of the dead? Why was I alone when all London was lying in state, and in its black shroud... The windows in the white houses were like the eye sockets of skulls.'

Arriving at the Katella Avenue command post, Angel went straight to the plate glass windows with a pair of field glasses.

Cabron pushed Holly into the room and she stumbled. "What... What am I doing here?"

"You are here to watch," Angel answered, making sure she

could see all the ribbons on his uniform.

Holly ignored Angel's strutting and thought about making a break for it. But she could see two guards, standing alert in the hallway, and Cabron started setting up his radio gear by the door. No chance of slipping by them! She moved closer to the window and made out the large colorful letters over the gate of what had to be the target. "You're going to Disneyland?"

Angel ignored the mockery in her tone and answered the question. "It has become a city in its own right, much larger and more heavily defended than the mini-towns we've been raiding. It will be a good demonstration of Ejercito Dragon's strength."

Scanning left and right with the binoculars, he spotted guards patrolling the fence—lots of them. The Disneylanders even had a couple armored vehicles of their own, just inside the main gate. They were expecting trouble. Had someone tipped them off? More likely they figured that there were no other targets left in the area for Angel to hit.

So, he was expected.

Did it matter? The reports estimated that the amusement-park-turned-walled-city had no more than five thousand inhabitants, and of those only half, at most, could really do any fighting. They had taken in many women and children—how could they possibly stand against a heavily armed force forty times their size? El Gringo was wrong, that's all there was to it.

Angel had some of his men on the inside again, but there weren't enough of them to take out the elaborate security systems the Disneylanders had set up at their gates. A try had been made to sabotage the little community's electric generators, but that attempt had failed. The generalisimo didn't know what they'd done to his man when they'd caught him, but he'd never heard from him again.

Oh well, no need for subtlety. "Plan C," he told Cabron, who relayed the order over his radio.

Through the field glasses, he could see his heavy armor moving out of places of concealment on nearby streets and taking up positions around Disneyland. Within fifteen minutes, the park was surrounded by a ring of armored vehicles. Twenty-six of them were armored personnel carriers and eleven were actual tanks he had managed to find and get running. It took another twenty-odd minutes for the rest of the men to finish forming up behind the armor. When they had, each vehicle was at the apex of an armed triangle, pointing toward a section of wall to be pierced. Once the vehicles had broached the walls, the men had orders to storm in and shoot only those who fought back. After many successful raids, the men all understood the importance of not killing the prisoners, especially the female ones.

Holly beheld the massing of troops without expression. She couldn't see the detail her captor could, and parts of the army on the other side of the little town were out of sight, but she could plainly see that the city was entirely surrounded by a huge force.

When Angel was satisfied everything that everything was in place, he turned to Cabron. "Ahora."

Cabron relayed the command, and one of the tanks assigned to the front gate raised a white flag and advanced. Good! By this time, the Disneylanders must realize that their situation is hopeless!

Angel fully expected them to surrender—seeing Ejercito Dragon completely encircling them, like a real dragon with a hapless knight in its coils. How could they hope to resist? The tank turned back to rejoin the formation.

"Dijeron que no."

"¿Que?" Angel couldn't believe it.

"They said no!" Cabron repeated the negative report from the parley tank.

How could they... Did they want to die? Switching mental gears before the thought that the gringo had been right could come to surface, he concentrated on his anger. If they wanted to be stupid and die, Angel would oblige them! "Da la orden. Attack at once!" Then he added in Holly's direction, in English, "They turned down their chance to surrender peacefully, so you'll get to see the Dragon Army in action!"

Cabron picked up his radio, but before he could relay the order, the building shook as though smashed by a fist. Glass shattered everywhere and a deafening roar drowned out whatever Cabron was going to say. Lacerated in several places by flying glass, Angel scrambled back to the window, where Holly was picking herself up as well. Somehow, she hadn't been cut. Was it an earthquake? That was not the rumbling of an earthquake!

He was just in time to see a second wave of explosions among his troops. The projectiles or bombs themselves were too fast to see, but—whatever they were—he could hear them tearing the air. Each explosion blew a large crater in the ground where it struck, and there were many explosions. In just two volleys, more than half of his heavy armor was destroyed, and the men were scattering...

Something was circling in the air overhead! Whether it had been there before and he just couldn't hear it because of the glass, he didn't know, but whatever it was had to be connected to what was happening to his troops.

What to do? Retreat?

Angel shied away from that thought, not just because it was unpalatable, but because everything he knew told him that if he retreated, it would be the end of his army. And what would Holly think if he retreated? No, whatever it was, they would not bomb their own people!

"¡Cabron!"

Cabron didn't move—he was still in shock over the sudden turn of events.

"¡Cabron!" Angel had to shake his adjutant physically to snap him out of it. "¡Da la orden! Attack! Anyone who doesn't obey, I will shoot, personally!"

Cabron fumbled with the radio and hastily ordered all units to attack. After pausing to catch his breath, he relayed Angel's threat to shoot anyone who didn't obey.

A third volley shrieked down on Ejercito Dragon, falling in a circle of death outside the craters already laid down. This pushed Angel's men in the opposite direction: toward Disneyland. First one, then all of the other vehicles that could, moved forward. Another volley fell on them, destroying five more vehicles and spraying gobs of dirt, metal, and flesh high into the air.

As Angel watched with the field glasses, one of the armored personnel carriers fell into a crater and got stuck. To one side of Disneyland, a tank suddenly veered off and left the battlefield, taking a column of men streaming behind it. The remaining vehicles smashed through the fences and walls in seven places. The men who were not maimed by the bombing surged into the breaches in the walls in disarray, more out of fear of the destruction falling from the sky than out of any desire to conquer, or even to obey orders. Angel didn't care about their reasons, just that they obeyed, and all but one tank commander had. He was also pleased to see that his choice to attack was the right one; once his forces were inside the walls, the shelling stopped.

Angel decided to go down and join his troops in securing the city. He signaled to the guards, who took Holly by the arms. Cabron gathered up his gear and they made for the stairwell. The party had barely descended two floors when another giant fist smashed the building, but this time it hit much harder. The building shuddered and groaned, and was pounded again. Everyone was knocked to the floor, and sunlight streamed into the stairwell from somewhere above.

"¡Dios!" Cabron gaped at the shaft of light in bewilderment, not understanding what was happening.

"Whoever bombed our troops is bombing this building!" Angel motioned for the guards to pick Holly up. "¡Vamonos!"

Careening down the stairs as fast as they could go, they descended flight after flight. The building continued to shudder and surge. Grinding metal and twisting stone moaned in ear-splitting tones, vibrating through the very bones of the structure.

Arriving in the underground garage out of breath, they all

piled into Angel's HUMVEE and held on while the self-styled general started the motor, floored the accelerator, and peeled out of his parking space and up the ramp into daylight. As they drove across the ruined parking lot, another round exploded just behind them. The HUMVEE rocked as the ground heaved, but they made it through the front gate before they could be bombed again. Behind them, the entire building they had been occupying was reduced to rubble.

But it was too late for Disneyland.

When Ejercito Dragon had poured in through the openings in their walls, the matter became a simple question of numbers, and the defenders were quickly overwhelmed. However, it took some time to mop up the resistance. They fought bravely, and several defenders with Molotov cocktails ruined two more of Angel's armored vehicles.

From a new command post—some kind of elevated control booth for an outdoor ride that had a good view of most of the park—Angel observed his men getting into the rhythm they had developed in other attacks. They quickly cordoned off one open space after another and filled them with prisoners, before marching them to the main pen, right below the new field headquarters. He noted with some interest that many of the Disneylanders fought on, individually, even when it was obvious that their city had fallen and they were way outclassed. Someone had *really* trained these people!

It took an hour and a half for his men to bring the captured Disneyland commander to Angel, but by that time even the last pockets of resistance in Space Mountain and Sleeping Beauty's Castle had been crushed. He tried not to look at Holly, who was leaning against a wall with her arms crossed over her breasts. He regretted now that he had brought her... But how could he have known the little city would have such a deadly defense? What *was* that defense?

Angel sat in a chair, Cabron beside him, while a number of guards surrounded the prisoner and covered the door. A cold wind blew in through the glass-less windows—every window within a mile must have been shattered.

"What is your name?" Angel asked.

The man did not answer. He just squared his jaw and pretended to inspect his shoelaces.

Angel pulled out his 9mm. "What is your name?"

The man still would not answer.

Tough guy. This must be the man who had trained the people to fight. Angel sighted carefully and shot the man's knee—it hadn't worked so well with Mario, but this man didn't know Angel so well. "Okay, never mind the name. What I really want to know is what those bombs were and where they were coming from."

Holly turned to look out the window, but that was little better; the subjugation going on behind her was the same as that before her. The children were being separated out to be kept as household slaves and as hostages—incentives for the cooperation of their parents. The women were being herded to a separate corral, where... Nausea rose in her throat and she struggled to keep from throwing up.

The man rolled on the floor, clutching his mangled knee. "Okay," the man gasped, "I'll tell you... But it won't do you any good..." In spite of the obvious pain, he did not cry out, and even managed a short laugh at Angel. "Those were...sixteen-inch projectiles...turret guns on the battleship *U.S.S. Wisconsin*." He stopped and concentrated on breathing.

Angel was stunned. "A *battleship*?"

After a few minutes, it was easier for the Disneylander to talk, though his voice was still shaky. "She was on one last tour of the Pacific before being mothballed when things fell apart. My people found her off the Long Beach Naval Shipyard. What's left of Pacific Fleet Command in Hawaii is sending everything they can this way, to help civil authorities maintain the peace. Well, there aren't any civil authorities left—at least, none of the old ones—but the *Wisconsin* was happy to offer to protect our little city, especially after we sent them some fresh food."

"A battleship?" Angel was having a hard time believing what he was hearing and didn't notice that he was repeating himself. "I had no idea their guns could reach this far inland!"

"They can reach much farther, and everyone along the coast knows about the vile gang of rapists you call an army, Señor Ortega."

"So, you know who I am!" Feeling proud to be recognized, Angel puffed up his chest, hoping Holly had heard, but she was still staring out the window, ignoring him.

"Yes, I know who you are, you son of a bitch! I've been expecting you. Our positions might well be reversed now, if your lousy excuse for an army had run in the opposite direction!"

Angel ignored the insult and tried to act as though everything had gone according to plan. "It was a good try, but not good enough... Tell me more about the *Wisconsin*."

Holly turned back to face the room, horrified by the interrogation, but also curious to know how the Disneylanders had handed Ejercito Dragon such a beating, even as their downfall overtook them.

"Well, the navy suffered less desertion than the ground-based armed forces. I guess their folks figured that their ships wouldn't be targets, since they can move them around. Still, they lost a lot of men from the ships that were ashore, because those men had families to protect, and they couldn't take their families aboard ship..." The man gasped and tried to keep from moving his ruined knee. "The *Wisconsin's* captain says that what's left of the Pacific Fleet will help any peaceful communities along the coast, though now that they've eaten most of the food they had on board when things fell apart, they're partial to people who are willing to trade supplies for protection."

The prisoner laughed at his inquisitor. "Hah! Those big guns must have taken out half of your men and most of your tanks before you even knew what was happening! No more easy victims for your scum to abuse, Señor Ortega. Did you hear that airplane? That was a Remote Piloted Vehicle from the ship. They traced your command post through your radio signals and almost blew you up when they hit the building, I'll bet! I was watching. They came *this* close to toasting your sorry ass when you were driving across the parking lot. The RPV has cameras, so they could see you running for cover. Next time you attack a peaceful community in California, the *Wisconsin*—or other ships like her—will shell your army right out of existence! And when they find out where you're based, they'll drop a Tomahawk missile right on your ugly head!"

Holly laughed. She didn't mean to, but she couldn't help it. Way to tell him!!

The great general of Ejercito Dragon snarled and shot the Disneylander, half-emptying the magazine into him before he could say anything that would cause Angel to lose any more face. Then he lashed out at Holly and punched her in the solar plexus with the barrel of his gun. His finger was on the trigger, but didn't exert enough pressure to cause it to fire. The effect, however, was still devastating. Caught by surprise, Holly made no effort to turn the blow or jump back. The unforgiving metal jabbed straight into the unprotected bundle of nerves, paralyzing her with hot sheets of electric pain. She collapsed to the floor, unable to breathe.

Cabron chortled with glee and licked his lips.

The sight of the redhead's quivering helplessness triggered an automatic response in Angel. He reached into a pocket and drew out his switchblade. With a practiced motion, he grabbed Holly by the shirtfront and sliced her shirt from collar to hem. The bra was next.

Holly began sobbing and gasping for breath, making frightened little noises as she tried to cover her breasts.

Angel was now fully aroused—the sight of abject terror all the more satisfying when it came from someone who had previously shown a will to fight. He put the knife down and undid Holly's belt, using both hands to peel off her pants.

It was the move the actress had been waiting for. The pain had been excruciating, but she had experienced worse before, and she knew that her survival was dependent on keeping a part of her mind alert for opportunities. She grabbed for the knife, finding it with her left hand and striking at Angel's head.

He was too fast. Snarling again, he lashed out with his right arm, smashing his fist against her wrist. The knife went spinning across the room. "Nice try, whore!" He cuffed her across the face, drawing blood from a cut on her lower lip.

Screaming was no good—there was no one in the entire city who could help her. Holly screamed anyway, not quite able to block out the sound of Cabron's cackling.

When he was done, Angel rolled off her and stood to one side. Holly was no longer kicking, but he was wary of her tricks now and didn't want to get too close while he pulled his pants back up. He retrieved the switchblade, folded it, and returned it to his pocket. "Cabron," he spoke calmly, pretending he'd meant for the interview to turn out the way it had, "call the captains. We must decide what to do about this *Wisconsin* threat."

"¡Si, General!"

"No, wait! First, while the men are still thinking about what they can find for themselves in Disneyland, send two columns to track down that tank that deserted. When they find it, their orders are to destroy it and any men left with it. No prisoners. Kill them all. The men must all learn that no one betrays Angel Jesus Ramos Ortega and lives!"

"Si, General." Cabron had been present at Mario's disciplining; he understood. "But what do I do with the woman?"

"Whatever you want. I don't care."

"¡Si, General!"

Angel had meant for him to amuse himself quickly and then kill her—she was obviously never going to appreciate him—so they could get on with business, but Cabron had more elaborate ways of playing with his toys. They involved knives, took much longer than Angel's simple beatings and rapes, and were always lethal. He decided to take Holly back to her cell and come for her later, when they'd have a whole day to spend together.

Cabron could be patient.

That evening, the captains gathered in an underground meeting room that had been set up for the purpose, in a building near the old Pomona base. The day's glorious victors were all somewhat subdued as they sat around an old Ping-Pong table. Apprehension permeated the room.

It wasn't the sixteen-inch guns Angel was worried about. They were more than thirty miles from the coast—surely they were safe from the shells this far inland? What preyed on his mind, and word of it had spread faster than fire in a refinery, was the threat the dead Disneyland commander had made. If word of his location got back to the captain of the *Wisconsin*, he could be in real danger; a cruise missile could travel hundreds of miles inland!

Ever since the old city government of Los Angeles had fallen apart, Angel had been so confident that no one could stop him, he had not bothered with much secrecy. The Pomona base was well guarded, but that made it conspicuous, and Angel had never issued any specific orders to keep the location of such facilities secret. What if someone had told someone who had told the captain of the *Wisconsin?* They had tried to avoid detection on their way back from Disneyland, but what if an RPV had followed them to the base?

Well, even if the *Wisconsin* did know about the Pomona base, Angel didn't think the warhead of a Tomahawk could reach this room, a half a mile away.

He started the meeting by asking for a report from the captain Cabron had sent after the deserters. With this new threat, there was a danger that others might think of deserting, and he wanted to make sure he stemmed that tide before it got going.

"Mi General," another captain began, in Spanish, "Miguel did not return. He found the other tank and opened fire on it. All of the deserters were executed, as you ordered, but someone threw a grenade inside Miguel's tank and he...didn't make it."

Angel cursed silently; two more tanks lost!

"Gracias Ramon." Well, at least the message was delivered. He decided to let everyone think about it for a bit before continuing.

"General," Ramon had apparently done some thinking already, "the wounded are dying. We have only two doctors—we've never needed more—and now there are thousands of wounded. They are dying before we can pick them up off the battlefield, and many of the soldiers sent out to get them just keep on going and don't come back."

"When we leave this meeting," Angel's voice was low and dangerous, "you are all to issue orders that anyone attempting to desert is to be shot immediately. In the future, if we ever see anyone who has left us, they are to be shot on sight." He glared around the room. "¿Claro?"

"Claro," they all replied.

"So, how many men did we lose?" This was one of the Asian captains. Angel had never learned to pronounce his name, but he, like all the other Asians in Ejercito Dragon, had learned a lot of Spanish.

"We're not sure yet." Cabron replied, without seeing the visual daggers Angel directed his way. "The men were all packed very close when the shells fell on them. It's hard to believe, but we think about thirty thousand bit the dust in the bombing. Also, there may be another ten thousand wounded, but it's hard to tell... We did try to count the living once, but we could only find about fifty-five thousand, with maybe another two or three thousand wounded who might live. And then there's our heavy armor! All but five of our tanks and APCs have been destroyed..." He trailed off when he finally noticed his general's angry look.

"Yes," Angel sought to redirect the conversation elsewhere. "It was an important victory, but at a terrible cost. We need to rethink what we are doing, now that we know about the *Wisconsin*, and the possibility of other ships like her."

"There are other ships like her?" Several of the captains asked at once. They did not care for that idea at all.

"Well, no. Maybe. We don't know." Angel had decided that it wouldn't be prudent to tell them what the Disneylander had said about the Pacific Fleet Command. "I've talked with some of our

men who used to be in the Navy. They say Navy bases had just as
many desertion problems as the other bases. A lot of crews would
not come back once they set foot ashore. Some captains let their
crews go when they asked leave to go and protect their families.
One man told me that some captains live alone on their empty
ships, waiting for who knows what. Others have disabled their
ships so that they can't be seized by the 'wrong people'. A few even
sank their own ships." He had their attention again. Good.

Now, a little distortion of the truth, and he should be able to
motivate them without panicking them. "The *Wisconsin*, however,
was out at sea when everything fell apart, and arrived with her
crew intact. That's probably how her captain held on to them. I
don't think there's any way we can know how many such ships
there are out there, but there are bound to be some more, and all
of them will be heading home, since there is no government in
Washington to order them to go anywhere else."

He let them think about that prospect only briefly. He didn't
want to lose control of the conversation again.

"So what we need is to move our operations inland, and come
back to deal with the ships when we have better equipment."

"Better equipment?" It was the oriental captain again.

"Yes, we've been getting M-16s, trucks, fuel, a few armored
vehicles, and other stuff from National Guard depots, but there
are other bases—bigger bases—where we can get better weapons."

"Like what?"

"Well, there's Edwards Air Force base north of here, but I don't
know how much useful stuff we can find there—I think they used
it mostly for landing the space shuttle. There was Camp Pendleton,
but they closed that base last year and turned it into an office
park. Our best bet is Twenty-Nine Palms Marine Corps Base."

"Isn't that in the Mojave desert?"

"Yes. A great place to keep tanks and artillery, don't you think?
Some heavy artillery I've seen would have no problem blowing a
hole in a ship's hull. And they'll have helicopters."

"Helicopters? Who are we going to get to fly them?"

In his mind, Angel decided it was time for him to have a private talk with this annoying Asian with the annoying name—a private talk that would take care of the problem *permanently*. "We have more than fifty-five thousand soldiers," he tried to keep his voice level, "some with U.S. army experience. What are the chances that none of them were trained to fly helicopters?"

No one answered.

"Even just a few would be a big help in taking on our next target."

"What target?" Again, several asked at once.

"The Mormons." Angel grinned. "I've been hearing for some time that they were hardly affected by The Collapse, and it's part of their religion to hoard food anyway. Their state police is still active, but what are a few hundred cops to an army as large as ours?"

He could see the expressions slowly changing from doubt and fear to hope and anticipation.

"And most importantly, they are hundreds of miles inland. The *Wisconsin* won't be able to help them when we attack!"

That got them thinking!

"Mormons are just like Quakers," someone asserted, "a weird pacifist cult. They shouldn't be any problem at all!"

The log-jam broke and the conversation started flowing again, but this time it focused on possibilities and tactics. Others had heard about the Mormons as well. One captain even said that there were more women in Utah than anywhere else, because of the polygamy. In the space of a few minutes, all of the captains— even the doubtful Asian—had stopped thinking about the Disneyland disaster and started thinking about future glories.

Angel sighed, hoping no one could tell how relieved he was. Now, all he needed to do was get them working on preparing for the attack on the Mormons. If he could keep them busy and rushing around—without a minute to spare for themselves—they might not think too much about the implications of the beating they had taken.

CHAPTER 49:
WEDNESDAY, MAY 17, 2000

"Lying, cheating, hurting
That's all you seem to do…
Your time is gonna come."
—Led Zeppelin, *Your Time is Gonna Come*

Jimmy leaned against the wall, her hands stuffed into her pockets, her eyes watching the scene in front of her.

The representative from Deseret was just wrapping up his speech, promising that Deseret would never attack Dollar Ranch or attempt to force its residents to become a part of that growing state. They just wanted to touch base because many ranchers in western Colorado were members of the LDS Church and were petitioning to have their land admitted to Deseret. If, some day, Dollar Ranch were to become surrounded by Deseret Territory, they should not fear for their freedom, as long as they did not aggress upon Deseret. Dollar Ranchers should also be warned that Deseret would defend its own, but did not have enough resources to help independent communities.

Dreamer had been asking the Mormon some pointed questions, and was getting the answers he wanted to hear, but was still uncertain. "Well, it all sounds nice, but how do we know that you won't change your tune in the future? The Romans told the Carthaginians pretty much the same thing and then turned around and sacked them!"

"They also extorted huge bribes from the Carthaginians before turning on them, if memory serves. We have done nothing to you and propose only to leave you alone. Besides, the President of the LDS Church, our living Prophet, has set it as official Church policy. That is not something easily changed. It is true that the government of Deseret is not composed completely of Latter Day Saints, but we are by far the majority, and we can be counted on to keep state policy in line with our beliefs."

The man spread his hands in a gesture of openness and good-will. "Personally, I can tell you that I have the greatest respect for what you have built here. This is a remarkable community—I heard about it more than a hundred miles from here! According to what the prophet has asserted, it would be a black usurpation of the role of our Heavenly Father to try to force you to join us in faith or in politics. God requires that his children be free to listen to His voice in their hearts. Any coercion of peaceful peoples on our part would blot out that voice and replace it with our own human and fallible voices. It would be a great sin."

The words of the traveling Ambassador were a great relief to many of those listening, but Jimmy was only slightly aware of what was being discussed. Her attention was focused on Michel and Razor, cuddling on a bench about fifteen feet in front of her, unaware of the young woman's scrutiny. Razor was leaning against Michel, who was tracing patterns on her thigh, occasionally making *sotto voce* comments that made her laugh—as he alone was able to do.

Jimmy felt torn. She knew she had a terrible crush on the Frenchman, but she had also developed a deep love for Razor, al-beit of a different kind. She admired the mysterious woman enor-mously and enjoyed every second she could spend with her—es-pecially when Razor was teaching her to dance and fight. She craved the love of both Razor and Michel, but they were in the process of discovering each other, scarcely aware of anyone else.

It had been an exquisite agony when the two had shown up, as a couple, to Jimmy's nineteenth birthday party. It had pained her to see them together, and yet thrilled her that they were both there to be with her. They had stood by, as proud of her as her father was, when she'd signed her contract with Merlyn, and become an independent member of the community.

For some reason Jimmy hadn't fully thought through, she had made a snap decision right as she was signing and had written the name she'd been given at birth: Eva. It had been her mother's name and she had not let anyone call her Eva since her mother, *the* Eva, had been laid to her rest.

Dawn had also signed, just last week. At seventeen, she was plenty old enough to take care of herself, even if she did waste too much time playing with her hair and picking the right clothes. Dawn could be very annoying, and actually thought that things like nail-polish were important, but she was all right. At least she could shoot!

Actually, Dawn loved to shoot, and was proud of her role as a sentry. All of Jimmy's siblings had been taught gun safety and marksmanship from an early age, but it was Dawn who had become the best shot. It was amazing that someone so prissy could be so deadly accurate! She had been really taken with the high power and long range of the Barretts when they had arrived at Dollar Ranch, and had made a point of practicing with them whenever she could.

The reason for this one weird exception to Dawn's silly obsession with femininity, Jimmy knew, was that her real love in life was mathematics—another 'unfeminine' side of her character she tried to hide. Because of her fascination and skill in math, the calculations other long distance shooters needed to do on paper, or complete on a computer, she could do in her head. This ability had impressed the other Dollar Ranchers to no end. Some of them even called her a 'prodigy' or a 'virtuosa.'

Jimmy had to give her credit; the girl didn't act like it was any big deal and didn't let it go to her head. The secret, Dawn had confided, was that she had figured out some computational shortcuts, that was all. She didn't actually do anything all that complicated. Anyway, in spite of the hairspray and junk in the bathroom,

Dawn made a good roommate in the apartment Jimmy had built for them out of the family's barn.

"Hey, tough girl."

Startled out of her thoughts about her heartache and her sister, Jimmy turned and saw that Ed—who had pointedly avoided her birthday celebration—had slid up next to her. He was now leaning on the wall with his hands in his pockets, in an unconscious imitation of her. She understood now all too well the jealousy he'd been feeling, and even though she had disliked his way of showing it, she realized that it meant that he cared for her.

"Ed," she tried to make some amends, "I'm sorry I've been so inconsiderate of your feelings."

"I thought you might come around. Let's go outside and talk about it."

She followed him out.

His truck was still warm when they got in. He drove them out one of the radial roads and up onto the valley rim. It was a place where a trench was being dug up and over, taking a pipe to a nearby abandoned oil and gas field. Jimmy got out before Ed could say anything. She didn't want to be alone with him in his truck.

He joined her, looking down at the lights of the town. "It's pretty up here, but none of it means anything if I can't have you."

"No one can have me." Even though Razor was no longer Prudence, the time the older woman had spent with Jimmy had affected the younger woman's thinking.

"What I meant to say is... Jimmy, I love you, and I..." He gulped. "Will you marry me?"

"Marry you?!" Jimmy was taken completely by surprise. "Ed, I meant what I said about being sorry about the way I treated you, and I do care for you, but..."

"Then marry me!" He took her by the shoulders and pulled her lips to his.

She pulled back. He pulled harder, brushing her lips with his. She jerked free, and slapped him across the face. The violent contact stopped them both for a moment, standing apart, breathing hard.

Then Ed advanced on her again. "You little bitch!" The light of reason had fled from his eyes.

Seeing the rage on his face made Jimmy truly afraid of another human being for the first time in her life. He grabbed her by the shoulders again, his fingers digging in painfully. He was bigger and stronger than she was, what should she do?

I should have worn my birthday present to the meeting! Michel had given her one of the Sig Sauers on her birthday, after finding that she was much better with them than he was.

Then Jimmy remembered what Razor had told her about the time to strike back being the very instant they start something. After that, they've got you in their power, and it's too late. She gripped Ed's shoulders and pushed against him, like a Sumo wrestler, with all her strength. He reacted just as she hoped, pushing back as hard as he could. She reversed herself, now pulling on him for all she was worth, and letting herself go over backward.

It worked better than she had imagined. He well-nigh flew over her head, as though he had jumped and been kicked at the same time, and landed heavily on his back. *Thump!!* He lay there, stunned and unable to breathe. It was only a few seconds, but it was long enough for Jimmy retrieve the dirk from her boot. She pulled Ed's head back by the hair and held the blade so he could feel its sharp edge on his neck.

"Not one move, or I'll slit your throat," she hissed.

Ed had started to tense, but now went completely lax—a puppet with his strings cut.

"Good." She moved the knife to make sure he could feel it. "Now reach into your pocket, slowly, and hand me your keys."

Ed complied. The will to fight seeped out of him as tears of regret ran down the sides of his face, mingling with the dirt.

Jimmy snatched the keys from his hand and dashed for the truck, but Ed made no move to stop her. She got in and locked the doors, but he still did not get up. She couldn't tell for sure in the

rear-view mirror, but for all she could tell, even after she accelerated back down the hill and into town, he did not move. When
she returned later with Merlyn, Razor, Michel, and her father, Ed
was still lying where she had left him, still spilling his tears silently upon the earth.

Ed's trial and sentencing were carried out immediately, delayed only long enough for the gathering of the evidence the plaintiff
wanted to present.

Merlyn sat at the table in the dining hall where he had played
the tape recordings of the radio broadcasts. The short notice notwithstanding, the room—the same one the Deseret Ambassador
had spoken in—was packed. It was warm and stuffy from too many
bodies being too close together. Dreamer stood watch over Ed
with a rifle, but it was hardly necessary; Ed was as still and lifeless
as when they had found him on the hill.

This time, Randy had brought Merlyn a hammer and a piece
of 2x4 to use as a gavel and pad, and Merlyn pounded the piece of
wood to good effect.

"First off," Merlyn was able to speak without raising his voice,
"I want to remind everyone of the social contract that binds us
together and governs these proceedings."

He held up a copy of the contract, the one Ed had signed.
"Every one of us is bound by this contract. We are not bound in
theory, not bound because some elected leader says so, and not
bound because of history, precedent, or cultural habit. We are
bound because of our consent to be so bound."

The room quieted so that each person's breathing was loud in
their own ears. Even the children present understood that this was
a very important occasion. It was a time when everything would
either begin unraveling, or the voluntary bonds they had accepted
would become tighter, carrying the authority and force of law.

"The accused is here," Merlyn continued, "because he agreed
to be here if ever accused. The accuser is here because she has also
agreed to be here. And I am here, because I, as Owner of Dollar
Ranch and a signer of the social contract, have agreed to preside

over these proceedings. Do any of the parties to this matter dispute any of these facts?"

Without looking at each other, both Ed and Jimmy shook their heads.

"Very well then," Merlyn wore the expression of a child forcing down a spoonful of castor oil, "Edward Lerta, you stand accused of an initiation of the use of force against Eva, daughter of Dreamer, also known as Jimmy. You also stand accused of third degree harm, or minor physical harm, as defined in the contract. Do you contest these accusations?"

Ed showed a brief revival of spirit. "I wasn't going to rape her!"

"Son, what you were or were not going to do is something only you—if anyone—can know for sure. That's not what we're concerned with here. Our concern is only with what you *did*—the facts of history, if you will. Now, do you dispute the accusations?"

"Well, I did start it. I admit that, and I regret it very much..." Everyone watching could see the fleeting spirit that had animated Ed draining away. Only Merlyn and those in the front row could see the tears return. "But I didn't mean to hurt her!"

"Again, what you meant is not a fact that can be determined by evidence, only what you did. And the doctor has confirmed that there are bruises on Jimmy's shoulders where you gripped her. That's solid evidence of third degree harm. Do you dispute that evidence or the accusation?"

"No, sir."

"So noted." Merlyn made some notes in a journal he had hoped he'd never have to use. The very blankness of the page on which he wrote made it all the more difficult to do. "Now, do you wish to make any counter accusations against Jimmy—I mean Eva?"

Ed thought it over. "No sir. She whipped me good, but I know I deserved it."

"So noted." More notations in the Journal of Dispute Resolutions. "Now, Eva, the crimes to which Ed has just admitted carry a serious penalty. An initiation of the use of force combined with physical harm of any degree has a sentence of expulsion from the community. I must advise you that you will have to live with what happens here tonight, one way or the other."

As much as Jimmy normally enjoyed attention, she now felt distinctly uncomfortable. Everyone was holding their breath to hear what she would say, and it was disconcerting to be referred to by her mother's name—even though it was also her own and she had chosen to use it for contract business. She knew that far more than the resolution of her conflict with Ed would depend on what she decided. This *much* attention, on something so important, was definitely not enjoyable. But it was her duty to do her best, so she did not flinch or whisper when she answered Merlyn: "I understand."

Merlyn nodded. "If you believe that Ed is truly repentant and that this will never happen again, you might wish to withdraw one of your accusations. I cannot be merciful—I am required to administer whatever punishment the crimes call for, as per the contract. Only the victim can show leniency on the guilty. Do you understand?"

"Yes, Merlyn."

"Very well. Do you wish to withdraw either of your accusations?"

Jimmy knew what her answer had to be, but she hesitated just the same. She couldn't look at Ed as she spoke. "Merlyn, I can't. I honestly believe that Ed is not a bad person—really—but he has always had more temper than he could handle. No sir, he was out of control, and if I let him off the hook, I could never live with myself if he lost his temper again and hurt someone. He did what he did, and I cannot pretend he didn't."

Merlyn drew a heavy sigh. "Edward Lerta, having pled guilty to the crimes of which you have been accused, and having failed to win leniency from your victim, I hereby sentence you to the punishment required by contract for your crimes: you are expelled from this community. Because the actual harm you have done is minor, and there was no loss of property, valuable time, or other such consideration, none of your property is forfeit for the repay-

ment of such debts. Under escort, you may collect your belongings and leave at once." He paused and Ed met his eyes for a
second. "I'm sorry this has happened, son, and I hope you choose
to make this something you learn and grow from, instead of something that destroys your life."

Merlyn banged his gavel.

"Dreamer, Optimist, if you would escort Mr. Lerta while he
collects his belongings and then to the gate?"

Both men rose and prepared to leave.

Jimmy finally turned to face Ed, tears brimming over. He was
no longer tearful himself. He stood abruptly, prompting Dreamer
to level his rifle. "*Bitch!*" Ed turned on his heel, his two guards
trailing him out of the room.

CHAPTER 50:
SATURDAY, MAY 27, 2000

"And you're rushing headlong
You've got a new goal
And you're rushing headlong
Out of control."
—Queen, *Headlong*

Rosalia was sitting with a book by the door of the room she shared with Holly, listening intently to the comings and goings outside. Something was happening—something big.

In this room, and in the other, she had always been able to hear people speaking in the hallway when they passed by her door. It didn't happen much, and the guards never spoke at all. But now, groups of people had been hustling back and forth for hours.

Since she understood both languages being spoken, the two prisoners had agreed that Rosalia should do the listening. She had learned much from the snippets of conversation she had been collecting over the last several hours.

Holly came out of the bathroom and whispered to Rosalia. "Okay, I think they're too busy to pay much attention to us, so let's compare notes." The dark blues and purples of Holly's bruises were fading to greens and yellows, and her split lip was healing, but the rage in her still smoldered. She was itching for action, even if it cost her everything.

Rosalia had tended to her friend's wounds as best she could, but knew that the deepest wounds were in her soul, and those would take time to heal. Holly's anger, she thought, was probably the healthiest reaction she could be having; it was much better than withdrawing into fear, or giving up the will to live altogether! Rosalia had seen such reactions in other abused women. She put a hand on the actress' shoulder and whispered back, "First, we seem to be in a room in some kind of base or something. All of those people are busy working on things *here*."

"That's interesting. I heard someone say something about a base in Pomona, when Angel took me to witness his great victory over Disneyland. Maybe that's where we are... But I didn't live too far from Pomona! They had me blindfolded in that car for hours... It must have been a trick to make sure I didn't know where I was."

"You could be right." Rosalia had never been able to figure out where she was being kept, but had always assumed she had been in some kind of permanent facility Angel maintained. "The other main thing I've learned is that they are working on preparing materials for some kind of invasion or something. Angel is through raiding little neighborhoods like yours—he is taking his whole army on the road somewhere. They also seem relieved about the Russians not bombing something, if you can believe that!"

"You haven't heard about the Russians?"

"What about the Russians?"

"Never mind. I'll tell you later... But that does explain all the running around. It takes a lot of work to take an army on the road—especially if you're in a hurry. I wonder if that son of a bitch who calls himself a general is up to it..."

Rosalia regarded her companion curiously. "How would you know about stuff like that? Uh, no offense."

"No sweat. My ex—Frank—he was a sergeant in the Army. He worked in logistics—always bitched and moaned about what a headache it was when they put on an exercise involving any more than a few hundred men. He wanted to go career Army, before they kicked him out. I bet things are a real confused mess out there!"

Leaning against the door as they sat, taking a moment's comfort from their closeness, both understood at once that they would never have a better chance to escape.

"So what have you come up with?" Rosalia asked.

"Well, that bread-white I saved from breakfast is still fresh in the plastic I wrapped it in, so we may be able to use that... If they ever feed us again."

It was strange, Rosalia had to admit, strange and more than a little alarming. As prisoners, she and Holly had always been well cared for. But today things had all changed; not only had no one come to clear their breakfast dishes away, no one had brought them lunch, and she was sure it must already be past dinner time.

All the more reason to concentrate on escaping!

"What else?"

"Well," Holly patted her waistband, "I've got a nail file and a half a pair of tweezers tucked in my pants. When we think they're not looking, we can try to pick the lock."

"Anything else?"

"A can of aerosol. Too bad they don't let us have any matches, or it'd make an even better weapon! Still, even without lighting it on fire, it'd sting like hell if you sprayed it in the guard's eyes."

"Me?"

"Honey," Holly took her hand, "you are a beautiful Spanish lady, but you have no experience distracting men. Me, I've been nothing but a distraction for men all my life. If we get a chance, I'll get the guard's attention, you spray him, and then we'll both jump him. Okay?"

"Okay." Rosalia thought that Holly might be taking the more dangerous role upon herself, but had to agree with her logic.

"You said those were the major things." Holly changed the subject in an effort to keep Rosalia from worrying about it too much. "Have you learned anything else?"

"I've heard two other things more than once, but I'm not sure what they mean."

"What things?"

"Several people mentioned 'Mormones' and 'veinti-nueve

palmas." Rosalia puzzled it over. "So I guess that whatever is going on has something to do with Mormons. There were once a lot of them around here, so I don't know how great a hint that is. The other thing means 'twenty-nine palm trees.' There hasn't been much else—mostly just talk about all the 'stuck up Mormon whores' they are going to...you know."

"Hmmm... There's a big Marine Corps base out in the Mojave Desert called Twenty-Nine Palms, could that have been what they were talking about?"

"Yes! 'Palmas' can mean 'palms' or 'palm trees' and I'm sure someone mentioned it in the context of some kind of fight Ejercito Dragon had won."

"They beat the United States Marines?"

"Maybe there were not many of them left. From Angel's bragging about his conquests, I think there are many military bases that have been abandoned."

"Yes. It got really bad when everyone anywhere near a base started worrying about the Russians bombing them..." Holly had a sudden thought. "Say, just how long have you been in here?"

"I don't know. I didn't think of counting, at first, and then it was too late to know for sure... But I'm pretty sure it has been over a year."

"More than a year!" Holly gasped in disbelief. "We have *got* to get out of here!"

It was the next day when Holly awoke in a pool of ink and repeated the same words: "We have *got* to get out of here!" The lights had been turned off, and the two had fallen asleep when exhaustion overtook them in the blackness.

Rosalia woke up to a vigorous nudge. "What?"

"This has gone on long enough. It's obvious that the power has gone out and we haven't heard a thing for a long time. I bet there isn't even a guard out there!"

"You really think so?"

"One way to find out." Holly made her way to the door by

feel. The light switch still didn't work, and the air in the room was stale. "Guard! Guard! Open up! We can't breathe in here!!"

No response.

"Guard!" Holly pounded on the door with both fists, yelling for the guard to open up.

There was still no response.

"I think you're right." Rosalia came over to stand beside her. "Let's listen again."

The two pressed their ears to the cool metal door, but heard nothing. It was unnerving. There was no background whisper of ventilation systems, no soft hum or muffled clank of machines at work, no thrum of the generator that had provided the building's electricity. The silence was so complete that the only thing they could hear—even when they were absolutely still—was the *shhh-shhh-shhh* of their own blood rushing through their ears.

"Fuck this!" Holly pulled the nail file out of her belt. "If there's no one out there, no one can stop us from picking the lock. I refuse to die in here, like a pet someone forgot to leave food for when they went on vacation!" She stuck the tip of the file between the door and the jamb, and ran it down until it hit the bolt. The sandpaper texture made it harder to work than a credit card, but the file was easier to angle because it was thinner.

"What were you going to do with the bread-white, anyway?" Rosalia had nothing to do while Holly tried to jimmy the lock, so she talked.

"I'd mushed it into dough, and I was going to try to squeeze it in the hole where the bolt goes into the door frame, the next time they came to feed us."

"Ahhhh!" That way the door would close, but not lock!

Some unmeasurable time passed.

"Shit!" Holly threw the file down. "This is hopeless. I can't even see my hand, let alone what the tip of the file is doing in there!"

"How about the tweezers?"

"Yeah, not having any light shouldn't make any difference to

picking the lock, but the tweezers aren't really the best shape...
Too bad nobody wears bobby pins any more! I could try turning
the lock with the tweezer-half while using a bobby pin to jiggle
the pins."

"Hey, there was a paper clip on a page in one of the books!
Would that help?"

"Yeah, that'd be great!"

It took a while to find the right book, but Rosalia managed it.
Like many people who love their books, she knew roughly where
they all were, their sizes, shapes, and kinds of binding. She recognized the right book by the feel of the cracks in its spine and
handed over the paper clip with both pride and fear.

It was good to be doing something, to be trying to escape—
but what if there actually was still a guard out there? What if he
was under orders to ignore any pleas coming from the room? What
if Angel had tired of them and had decided to starve them to
death? Or worse yet, what if everyone really had gone and forgotten all about them, and they were unable to get out?

With each passing hour, the air got mustier in the room.
Rosalia's stomach had given up growling, but she could hear Holly's
still making odd grumblings as she worked on the lock. Occasionally Holly would curse Frank for only letting her watch him pick
locks, and never explaining how it was done or letting her practice.

"This Frank of yours sounds like an...interesting person."

"Oh," Holly chuckled, "you could say that. He was nothing
but trouble. He got busted more than I did when I was out on the
streets, before I got into making movies. For all I know, he's in
even worse shape than we are, abandoned months ago in some
forgotten jail cell somewhere. It'd serve him right."

When Rosalia asked why, Holly didn't answer. But there was a
renewed ferocity in her efforts when she attacked the lock again.

More than an hour later, Holly bent the paper clip one time
too many and it snapped, leaving half inside the lock. "Goddamn
mother..." She slumped against the door in defeat. "Rosy," she was
nearly crying, "I don't want to give up, but I don't see any point in

fumbling around in the dark any longer. I wasn't getting anywhere with the damned lock even before the paper clip broke!"

Rosalia slumped against the door, next to her friend. The hinge dug into her back, and she moved to one side irritably. Stupid hinge... Hinge? She turned around and fingered the offending piece of hardware carefully. Of course the pin would be on the inside, the door swung inward! "Holly, can you think of anything like a nail we could get hold of?"

Holly considered the question before answering. "The bookcases are made of wood. They probably have lots of nails or screws holding them together."

"Good thinking." Rosalia nodded, felt but not seen. "They're probably held together with screws. They might work, if they're long and thin enough, but we don't have a screwdriver... I'm not sure how we would get them out."

"Work for what?"

"The hinges are on this side of the door."

"So?"

"So, I remember reading an illustrated explanation of how different hinges work. It was in an encyclopedia. My father had replaced a door my brother Jorge had broken in our apartment and I got curious. I remember it because I was surprised that the tube-like part of a hinge—the part you can see when a door is closed—is actually two sets of smaller tubes, held together by a pin. The part that's screwed to the wall is held to the part that's screwed to the door by a pin that also functions as a pivot. You use a nail-set, or something else thin and hard, to hammer the pin up from the bottom, and it pops right out of the hinge."

Holly now thought she remembered seeing something similar done once. "We could pull the door right out of the wall without having to unlock it! Rosy, you're a genius!"

"Oh, I read a lot."

"Whatever. So now we need a screw." Holly chuckled. "God, I really could use a great screw—it's been too long!"

Rosalia blushed. She hesitated to say anything, but Holly's

remark struck her as...extraordinary, given what had happened to her. "You...still want to have sex with men?"

Holly hesitated before answering, but when she did, her tone was firm—if somewhat hard-edged. "Rosy, sex is a great thing. I loved my job—can you imagine getting paid to do something that feels good to begin with? Sex with women is fun, but for me, there is nothing that beats a good fuck with a man I like." She fell into a thoughtful silence before continuing more quietly. "What Angel did... That wasn't sex, it was domination. The two have nothing in common. Handshakes and punches both involve hands, but they are two completely different things."

"Oh." Rosalia took Holly's hand in the blackness.

"I'm not saying I don't care—nor that I wouldn't like to settle the score with the bastard! But just because some sick asshole uses his dick to take out his aggression on me, that's no reason to go hating sex."

"I think I understand. Making love is a beautiful thing, and that makes it doubly ugly when someone takes that beautiful thing and warps it into a weapon. The domination is bad enough, but the corruption of something beautiful makes it worse..."

"No!" Holly sat up straight in the blackness, enunciating each angry word clearly. "It's not something beautiful corrupted. The two haven't a goddamned thing in common—*not a goddamned thing!*" Holly could feel Rosalia's hand tense in response and took a couple deep breaths to calm herself before continuing. "Rosy, it's not your fault, but you just don't know. You can't know. You've never experienced the utter violation of it—and I hope you never do!"

"Oh Holly, I'm so sorry!" Rosalia hugged her friend, wishing there were some way she could reach into her mind and erase the hateful memories.

"It sucks, Rosy, it really sucks to be used like that, but I'm alive and I know how to enjoy life. Angel is dead—he just doesn't know it—and he'll never find happiness. I'm much better off than he'll ever be!"

Rosalia had known girls who had been completely devastated by things such as what had happened to Holly. "Holly, how do you do it? How can you keep going like nothing bad happened?"

There was a brief silence.

When Holly did answer, it was very softly, almost a whisper. "Well, it's happened to me before."

The blackness pressed in and Rosalia could think of nothing to say.

Holly considered her next words carefully, speaking only when she was sure she had herself fully in control. "And I am not keeping on like nothing bad has happened. Something awful happened and I'll put the son of a bitch on the first express train to hell, if I ever get hold of him! But if there's one thing I've learned, it's that curling up and crying doesn't do any good—that only makes their domination more complete. Fuck that! I'm not going to give him the satisfaction of beating me, inside, where it really counts! He may have dominated my body, but he'll never dominate my mind!"

Rosalia realized that she would never completely understand what Holly had been through, but thought she understood what her friend was saying. "I think I know what you mean. There's a difference between accepting what's happened—that's unchangeable anyway—and acquiescing to his will." She pondered it in the inky stillness. "You know... In that sense, he's been doing the same thing to both of us... The sex isn't really central to what he wants, it's the breaking of our wills. It *is* about domination, and he's been trying to break both of us."

"Well... In a way, yes."

Rosalia startled herself by remembering that she had told Angel something along these lines herself. "When he first kidnapped me, he told me that he had my life in his hands. I told him that he could kill me—which only destroys my body—but that he had no power over me. That's how I got the scar over my eye. Instead of shooting me, he hit me with his gun and cut me."

There was a longer silence, in which the two considered the similarities and differences between their experiences.

After several minutes, Holly brought them back to their original subject. "So, uh, you think we can find a screw around here?"

Rosalia thought it over. "I have another idea that might be easier." She stumbled back to the bed with her hands out before her and fumbled around on the night table. "Ah-ha!"

"What is it?"

"My pen."

"Your pen? Rosy, we're trying to escape, not write letters!"

"This is *my* pen. It's a really good one, not a cheap ball-point. It has a metal ink cartridge inside that's made of steel and it has a sharp tip. I bet it'd make a great nail, if we could find a hammer."

"How about a shoe?"

"Okay." Rosalia groped around under the bed for one of the ugly retro-seventies shoes Angel had brought for her; it would probably be heavy enough. She found one and returned to the door.

In spite of their circumstances, she experienced a pang of sadness when she took her pen apart. It was probably going to get broken. When she had the ink cartridge out, she stood and fitted the narrow tip into the opening in the bottom of the upper hinge. It fit perfectly. "Okay, here goes!" She held the cartridge with one hand and banged upward with the shoe in the other, as hard as she dared.

She missed, hitting her fingers instead. "¡Mierda!"

"Why Rosy, I do believe that's the first time I've heard you cuss. Want me to help?"

"It's my idea, I'll do it."

Trying to gauge the distance more carefully, Rosalia hammered again. This time, she hit the cartridge, but nothing happened. She hammered harder. Still nothing. She swung upward as hard as she could, and the cartridge split apart, causing the shoe to hit her fingers again, and ink to ooze all over them. "¡Mierda! Hijo de la..." She cradled her wounded hand.

"What happened?"

"The cartridge broke and I got ink all over my hand."

"And the pin?"

"The pin didn't budge."

"Shit!"

"That's what I said!" They both laughed miserably and slumped back down against the door.

"Well," Rosalia proposed after a while, "I guess we're back to the screw idea."

"Yeah," Holly agreed, "I bet Angel would love to watch us do that..."

There was a silent pause, in which neither could see that they both turned suddenly toward each other. "The mirror!" They both shouted it at once.

"My turn this time!" Holly got up and hunted her way back toward the bed. There was a heavy lamp on the night table. She picked it up and grabbed a pillow. The lamp was plugged in somewhere behind the bed. Rather than take the time to find the plug, she jerked the lamp free.

She found the mirror by feel in short order and set the pillow down. Then she leaned against the wall beside the mirror with one hand and pulled back with the lamp in the other. "Here goes!"

Rosalia held her breath, unconscious of her own action.

Holly slammed the lamp forward, base first, as hard as she could. It was overkill. The mirror turned out to be of ordinary thickness and the lamp sailed right through, hesitating slightly in Holly's hand as it shattered the glass, and then getting tangled in a piece of fabric that was hanging behind the glass.

Cooler, fresher air wafted into the room through the opening.

"Well I'll be." It was equally lightless in the room behind the mirror. Holly picked up the pillow and broke off the jagged shards that hung from the mirror frame with it. "Anything you want to take with you? Time to go!"

Rosalia turned to look, then remembered that there was nothing to see. "No. I'm dressed, and my pen was about the only thing that was really mine in this room."

"Right." Holly stepped carefully through the hole in the wall.

"Watch the edges, there's still some sharp glass that I didn't get—shit!"

"What?!"

"I tripped over something. A chair. That son of a bitch must have sat here watching us!"

Rosalia grinned. "I wonder what he made of all the time we spent reading together on the bed."

"He probably thinks you were ruining me."

The chair grated on the floor as Holly pushed it out of the way. Rosalia tried to be careful coming through the opening, but scratched her shoulder on a thin glass blade Holly had missed. She didn't let herself cry out.

The women followed the wall until it came to another door. It locked from the inside. In seconds, they were out in the hallway. It too was pitch dark.

"Which way?" Holly asked.

"Either."

They followed the near wall again, until it came to a fire door.

Rosalia listened, her ear pressed to the door. "You think we'll find the Minotaur?"

Holly wouldn't have known what she meant before Angel had kidnapped her, but Greek history was one of Rosalia's passions and the actress had picked up quite a bit of it without intending to. "Are you kiddin'? With two beautiful women all locked up and helpless in his underground tunnels? I'm sure he would have found us—and we'd have kicked his ass too!"

Rosalia couldn't help but laugh.

Opening the door, they were blinded by a light that, when their tear-filled eyes adjusted, turned out to be only a soft reflection of sunlight filtering down a stairwell from several floors above.

"So, we were underground!" Rosalia's heart leapt at her first sight of sunlight in over a year. "Let's go!" She dashed up the stairs before Holly could stop her.

Running up several flights of stairs, she came to the ground floor and burst through a fire exit, out into a parking lot. The full strength of the afternoon sunlight was too much for her, and she had to close her eyes, but so great was the relief of freedom that she laughed and pranced in the fresh air.

Holly emerged more cautiously, blinking. Seeing Rosalia dancing in the deserted parking lot, she rushed to join her and gave her a tight hug. They had had electric light not too long before, but it just couldn't compare to the liquid gold pouring down on them from the open sky. It was the light of freedom! They both laughed and Holly kissed Rosalia, full on the lips.

Rosalia flushed crimson—that was no sisterly peck on the cheek!—and stepped back. "So...uh...what do we do now?" She squinted about, taking in her surroundings. There were a few cars in the parking lot—all of them wrecks—but no people. "And where are Angel's soldiers?"

"Maybe the people Angel left behind as guards deserted him." Holly answered. "He really took a beating at Disneyland, and maybe the folks here didn't want to be around after he pissed off the Mormons. Or," her face brightened, "maybe his slaves rose up against their guards after the main force left!"

Rosalia's mind was calming down after the exhilaration of release and the unexpected kiss, settling into more methodical thought patterns. "Let's check these cars. They all look wrecked, but maybe we can get one running. Then we can go look for something to eat."

"Good idea. I had some stuff stashed in the walls at my old place—I bet Angel's thugs didn't find it. We could start there."

"Great, and when we have enough supplies, we can go after him."

"What!?!"

"Angel must be stopped. You know it as well as I do. He's going to meet a violent end soon, and I want to be the one to deliver it! The sooner I can do so, the fewer people he will hurt... I wish I'd done it a *long* time ago!"

"Well, that I can understand," Holly had a strong desire of her own to see the worm squirm, "but that's crazy! You want two unarmed women to go chasing after a whole army?"

"If what you said about Disneyland is true, that army may well be scattered and confused when we catch up with him. Or, at the very least, they won't be expecting any attacks from behind. We can find some uniforms and dress like Angel's men... Or do you have some other pressing engagements? A movie to shoot?"

Holly laughed. "You *are* crazy, but maybe you're right." She regarded Rosalia with renewed respect. "No, I don't suppose I have anything I'd rather do than settle the score with that scum... And, besides, I can't let you go alone!"

"Okay then, let's go back inside and see if there are any left-over supplies or uniforms. This was supposed to be a base, right? Maybe the deserters left a few things."

Holly and Rosalia searched the entire building without finding anything useful. They spent more than an hour at it, but turned up only an empty package of cigarettes, with a half-used matchbook tucked in the cellophane. They lit some scraps of paper with the matches, to shine light in the basement levels, but it didn't matter—there was nothing left.

They did find that their door had been bolted and could not have been opened from either side without a key. Perhaps Angel had meant to starve them to death, but if so, his intentions—and the steel door—might have saved them from being taken by whomever had looted the Pomona base. They also found Rosalia's first bathrobe, encrusted with brown spatterings, in the room with the chair. Holly didn't ask, but suspected from her friend's expression that the robe had to do with some violence of Angel's.

Returning to the parking lot, they rummaged through the pile of abandoned vehicles with but scant hope of finding one they could get working. On the edge of the lot, away from the building and among the last vehicles in the heap, the two escapees came across a city bus with a serpentine line of bullet-holes perforating it from front to back. Walking dejectedly around the bus, they came upon a garage-type building. It had no windows, and a solid metal door with a large padlock on it.

"Rosy, if it's got a lock on it, it's got to have something valuable inside, wouldn't you say?"

"Yes!"

Setting off with greater purpose, they rushed to look for something to use on the lock. In the trunk of the third wreck she searched, Holly found a sturdy tire-iron. She called Rosalia and the two returned to the garage. "The lock looks pretty tough, but I bet I can pry the hasp off."

The metal squealed in protest when Holly applied the iron, but on the fifth heave, the screw heads popped loose and the lock and hasp swung free of the door.

"All right Holly!" Rosalia bent to the handle and lifted the door. Inside they discovered two Jeeps, uniforms, and even a supply of food and water, which became their immediate priority as soon as they set eyes upon it. Afterward, when they checked the cache over, they found that the Jeeps were fueled and ready to go.

Each Jeep had a spare tire and a double bracket with two large jerry cans attached to the rear. Rosalia took the two cans from one of the Jeeps and put them in the back seat of the other, also transferring the supplies and rations. Holly searched for plastic jugs, jars, buckets—anything she could find into which to siphon the gasoline from the Jeep they would be leaving behind.

When everything was ready, they set off toward the Mojave and the last known location of their quarry, laughing at their insanity.

Chapter 51:
Monday, May 29, 2000

"I'm a loser, and I lost someone who's near to me
I'm a loser, and I'm not what I appear to be."
—Beatles, *I'm a Loser*

Feeling more than a little guilty, Ed peered through Ms. Abel's binoculars at the watchtower to the south, then the one to the north, and finally to scan the ground for the gun emplacement they would have to go over. The Rifle Gang had approached the little valley of Dollar Ranch from the southeast, through wooded land that had belonged to the National Forest Service. Using firebreaks as roads, they had arrived at a small hill to the east of the valley without alerting the town's sentries and scouts who monitored the local roadways. The gang was now gathering its forces behind the hill.

Ed handed the glasses back to Ms. Abel. Whatever happened, it was all Jimmy's fault—she shouldn't have had him kicked out of Dollar Ranch! "It's like I told you. This hill, and the gun in front of us, are close to being right between the two watchtowers. That means the tower sentries will have to make their longest shots to hit us, and both towers may not be occupied—they think they've scared you off for good. We could wait longer to see if anyone moves in the north one, but the only movement there's been since we got here has been in the south one. We're a little closer to that one, but we're still talking about long shots—as good as quarter-mile shots—at moving targets."

"No." Ms. Abel swiveled her bucket-shaped head once to the

left and to the right once. "Dusk will be setting in soon, and I don't want to attack at night; they know the terrain inside the valley better than we do. Where's the gun you say is in front of us?"

"Right there, where it looks flat. Since they don't know we're here and we're out of range of the sensors, the gun is in the ground. If you look carefully, you'll see a cement pad. The gun will rise up out of it when the sensors pick up our movement. When that happens, the alarm will go off in the Big House and the PA system will warn us away. The automatic guns will begin firing thirty seconds after that."

"And you're sure the gap will be big enough if we take out the automatic rifle?"

"No, there will be some overlap in the fields of fire of the two guns flanking the gap, but it'll be brief. They are designed not to turn all the way to right angles so they don't start shooting defenders in the trenches. So, if we take out that center gun, and the men all double-time it, most everyone should be able to get through."

"What about the tower guns?"

"Like I said: it looks like there's only one tower manned right now, the one to the south, so the 'dozer needs to make that its first priority. Once it takes out the automatic gun, it should swing south and demolish that tower. Most everyone should get through."

"Acceptable losses, is that what you're saying?"

"It's the only way, unless you have a third 'dozer somewhere."

"All right." Ms. Abel put her binoculars down. "And you're sure the machine guns are only 30.06es?"

"Positive. But they're not machine guns. They're TJC-30s modified to be fired at a high speed by computers. I helped wired the system myself. Keep the guys without the body armor you took from the police station inside the vehicles, and they should be okay. The automated guns only look for man-sized moving objects that radiate heat."

"Computers! After all that man's machines have done to the

earth, how could they use computers!" The burly woman hated the machines. Two hundred of her men had fled the front gate the other night—no wonder! They were up against pure evil! Anyone who liked computers deserved to be shot, but now she had only about half as many men to do the job...good thing she hadn't been driving the first 'dozer, with its inadequate armor! She wouldn't get another chance, so the information she based her plans on had to be accurate—hence her final debriefing with the traitor.

"Uh, right." Ed supposed that anyone who didn't like technology before Y2K would only hate it worse now... But there wasn't any point in arguing about it with anyone who was religious about it. "So, after we break through, remember that we need hostages, as a first priority. Just the adults in the valley outnumber the force you have left, and even the kids will fight you. They also have a redoubt, and hostages are the only way you'll get them out if they take cover there."

"You didn't say anything about a redoubt before."

"They won't retreat there unless they're being bombed from the air or overwhelmed. We can't do either of those things. Our plan is to break in and seize hostages."

"Right, I'll brief the men." Ms. Abel drew her revolver and checked to make sure it was loaded.

"And I get the blonde girl."

"Wrong."

Ed turned in surprise—Ms. Abel had the revolver aimed at his chest. Her face dared him to rush her. "But you promised that I could have her if I helped you get in!"

"You betrayed your own people. You think I could ever trust you?" She didn't bother waiting for an answer; the bullet hit him right above the heart, passing through his left lung and out the back of his body. "Traitor!" She spat on him and left to brief her lieutenants.

Ed lay in the dirt, motionless. The pain was beyond anything he had imagined and he knew that nothing could prevent his death now. He might have tried to draw his own gun and get revenge before losing consciousness, but Ms. Abel's words had wounded him deeper down inside than her bullet had. As his life bled into the earth, he admitted to himself that he deserved it. He lay as still as the night Jimmy had bested him.

Thinking of that night brought back the painful humiliation of his expulsion from Dollar Ranch.

The faces of the people as he left the dining hall, the palpable hostility, and the even more intolerable expressions of pity... Tossing his things into the back of his truck... Being escorted to the gate at gunpoint... Driving out, leaving everyone he knew in the entire world... Arriving at the Rusty Cannon Motel and pulling over to bawl like a baby where nobody could see him... Looking up with bleary eyes to see his truck surrounded—the Rifle Gang had returned to town... Being dragged out and held, spread-eagled, on the parking lot... His rage at their sacking of his truck... The greater rage of being seen in a moment of weakness... Ms. Abel's gun at his temple... His voice speaking as though on its own, offering them information on how to get around Dollar Ranch's defenses...

It was not his life that passed before his eyes, but his descent into hell.

With each weakening pulse of blood, he understood that he had lashed out in anger at the one girl he had ever truly loved—a girl he may well have just delivered into the dirty hands of some vile gangster... Someone as vile as himself.

Ed's last conscious thought was that he had proved that Jimmy was right to have refused him leniency.

Ms. Abel kicked his body when she came back with her lieutenants to show them where the gun emplacement was. "Look carefully, men. I checked everything over with the traitor before I put him out of our misery. He worked with computers, so it served him right—after everything his kind have done to the world!" She realized that she was about to break out in a spontaneous lecture and reined herself in. "Anyway, the hole in their defenses will be right there, after the 'dozer takes out the robot gun, so that's where everyone needs to charge. Remind the men that the farther away they are from the flanking guns, the easier it will be for those guns to hit them, so, once the guns start firing, the safest direction will be straight forward. Once I'm inside the perimeter, the *computers* won't have a target and will stop firing. That's when you charge— it'll give you an extra thirty seconds without any *machine* shooting at you. I'll be on my way to take out the sniper in the tower. Got it?" The words 'computers' and 'machine' dripped with hatred. "We've got to stop these hellspawn *computer-lovers* before they ruin what's left of the world!"

The squad leaders split up and returned to their vehicles to brief their men. Most of them couldn't have cared less about the computers, but knew that they could extort a huge amount of supplies from the wealthy Dollar Ranchers.

This time the men in the backs of pickups wore body armor, and those without were crammed into an assortment of sport utility vehicles. The windows had been removed from all the vehicles, and slats of iron and steel had been welded over the openings, affording some visibility and some protection.

Ms. Abel climbed up onto the second armored bulldozer the gang had rigged. She had tripled the thickness of the slitted iron plates welded across the front of the glass-enclosed cab—thick enough to stop even a .50 BMG!—and had added welded slats around the sides and rear. She was well pleased with the results and was confident that she could both lead her men and be safe from the defending guns—now that she knew exactly what kind of guns they were.

Standing in what she supposed was a dramatic pose on the back of her 'dozer, Ms. Abel addressed her forces. "All right men, it's time to take what should have been ours a long time ago, time for revenge against these *technologists!* Follow me as soon as I take out the center gun!" She hunkered down into her seat and revved the diesel engine before engaging the caterpillar treads. The armored machine lurched forward and took her over the top of the little hill.

A bulldozer cannot exactly charge up a hill, so Ms. Abel contented herself with pushing hers as fast as it would go. It was a good pace, since she had the blade lifted to protect the machine's motor. As she advanced on the concrete slab the traitor had identified as the location of the hidden gun, the automated weapon rose from the ground and the PA system began warning her to withdraw. She recognized the voice with the island accent from the previous attack and spite flared in her heart.

When the alarm shrilled—slightly behind a signal from the nearest watchtower—Merlyn was on duty in the control center. He observed the bulldozer approaching gun number thirty-one on a monitor that had been activated by the same sensors that triggered the alarm and activated the guns. Using the Big House's own PA system, he put out the alert. "Gun number thirty-one! We are being attacked at thirty-one! This is not a drill! I see another armored bulldozer, so there may be Rifle Gang vehicles nearby. Those on watch are to report to gun thirty-one, reserve teams are to report to the Big House and stand by, in case this is a diversion!"

Anna came into the study, strapping a broad gun-belt around her slender waist. "Rifle Gang again?"

Merlyn shrugged. "I'm not sure, but they have an armored bulldozer like the one that attacked the gate." He took her hand and kissed it. "I wish it was your turn to stay here in the command center."

"And have me worrying about your safety the whole time? No thank you. We have an agreement, and it's your turn!"

"If it's them, it's a good thing you reprogrammed the guns after the battle at the gate. They'll probably be riding in 4x4 trucks again, and we'll need the automatic guns to keep them busy until our people get up there!"

Anna's new program for the guns recognized different kinds of vehicles, including bulldozers, and was programmed to place a ten-shot spread in an area where the driver was most likely to be. She had even found specs on some armored military vehicles and had programmed the guns to squirt their ten rounds into slits, hatches, and other vulnerable spots. Remembering how the 'dozer had continued moving after she had shot the driver at the gate battle, she had written the program to then seek out other targets and only return to a still moving vehicle if there were no other moving targets.

"No time for talk. I'm contract-bound to go help." She headed for the stairs that led directly up into the garage. "I just hope the new program works—I haven't had time to test it and we didn't get the best kind of cameras to use with this type of pattern recognition routine!"

Merlyn called after her: "If it doesn't, I can always take over one of the guns from here and fire it manually!" But she was gone.

Razor and Michel were in the armored car already, returning from a reconnaissance drive all the way up to Craig. They were pulling up to the Big House to refuel when people started boiling out and taking off in all directions. Opening his door to ask what was going on, Michel heard the alarm and slammed it shut again. He turned the wheel hard and sent the truck roaring up the radial road that led to gun thirty-one. In his side mirror, he caught a glimpse of Dreamer and Jimmy in their family's Ford Expedition. Other cars and trucks were also joining the race to the hill crest.

All of this was not visible to the attackers, who were preoccupied with the chattering of the machine guns that picked up after the warning cut off.

When Ms. Abel had passed through the electric fence, gun number thirty-one recognized the oncoming shape as a vehicle and started on its ten-round grouping. The ten rounds included a number of different kinds of bullets, three of which were armor-piercing, but none of them penetrated the iron slab. Even though she had been expecting it, the racket of the rapid-fire impacts startled the Rifle Gang's leader. She recovered quickly and, certain that her armor was impervious, pressed on.

The sentry on duty in the south tower turned out to be Dawn. She had been applying a sparkling fingernail polish to her toenails when the bulldozer cleared the hill. She had taken pains to make sure that she could keep an eye on the hills outside the valley, even as she applied the polish, but still felt a pang of self-doubt. Had she been careless in letting an enemy get this close? No, they had obviously gathered out of sight and traveled under the cover of the old logging roads through the forest. She didn't know it, but her signal to the command center arrived even before the automatic sensors picked up the bulldozer.

All of the watchtowers had portable instruments that reported the wind speed and direction to their occupants, as well as the temperature and even the humidity. Following her mathematical short-cuts, Dawn lined up the sights on the side of Ms. Abel's chest and then adjusted her aim to compensate for the distance, wind, and air conditions. Her target was not quite a quarter mile distant, and side-on to her, but it was moving relatively slowly and steadily. Holding quite still, and squeezing the trigger with a smooth, practiced motion, the girl placed a 750-grain slug in Ms. Abel's left ear.

To the girl, it was a disappointment. She'd meant to hit lower, but had overcompensated for the distance. To Ms. Abel, it was a death that didn't even give her time to be surprised. The bullet was an incendiary round, not a solid slug, so it began deforming when it grazed two of the slats and passed through the 'dozer's left window. When it struck Ms. Abel's head, it came apart further and liquefied all the flesh and bone it encountered in its expand-ing path, spraying the gory mess through the now-shattered right window of the cab.

This time, because the machine was traveling up a steep hill, the body of the driver slumped back, away from the control levers, and the machine kept advancing on gun thirty-one. Several mem-bers of the Rifle Gang heard the distant report of the Barrett, but the 'dozer continued on its way and they couldn't see that Ms. Abel had ceased to move. The machine reached the crest, after having veered left once and right twice, because of curvatures of the ground. Its course altered, it didn't hit number thirty-one straight-on, but gave the TJC-30 a glancing blow to the right.

Glancing though it was, it was a blow from a bulldozer, and the gun toppled. The 'dozer kept going, unmanned, down into the valley.

Not knowing it was leaderless, the Rifle Gang charged. Their vehicles swept over the hill, down, and up again, aiming for the gap in Dollar Ranch's automated perimeter. Remembering what they had been told about the defense, the attackers surged up the hill, as fast as they could—thinking they would be safer that way.

As soon as they cleared the first rise, Dawn went into action. She had just killed a human being, and thought she should feel something, but her heart was numb, and she didn't have time to dwell on it. She sighted on the first truck, a red 4x4 pickup with five black-clad men crouching in the bed, and shot the driver. The truck hit a rock and bounced upward as she pulled the trigger, so her bullet punched a hole low on the door, passed through both of the driver's legs, and drilled through the bench seat before exiting even lower on the opposite door.

By this time, several of the nineteen remaining vehicles were making their own holes in the electric fence and driving for the spot where the bulldozer had cleared gun thirty-one. Thinking that the automated guns would pick off those closest to them, Dawn sighted on the vehicles in the center of the pack. She picked a dilapidated old Suburban for her next target, estimated on how far she needed to lead it, and pulled the trigger. This time she missed the driver completely, but would have been satisfied to learn that her bullet incapacitated two of his passengers. She recovered quickly, but it still took her two more shots to get the truck to stop moving.

As she had expected, guns thirty and thirty-two began raking the advancing column from both sides. Both TJC-30s stitched the front driver's side of the first vehicle nearest them with ten-round groupings, then moved on to their next closest targets.

The lead vehicle on the south side of the charge, a Chevy Blazer, rang with the whizzing of ricocheting bullets. Many of the rounds were deflected by the steel slats, but a few made it through. When the driver was hit, the vehicle slowed and stalled. It would have rolled back down the hill until it turned sideways, but the driver of the pickup truck behind it was wounded and didn't react fast enough. The collision of the two vehicles forced those following behind to go around to one side or the other, which brought half of them closer to the flanking gun, and the other half into Dawn's line of fire.

The lead vehicle on the north side, a Ford Bronco, took the heat from the .30 caliber guns and kept going. As programmed, the gun moved on to the second vehicle, wounded its driver, and moved on again. Dawn caught the driver of the Bronco, a clean 500-yard shot that bored through his chest, as well as that of the man beside him. Hah! Now she was getting into the swing of things!

The hillside where gun thirty-one had left a gap in Dollar Ranch's defenses was now cluttered with wrecked vehicles. The trucks still charging up the hill did not want to get too near the automatic guns, so they tried to work their way around the wrecks and keep on a heading that would take them through the middle.

Dawn replaced her magazine with a fresh one and took advantage of the enemy's tactical blunder, dispatching four more drivers as they slowed to maneuver. The growing mass of wreckage in the center eventually forced the attackers to the sides, closer to thirty and thirty-two. The southern gun took out four more drivers while the northern one stopped three. A Toyota T-100 actually made it to the top and passed over the rim into the valley, on the north side, while Dawn was changing magazines again and wishing she had one of the belted Barretts. The four remaining vehicles turned to flee.

To the fire-control computers, they were still moving targets and both TJC-30s stitched the backs of the departing vehicles with ragged lines of bullet holes. Only one got away.

Out of the wreckage of the Rifle Gang's 4x4s crawled the sur-

vivors who could move. Now in deathly fear of the automatic fire
on the outer hillside, they surged forward. Thirty-six men cleared
the top, leapt over the breastworks, and were about to charge down
into the valley, when they were brought up short by the sight of a
dozen vehicles storming up the side of the hill. And the first one
was that damned ice cream truck that had gotten away from them
in Rifle! Instead of charging, they took up defensive positions outside of the breastworks.

Michel was thinking about how, even though he had practiced, he was still not a very good shot. Seeing one of the invaders
storming down the hillside with no cover, he decided to use the
armored car for a weapon as much as he could—it had worked for
him before! Veering off the road, he headed straight for the T-100.
The Toyota's driver turned aside, as the drivers had turned aside
on Colorado 13 when Michel had played chicken with them. Only,
this time, Michel wasn't trying to get away—he also turned and
rammed the pickup, crunching its entire left side and ruining its
left rear wheel.

Turning the armored car around on the loose-packed dirt and
sand of the valley-side was a chore, but the extra-wide tires Max
had installed prevented it from sinking in too deep and getting
stuck. Ave Max!! Having turned, the Frenchman scanned the hilltop, and—seeing the clumps of attackers crouching outside the
breastworks—considered his options.

In the command center, Merlyn took one of the guns off automatic and swiveled it around to point back toward the attackers
lining the outsides of the breastworks. The fire-control program
was written not to turn the guns more than 90 degrees, but the
guns could turn a full 360 degrees on manual—a detail that had
escaped Ed. Unfortunately, he couldn't get a clear shot that wouldn't
also endanger the defenders now arriving at the hilltop.

For their part, the Rifle Gang members did not see that they
had any options, and opened fire upon the approaching defenders.

Dawn was still dropping them as fast as she could, causing the

invaders to huddle in two clusters, behind the spots with the best
shelter from the leaden south wind. She was starting to feel it now.
How many people had she struck with a bullet so far? She was just
a kid, and now she was shooting people! But instead of feeling
compassion for the attackers, as she might have expected if she'd
thought about it in advance, all she could feel was anger. Not
defending herself and her family was unthinkable—not an option.
It was the *their* fault they were dying, it was *they* who were trying
to hurt innocent people, *they* who were forcing her to kill...in self-
defense! Still, she could see some of the men she'd shot writhing
on the ground—how would she ever get to sleep without seeing
them in her nightmares?

Pleased with the continuing success of his armored-vehicle-as-
weapon tactic, Michel drove the armored car right up to the crest
of the valley side and smashed through the breastwork wall he
thought was sheltering the most shooters.

The men scattered, but did not run—for fear of the automatic
fire outside the valley. The truck's front wheels went over the edge
of an outcropping of rock, immobilizing the armored vehicle. Some
of the Rifle Gang fired on the metal beast in their midst. Others
fired upon the still-approaching vehicles of the defenders.

Michel and Razor tried to shoot back through the gun ports
in the sides of the truck, but neither of them was an accomplished
marksman, and they could not angle their guns to aim well. Through
her little bullet-proof window, Razor could see several of the remaining gang members sighting on the first of the approaching
vehicles—the Expedition.

Before Razor's eyes, one man after another fell—must be the
sharpshooter in the tower—but there were too many of them.
They were going to shoot Jimmy and Dreamer!

Razor had her gauntlets on—she had insisted upon it—even
though she knew that they would make it harder for her to shoot,
and her experience on the highway had taught her that a weapon
that let you deal with your enemies from a distance was always to
be preferred. Now, seeing the threat to someone she had grown to

love, she forgot the lesson; she simply *reacted*. Kicking the passenger door open, Razor fell upon the men behind the breastworks.

For the Rifle Gang, it was as though a deadly ghost had returned to haunt them. Several had seen Razor mangle their fellows, and the rest had heard about it. With an astonishingly quick series of moves, she had slit one man's throat and put another's eyes out. Some of them fled down the outer hillside, right into the line of fire of the gun Merlyn returned to automatic fire. Others started to recover from the shock, but she was among them, dancing out death. She laid three more flat before the last one finally brought his gun to bear and shot her.

She went down, a hole—a much bigger hole—through the same shoulder where she'd been wounded before.

The man who shot Razor stood over her, with a relieved expression on his face—an expression that turned to agony as Michel fired one of his rifles through the passenger door of the armored car and put a bullet through his stomach. Before he could fall, a .50 caliber slug caught him from behind and spun him to the ground.

On the other side of the truck, Dreamer had imitated Michel's tactic and had rammed the breastworks where the last remaining attackers had taken refuge. One was crushed under the car, and the others dropped their guns and raised their arms.

Jimmy wanted to shoot them where they stood, but couldn't do it, now that they had surrendered. The Contract allowed for capital punishment—lethal self-defense—only in the case of a threat to one's life, but these wretches were obviously no longer a threat, even if they deserved no pity. She waved at her friends in the armored car, but no one was in the cab.

Getting out of her father's car and trotting around to the other side of the stranded truck, she found Michel—tears streaming down his face—cradling Razor in his arms.

Jimmy ran to him. "Razor! Is she..."

Michel shook his head. "No, she is only hurt. In ze same shoulder as last time. We 'ave to get her to ze doctor immediately, and ze truck is stuck. Bring your fazer, and your car, we *must* get her to ze doctor immediately!"

Jimmy was off before he was done talking. Dreamer was away from the Expedition, holding the prisoners at gunpoint. The young woman jumped into the driver's seat and slammed the 4x4 into reverse, unaware that she was spraying her father with gravel as she swung the big sport utility vehicle around.

She and Michel loaded Razor into the car and drove her to the doctor's clinic—again. But this time was different. This time, though Jimmy perceived Razor to be something of a rival, she was also someone she loved. She pushed the Expedition as fast as she dared, blinking furiously to clear tears from her eyes.

It wasn't until much later that night, while Jimmy and Michel were watching over Razor's sleeping form, that they heard about Ed. His body had been found among those of the enemy, just outside the perimeter.

Even though it was clear that by expelling Ed, Dollar Ranch had been exposed to the nightmare of treason, everyone was talking more about how wise Jimmy had been. Many who had previously thought she should have shown Ed mercy now praised her for refusing to allow such a poisonous traitor to stay among them.

The other two stories that were circulating were various versions of how Dawn had all but single-handedly stopped the attack in its tracks, and the one about The Optimist's greenhouses. The defenders on the hill had ignored Ms. Abel's bulldozer after seeing that it was no longer a threat to them and concentrated on more immediate concerns. Unhindered, the machine had continued down into the valley, smashed through a fence, and had been headed straight for the greenhouses when Goya had spotted it. She wouldn't talk about how she had stopped it, but from the location of Ms. Abel's corpse, Goya had obviously climbed on board and pulled the woman's remains from behind the controls. In spite of the horror of it, the feisty Peruvian was clearly pleased to have The Optimist's effusive gratitude.

When Razor awoke, they told her the news. She grumbled

about being stuck in the clinic again, but was glad to see Jimmy unharmed. "Ahhh... The same shoulder again! God, it really hurts!" She winced. "I... I guess that was kind of stupid of me..."

Jimmy was the first to respond. "Maybe. My father says that bladed weapons are for when you don't have a gun handy, but you sure scared the heck out of those guys... I know it sounds like an excuse, but I think more people might have been hurt if you hadn't gone berserk... How many do you think you could have hit through your open door before one of them got you?"

Razor conceded that Jimmy had a point, but still thought she might deserve what she'd gotten for thinking with her feelings.

"Ze doctor," Michel fiddled with the blanket on Razor's bed, "he says zat you will probably never be able to move your left arm as freely as before, but zat for most purposes it will not matter."

"Most purposes! I'm a dancer!" Razor reigned herself in. "Well, I used to be... I mean, I guess I won't be teaching dance lessons anymore..." She fought back angry tears. "Thank you two for taking such good care of me. It feels better than I ever imagined it could, to be loved by two such good friends!"

Jimmy blushed and Michel kissed Razor's hand.

"Say Jimmy, how would you like to take over my gauntlets?"

"Oh, I couldn't!" Jimmy was both pleased and horrified.

"You have to!" Razor tried to sound stern and failed. "I'll never have the movement in my shoulder to use them properly, and you're getting pretty good with them—it was a happy coincidence that our hands are about the same size. If you don't take them over, they'll go to waste, and we wouldn't want that to happen, would we?"

"No, we wouldn't want that!"

"But," Razor caught Jimmy by the hand, "only use them when you don't have a gun handy!"

All three laughed and both Michel and Jimmy hugged Razor—being careful of her damaged shoulder.

It was an all-too-brief moment of shared peace.

CHAPTER 52:
MONDAY, MAY 29, 2000

"I'm on the highway to hell,
Don't stop me!"
—AC/DC, *Highway to Hell*

"It looks like a roadblock."

The early light of dawn revealed a massive concrete-reinforced earthwork across the highway. People in and out of uniform were still working on the walls of something apparently meant to be a holding area for cars forced off the road.

Holly peered ahead. "And it looks new. I bet you were right about Angel's army coming this way."

"Let's take off our hats then." Rosalia doffed her cap and plucked Holly's from her head.

"Hey, now I'll have hat-hair!"

"It's better than a bullet through the head, which is what we might get if they think we're with Ejercito Dragon!"

"Oh, all right." Holly chuckled and parked the Jeep before a stout gate that blocked their way back onto I-15.

The two surveyed their surroundings and found that everyone had stopped working—the better part of a dozen guns were pointing in their general direction. Holly ran her fingers through her long red hair while Rosalia unconsciously imitated her with her own dark curls.

A man wearing a highway patrol uniform and a puzzled expression approached them, with his gun drawn. "Would you ladies please step away from the vehicle?"

"Have we done something wrong, officer?" Holly didn't use her most seductive voice, but it nevertheless came out huskier than usual. Rosalia suppressed a laugh when the man visibly changed his mind about whatever he had been going to say.

"Maybe," he finally answered, "and maybe not. I don't know—but a bunch of murderers dressed like you two busted through here yesterday."

Holly and Rosalia turned to each other. They were definitely on the right track.

"Please step away from the vehicle." The man repeated.

The women complied, holding their hands out to show that they were unarmed.

"What's that on your hand?" The trooper pointed toward Rosalia.

"Ink."

"Ink? How did... Never mind." He sauntered around the open Jeep, peering at its contents while asking his questions. "May I ask what brings you to Deseret?"

"We're looking for somebody." Holly answered.

"Who?"

"Someone who owes us something."

The policeman stopped. He discovered nothing more dangerous than gas, food, and water in the Jeep, unless maybe a handgun was hidden in a compartment somewhere. "Who are you looking for and what do they owe you?"

"It's personal."

"Look, ladies," the man raised his voice in exasperation, "A little more than twenty-four hours ago, an army of men dressed as you are, in military vehicles like yours, swept over the border here, killing everyone in their way. Deseret has a policy of open borders, but not to known criminals. Give me a reason I shouldn't arrest you and hold you for trial with the rest of them!"

Rosalia spoke up. "Were there any women in that army?"

"None that I've heard of, but you could be spies, or messengers, or...something."

Rosalia didn't see why he should care about their story, or help them, but she didn't think she could invent anything better, so she told him the truth. "We are following—hunting for—Angel Jesus Ramos Ortega, the leader of that army that came through here yesterday. He held us prisoner and we have a score to settle with him."

The officer laughed. "You must be jo—" He stopped when he realized that both women were dead serious. They were also tired-looking and somewhat gaunt. The one with the ink on her hand had a bloodstain soaking through the right shoulder of her olive shirt. And the redhead—she was vaguely familiar, in a way that was both exciting and frightening—had a bruise still visible on her jaw... "You two set out to hunt the leader of an entire army all by yourselves? Just the two of you?"

"Well," Rosalia would not be cowed, "we didn't have an army of our own handy, and weren't likely to find one as big as his anyway. We thought something a little less direct might work; that's why we're in uniform. If we could approach Ejercito Dragon at a time when things are confused, we might be able to get to Angel and slip away before anyone caught us."

"Ehersito what? Never mind. What were you going to do when you caught up with him?"

The two women looked at their feet.

The man shook his head. "I ought to send you back just for coming up with such a half-baked plan. And besides, murder is still illegal in Deseret, even if the guy deserves it!"

"Then he *is* here?" Rosalia took a step forward.

"Well, no, not any more, but..." The border guard retreated a step.

"You said something about awaiting trial with the rest of them; what did you mean?"

"We've captured some of his men, but the leader—Anhel, I guess—got away. He's definitely not in Deseret any more."

"Then we're only travelers passing through. You have no reason to detain us."

"Well, I…"

"Pleeeeease?" Now Holly really turned on the charm, advancing on the man and using the pouting look that had made her a star.

The trooper grunted and backed away, as though Holly had suddenly become dangerous. "Wait here." He turned and tramped through an opening in the wall, waving off the watching marksmen as he went.

Holly turned to Rosalia. "Did I say something wrong?"

Rosalia shrugged. "I'm not sure, but I got the impression he might have recognized you…" She laughed. "I don't suppose a good Mormon should be *able* to recognize you!"

Before they could speculate about it more, the officer returned with a clipboard and a green sticker, which he attached to the Jeep's antenna. "I'm probably crazy for doing this, but you can go on through. Make sure you leave that sticker on the antenna as long as you are in Deseret. With all the recent excitement, you could get shot at if you take it off." He moved off to open the gate.

"But…" Rosalia wasn't sure what to do. "Can you tell us what you know? How will we find him?"

"Oh, just follow the trail. You'll see where he went plain enough." He motioned for them to drive through.

Holly hopped back in the driver's seat and Rosalia got in beside her. As they passed through the gate, the actress stopped the Jeep, leaned out, and kissed the surprised trooper on the cheek. "Thanks!"

Blushing intensely, the man stammered, "Don't mention it." Then he stopped and blinked. "Do either of you have any weapons?"

They both flushed with embarrassment, not wanting to admit the truth.

He rolled his eyes. "I don't know if I'll ever forgive myself for this but…" He drew his sidearm and handed it to Holly. "That's a 9mm. Here's a couple extra magazines. Never was my favorite caliber! If you do catch up with Mr. Ortega, and get the chance, you tell him you've got a nine-millimeter message for him from Parley."

"Okay, but... Who's Parley?"

"Parley was my best friend. He was manning the lighter barricade we had here before, when that son of a... When Mr. Ortega came through here with his army. Parley saved my life once..."

"Oh." Holly tucked the gun into her pants. "Thanks!"

"It's nothing major. I've got a 10mm I like better anyway. But don't tell anyone, okay?"

"Okay." Holly leaned out of the Jeep again but he jumped back before she could touch him. She chuckled. "So, which one did you see? *Redhead from the Red Planet?*"

The man was speechless for a few seconds, then stammered, "All of them!"

Holly couldn't keep from laughing at the officer's horrified expression.

"I didn't say that! Uh... Remember: *please* don't mention it!"

"We won't!" She winked and pulled ahead. The officer did a Homer Simpson in the rear-view mirror, smacking his forehead before turning to close the gate. As soon as they had driven around a curve and the barrier was out of sight, Holly pulled the Jeep over to the side of the road. "Let's get out of these uniforms—I don't think he would have let us through if he hadn't recognized me."

Rosalia concurred and rummaged around in the back for the clothes they had been wearing when they escaped. "It sure would be nice to find a place we could wash these!"

Holly laughed. "Better smelly than dead!" Once changed, she pulled the Jeep back onto the highway again.

Several hours later, when Rosalia was taking a turn driving, the first sign of battle detached itself from the featureless horizon and flowed up to meet them. They had passed through St. George and Cedar City, and had seen no sign that the army had stopped. The last town they had passed was called Beaver. Angel seemed to have been intent on a headlong drive for the Capital, not wanting to spread his forces thin by leaving garrisons at towns conquered along the way.

"Look," Holly pointed, "there's some kind of wreck off to the side ahead!"

"Yes, I see it." Rosalia slowed down as they drew alongside a burnt-out hulk they could not identify. "Wow, there's not much left of it!"

The next evidence of Angel's passing they encountered was a tank, parked right in the passing lane ahead of them. They approached it cautiously, because it was still intact, but it turned out to be empty—or, at least, any occupants it had ignored them completely when they passed it by. Rosalia regarded the menacing turret with its big gun in the rear-view mirror. "What do you suppose was up with that?"

"It's probably broken down." Holly turned back to look at the receding machine. "Frank liked to say that tanks are tough, but they need so much maintenance that they're also fragile. If Angel drove the things up here on their own power—and I can't imagine where he'd get enough big-rig trucks and drivers to do it any other way—they'd end up needing a lot of maintenance pretty fast. I doubt he has many tank mechanics among his men."

"Probably not. He likes to think he's a great general—did you see that ridiculous, over decorated uniform he came up with? But he's really just a scared kid who grew up to be a back-street thug. Intimidation is the only skill he's developed. From what you told me about Disneyland, I doubt he'll make it long as a general..." Rosalia lapsed into thought, probing painful memories, and the conversation came to a stop.

A few minutes later, Holly called out again. "Look, there's another wreck—no, two up ahead!" This time, the blasted remains were closer to the road, a pair of black smears near the other side.

Rosalia stopped the Jeep when they drew along side. "I think that's a piece of helicopter blade. No wonder these don't look like much; they must have fallen from pretty high up in the sky. Do you think Angel shot down helicopters the Mormons sent to check on him?"

"If he raided Twenty-Nine Palms successfully, he could have his own helicopters."

Rosalia put the Jeep back in gear. Over the next ten miles they passed another broken-down tank and five more melted heaps of debris fallen from the sky, all looking similar to the first three. Then they started passing the wreckage of tanks, many of them on the road or very near to it. They had to drive around twisted piles of caterpillar treads and other less identifiable pieces of blackened metal. Scattered in among these were lighter-weight vehicles that gave the appearance of being able to threaten aircraft—some had large guns mounted on them, others had boxy attachments that resembled missile batteries of some kind. After that, they started seeing exploded armored personnel carriers, and various pieces of overturned field artillery.

Neither Holly nor Rosalia could think of anything to say.

In some places they could see charred corpses, not quite contained by their mangled steel coffins. Occasionally the wind would bring the smell of burnt meat. Holly wondered if this was how more places would look if the Russians had attacked again. Whatever happened to the second wave of Russian missiles anyway?

The devastation now spread wide on either side of the road and showed no signs of ending. Rosalia tasted bile and would have stopped to vomit, but there was nowhere to stop that would not be near something dead. She was sure the smell would get worse if she stopped, so she forced her stomach not to heave.

Just before a town called Fort Cove, the swath of carnage veered right, onto I-70, eastbound. Next to the road, a long furrow sliced into the ground. As they drove by, it grew deeper and ended in a blackened pile of scrap-metal and dirt, right up against the road. Rosalia took the turn slowly. They passed the remains cautiously; there were pieces of tail-fin and wing scattered around, some on the road. "I wish we could keep going north. Those Mormon towns looked so nice and clean, and...normal!"

Holly put her hand on her friend's shoulder. "We could, you know. We could give up on this crazy idea of ours."

Rosalia's eyes misted over. "I want to, I really do... But I can't. I may be crazy, but I have to confront him." Her voice dropped to a whisper. "I just have to."

Holly grunted. "Well then, step on it. It smells here."

Rosalia drove as fast as she dared. The remains of bombed military vehicles were as thick as ever, and craters in the roadway made for obstacles that were harder to see in the distance.

A few miles past a town called Richfield, the two started seeing fewer and fewer tanks, until the road cleared of wreckage for a time. Then something new separated from the horizon and approached: destroyed trucks. There were many more bodies around the burnt trucks than there had been around and in the other vehicles. Near the town, they had seen people collecting bodies and digging what they assumed would become a mass grave. But farther from the town, the bodies had not yet been tended to, and birds and other scavengers were pecking and tearing at them.

For some odd reason unknown to both women, the feasting animals included a large number of seagulls. And where the ruins of the tanks had been silent, the human and mechanical debris along this stretch of highway was alive with animal movements, squawkings, and barkings. At one point, Holly thought she glimpsed a bald eagle among the scavengers, but she'd never actually seen one before, so she wasn't positive.

The count of destroyed trucks and dead bodies was unimaginable. There was no place to stop where some wreck or another was not close by. In spite of having no love to lose for members of Angel's gang, Rosalia could not prevent her eyes from tearing up.

"Jesus!" Holly breathed, "how many men did he have?"

Rosalia swallowed. "I'm not sure. He bragged to me once that he had more than 100,000, but he must have lost many at Disneyland."

"Yeah, but not more than half his force. How many trucks does it take to carry fifty thousand men?"

"I don't know, but I never imagined I would see so many dead people in my life!"

They fell silent again, while the macabre scenery went on…and on…and on.

About halfway between Salinas and Green River, they had to stop to refill the Jeep's gas tank from their third jerry can. As the fuel gurgled down the tube, a jet flew overhead. Holly shaded her eyes and peered at the plane as it banked and came over them again. It banked again and disappeared to the north.

"I don't know much about war planes, but it seems to me that that thing sure had a *lot* of missiles underneath!"

"That must be what did this." Rosalia got back in the Jeep and settled into the passenger seat, letting Holly take the next turn driving.

The redhead got in on the driver's side. "That plane, and its brothers and sisters, must have flown over Angel's army, bombing it until it turned aside, and still bombing it as they ran away. All we've seen so far are bombed tanks, trucks, and stuff like that—no sign of fighting on the ground. The Mormons back at the border must have sent a message before they were overrun, and the ones in their headquarters must have sent airplanes to bomb Angel until he gave up… But why did they continue bombing him after he turned aside?"

"Maybe," Rosalia tried not to look as Holly drove around yet another blackened truck full of bodies, "turning aside wasn't good enough. Maybe they wanted revenge."

They fell silent again, until some time later when they heard the distinct thup-thup-thup of an approaching helicopter.

It came from behind them and swooped low overhead. Pivoting sharply, it came back toward the Jeep, machine guns and missile launchers clearly visible under stubby wings on either side. The war machine had an insectile appearance that radiated hostility.

Faced with the intimidating sight, Holly eased up on the gas and let the Jeep coast to a stop. Fortunately, the destruction had thinned and there were no remains of burnt corpses nearby.

At first, the chopper hovered, blocking their way. Then it settled to the side of the roadway. Someone got out from the opposite side and came over to the Jeep, where the two women tried to remain calm and make no threatening moves. The approaching figure removed its helmet and turned out to be a woman as well. "Who are you two?"

"We're just two girls from California passing through." Holly prattled in her 'bimbo' voice.

The woman from the helicopter scowled. "Where did you get that green sticker?" She took it in her hand and read the number it had written on it.

"Why, that nice officer back at the border gave it to us. He told us no one would shoot us as long as we left it alone. He wasn't wrong, was he?"

Instead of answering, the woman returned to the helicopter, coming back a few minutes later. "I don't know what you two are up to, but you have a valid travel permit and the Mesquite border guards say you're okay. I have to warn you, however, that you are headed for trouble. The army that came through here is camped right outside our new border, past Grand Junction. You don't want to go that way."

Rosalia changed the subject. "Can you tell us what happened? I'm no friend of these people you bombed—many certainly deserved to die—but why did you continue bombing them after they turned aside?"

The woman's face changed—softened and sagged—showing her own sense of horror at what she had witnessed. "We sent a chopper to warn them off, but they shot it down with a Stinger, or something from below. So we sent in the planes to take out their choppers—they only had a handful of them. Then we tried again. I was on that flight, actually, I was the one on the microphone. But they wouldn't listen—tried to shoot us down! They missed, but their answer was clear. So the planes came back in and started taking out their heavy armor and anti-aircraft vehicles. How could they think they could come storming through Deseret and we wouldn't try to stop them?!"

She stopped talking and stared westward, the loathing of what she'd been a part of engraved on her face.

"And then?" Rosalia prompted as gently as she could.

"And then we tried again, and they still wouldn't listen—tried to shoot us down again. And you know, a lot of their stuff wasn't working. I don't know where they got all that equipment, but the officers must have ditched all the firing pins into a river or something, because they all they did with their heavy armor was ride around in it—maybe they hoped to use it for intimidation also. Anyway, we took out all their APCs, artillery, and other serious equipment. That was after they turned aside, as you could probably tell, but we couldn't let them take their weapons of war with them—they might turn around and try again."

The woman hesitated, visibly struggling with nausea. "When there were only trucks and cars left, we tried one more time... Not too far west from where we are now. All we wanted was to get them to lay down their weapons. We would have let them all go, if they had surrendered and turned over their weapons. But they wouldn't. They fired on us again, with small arms and RPGs. They had to have known that there was no way they could beat us, but they fired on us anyway!"

"So you started bombing trucks full of men?"

"They still had some stuff we were not willing to let them use against us in the future, and they had big tanker trucks full of fuel to enable them to do so. They were showing very clearly how irrational and hostile they were willing to be—we couldn't just let them go and take their weapons with them!"

No one spoke until Rosalia broke the awkward silence. "The border guard mentioned something about putting some of them on trial, so some must have eventually surrendered, right?"

"Yeah, some of them—about fifty miles east of here. When you go by, you'll see a big prison camp. I think they finally got the

message when we blew up the tanker trucks. In fact, most of the
ones left alive surrendered, but some of them must be real hard-
core psychopaths; they kept on going. I guess it was a mistake to
lay off the Jeeps, HUMVEEs, civilian vehicles, and other smaller
stuff—I think now that that's what the command staff were in."
She gazed eastward, scanning the horizon.

"Angel Ortega, their leader, was probably in one of those vehicles. He would never surrender."

The woman eyed Rosalia suspiciously, but finished her story.
"We kept bombing them right up to the border, and then let the
rest go. By that time they had no trucks left and no RPGs. Maybe
five thousand escaped over the border with their small arms—not
enough to threaten Deseret again." She paused. "Did you say that
the man running that lunatic show's name is Anhel? That means
Angel, doesn't it?"

The two nodded.

"That's sick. Really sick."

Rosalia shrugged. "It's a common name in Spanish-speaking
countries. Can we go now?"

"Yes, but whatever you do, don't take that sticker off. Some of
Ortega's vehicles strayed from the main force and we're still mop-
ping up. If you hadn't stopped, the pilot would have blasted you,
and if I hadn't seen that sticker, you'd be under arrest."

"We understand."

"I don't think you do. You are driving into a *war* zone."

"We've been in a war for a long time. We are now looking for a
way to end it."

The woman clearly thought they were not right in the head,
but evidently decided it was none of her business and returned to
her helicopter.

As they had been told, they left the state of Deseret after passing the town of Grand Junction, formerly of the state of Colorado.
The beefed-up cement block and earthwork barricade was still
being built when they arrived.

When they stopped, a trooper in a uniform with a large beehive patch on his sleeve, and another on his chest, removed the green sticker from their antenna. He tried to persuade Holly to turn back, while Rosalia was filling the Jeep's tank out of the last jerry can. When it was full, there was still a little fuel left in the can, but not much.

The officer gave up and waved them through.

"So, what do we do now?" Holly asked as she drove them away from the security of Deseret.

"I'm not sure. We should go ahead and put our uniforms back on, for one thing. If we do happen upon what's left of Ejercito Dragon, they might mistake us in the same way everyone else has."

"We're not planning to drive into their camp, are we?"

"No, but we should be prepared in case we meet up with them sooner than we expect."

"I'll go along with that." Holly pulled off to the side of the road again, and the two women took turns keeping watch while the other changed clothes.

On the trail of a dangerous quarry, the mountains that might have appeared beautiful under other circumstances were now ominous. The loomed overhead menacingly, like the ancient fortresses of the evil wizards in Rosalia's fantasy novels. An eventless but dispiriting half-hour later, they came to signs announcing the town of Parachute. "Maybe we should stop here until we work out a plan. The border guard said he thinks Angel is camped in the next town, a place called Rifle."

Rosalia agreed and Holly pulled off the highway at the exit. They sat in the idling Jeep by the stop sign at the end of the ramp, thinking. They were getting closer to their prey and neither of them had really come up with a good plan yet.

"Hands up! Don't move!" A young voice interrupted their thoughts.

The two complied, Rosalia silently, Holly cursing under her breath.

"That's good. Hold 'em high an' don't try anything funny."

The proprietor of the voice came into view as he spoke. He looked to be about ten years old, sandy-haired and brown-eyed. He was bearing a rifle that was large in his hands, though he was obviously comfortable carrying it.

Holly rubbed her head against her raised right arm, making her hat tumble off.

"A girl!"

"Yes, both of us." Rosalia took her own hat off.

"Hands back up!" The boy shouted, clearly confused. "Hey, what's that stuff on your hand?"

In spite of the gun, Holly giggled and Rosalia sighed. "It's ink. I broke my pen...trying to get away from the army that came through here yesterday."

"You're not with them?"

"No! We're not with them!" Rosalia considered the possibility that a frightened child with a gun might actually be more dangerous than a full grown man. A man would be more prone to over-confidence. "These uniforms are disguises." She could see in his eyes that the boy desperately wanted to believe her.

"Well..." He shifted his rifle to one arm and scratched a grubby finger at his temple. "You don't look like the those people. Why are you disguised like them?"

"Their leader is a very bad man." Rosalia answered. "He hurt us—both of us—and we want to make sure he doesn't hurt any-one else."

"You mean it?" The little guy was on the verge of crying. "I want to stop him too!"

"Cross my heart and hope to die!" Holly held out her hands to him. "Why don't you come here and tell us what happened?"

The boy climbed up onto the hood of the Jeep, holding his rifle so he could point it at them quickly if he needed to. "You can put your arms down now, lady," he waved at Rosalia with his weapon.

"Thank you."

"Tell us what happened," Holly prompted.

"My family lived here, north of Parachute. When we heard that the folks up at Dollar Ranch wiped out Ms. Abel and most of the Rifle Gang, Dad decided we should go and see if they'd let us join them, up there on the ranch. We'd just gotten on the road," he pointed at the ramp that lead to the eastbound lanes of the highway, "when all of a sudden all these cars came zooming around the corner. They were going real fast! And they had *lots* of cars. And some of them were the same ugly color as yours—that's why I thought you might be with them. And..." Tears began welling up in his eyes.

He turned his head, ashamed to let two girls see him cry. After a brief struggle he got his tears under control. "And one of them shot Dad while he was driving... For no reason! He just shot him! Our car crashed and my seat belt was stuck—I couldn't get out." The boy started crying again, but continued with his story. "Mom and Tommy and Janie got out though, and those mean men in their cars shot them as they drove by. For no reason! They just shot them... By the time I got out, the men were gone, but it was too late, Tommy and Janie and Mom were all dead! And Dad, all dead..." Now he couldn't stop the tears.

Holly got out of the Jeep and went to the boy. He didn't resist when she hugged him and kissed him on the top of his head, but soon enough he pushed her away and wiped his nose on his sleeve. "So, are you going to kill him? I want to help!"

"Of course you do," Holly parried, "but don't you have other family around here? Won't they be worried about you?"

"Nope!" He shook his head fiercely. "I buried all of my family yesterday. I've been waiting under the overpass ever since. When they came by again, I was going to get even!"

Neither woman answered immediately, being uncertain how to handle the situation. They didn't want to just leave the boy on his own, but wouldn't it be wrong to encourage him to seek revenge? On the other hand, as they themselves were bent upon revenge, were they in a position to be critical of the boy?

Holly tried one more time to discourage him. "How were you

going to get even with them when there's thousands of them and only one of you?"

"I'm a pretty good shot, and this is Dad's Ruger 10/22. It's only a twenty-two, so it doesn't kick much, and I can hit a tin can at fifty yards! Watch!" He turned and sighted on a streetlight across the road. Before the two women could stop him or even protest, he flicked off the safety and pulled the trigger. A loud *crack* was followed by the tinkle of falling glass. "This magazine," he held up a small plastic box, "holds ten rounds." He puffed up his chest with pride. "I could take out a whole carload of bad guys before they could figure out where I was hiding under the bridge. If I got 'em one car at a time, I could get lots of 'em before they got me!"

Holly and Rosalia both had to chuckle at his fierceness, even though they now regarded him with considerably greater respect. Rosalia decided to take a different approach. "What's your name?"

"Joseph."

"Well, Joseph, My name is Rosalia, and she's Holly. Holly calls me Rosy because she can't say the Spanish R." She made a face. "You know, it could be lucky for us that we met you. We understand that the bad guys are staying at a place called Rifle. Do you know where that is?"

"Sure!" He beamed at the prospect of being useful, then frowned. "That's where the Rifle Gang was from. Boy, that's really bad luck—we just got rid of one gang of bad guys and now we've got an even bigger one!"

"Right. So we need to be smart. If we want to stop the leader of the bad guys, we can't just show up and start shooting. We might get a lot of them with the help of a gun-man like you, but they'd get us before we could finish the job. What we need to do is scout ahead, see what they're up to, and come up with a plan that we know will work. Do you think you could help us with that?"

"You bet!" He leapt to his feet, ready to leave for a scouting mission that instant.

"Wait! Wait!" Rosalia tried not to laugh. "We'll go scouting, but we've come all the way from California, taking turns driving, without any real rest. What we need first is a safe place to sleep, and then to plan the scouting mission. Some maps would really help..."

"You can stay at my house. I'm sure Mom and Dad wouldn't mind if..." He veered away from that thought. "I haven't been back there since we left for Dollar Ranch, but I'm sure nothing's happened to it, and there's plenty of beds for you. And Dad loved to hike. He's got—he had all kinds of maps!"

"Sounds wonderful!" Holly winked at Rosalia. "Can you guide us back there, Scout?"

"Let's go!" He hopped over the windshield and into the back seat of the Jeep.

Holly got into the driver's seat and asked the young guide which way to turn.

"That way. Over the bridge, and then keep on going for about three miles on this same road."

"Got it." She eased the clutch out and accelerated the Jeep toward their new destination.

"So tell me," Rosalia asked, "what is this Dollar Ranch you keep talking about?"

"I'll tellya, but first you gotta tell me how you were going to get away from an army with a pen. This I gotta hear!"

Holly laughed.

Rosalia swatted her shoulder in mock anger. "Haven't you ever heard that the pen is mightier than the sword?"

CHAPTER 53:
WEDNESDAY, JUNE 14, 2000

"Whatever you're looking for
Don't come around here no more."
—Tom Petty & the Heartbreakers,
Don't Come Around Here No More

The *Alexa Petrova* sailed into the Strait of Juan de Fuca a little after 8:00 a.m., on a beautifully sunny day. It promised to be pleasantly warm.

Alexis could appreciate the scenery, but was unable to fully enjoy the sail, as uncertainty about what lay ahead mounted in her. Even at this close range, Lieutenant Daniels had been unable to raise SeaTac International Airport and had gotten no response from McCord Air Force Base.

They were close enough now that, if they could only find enough fuel, they could get back to Deseret in a single flight! She gazed over the flat covers of the cargo holds, where the helicopters were tied down. Three Blackhawks, the Hind, and the Apache. She grinned. The Apache had barely had enough fuel left in its tanks to make it to the old Russian ship, but it was hers now. Finders, keepers! And now, if they could dig up enough avgas for four helicopters, they'd probably find enough for five... That still worried her. They'd struck out on finding fuel for the choppers several times in a row now—lucky for them that diesel for the ship was easier to find!

Looking into the water that rolled by beneath the ship's railing, Alexis could see the sun's slanting rays penetrate the surface only to dim and disappear into the murk a few feet below. That fit! Gazing into the future was always a risky business, but usually she could see lots of things coming months and even years in advance. Even during this insane time of the world falling apart all around her, she'd known what she had to do and where she needed to go. But now... Her vision dimmed and disappeared a few feet ahead. She had no idea what might lie around the next corner, let alone in Deseret...or the Dollar Ranch—if she ever got there!

It was about 3:00 p.m. when the ship hove into view of Lynnwood, at the north edge of the Seattle sprawl. There was no smoke in the air, as there had been at Anchorage, but the city was thoroughly destroyed. Not all of it was burnt, though fire had obviously swept through large sections of the metropolis. In some places, simple neglect had left the streets strewn with stripped cars, fallen trees, and other debris. In other places, clogged sewers had resulted in lakes and ponds of various sizes springing up.

Allen stood at the rail beside Alexis and Petrov, not standing too close. He knew that she didn't want any public displays of affection while she was still in uniform. "Jesus... It's as bad as if those missiles had gone off!"

The Russian grunted in dissent. "No. The cities, they may be dead, but the people, most of them are alive."

"Pavel's right, John." Alexis was glad all over again that Petrov had elected to come with them. He had a keen mind, could fly a helicopter in a pinch, and—having brought the Hind, a pilot, and a mechanic—added the equivalent of a flying tank to her squadron, as well as the expertise to keep it running. He was also great at telling stories. "Remember the tent cities in the Chugach Range? Some of those places were turning into forts, even as we sailed by them. Our old ways of living may have gone with the twentieth century, but I think our people—the human race—are digging in and figuring out new ways of doing things."

For two hours, the desolation appeared ahead and slipped astern with a melancholy rhythm made hypnotic by the gentle rocking and ever-present vibrations of the *Alexa Petrova*. When they rounded the point north of Normandy Park, the ship disengaged its engines and drifted forward. They were within one and a half nautical miles of SeaTac.

Alexis climbed to the aft crows' nest with a pair of field glasses to assess the situation herself. John Allen joined her, enjoying the opportunity to have an excuse to get closer to her. Alexis was enjoying his company more and more, but didn't want to 'go public' until she had discharged her duties to her subordinates, and made a face at him.

Allen put on his most innocent expression and asked, "What? Can't I want to have a look too?"

His joking tone always made her laugh. "You're not fooling anyone, you know. I think Petrov already knows, and Captain Stewart, but he's too reserved to let on. If the Okie found out, everyone would know!" She peered through the binoculars toward the airport, adjusting the focus as she spoke. "Oh well, hopefully it won't matter soon... Hmmm, it looks more trashed than Anchorage International was, but there are lots of intact aircraft, including some helicopters. Some of them might have fuel in their tanks we can use."

"Should I ask Captain Zaitsev to stop here?"

"No, I want to check on McCord first."

"Okay, I'll ask him for best speed to Browns Point." He climbed down the ladder and disappeared into the bridge.

Alexis had decided to stay in the crow's nest for a little longer when she caught a flash of light from the shore. There it was again! Three longer flashes, a pause, three shorter flashes, a longer pause, three short, three long, three short: an S.O.S. signal! She climbed/slid down the ladder and nearly collided with Allen and Captain Zaitsev coming the other way.

The civilian grinned. "Yeah, we saw it too. Who do you think it is?"

"I don't know, but let's get Daniels to scan the CB and ham wavelengths to see if they're talking." She turned to the old sailor and addressed him in Russian. "Captain, if you wouldn't mind bringing us in a little closer?"

"Da." Zaitsev turned to go back to the wheelhouse, not bothering with any questions.

Lieutenant Daniels had been making repairs on the equipment built in to the old ship and had temporarily set up his own gear in the same cabin. In the few minutes it took Alexis and Allen to drop a deck and head forward, Petrov beat them to the radio room.

The lieutenant raised his hand and motioned for silence. "I've got him! He's a ham operator all right! He says his name is Matthew Stokes." He picked up his mic and switched on a speaker. "This is Lieutenant Joshua Daniels, USAF. What is your situation?"

The tinny voice cackled back immediately. "Boy are we glad to see you, Lieutenant! Uh... Did you say you were with the Air Force?"

Daniels laughed. "Roger that. How I got on this ship is a long story. But what is the nature of your emergency?"

"Are you kidding? I had to barricade my family for weeks inside the bomb shelter my old man built back in the fifties, found everything deserted and destroyed when I came out, and you want to know what my emergency is? My life is an emergency right now!"

"You've got a point there, Mr. Stokes. But the nuclear threat was over weeks ago, didn't you hear about that?"

"Yep. But that was only the first problem. Then we had gangs wandering the streets robbing anyone they could find. I guess they ran out of food a while ago, because it's been pretty quiet for the last couple weeks and we've been able to live in the house again."

"Understood. So, why did you signal us?"

"A ham operator in San Jose told me that Silicon Valley has held together. The area is actually thriving; trading computer stuff that still works—or stuff that can get older computers working again—for gold, food, and protection. They've got a good thing going there, and I'm an engineer. I think I could find work there. I was wondering if you might be headed down the coast, when you're done with whatever you're doing in this ghost town, and if you could give me a ride. I've got food and some gas I could trade, but no wheels, so we're stuck here. What do you say?"

Daniels turned to Alexis.

"Tell him that Tacoma is our destination, at least for now. If we find enough fuel here, we might take off over land for Deseret, at which point it's between him and Captain Zaitsev. If we can't find enough fuel, we might be heading down to the San Francisco bay area ourselves!"

"Yes, ma'am!"

One way or another, their journey was nearing its end, and as the news about Silicon Valley spread through the crew, everyone's spirits lifted.

CHAPTER 54:
THURSDAY, JUNE 15, 2000

"Don't wait for answers
Just take your chances
Don't ask me why."
—Billy Joel, *Don't Ask Me Why*

Rosalia and Holly awoke with a start in the back of their Jeep, stretched, and rubbed the sleep from their eyes. Scout should be back soon... Jumping from the Jeep, they scrambled up the incline to the overlook from which they had been spying on Angel's camp for the last week and a half. They lay on their stomachs, as Scout had taught them, and lifted their heads only enough to see over the edge of the cliff. Holly had a pair of binoculars the boy had lent them.

Early morning light was pouring through the eastern gaps, filling the valley below them with pastel purples, pinks, and oranges. Wisps of mist curled off the Colorado River as it wound along beside the highway. Above and to the west, mountain peaks were already aglow with golden fire.

There were several hotels in the town of Rifle, but even with five or six men to a room, it was not enough to house Ejercito Dragon. Almost every building in the little town had been commandeered for use as a bunkhouse, and the streets were choked with all the cars, Jeeps, HUMVEEs, and light trucks that had carried the survivors of Angel's army out of Deseret and into Colorado.

As had happened on several previous mornings, a confused

mass of several hundred men was milling about in the parking lot of the Rusty Cannon Motel—another hunting party was preparing to search for another house, farm, or ranch to plunder.

"I still can't believe we let him talk us into this!" Rosalia peered through the binoculars Scout had lent them. "I don't see any sign of him, but I don't see any sign that he's been caught."

"He's a smart kid, Rosy. With all that his dad taught him about hunting, he was probably more prepared to do what we set out to do than either of us were. And besides, we've been camped at his place for two weeks and no one has come up with a better idea."

"Yeah, but letting him sneak into their camp, all by himself! He's smart, but he's only a kid!"

"Hey, I'm not saying I'm not worried. I really love that little guy, but we would never have figured out the all dirt roads around here, and we would definitely not have found this great place for spying on the valley. He's littler and better at sneaking than both of us put together. *We'd* probably be the ones caught by now, if it wasn't for him!"

"I know, I know. I just feel that there's something not right about sending a child off into a dangerous place."

"Rosy, we didn't send him. This 'recon mission' was his idea, his plan. I think they're running out of food down there; they're more and more disorganized every day and will have to make some kind of move soon. He was right about it being a good time to go in for a closer look. Besides, I don't think we could have stopped him if we'd—"

"*¡Manos arriba!*"

The two froze, mid-argument. Before they could decide what to do, they heard laughter behind them—young laughter. They relaxed, but remembered to scoot away from the edge of the cliff before turning around.

"You little monster!" Holly tried to scold him, but she couldn't keep herself from laughing—more from relief than from actually sharing in his joke. "Scout, don't you ever do that to me again! I woulda peed in my pants if I'd had anything to drink recently!"

The boy thought this was uproariously funny and laughed until he had tears in his eyes. Both women hugged him, poking and prodding to make sure he was okay. He tolerated it only for a moment and then pushed them away. "Aw, cut it out!" He restored his dignity by messing up his hair. "And Rosy, I'm surprised at you for even thinking about trying to stop me. Holly's right; you couldn't."

"I didn't mean to doubt you, Scout, but I would feel really sad if something happened to you."

"Yeah, well, I'm not a kid anymore. I'm my own man, and I can take care of myself. I let you two join up with me because I thought you'd be good to have on my team, not because I wanted someone to baby me."

"But you're only..."

"But nothing! Who's the one who brings home meat to eat? Who's the one who knows where there's water that's safe to drink?"

"You, of course, and I don't want to baby you." Rosalia could see that he was genuinely upset and wanted to mollify him. "It's just hard, Scout. Most kids your age aren't as grown up as you are. It's hard to get used to someone so little being so grown up."

"Well you better get used to it!" His tone didn't soften a bit. "Rosy, you have to promise me that you won't treat me like a kid anymore. I mean it, I want your most excellent promise, or I won't help you any more and I won't let you be on my team!"

When had this become his team? No matter, he was serious, and she knew she needed his help. "Joseph," she looked him square in the eye, "I'm sorry. You are right and I was wrong. I promise— I swear that I will treat you with the same respect I treat any other independent and responsible person."

His forgiveness was immediate. "Thanks!" He hugged her.

"I swear it too, Scout." Holly wasn't sure what prompted her to say it, but she meant it.

He hugged her as well.

"So, what did you find out?"

"Not much. I couldn't understand what anyone was saying. 'Wirree-tirree-mirree'—they kept talking in Spanish!" He made a face. "But I did find some things. First, they're stupid. The Rifle Gang was a mean bunch, but they were smart. They left everyone alone as long as they would pay 'taxes.' Dad said it was like taking a cow's milk but not killing the cow—that way you get milk for a long time. From what I could tell, these Ejercito folks are killing the cows for one day's worth of milk."

"What do you mean?" Holly asked.

"They don't know anything about finding food for themselves. They are finding the folks the Rifle Gang used to 'tax' and killing them to take everything they have."

"Is that what the groups of men that go out every morning are doing?"

The little man nodded. "They were unloading a truck after yesterday's raiding party came back last night. It must have taken them some time to kill everyone, 'cause they didn't get back 'til after dark. And I'm not sure, but I think a lot less men came back than were sent out."

"How does that tell you they're killing everyone?"

"Well, they had a couple prisoners."

"Didn't you say they killed everyone."

"They do, except for girls." His face darkened. "You remember your promise?"

"Yes, but..."

Scout shushed her to silence, then turned to face down the hill and made a waving motion with his rifle. Two girls scrambled up the hill from where they'd been hiding behind the Jeep. They both had long brown hair tied in ponytails, striking blue eyes, and very light skin—twins, maybe twelve years old. They were wearing home-made dresses in a floral pattern and actually curtsied when they were standing before Scout and the two astonished women.

"Penny," declared one.

"Patty," echoed the other.

"We are pleased to meet you," both intoned in a well-rehearsed duet.

"Now don't be mad," Scout shifted his weight anxiously from foot to foot, "and remember your promise. I know our mission is important, and I might have tipped 'em off by rescuing these two, but I couldn't leave 'em there!"

Rosalia and Holly stared at the twins, having no idea what to say.

"I didn't let anyone see me, and didn't use my knife on the ropes they were tied up with." Scout was all but pleading now. "I made bed-sheet ropes to make it look like they climbed out their bathroom window. Those Ehersito stooges should think they escaped on their own and climbed out the window. If they even look for 'em, they'll look in the wrong direction. They won't know we've been watching them!"

"Scout, it's okay!" Holly put her hand on his shoulder.

"We're just surprised is all," Rosalia agreed. "You are an amazing young man!"

"I don't know if I would have been brave enough to try what you did last night!" Holly added.

Scout flushed a deep scarlet and changed the subject. "Anyway, they shot Penny and Patty's parents and took everything from their farm."

The two girls bowed their heads.

"I found out one more thing, Rosy, but it's not good news."

"What's that?"

"Those guys are really mad about something. They keep arguing all the time. And that one you told me to keep an eye out for? Anhel? He shot someone last night—at least the guy doing the shooting looked like you said Anhel would. I think everyone's mad at him and he goes around with lots of guards. I even found out where he's staying, and there are lots of guards there. Getting in and out of Rifle is easy—the nincompoops only have guards on the roads!—but getting at Anhel...that will be harder."

"Can you show me the route you took?"

"Sure!"

Rosalia, Scout, and Holly crawled up to the edge of the cliff again, while Patty and Penny sat among the rocks a short way down the slope.

Rosalia scrutinized the town with the binoculars while Scout pointed out landmarks. When she had the route fixed in her mind, the three pulled back from the edge. "I'll go in tonight and finish Scout's recon mission," she told her companions.

"Are you sure you should?" Scout took his turn doing the worrying. "I mean, I don't *think* they know I was there last night, but they might. It could be more dangerous tonight, and you can't hide as easily as I can."

"Scout, you did a great job, but we need to know what they are planning, and I'm the only one here who speaks Spanish."

He was still doubtful, and it showed on his face.

"And besides, they look as disorganized and lazy as they have every other day. I think we should take the girls back to your house and we should all eat some food, and get some rest. Holly can drive me back here tonight and I'll slip in the same way you did."

Scout planted his fists on his hips. "You're not leaving me behind!"

Rosalia waved a placating hand. "I'm not trying to baby you, Scout. I'm done with that. I keep my promises. But think about it for a minute. You can't drive and someone has to look after the girls you rescued. They're still in shock and need some rest. You can't rescue people and then just leave them on their own!"

Scout wanted to argue, but he could see that Rosalia was right. "Okay..." He kicked at a rock. "We'd better get going then."

"Now that I think about it," Rosalia added, "we should teach you how to drive when we get a chance—never know when you might need to know how!"

That idea cheered Scout up. Having reached agreement, they all picked their way back down the hill to the Jeep. Holly got in the driver's seat while Rosalia took the front passenger seat. The two girls sandwiched Scout in the back seat, pressing close to him.

After winding down the dirt road from the hilltop and starting back toward Parachute, Holly took a quick look in the rearview mirror—the two girls had already fallen asleep. Their heads were lolling on Scout's shoulders, and the gallant young man had put an arm around each to keep them from falling over. He was struggling to keep awake himself.

That evening, Rosalia felt distinctly on edge when she and Holly returned to the overlook. Her nap had was all too brief, and—she had to admit—she was scared. Looking down at the twilit town, she wished she could give up on her mad quest. But even the thought of giving up fired an angry ball of heat in her chest, and she knew she'd never abandon her task.

"Still looks all peaceful." Holly was using the binoculars. "They probably do think they didn't tie the girls up well enough and they ran away—not worth chasing."

"God, can you believe our Scout? He's got more courage and spirit in his little body than every single one of those men down there put together!"

"Yup! He's some kid!" Holly chuckled. "I mean small grownup. Or something. I don't know what to call him, but he's done a lot of growing up these last days."

"How old do you think he is?"

"I don't know—he won't tell me either." Holly chuckled. "He looks about ten, but he acts much older. He did even the first day we found him. Maybe he is older, but is small for his age?"

The two women drew back from the edge and waited for night to fall completely. The sun had already set behind higher mountains to the west, but was still high enough in the sky to provide a fair amount of light. The sky overhead was a deep luminous blue, through which some of the brighter stars and planets were already showing. To the east, several mountain peaks shone with a ruddy glow, the last rays from the sun not having left them yet.

"Holly, I'm scared."

"You should be!"

They were both silent for a while, watching as more and more stars appeared in the deepening void above.

"How can that little guy have been so casual about strolling down there in the middle of the night, among the very people who slaughtered his family?"

"Maybe," Holly drew the words out, "he doesn't really understand how twisted they are. Maybe, in spite of everything he's been through, he still thinks that shooting someone only blackens their face, like in cartoons." Her voice dropped to a whisper. "Maybe he doesn't fully understand the terror and pain he rescued those girls from."

"Maybe." Rosalia stood. "I'd better go, before I have a chance to chicken out. How does all this charcoal stuff Scout put on me look?"

"You look blacker than the Dark Knight. Hurry Rosy, and be *careful*! I'll be waiting here." Holly hugged her.

They kissed and Rosalia stepped carefully down the hillside, following Scout's directions to where she found a path. Scout had told her that it would take her down the hill and to the water tower on the northwest edge of the town.

Even though the moon had not yet risen over the mountains, she could pick out stones and other obstacles in her path easily—the thin mountain air let in a lot of starlight. She moved as silently as she could and encountered no sign of any other person along the entire path. The charcoal Scout had rubbed on her exposed skin itched like crazy, but, other than that, she was fine when she reached the water tower—not even winded from the hike. Good old Scout!

The town had no electricity. The street lights were out and there were no rectangles of yellow cast from windows. Nor were there any flickering shadows cast by neon signs. The sad streets and battered vehicles were bathed only in the still blue light of the stars, which did nothing to soften the alien look of the dead town. And it *was* a dead town. Ejercito Dragon's occupation was an evil force that animated it with the false life of a zombie. The men around Rosalia were all, temporarily, undead. As Holly had said of their leader, they just didn't know it yet.

She found her non-visual senses heightened by the ebon stillness around her. The flapping of bat wings was clear and loud, and she could feel small cracks in the pavement beneath her shoes.

It was ridiculously easy to avoid the places where Angel's men sat by campfires in the streets. Groups of men wandering about were universally noisy—where had they dug up any alcohol to get drunk on?—and even lone men could be heard a block away, as they trudged sullenly along.

Hiding in doorways and between cars, or simply walking along empty streets, Rosalia made her way to the building Scout had identified as the place where Angel was staying. Peering from inside a clump of bushes by a house across the street, she determined that there were indeed many guards about the place—a small two-story house away from any other buildings. She could feel her blood pounding in her ears.

Her heart stopped beating when one of the guards shined his flashlight right on her. She froze, but it didn't matter. The man was only on patrol, shining his light around. The beam had passed over her hiding place, as it had other places, without pausing.

Reminding herself to breathe again, Rosalia crept back as silently as she could and made a wide detour to approach the house again from the rear. She got to within fifty meters of the house by following a dry irrigation ditch that bordered the field behind the house, but then was stuck—the only way to get closer was across an open field. ¡Caramba!

She scurried up and down the ditch, but found no way to get closer to the house that was not equally exposed. Returning to the point where the ditch was closest to Angel's headquarters, she stopped to think about what to do next. It would be a shame to come all this way, only to have to give up and go back. She didn't mind that Scout had accomplished more, but they needed to know what was happening—find some way to finish what they had come to do!

Rosalia was still trying to figure out what to do when a group of men led by one with a flashlight approached the front of the house. As she watched, with only the top of her head above the rim of the ditch, an inky shadow detached itself from the rear porch and headed around the side of the building to join the other guards. After a short conversation, two of the new arrivals were allowed to enter, and the shadow returned to the back porch.

So, there *was* a guard in back! She hadn't been able to see him because he was sitting or leaning against the building and, unlike the other buildings in the town, light was streaming out of the windows of this one. Realizing why she hadn't been able to see the guard at the back door, Rosalia understood her own invisibility when the other guard had shined his light on her.

Not only that, but it was a warm June night and the windows of the house were wide open! If she could creep close enough, quietly enough, while staying out of the light, she just might be able to hear what was going on inside...

Slithering on her belly as Scout had taught her to do, she made her way closer. To her surprise, what had appeared to be an open field from the security of the irrigation ditch was actually dotted with tall clumps of coarse grass—even an occasional small juniper bush. Lying flat on her stomach, these things actually provided more than enough cover. She doubted that anyone could see her, unless they were above her...

What if there was a guard on the roof?

She froze at that thought, trying to make out the roof in the gloom. A tuft of grass blocked her view and a gentle breeze brought her the distinct fresh scent of wild sage. Well, if she couldn't see the roof, no one on the roof could see her...right? Maybe. Shrugging inwardly, she inched forward again.

Rosalia was actually not yet as close as she dared to get when she heard voices. They were raised in anger.

"Geez, what the hell made you go and invade Deseret?!" She

did not recognize this first voice.

"We didn't know they had their own goddamned Air Force!" This was Angel's voice—she recognized it easily.

"Christ! Hill Air Force Base was only one of the biggest fucking bases in the Rockies. Where do you think the planes came from that did practice bombing runs in the Great Salt Lake Desert?"

"Our intelligence reported that the base was abandoned."

"Sure, the Mormons were as afraid of the Rusky missile hoax as anyone else was, but they weren't stupid. They moved all the airplanes off the base, and then moved them back again after the missile scare was over. They took them out into the desert—they even announced it on the radio to make sure nobody got any crazy ideas about attacking them."

"On the radio?"

"Oh for crying out loud, you invaded Deseret and didn't even bother listening to Beehive Radio?! What kind of—"

Rosalia couldn't hear what happened, but the unknown voice stopped abruptly. Then Angel's voice was raised again:

"¿Cabron, para que me traes este idiota? I don't need his shit. I thought you said that he had information about where we might find the gasoline we need to get back to Los—El Angel!"

An answer was mumbled that Rosalia couldn't make out, but she recognized Cabron's voice. Cabron rarely spoke in English, partly because, unlike Angel, he had never worked on making his English an effective tool for getting what he wanted. She had only seen him twice during her imprisonment, but he too was someone she had known since childhood, and thought him to be someone who deserved death more than Angel himself. Cabron's was a voice she could *never* forget. He was muttering in Spanish to Angel now, too low for her to make out the words.

A few minutes later, Angel spoke again in English: "Well why didn't you say so!" Not long after, the tinkle of bottle caps thrown out a window and onto pavement rode the wind back to Rosalia.

She waited as patiently as she could, taking the risk of raising her head above the little juniper bush she had chosen for cover, but still couldn't hear anything clearly. She had just made up her mind to try to get closer when a pair of floodlights came on over the back porch.

¡Mierda!

Rosalia crouched behind her bush, feeling certain that she'd be seen. The plant was not very thick and was brightly outlined by the lights. She pulled into a tight ball, looking at the shadow the bush cast to make sure that no part of her stuck out into the light.

A door slammed, but the slamming of her heart against her ribs was louder in her ears. God, could they hear her heart?

Next, she heard male laughter, and then a soft hiss. Angel and his guests were urinating in the back yard. The plumbing was probably not working inside... They were pissing right at her and hadn't seen her!

"So, you think they have enough fuel for us at this Dollar Ranch?" It was Angel.

The unknown voice answered. "Gas, trucks, even an armored car. They've stored up plenty of food and won't share it with anyone!"

"Well, we'll have to teach them to be a little more neighborly then!"

"It won't be easy..."

Was that something crawling on her foot?

"They're a tough bunch. They wiped out the Rifle Gang..."

There was definitely something crawling on Rosalia's foot. It wasn't just crossing over her shoe, but was now working its way up her sock! If only the boots she had found with the uniform had been her size, she could have tucked her pants into them. It took all her effort not to scream.

"But you've got a lot more men. You should be able to pull it off..."

It must be a centipede or something... Oh God! All those legs on her skin, clawing their way up her calf! Not shaking it off—not making any movement or sound at all—was unquestionably the hardest thing Rosalia had ever done. She didn't breathe, didn't dare tremble. Tears of effort and fear ran silently down her face.

"There can't be more than a few hundred people in their whole valley. If you surround them and attack them from all sides, you should be able to spread them out too thin for them to be able to hold up against you."

The thing crawled up against the place where the fabric of her pants was pulled taut against her calf. It started wiggling and...were those pincers?

"Ahhh..." Angel again. "I have some maps inside. Can you show me their location?"

"Sure can, Mr. Ortega!"

"Excellent! Another beer?"

"Sure!"

Rosalia heard their footsteps retreat and the door slam again, but still didn't move. Her multi-legged tormentor hadn't given up and was struggling to go higher between her leg and her pants. She forced herself to count to sixty—slowly—a full five times after the light was extinguished, before beginning to move cautiously back, away from the house.

The movement reduced and changed the places of tension in the fabric of her pants, allowing the thing to move freely again. Rosalia bit her lip to keep from crying out as it climbed to the back of her knee and tickled the soft skin there.

Finally, back in the ditch, she tugged frantically at her pants until she got them off. Seeing nothing, she turned them inside out and a cricket sprang from the cloth and hopped away.

A cricket!

It was laughter she had to stifle now. She would have sworn—up to the moment she caught sight of the insect—that it had had to be at least ten centimeters long and have ten times as many legs! She breathed deeply to calm herself and pulled her pants back on, glad to be rid of the little invader.

Rosalia thought about trying to go back to the house, to kill Angel herself without risking her friends. The idea was appealing, but she didn't think she could get past the guards, so she reluctantly dropped it.

She made it back to Holly with only one more close call: someone hailed her from half a block away, asking if she knew of anywhere he could get a drink. She had simply ignored him and kept on walking. The man had not bothered to follow her.

"Girl, I am so glad to see you!" Holly greeted Rosalia with a hug.

"It's only been a couple hours...and I wasn't due to come back until dawn."

"Just 'cuz you aren't late doesn't mean I can't worry. I've been sitting on my ass up here for more than four hours, imagining all kinds of horrible things he could be doing to you if he'd caught you!"

"Well, I did have a bad experience with a cricket."

"A cricket!" Holly laughed.

"Laugh all you want, but it was a nightmare. The damned thing was crawling up my pants and Angel was peeing in the grass less than ten meters in front of me!"

"I'm sorry, Rosy!" She tried to stop laughing, but only managed to get it down to a chuckle. "But that *is* funny!"

Rosalia knew that it would do no good to get mad at her friend, so she waited for her to get it out of her system.

"I *am* sorry Rosy," Holly apologized again, "I just can't help it. A cricket!" She giggled a while longer and then settled down. "So, you must have found something out, or you wouldn't be back here so soon."

"Yes. They are going to attack Dollar Ranch."

"The kid was right!"

"That's not the only thing he was right about."

"What else?"

"There are guards all around Angel. Our only chance to get him will probably be when he attacks the ranch."

"So what do we do? Sit around until he makes up his mind to attack?"

"No, I've got a better idea: we warn them. Maybe they'll help us if we help them."

"Now you're talkin'! I'm tired of hangin' out here in the wilderness. You know what Scout says?"

"What?"

"They have electricity and running water—hot water!"

Rosalia eyed her friend. "Before you get too excited, there is one small problem we need to fix."

"What's that?"

"We're almost out of gas. Even with the two liters Scout salvaged from his family's car for making Molotov cocktails, I don't know if we can make it all the way there."

"So we'll hike the rest of the way. How far can it be?"

"I don't know, we'll have to ask Scout."

Holly did not reply right away. "Rosy, didn't he say that he'd never actually been there?"

Rosalia also paused before answering, "Holly, you know what?"

"What?"

"He's right about something else: he is definitely *not* a kid. Whether he's been there or not, I believe he can help us find Dollar Ranch before Angel does. I know he can!"

CHAPTER 55:
WEDNESDAY, JUNE 21, 2000

"Riding the storm out, waiting for the fallout
And I'm not missing a thing... riding the storm out."
—REO Speedwagon, *Riding the Storm Out*

Angel checked his good luck charm—nine brass circles! Everything was ready. "Cabron, da la orden."

Ejercito Dragon, all three thousand seven hundred or so members left to it, was on the march again. Cabron relayed Angel's order and the rag-tag column of vehicles on Colorado 13 started to pull out of Rifle. As it advanced, more Jeeps and pickup trucks slid out of parking lots and side streets and filled in behind.

Angel viewed the meager column behind him and cursed silently. Only he and Cabron knew the full extent of the desertions they had suffered since arriving in Rifle—nearly a thousand men!— but everyone knew that there had been many. All he had left, he was painfully aware, were those miserable wretches who were so lacking in imagination that they could see no other way to survive than to plunder. Most of the real soldiers had left him after Disneyland. Of those remaining, most of the more intelligent ones had surrendered in Deseret. He didn't let himself think about how those two facts reflected on him.

These would have to do. Angel didn't care what happened to them, as long as they got him what he needed to get back to L.A. The thought had crossed his mind of loading his Hummer with jerry cans and taking off for L.A. on his own—where he thought there were still loyal troops and supplies awaiting his return—but he was sure he would be pursued if he tried. And he had taught them well what to do with traitors! So, for now, he was stuck with trying to get everyone who stayed with him back to California. After that, he could make new plans, find a way to rebuild his army where the warships couldn't get at him...

He was still musing on visions of future glory—maybe they could take over Silicon Valley after all!—when the column came to the turnout. It was just a dirt road near Rio Blanco, but his scouts told him that there was a ranch that probably had supplies at the end of the lane. Cabron tapped him on the shoulder to bring it to his attention, and Angel issued orders.

With no real organization, Ejercito Dragon, the entire force, wrapped its slovenly aggregate body around the ranch house. There were no animals in the stockades, no signs of life anywhere.

Cabron took the thin sword he had found back in Rifle and impaled a white kerchief on the end. He advanced with his white flag until he stood before the front porch. "¡Atencion! Peeple eenside! General Angel Jesus Ramos Ortega orders you to surrender. Eef you turn over all your supplies of food and gasolina, you weell be allowed to leev!"

There was no reply.

He called again and there was still no reply.

Sheathing the sword and tucking the kerchief in his belt, he returned to the encircling forces and borrowed an M-16 from one of the soldiers. Moving the lever to full-auto, he stitched an uneven line of bullet holes across the front of the house.

Still no reply.

"Cabron," Angel rebuked his minion, "don't waste ammunition. We have barely enough as it is, and you're setting a bad example."

Cabron resented being chastised in front of subordinates, but didn't argue with Angel. He'd get his chance to let Angel know what he really thought soon enough! For now, he saluted and turned to order a team to storm the front door, which they did, encountering no resistance. They emerged a minute later. "¡Esta vacia!"

A quick search revealed that nothing of value had been left behind. No fuel, not a scrap of food, and no useful supplies. The empty house mocked the attackers, its open door a mouth thrown wide in laughter.

Angel frowned. How could it be empty? There had been a family living there the day before... Perhaps they had heard of his coming and taken flight? But how would they have had time to clean the place out?

He had Cabron give the orders to withdraw and proceed to the next target. This turned out to be a neat white cottage on an obviously well-tended farm.

Angel ordered it encircled.

White curtains flapped in the open windows, but there was no other motion to be seen.

Cabron reaffixed his kerchief to his sword and approached the cottage. "¡Atencion! You eenside! General Angel Jesus Ramos Ortega orders you to surrender. Eef you geev us all of your food and gasolina, you weell be allowed to leev!"

In reply, a gunshot thundered from one of the windows, leaving a hole in the middle of Cabron's kerchief as the bullet tore it from his sword. The white flag's owner scurried for cover before the cloth itself had settled in the dust. Trying not to look embarrassed and bristling with anger, he returned to Angel's HUMVEE. "¿Doy la orden?"

"Si." The gang leader cursed while Cabron relayed the order.

At his call, Ejercito Dragon left the cover of its vehicles and stormed forward. The farm house's white walls were soon peppered with bullet holes on all sides. It was unimaginable that anyone inside could have survived, but Angel's men continued to fall— the idea that lethal friendly fire might pass all the way through the house never crossed their minds. The earsplitting rat-a-tat of continuous gunfire blanketed the area and the smell of burnt gunpowder was everywhere.

If he'd had any military or police training, Angel would have realized that he was providing the defenders with what is called a 'target-rich environment,' as he had in Disneyland. The people in the house didn't even have to aim carefully—just pulling the trigger virtually guaranteed them a hit. In contrast, the Californians had to either try to aim into the shadows behind the windows while running forward, or stop and attempt the same feat while making easier targets of themselves. Neither of these options was appealing to the men, especially given that they could see their comrades dropping around them. Instead, they ignored their orders and switched their M-16's to full-auto, pouring thousands of rounds into the house.

Eventually, the attackers would have overwhelmed the defenders by simple brute force, but those inside the house had no intention of letting the attackers steal their supplies. They had brought a barrel of gasoline up to the living room and set it about twenty feet behind the front door, with a candle burning behind it. A bullet had already pierced it from side to side, near the top, dousing the floor with several gallons of the flammable liquid. When a group of Angel's men gained the porch, they sprayed gunfire through the front door before attempting an entry. Eleven bullets hit the barrel straight on, spewing gasoline backward and over the candle. The fuel ignited in a huge fireball that engulfed the house and blistered the men on the porch.

Ejercito Dragon fell back.

For the first time since his last argument with Rosalia, Angel Jesus Ramos Ortega was struck speechless. The heat from the blazing house forced him to turn away and climb back into his HUMVEE. Realizing what would happen if his men became aware of how many of their comrades they had lost to a single house, Angel ordered an immediate withdrawal. Ejercito Dragon withdrew, with only Angel, and possibly Cabron, aware that they had lost more than eighty men and gained nothing from their second detour.

Angel was unsure of what to do. On the one hand, they needed

the supplies they could get from such farms and ranches to take on
Dollar Ranch. On the other hand, a few more fiascoes like this,
and even these witless fools would desert him!

The reason he had decided on a massive attack was precisely
because of the heavy casualties the smaller raiding teams had taken
from similar targets. Now he wasn't sure that any strategy would
get them the supplies without morale-destroying losses, and that
was just from stand-alone houses! What if the occupants of Dollar
Ranch wouldn't surrender, even when they were surrounded and
outnumbered?

For the first time, Angel contemplated the possibility that he
might not win, but the thought was too unbearable, and his mind
shied away from it. He gave the order to bypass the remaining
smaller targets and to proceed at once to Dollar Ranch.

*   *   *

Patty and Penny stumbled along behind Scout, trying hard
not to complain, but obviously on the brink of exhaustion. Rosalia
and Holly weren't feeling much better themselves.

The Jeep had run out of gas the day before, near the burnt
shell of a house they had passed on the road. It had taken a lot of
work, but Scout had insisted that they push the Jeep off the road
and hide it. Holly had not wanted to spend the time, but Rosalia
had weighed in on Scout's side, saying that it would be bad news
for them all if Angel IDed the abandoned Jeep and became alerted
to their presence. He had outfitted the Jeep, after all, and might
recognize it. If he did, he might try to find whoever had brought it
to Colorado.

After hiding the Jeep behind a piece of blackened wall that
was still standing, they had set out on foot. At first, the pair of
plastic two-liter bottles full of water, paper-wrapped pieces of
cooked rabbit, and other supplies they carried in their backpacks
had weighed heavily on their backs, especially to the younger three.
Scout, of course, had refused to let on that his pack—much larger

than either Penny's or Patty's—was heavy, and the two girls had tried hard to follow his example.

The remainder of the day had been one long, hot, and dry march. The high mountain air had ensured that the five searchers spent a bitter cold night, even in the abandoned ranch house they took refuge in. Scout had lit a small fire in the fireplace—more than that might increase the risk of detection. The place had been stripped clean. They only had two blankets and Scout's sleeping bag between the five of them.

Now, Holly stared at the puffs of dust kicked up by her feet. With each plodding step she took along the deeply rutted dirt road, doubt grew in her about their choice of direction. She told herself for the fiftieth time that they had to be on the right track, but she couldn't feel confident that it was so anymore. Scout had remembered his father saying that the turn would be past a burnt house, and the dirt road certainly appeared frequently traveled...

But what if it wasn't the right one? Holly knew she was no expert, but the land did not look like good ranch land to her, it was too dry. They'd only been at it for a day, and already she was wishing her backpack was heavier again; the water would not last much longer. How far could it be?

The mid-morning sun was already searing hot.

Better not to think about that. It only made her feel more exhausted. Better to think about something else. Maybe get everyone's mind off their predicament... Holly's thoughts naturally turned to the one subject that occupied more of her and Rosalia's attention than any other. "Hey, Rosy, what's up with this Angel prick anyway? Why did he attack me—my little town, when he could have made one of his own just as easily? And, after almost getting beaten at Disneyland, what made him go and attack the Mormons?"

Rosalia was tired herself, and only made a tossing gesture with her hand, dismissing the subject.

"And he still hasn't learned his lesson. I mean, now he's got to go and attack someone else! Is he just plain psychotic, or what?"

"It's a long story."

"We don't seem to be short on time... Or do you have some other pressing engagements? A movie to shoot?"

Rosalia laughed hoarsely and called for a break. The girls collapsed gratefully onto the embankment on the north side of the road and Scout—after pretending to take a long sip of water—offered them some of his supply. He had husbanded his stock more carefully than they had.

Seeing that Scout had not swallowed, Rosalia smiled and started her explanation. "I've known Angel since we were little kids. We lived next door to each other, on the same floor, in the same apartment building." She could scarcely believe that so much time had passed. She remembered how weird it had felt when the year 1984 had arrived—a year that had always been part of a fictional future in her mind—and now it was already the year 2000! "When he was nine and I was seven, he asked me to marry him, and I agreed. He was an only child and came to play with me and my brother, Jorge, who was the same age he was."

She nudged Scout. "Angel loved the stars. For a child, he knew a lot of them by name, and could tell you where to find them in the constellations. Did you know that there's a star called 'beetlejuice'?"

The little man shook his head.

"It's not spelled that way," Rosalia continued, "but that's how you pronounce it. It's a red giant—Orion's left shoulder, actually. Angel taught me that, and showed it to me in the telescope he and Jorge bought with money they got from a paper route they worked together. Angel used to say that he was going to sail between the stars in a starship when he grew up—he loved stories about space. He's a lot smarter than your ordinary street gang leader!"

"Sounds like he was a neat kid," Holly commented. "So, what screwed him up?"

"Let's get moving again, and I'll tell you."

Everyone groaned, but they got to their feet and started down the road again. The twins were quite interested in the story and increased their efforts to keep up.

"When Angel was ten, the police raided our barrio. It was a big sting operation and they were supposedly rounding up three major 'drug king pins' that night. They did actually grab one family that was selling cocaine through a laundry service they were providing other residents of our apartment building, but it didn't turn out the way the police planned. They got mad, and I guess some of them got confused... I don't know why or how, but one team was on the wrong floor and kicked in the door to Angel's apartment.

"His parents were honest, hard-working people. In fact, Angel's father hated the drug dealers in the building and had been asking the police to do something about them for a long time. It was because the police never did anything that he bought a gun, and because the police busted through his door without announcing themselves that he shot at them. He thought they were members of a gang, come to hurt his family because he wouldn't play along.

"I didn't see what happened, and Angel never talks about it, but I could hear it through the wall. First there were a few separate shots, and then there was a terrible ripping, as loud as if the Devil himself were tearing the roof off the building. I know now that it was the sound of machine guns, but, as a little girl, I thought it was the end of the world." Rosalia spoke as if in a trance, deep into her memories. "The noise made by the police before they crashed into Angel's apartment had already awakened me, and I had wandered into the living room with my teddy bear. I remember exactly the way my bear looked when a row of bullet holes appeared in the wall, over my head, letting some light in. I screamed and threw myself on the floor, covering my ears with my hands, but I could still hear and it wouldn't stop...wouldn't stop..."

Rosalia covered her ears, as though she could still hear the screams that had been cut short, the gunfire that went on and on, and behind it all, the keening of a terrorized child.

"When it was over, they had cut Angel's father in half and shot his mother seven times. The only reason Angel didn't get shot is probably because he was hiding under his bed and didn't come out until things had calmed down. He could see police in the apartment. He thought they were there to help him."

The young people were listening with wide eyes, and even Holly's expression hinted at a little sympathy for Angel—but only for the boy he had been, not for the man he was.

Rosalia continued after a short pause. "And you know, the police never apologized. They insisted that it was an honest mistake and that they had followed all their guidelines in conducting the raid—as though their stupid guidelines were more important than the people they had endangered—murdered!"

They all trudged along in silence for a while.

"So," Holly asked, "that's what twisted him all up?"

"Well, he was never the same after that, but that was only the beginning, I think. The government placed him in a foster home with some other kids, and some of them were into drugs. They taught him the business and showed him how much money he could make, even as young as he was. That's when things started getting really bad. He eventually got kicked out of high school, but by then he was making so much money, he didn't care. I think his gang—he called it Ejercito del Norte, the Army of the North, back then—was a way to get back at the police.

"My brother, Jorge, tried to warn him, tried to help him, but Angel wouldn't listen. The more Angel tried to solve his problems with anger, the more Jorge understood that that was not the way to solve problems. Jorge explained it to me, showed me how stupid and destructive Angel was being, and how much better things would be if he'd just use his head and *think* about his choices. My brother told me to study hard and read lots of books—he told me that I was smarter than both of them put together, and that if I learned enough, I might be able to figure out a way to stop things like what happened to Angel's parents from happening anymore. Jorge gave me a mission, a purpose, and I think that's the only thing that kept me from getting dragged into the hatred and violence that consumed Angel." Rosalia covered her eyes. "I miss him—my brother—even after all this time!"

Scout could see that his friend was upset, but, for all his early maturity, was too inexperienced in understanding other people's pain to refrain from asking the obvious question: "What happened to Horhay?"

A sharp sob escaped Rosalia before she could catch it. But...it was okay...she had agreed to tell the story. "Right before he got kicked out of high school, Angel's gang got in a big fight with a rival gang. Jorge tried to stop the fight. He got right between the two sides, in one of the streets near the school, and told all of them they were being stupid and that neither side would be better off if they fought. It was one of Angel's own gang members, a violent and hateful kid everyone called El Cabron—that means 'jerk' in Spanish—who pulled a gun out and shot Jorge."

"Rosy, that's terrible!" Holly put an arm around her friend's shoulders. "Is that the same Cabron that came for me when...when Angel wanted me to watch his attack on Disneyland?"

"Yes." There were bitter tears in Rosalia eyes.

"Anhel attacked Disneyland?" Scout couldn't believe it. It was a kind of sacrilege he could understand—a violation of things he cherished, personally.

The two women nodded and Scout picked up his pace. He was more determined than ever that this Anhel needed to be stopped. After another few minutes of trudging on miserably, Scout had one more question: "So, now you're after Angel because of what he did to you *and* because of what happened to Horhay?"

Rosalia thought it over before answering. "Yes, Scout, but there's more. I'm also doing it because there is a lot of blood on my hands—all the people Angel has harmed since the day Jorge was shot!"

"Rosy, that's ridiculous!" Holly swung around in front of Rosalia, making her stop and look into her eyes. "You were just a kid. What were you supposed to do? Jump into the fight and get blown away like Jorge?"

"You don't understand."

"Like hell I don't! You know I've got an excellent reason for wanting to nail him myself... But you can't go around blaming yourself for what someone else does!"

"No, you really *don't* understand." The tears returned to her eyes. "You see, I witnessed the whole thing: the fight, Cabron shooting Jorge... I could have told the police, and maybe things would be different—Cabron, at least, might not be helping Angel to do so much evil. But Angel asked me not to tell. He swore it was a mistake, and that he would die in police custody. I don't know why I listened to him. He'd grown quite nasty since his parents' death, but I suppose I still loved that part of him that was the little boy who'd shown me the stars. Over the years, that part of him has grown smaller and smaller. I think it's probably entirely gone now."

She drooped sadly and Holly hugged her tight, holding her up.

"Right before he kidnapped me, I'd told him that I'd given up on him and that I should never have agreed to keep the truth from the police about Jorge. Maybe he decided that I was going to tell. After all these years, I don't think the police would have been interested, but I'm sure he didn't want to take any chances that they might start looking into his business more carefully, so he kidnapped me." Rosalia leaned against Holly and let herself cry.

Scout joined in on the hug and, after a brief hesitation, Penny and Patty did too.

Rosalia shook them loose when she'd regained her composure. "Thanks guys, I love you all... But we're going to die if we stay out here in this desert, and I'll never get to set things right with Angel, so we've got to move on. Scout, are you still sure this is the right road?"

The boy-man didn't answer directly, but started walking again.

"All right then, let's go. We've got to get there before Angel does!"

Some time later, when the two women were walking a little apart from their younger companions, Holly nudged Rosalia. "Rosy,

I'm as determined to stop that fucking bastard as you are, but I want it because I'm pissed. You want it because you feel guilty. If we do get a chance to stop him from ever hurting anyone again, and it could be either of us pulling the trigger, I'll let you go first. I'll never forget what he did to me, but being pissed won't stop me from living my life. You've got to deal with this guilt bullshit you're carrying around, or it'll eat you up. Okay?"

Rosalia had thought that Holly had already smashed all her stereotypes about what kind of woman might star in pornographic films, but found herself surprised all over again by her friend. Under her often crude exterior, Holly was one of the most warmhearted and genuine people Rosalia had ever met. She had no idea how to respond to such generosity, so she simply mouthed, "Thank you!" and hugged her friend.

She would always remember the feel of the actress' warm body in that embrace, the flinty odor of the dust from the road in her hair.

*　　*　　*

It was well past noon when Ejercito Dragon arrived at the Dollar Ranch front gate and parted, as water splits on the bow of a ship. Half of the vehicles swung to the left and half swung to the right. The impression of those behind the gate—now fitted with steel plates welded over the bars—was that the army poured over them forever and ever. Dollar Ranch might drown in its enemy without a single shot being fired.

To Angel, the situation appeared hopeless. The valley was more than three kilometers long and his men would be spread too thin to make much of an offensive force anywhere around its perimeter, but massing in one place would enable the defenders to concentrate their fire, as the people in the burned cottage had done. El Gringo's words about why such little towns would never surrender to him came back to Angel, but he brushed them aside. He'd worry about having to attack only if he had to.

For now, the task at hand was to impress those inside. He even spent some precious gasoline ordering the first vehicles that had arrived to swing around—out of sight—and drive by the gate a second time.

When everything was in place, and he was sure the defenders could see themselves surrounded on all sides, Angel approached the front gate himself. He didn't have a white flag, so he approached alone, his hands open wide. He stopped twenty feet shy of the gate, where he sensed that there were a large number of armed people behind the metal plates. He could see the muzzles of many rifles pointed at him through the slits.

"I am Angel Jesus Ramos Ortega! I am the general of Ejercito Dragon and I have your entire valley surrounded by a force of ten thousand men!" He paused to let the lie sink in. "If you will all put your weapons down and leave this place, we will allow you to live. If you give us any resistance whatsoever, or try to attack us, we will overwhelm your defenses and not a single person will be spared...except, perhaps, for some women who will wish they had died. I give you twenty-four hours to think about it!"

He turned to go, but a voice with a slight island accent answered him immediately. "We don't need twenty-four hours—our minds were made up before you got here. Rosalia has warned us and we are prepared. We will not surrender, and if you do not get off our property at once, we will consider your presence an act of aggression. If you do not leave, you will die, Angel Jesus Ramos Ortega!"

Angel tripped over a rock that wasn't there, not quite falling. Rosalia! It was impossible...but how else could the man have known Rosalia's name if she hadn't somehow communicated with him? But how could she even know where Angel was, let alone what he was doing?

Impossible!

Angel heard laughter behind him, female laughter. He spun on his heel, but could not see Rosalia through the armor on the gate. She was *here*? How?!

Struggling to get a grip on his shock, Angel shouted, "You have twenty-four hours," and retreated. He needed some time to think about this.

Behind the gate, Holly continued laughing.

Scout turned to Merlyn. "He's lying." He poked a thumb at Holly. "The Mormons told Rosy and Holly that they only let about five thousand escape Deseret. He's such a crummy commander and has made everyone mad at him, I bet he doesn't even have half that many left!"

Merlyn couldn't help but chuckle, but he took the young scout's assessment seriously. "And they have no armor. If they attack us, they'll get hurt bad. But still, five thousand—or even two thousand five hundred—are a lot of troops. Even with the people from the surrounding farms and ranches who decided to join us for this fight, we only have about three hundred. I wish more had joined us!"

Holly sobered up. "Maybe they won't attack. Maybe they'll try to wait us out. We can sit here until reinforcements arrive."

"There won't be any reinforcements. We turned down Deseret citizenship, and they told us they wouldn't be able to spare resources from protecting their own people if we were attacked. No... It was worth asking, so I had Randy radio a ham operator he knows in Deseret, but I don't expect help—and I think Angel knows we can sit here for years. He'll attack all right...unless Rosalia is successful. That might change their minds. Otherwise, it's back to plan A."

Everyone present agreed.

"Well then, let's get going!"

While the defenders of Dollar Ranch were fine-tuning their preparations, Angel was reconsidering his own. There were two tall hills overlooking the west wall of the hidden valley. He picked the closer of the two for his headquarters and sat in his HUMVEE until the men had dug a trench and built up a breastwork. When he was sure it was safe, he entered his new command post, surrounded by a personal guard of the most trusted soldiers he had left.

Soon, he was sending out orders from the hilltop command center: everyone was to make a show of digging trenches within eyesight of the valley walls, on all sides.

Grumbling, Ejercito Dragon complied.

As they worked, a soldier would occasionally stray too close to the defensive perimeter. When that happened, the automated guns could be seen rising from their bunkers and the PA system would warn the intruders off. It didn't take them long to learn how close it was safe to get—few things focus the mind as sharply as the sight of a belted weapon aimed between the eyes.

CHAPTER 56:
THURSDAY, JUNE 22, 2000

"You have shown me the sky,
But what good is the sky,
To a creature who'll never do better than crawl?
Of all the cruel Devils who've badgered and battered me,
You are the cruelest of all!"
—Man of La Mancha, *Aldonza*

Rosalia crouched outside the breastwork surrounding Angel's command post, still not seeing any guards, other than the one patrolling the side of the wall facing Dollar Ranch.

This is really stupid, she told herself—not according to plan! She was supposed to stay safely hidden on her own hilltop, the one behind Angel's. She'd been hiding in her own little breastwork of dirt and rocks since before Ejercito Dragon had arrived.

The mission she had persuaded the ranchers to let her undertake was to kill Angel before he could launch his final assault. With their leader dead, the rest might scatter.

In spite of all the lives it might save, it had not been an easy sell; the ranchers had moral problems with firing the first shot. She appreciated their civilized stance. They hadn't budged until she pointed out that Angel had already initiated the use of force against her and Holly, and had sacked Patty and Penny's farm, as well as killing Scout's parents with no provocation. That had persuaded them that Rosalia's proposal might be the best way to resolve the crisis, but they had still demurred. Their social contract—of which she had been shown a physical copy!—prevented them from firing the first shot. It was amazing to find such scruples in such uncivilized times.

The impasse had been settled when Holly had pointed out that she and Rosalia had not signed the contract, and personally had no moral qualms with using a *delayed* retaliatory force to prevent Angel from doing more harm. The question then became, would the ranchers help them?

Merlyn had agreed to help, as long as it was done in such a way that Angel had to transgress first. They couldn't simply shoot him when he showed up. He had to trespass, do some kind of harm to the ranchers or their property. This was why Merlyn had made it clear to Angel that Ejercito Dragon's presence on Dollar Ranch land would be considered an act of aggression—the gang leader's subsequent decision to stay was a latent act of force and justified a retaliatory response against him.

That was the plan, and, of course, Angel had removed any moral ambiguities by showing up and threatening the Dollar ranchers with violence... But Rosalia had never had a chance to pull it off! She had watched Angel arrive at the closer of the two hills, exactly as Merlyn had predicted, but had not been sure which vehicle was the gang leader's. Not wanting to expose herself until she could get a clear shot at her target, she had waited. It had turned out to be the HUMVEE, but he was moving when she spotted him, and she knew she wasn't good enough to hit a moving target.

Merlyn had showed her how to use a Barrett, and preset the gun's telescopic sight with a computer so that the cross-hairs would show exactly where the bullet would hit on the other hilltop, provided there was no wind. She knew that she was no sharpshooter, but wouldn't hear of letting anyone else take on the mission. She had hunted Angel this far—she wasn't about to let someone else finish the kill! It had taken a lot of argument, finally appealing to his duty to protect the twins, to persuade Scout that she needed to do it alone, but in the end, everyone had agreed.

So, Rosalia had accepted Merlyn's help, and he had set things up so she could hit any stone the size of a football, or larger, on the target hilltop with only a little movement of the rifle. She had even learned a little about compensating for the wind with her practice rounds. She was not the best, but she was confident she could hit something as large as a man—if he was standing still and she could get a clear shot.

Holly had cried when word of the approaching army was radioed out to them on Rosalia's hilltop, and she had given her friend a last hug. "I know there's no sense in risking both of us out here, and I know there's no way I can talk you out of this, but I can't help myself... Please come back with me?"

Rosalia had hugged her back and said nothing.

"I wish I hadn't promised to let you pull the trigger first!"

"No you don't."

"I..." Holly stopped and gave her friend a sharp look. "I guess you're right—I meant what I said back on the road. It's just that I... I feel that I'm never going to see you again!"

"Oh, don't be so melodramatic." Rosalia had pulled back and held Holly at arm's length. "I'll kill the murdering son of a bitch and then come back and join you as soon as it's safe."

Holly laughed. "You need to practice cussing—you're still not very convincing. And you'd better shoot him quick, 'cuz if I see him first, I'll nail the SOB myself!"

Rosalia had kissed her, full on the lips, and hugged her again. "Whoever gets him first is fine with me." They hugged again. "You can show me how to cuss when I get back, okay?"

"Okay." Holly wiped her eyes. "Here, you keep this." She stuffed the blushing border guard's 9mm pistol into Rosalia's waistband and turned to leave, not letting herself look back.

Much to Rosalia's frustration, her quarry had stayed behind his breastworks or in his tent, since the time he'd scurried out of his HUMVEE. Scout was right. Angel must be really scared of his own men to take such precautions; *nobody* could get a clear shot at him!

Well, she was tired of waiting. And with all of Angel's men

focusing on Dollar Ranch, it had been easier to sneak up behind his command post than it had been to get within earshot of the house in Rifle. It was now a few minutes before 3:00 a.m., and she was crouched outside the same breastwork that had frustrated her for so long, looking for signs of guards by Angel's tent. There were none. They must be all fanned out on the hillside, between Angel and his sleeping men.

She listened carefully, her heart hammering like a rabbit's when she hears the howling of the hounds—but she was the huntress this time! All was still, save the occasional scraping of the pacing sentry's boots on the rocks on the other side of the hill top. Rosalia took several deep breaths to calm herself.

Okay. Breathe... That was better.

Reaching down to her right boot, she pulled out the dirk she'd been given by a young blonde woman in the ranch. Whoever she was, she had said that she had a better set of blades now. With her left hand she reached across her waist and drew the 9mm pistol. Gripping both firmly, Rosalia braced herself. This was it!

She slipped silently over the wall and crouched between it and Angel's tent. Still no alarm, no sign of guards. A weak light was coming from some kind of lantern turned low inside the tent. It shone out through several of the window flaps and made the walls glow.

Creeping cautiously up to a window, Rosalia peeked inside. God must be smiling on her: Angel was alone. He must not even trust Cabron anymore! He was all twisted up in his sleeping bag, half off his air mattress, mumbling in his sleep. Hah! Served him right—she fervently hoped he was having a nightmare about being stalked by one of his own men.

Hmmm. The door was zipped shut and would probably make too much noise if she unzipped it. She examined the knife in her hand. It was obviously sharp and well cared for... She poked the tip through the side of the tent—the nylon fabric parted with only the slightest quiver, and almost no resistance. Before she could lose her courage, she slid the knife down the wall, making a gash big enough to climb through.

Still no sign of alarm.

Holding her breath, Rosalia slipped inside.

Angel *was* having a nightmare, but not about his men. He was dreaming that Rosalia had kidnapped him, and was torturing him with passages from books he could not bear to hear. In his dream, she took a paperback on ethics by some female philosopher and stuffed it in his mouth. He tried to turn aside, but the chair she had tied him to wouldn't let him. He tried to scream, but couldn't get any words out around the book.

Angel opened his eyes with a start, and found that his mouth was indeed covered. He could feel the unmistakable presence of a knife at his throat, and, when his eyes focused in the dim light, Rosalia's face was hovering over his own.

"¡No te mueavas!" She hissed in his ear. "One wrong move, and I'll kill you where you lie!"

He nodded his understanding. If he could get her to move the knife from his neck, he could grab her and hold her until a guard came...

"Now, before I uncover your mouth, I want you to understand a few things. The first is that I also have a gun. My life as I knew it ended when you kidnapped me, so I have nothing to lose. You do the slightest thing to make me nervous, and I'll kill you. I'll use the next bullet on myself, so not even your guards will get anything out of any stupid move you might make. After what you did to Holly, nothing matters more to me than stopping you, understand?"

He nodded again, mentally discarding his idea of trying to grab her—unless she made a mistake.

"Good. But the main thing is that I came here to kill you." He jerked, but she held him firmly, pressing the knife flat against his skin until he subsided. When had she become so strong? "If I was like you, your throat would be slit and your lousy blood would be running over my hands, right now. But I'm *not* like you. God knows you don't deserve it, Angel, but I've decided to give you one last chance. If you betray me, I will kill you personally—without the slightest hesitation." She looked into his eyes without speaking, trying to think of a way to get him away from his guards. "Now, I'm going to take my hand off your mouth, and you're going to tell the guard that you need to go to the bathroom, and order him to stay away from the back of the hill. Then we're going to go for a walk. Got it?"

He nodded a third time and she uncovered his mouth. "¡Raul! I'm going to take a crap. Don't let anyone disturb me on the back side of the hill."

The response was not immediate—Raul might have dozed off. "¿Eh? ¡Si, General!"

Holding the knife to Angel's skin until the last second, Rosalia jumped back from him. She put as much distance as she could between them and, while transferring the knife to her left hand, drew the gun with her right—she'd tucked it into her pants again in order to clamp a hand over Angel's mouth. She needn't have bothered; it took him a while to extricate himself from his sleeping bag.

As he disentangled himself, Angel groped under the covers for his gun, which he always kept by his side, until he saw it on the tent floor between Rosalia's feet. He thought about rushing her, but he could see that her gun was steady in her hand. It had already been cocked and was ready to fire. Where had she learned anything about guns?

No matter, if she was here to 'give him a last chance,' he might be able to get out of this by simply lying. Without a word, he grabbed a shirt—making sure she could see that it was only a shirt—and unzipped the door.

Under Rosalia's watchful eye, Angel marched back to the breastwork wall, climbed over, and continued down the back of the hill. Toward the bottom of the hill, Rosalia ordered him to stop and sit. He did, and she sat about three meters uphill from him, covering him with the gun.

"If you're planning on taking me back to the valley with you," he told her, using the barrio dialect he had never outgrown, "it won't work. I don't know how you sneaked out past my soldiers, but there's no way you can walk me all the way back there. They are loyal and would notice something wrong."

"I know. I came here to kill you, remember?"

"But you're not going to, so what do you want?"

"I want you to make the first good decision you've made since the deaths of your parents. I want you to stop this fight before it starts, before anyone else dies!"

He laughed. "You don't want much, do you?"

"Angel, you are a better person than you have made yourself. You failed to create a community because you were using the wrong tool: force. In spite of that, you are a very creative and intelligent person. You don't show it, but I know it. I remember. You don't have to be a murderer and destroyer of things other people make; you can make your own things. You don't have to fight like a pig for scraps in the mud; you could use the power of your mind to build the starships you once told me you would fly among the stars!"

Rosalia could see that she wasn't getting through—his blank face betrayed no emotion at all—but she had to keep trying until she knew with absolute certainty that there was no hope. "Every time I give up on you, I remember the beautiful child you once were... Angel, you are still young! You can stop all this madness and choose to live a life that adds value to the world—gold to the bag—instead of draining it. I know you can!"

Angel laughed derisively. "Stupid idealistic whore! You are so full of shit, I can't believe I wasted any time on you. The world doesn't work that way—power is all that matters! Jorge was full of it too, and I guess he left it to you when he cashed in."

With a sinking heart, she lifted her 9mm and sighted on his chest. "You can keep denying the truth as long as you want, but consider this: I have the power you say you believe in—right here in my hands—so what does it say about you that you still won't listen?" He was shivering in the cool desert night, with only his shirt and pants on... Or did he actually realize that he could be dead soon? "Listen Angel, this is my offer. You've got one chance to live: call off your attack on Dollar Ranch. That's my price. Call it off, or you die here in the dirt. Your choice."

He tried changing the subject. "How did you get away from my guards in Pomona?"

"I'm not joking, Angel. You make your choice—you give me your word as general of Ejercito Dragon that you will withdraw, or I pull the trigger."

Angel was about to tell her that she didn't have the guts, but thought better of it. She had shown a great deal of spine when she had been his prisoner—too much! He tried another approach. "I thought you said you weren't like me, and now you're telling me you're going to shoot me in cold blood?"

"If you don't agree to call off the attack, it will be self defense... But you never understood the idea of self defense. Jorge tried to tell you, but you wouldn't listen. Instead of fighting back and fixing the problems that led to your parents' deaths, you've become as bad as the cops you hate—worse!"

"That's a lie!"

"Is it? You kill indiscriminately, don't admit it when you're wrong, and never apologize. Now who does that remind you of?"

"No! You're wrong! I was going to build a better Los Angeles, and I would have, if it hadn't been for the Y2K thing!"

"Angel, we've already been over that!" She was half tempted to shoot him just for being so obstinate, but killing an unarmed man where he stood was not something she could do. "We both know that was a lie the first time you tried it on me and neither of us believes it now. You can stop bad things from happening with a gun, as I am going to stop you, but you can't build good things with guns. Communities cannot be forced into being; they result from the free decisions of individuals to associate and cooperate."

"No! Rosa, you've got to believe me! I was only..."

"Enough!" She motioned with the gun. She half wished he

would rush her, so she could shoot him in an act of self defense with no qualms. "I've got to get back...to the ranch...or they'll attack your troops while they sleep!" She was not very good at making things up on the spot, but hoped he couldn't tell she was lying. "And my hand is getting tired, so swear your surrender to me now, or you'll get what you've so richly deserved for so long!"

"Rosa..."

"Now!!"

"All right! All right! I swear it!"

"You will order your troops to withdraw in the morning?"

"I will, I swear it!"

"Okay, turn around."

"But I thought—"

"Do it! And stick your hands in your pants, behind your back!"

Angel obeyed.

Rosalia moved up behind him while he was wedging his hands into his pants. She raised the gun, meaning to hit him on the back of the head. "This is a nine millimeter message from Parley!"

He heard her voice in his ear and turned his head, thinking she meant to shoot him after all. The blow fell above his right eye.

Inspecting Angel's crumpled body on the ground, Rosalia found blood welling up in a cut she'd given him over his eyebrow.

"Eye for an eye, you bastard!" She kicked him in the stomach. "And that's from Holly." She kicked him twice more. "And that's from Scout and the twins. If you double cross me, I *will* kill you!"

CHAPTER 57:
FRIDAY, JUNE 23, 2000

"Well, the talk on the street says you might go selling out…
I need to know
I need to know."
—Tom Petty & The Heartbreakers, *I Need to Know*

Cabron bent through Angel's tent-flap with the requested maps. They needed to come up with a foolproof plan that even the fools they had left for soldiers couldn't mess up.

"¿Estas bien?" Cabron waved at the bandage on Angel's forehead.

"I told you, I slipped on a rock going to the bathroom yesterday morning. It's nothing major." Silently he fumed, and ached in several places. What had she done to him while he'd been unconscious? It was utterly intolerable, the thought of her doing things to him when he'd been senseless, helpless… His thoughts twisted away from recognizing that inflicting that same kind of helplessness was exactly what he had built his life around—his mind veered so sharply to avoid the recognition that the room actually spun and he had to sit down.

His greatest satisfaction—his only satisfaction—came from having lied to Rosalia. Though, in truth, he didn't have enough fuel or other supplies to retreat. So he had no choice but to fight. But still, as amazing as it was that she had managed to sneak all the way out of the ranch and into his command post, it was even more amazing that she'd been stupid enough to believe him.

Rosalia, of all people, should know better.

Cabron shrugged and rolled out the maps on a folding table he'd brought earlier. If he thought there was anything odd about the duct tape running down the tent wall, or the extra guards Angel had posted, he didn't mention it.

"First," Angel brought his mind back to the problem at hand, "tell me about the trouble makers. What did you do with them?"

Cabron shrugged again. "They were spreading unrest among the men, telling them that we don't have more than two days' food left and grumbling about not having enough sleeping bags. The worst was that black guy who kept telling everyone we don't have enough ammunition left for anything but a very short battle with the Dollar Ranchers."

"But... We *don't* have enough ammunition left."

"I know that," Cabron stopped himself from rolling his eyes, just barely, "and we don't want them to waste any more, but we also don't want them so worried about it that they won't attack. Right?"

"Right." Was Angel imagining things, or was Cabron getting a bit of an attitude?

"So," Cabron continued, "I sent them out to attack the surrounding ranches, supposedly to bring back supplies. It was a great way to get rid of them without encouraging desertions from the rest of the men. Maybe they'll get shot up, or maybe they'll run off. Either way, they won't bother us any more."

Angel didn't care for the idea of letting deserters get away, but could see the simple effectiveness of Cabron's solution. "Good. Well done." He toyed with the maps on the table. "When we're done here, send out word that the Dollar Ranchers have huge hoards of food and enough houses with real beds for every man to get one of his own. And send out an 'official' pronouncement that every man who leads a successful charge over the rim will have his pick of the hundreds of women and girls who are inside."

Cabron raised his eyebrows. "There are hundreds of girls in there?"

"I don't know, but there should be plenty for the few men we have left when we get in." Angel grinned. "Also, spread a rumor that at least one of my most loyal men is in every group, with orders to shoot anyone who deserts. Then send someone, maybe one of the surviving Asians, back to Rifle for something—anything. Don't tell anyone, and when he leaves have him shot. This will give the impression that we really do have people watching for deserters in every group of men. Understand?"

"¡Si, mi general!"

Was there a slight trace of sarcasm in Angel's response? He must be letting his fatigue catch up with him—Cabron had been his right-hand man since the very beginning. He'd even shot Jorge at Angel's request. If there was anyone he could trust, it was Cabron.

Angel pushed his doubts aside. A truly foolproof plan was now the first order of business. "The way it looks to me," he pronounced, "is that if we can force the men up over the rim—even with heavy losses—we can overwhelm the defenders. Then we'll have everything we'll need to return to L.A., or stay here until we think of something better to do."

Cabron agreed. "Our best bet would be to have a few small groups of men attack different places at the same time, all around the valley. When the ranchers spread out, we attack with the rest of our forces at a single place, concentrating enough firepower to get through."

"¡Bueno!" Angel thought it over. "That way, while they're spread all around the valley, we'll have over three thousand men at one spot...but...no; we shouldn't put them all at one point. When they realize what's going on, they could all try to defend that one place. If we attack along a stretch, they'd still be spread out, even if every single one of them were there. Suppose we make it a long stretch, but not longer than a kilometer?"

"Yes! That's perfect!"

They spent more than an hour working out the details and the exact orders that would need to be given. Finally, Angel was satisfied. Visions of Achilles and the sack of Troy returned to his mind—particularly vivid was the image of all the women slaves the Greeks had carried off. "Excellent! We'll attack tomorrow. We have enough food for one more day—when the men are fighting, I want them to know that they only way they are going to eat is by winning the battle. Tell them that all they have to do is follow orders, and they'll be sleeping well tomorrow night, with full stomachs and maybe something else for their other appetites, yes?"

"Yes, but I wish the man who told us about this place were still alive. He might have been able to tell us more about their defenses."

Angel frowned. "He insulted me, and he was done. He said he was never inside Dollar Ranch, remember? He could not have told us anything more."

"Si, mi General." Cabron saluted and left to deliver the necessary orders. He knew better than to argue with Angel, but disagreed—the man had been in a group that had attacked and lost. He had seen the defenses in action. Angel was showing increasing signs of irrationality. Maybe it was time for him to have an accident... Perhaps a stray bullet during the fighting? God knew Angel had lost it—Everything had gone downhill since that stupid business of trying to start a government! It was time for someone with more brains to take over.

After Cabron left, Angel's thoughts reverted to Rosalia. Why hadn't he slit her wrists and dumped her out in the Pacific Ocean when he'd had the chance? And what did it mean that she appeared here, now?

He fingered the bandage over his eye, staring out through a tent-flap.

How had she escaped? How had she found him? And where on earth had she learned to crawl through enemy lines on assassination missions?

Maybe it had been a mistake to put that redheaded whore in with her... Why had he done that?

Enough fooling around! He'd issue orders that she was to be taken alive, and then, once the ranch was under his control, he would do what he should have done in the first place: rape her until she no longer amused him, and then kill her. Even though he enjoyed forcing himself on women, the thought of raping Rosalia had always been repugnant to him. He'd never allowed himself to recognize the fact that he still loved her, but that feeling finally expired in the furnace of his humiliation.

His emotional polarity reversed itself and he experienced the most passionate hatred he could remember feeling since the night of the police raid on his parents' apartment. To think of all the time he'd wasted reading Shakespeare and other garbage, and perfecting his English—just to impress her!

Hold a knife to his neck, would she? He'd show her!

CHAPTER 58:
SATURDAY, JUNE 24, 2000

"You don't get something for nothing
You can't have freedom for free!"
—Rush, *Something for Nothing*

The morning dawned cool and clear. It was going to be a very hot day.

Good! Angel smiled as Ejercito Dragon assembled itself behind his headquarters hill. If they were thirsty, that would remind them that food and water would only be available to the victorious. He was lying behind the breastwork that crowned his hill, peering over the wall with a pair of binoculars. What a pathetic bunch!

After some time, all the men in their vehicles were assembled in a long crooked column, hidden from any watchers on the valley rim by Angel's hill. Angel turned to Cabron, the only man he trusted to be near him when bullets were flying. "Da la orden."

Cabron relayed the signal and the dozen decoy teams posted around Dollar Ranch began firing on the valley rim. They engaged the occupants of the watchtowers, not really trying very hard to hit them, but pinning them down while they moved around and tried to appear as though they were about to attack. It was an odd thing they had been ordered to do, but it was better than actually trying to get closer. Getting closer would activate the belted guns—dark skeletons rising from black crypts. They had no interest in seeing that happen.

After five minutes, Cabron relayed the order to charge.

Most of the Jeeps, cars, pickup trucks, and other vehicles that made a sort of light cavalry out of Angel's army had so little fuel left, they probably wouldn't last for long—but it didn't matter; they had less than two kilometers to go to get to the center of Dollar Ranch.

They roared around the headquarters hill, an incoming tide of hundreds of machines that shook the ground as they fanned out to attack a one-kilometer stretch of the valley wall. They charged as fast as they could bounce over the rocky terrain. Angel changed his position to the breastwork facing the valley. He could see the formation of vehicles actually taking on a linear shape, so as to attack the entire defending stretch at once. He smiled for the first time in days; for once the men were following orders and acting like a real army. This might actually work!

The line reached the bottom of the valley wall and started working its way up. The vehicles not equipped with four wheel drive were having a harder time, but still making progress. When they reached halfway up the hillside, Angel heard God open His mouth and scream at him. This was no mere warning from the PA system he'd been told about, nor the firing of a few machine guns! The entire kilometer-long stretch of valley rim erupted in fire at once, and several dozen explosions along the halfway line hurled no fewer than fifteen vehicles into the air. The steady chattering of automatic weaponry, punctuated by the sharper crack something very high-powered, was resounding, even at his distance.

Through his binoculars, Angel could see that the belted guns had arisen from the earth, and were spitting death at a furious pace. This he had expected, but the entire length of the rim-top breastwork was also crawling with defenders! Some of them were shooting bipod-mounted, belted versions of the big black guns Angel's scouts had seen in the watchtowers. Before his disbelieving eyes, they leveled a withering barrage on his men, concentrating on the drivers of the vehicles.

In short order, every single vehicle had either stopped moving, or been overturned. A few of those blown up by the land mines

even managed to catch fire, though they did so without enthusiasm. Ejercito Dragon's advance faltered, but Dollar Ranch's electric fence was broached in scores of places.

They knew!

They knew about his plan! But how? Was there a traitor among
his ranks? But even if there was, it was doubtful the Dollar Ranchers would believe any story he told... And the orders had not been
given until that morning—not enough time to prepare a defense
like this! How could they know?

In the deep recesses of his mind, he was sure it had something
to do with Rosalia, but he couldn't figure out what. The thought
preyed on him that she had warned him not to betray her, but he
didn't have time to think about it.

Cabron drew his attention back to the battlefield. "¡Mira,
General!"

Before Angel's astounded eyes was an even greater surprise than
the unexpected strength of the defense: his men were regrouping!
Those who had not been too badly injured by the ambush on
their vehicles poured through the openings in the electric fence
and spread out, struggling up the hill, while trying not to present
any target-rich pockets to the defenders... And—Por Dios—they
were advancing! They could see that turning to run was no protection from the machine guns and must know they'd be out of ammunition soon, and were struggling to finish the fight before that
happened.

In his binoculars, man after man went down, some of them
knocked off their feet—that must be what the big guns did—but
the rest climbed upward. Cabron had been right, even with their
breastworks and their machine guns, and whatever the big black
weapons were, the defenders were still greatly outnumbered and
could not stand forever.

Angel whooped and clapped Cabron on the shoulder. They
were going to win! For the first time since Disneyland, something
was going their way! Through the field glasses, Angel watched his
men getting close to the top.

The defenders were retreating!

Angel could see them falling back into the valley. His elevation was not high enough to see well into the part of Dollar Ranch that faced away from him, on the other side of the ridge, but he was sure the ranchers were running like hell. His men were over the top, chasing them down into their valley—they were being routed!

Suddenly, a series of many explosions sent tremors through the ground. Huge quantities of smoke, dirt, and other debris were hurled into the sky from the other side of the ridge—it was maddening not to be able to see what was happening.

"Cabron! Get on the radio and find out what the hell is going on!"

"¡Si, General!" Cabron fiddled with his radio a while before finally getting a report. "It's confused, Angel. It looks like the defenders planted a large number of land mines and booby traps on the inside wall of the valley. According to Ramon, hundreds of men have been blown up, or are injured." He stopped and listened intently for a moment. "He says he thinks there are about 500 men left, and they are still advancing, pushing the defenders back! He says...wait a minute... It's someone else now—Ramon's been shot. He says that the ranchers have all fled into a mine shaft in that ridge there in front of us."

Angel cursed and paced while Cabron queried the man on the other end of the radio link.

"He says that they seem to have all gone down the mine shaft—we can take their houses and supplies! What? The guns on the hills have turned around and are shooting down into the valley! The men are storming the entrance to the mine anyway..."

The two heard a deep throated double *BOOM!* from the other side of the hill. A blazing liquid was visible briefly, arcing up and down again behind the top of the ridge, and then nothing could be seen but a billowing black cloud of smoke.

"What?" Cabron turned to look at Angel. "He says that two giant gouts of some kind of burning liquid just exploded from the mine opening and doused the men. There are only, maybe, four hundred men left, but they're still attacking the mine..."

Thup-thup-thup...

At the same time, Angel and Cabron both heard something new: a palpable vibration that rose above the din of battle. What the Devil!?!

Three airborne shapes swooped into the valley, falling on Angel's men, as falcons might appear in the sky and pluck field mice from the grass. One was boxy and green, with a red star painted on the side, one was angular and jet-black, and the third had camouflage patterns adorning its sleek shape, except where it bristled with guns and other weapons, as did its companions.

"Petrov! Okie!" Alexis sent to her sister ships, "the good guys have been forced down into that mine—see all the bodies piled up by the entrance? Anyone you see engaged in hostilities outside the mine entrance is a bandit. Fire at will! Repeat: *FIRE AT WILL!!*"

"Yeeee-haw, Major Tom!"

"Da, Major Tom!"

Leading the formation in the Apache she had picked up in Alaska, Alexis dove on Ejercito Dragon. John Allen held the trigger down on the forward gun—having matched his book-knowledge of the weapons systems with more practical instruction from Alexis—and chewed up a line of attackers as they went. The three helicopters banked sharply for another pass, the Hind a little less elegantly, but keeping up.

For once forgetting his personal safety, Angel climbed to stand on the breastwork and stared at the three helicopters diving on his men on the other side of the ridge. On their second pass, the Hind and the Apache fired scores of rockets from their rocket launchers, while the Blackhawk broke from the formation to plant a larger missile in the middle of a group of Ejercito Dragon soldiers that was gathering to attack some of the defenders who'd been caught in a watchtower. Angel couldn't see it, but he knew his men were being scattered in every direction—there was no way they would stand up to such a rain of fire.

It was the opportunity Rosalia had been waiting for.

Her supply of food and water was gone; it was her anger at being lied to by Angel once again that sustained her. She had returned to her hilltop, unwilling to risk trying to get through Angel's men and not certain he would keep his promise. After he had broken his word, she'd known that his personal security would be tighter and she'd never be able to sneak back in and kill him, so she had been waiting patiently for a clear shot. As before, he'd never stood still long enough in an exposed place for her to line up her sights on him. She should have put a bullet in his head when she'd had the chance!

And now, finally, he had been flushed out. Merlyn hadn't mentioned anything about helicopters! Rosalia thought about radioing back for an explanation, but didn't want to take her eyes off her target. The three swooping shapes were devastating the last remnant of Angel's once-fearful Ejercito Dragon. Maybe the messages Merlyn had sent to Deseret had been answered after all? It didn't matter. What mattered was that Angel was so surprised, he had left his cover.

She placed his back in the middle of the cross-hairs and tried to feel for wind. She wasn't sure, but there might be a very slight wind from the right, so she moved the cross-hairs to center on the right side of his back. Angel moved, waving his arms, and then stood still again. She adjusted the gun, held her breath while saying 'squeeeeeeze' in her mind, and pulled the trigger as smoothly as she could. "And this one's from me!!"

On his hilltop, Angel was watching the unfolding disaster. The choppers came back for a third run, this time targeting the men lowest down on the hill, perhaps attempting to drive them away from the mine entrance. Whatever the reason, it impelled the remaining men back up to the top of the ridge, fleeing in complete panic.

Standing still, he steadied his binoculars. The pitifully small contingent of men he had left—obviously out of ammunition— backed up around one of the towers. They were still fighting, with knives and even their bare hands. Served the idiots right for wasting their ammunition!

Maybe he'd be able to go back to Los Angeles on his own after all. If the ranchers captured his men, he could take his Hummer and leave before they could chase him.

The defenders surged out of their mine shelter—from several concealed openings near the top of the hill where Angel could see them—and charged at his remaining troops. The helicopters hovered over the scene, no longer able to concentrate their fire exclusively on the invaders. One of them headed off to deal with the decoy attackers. Angel smiled grimly, and then stopped. There, at the base of the besieged tower, a girl was *dancing* through his men. He could see her long blonde hair clearly. Her hands were made of metal. She was spinning, jumping, and kicking through his men— a reaper making a long furrow in a human field. Por Dios, men were writhing on the ground behind her! What the hell was she?

CRACK!

Something traveling at supersonic speeds ripped through Angel's left elbow—from behind!—spinning him around violently and tumbling him from his perch on the wall. Rolling in agony in the dirt, he found that his arm had been ripped completely off at the elbow. Unheeded, his 'lucky' 9mm slipped from his belt and into his pants. Howling with pain, he clasped the arm stump with his right hand, and noticed the hilltop right behind his own. It was about the same height as his own—right there behind him the whole time!

Rosalia!

He was certain that Rosalia was up on that hilltop. She'd been spying on him and had radioed the defenders when she'd seen his troops forming up behind his hill. That was how they had known! And that was how she'd been able to get past his sentries—she'd been waiting for him outside the valley from the beginning!

"Rosalia!" He screamed in her direction, as though he could strike her down with pure rage. "Rosalia!!!" What was that threat she'd made? *'If you betray me, I will kill you personally—without the slightest hesitation.'*

Cabron beheld the great General of Ejercito Dragon and laughed. Seeing him scrabbling among the rocks, trying to get under cover—it was funny! "¡Mi General! Your uniform is dirty! Should I have the battle stopped so you can get a clean one on?"

Angel gaped at his most trusted lieutenant, bewildered, not understanding what he was hearing. "Cabron, help me, we can get to my Hummer and escape!"

Cabron laughed again and kicked the stump of his former leader's arm. "Help you? For twenty years you've called me 'El Cabron'—why should I help an incompetent like you who can't even appreciate a friend like me?"

Angel's erstwhile toady pulled out his knife and moved forward, the battle forgotten. So engrossed was he in a chance to play one of his favorite games, he failed to see the Apache turn from the melee below and head in his direction.

"Cabron," Angel panted as his former adjutant advance on him, "wait, you need me! We can still escape... You're insane!"

A disappointingly short while later, when Angel lost consciousness, Cabron heard the approaching helicopter. Frowning at the interruption, he scaled the south breastwork to see if it was indeed time to escape. His head cleared the wall just in time to see the helicopter loose two missiles. He lost his balance and fell back onto the ground behind the breastwork wall. Riding twin lances of white smoke, his death streaked straight at him.

Alexis whooped in satisfaction as the enemy command post was transformed into a geyser of fire and shattered stone. Frustrated that she could not help the defenders on the valley rim any longer, she circled the hilltop where she had seen the enemy's HQ. "Hit 'em again John, the enemy HQ must be completely neutralized!" Allen fired a stream of the M261 MPSM missiles as Alexis circled farther around. Angel's command center was shattered by more than one hundred separate explosions.

When the smoke cleared, Alexis could see nothing left of the hostiles' command post. "Petrov, Okie, we've taken out the enemy HQ. Okie, while Petrov is cleaning up the perimeter, you use your PA speakers. Fly over any remaining hostilities and inform the attackers that their leaders are dead, and that they had better surrender if they don't want the same thing to happen to them. Tell them to put their weapons down and hold their hands up high where we can see 'em. Anyone who tries to leave with his weapons will be shot! Got it?"

"Roger that. Good shootin', mayum!"

"Da... Roger that, Major Tom!"

Rosalia stared in disbelief. She had been certain she had missed, and then the entire hilltop had leapt for the sky! The reason why presented itself a few seconds later, as one of the helicopters rose above the smoke. It calmly circled the hill, letting loose a barrage of missiles. By the time it was finished, the hill had a new top, slightly lower than the original one.

YES!!!

She found that she didn't care who had done the deed after all. She had taken her shot, and Ejercito Dragon was obviously never going to bother anyone again. Looking down at the thirty-pound Barrett, she decided to leave it where it was and head back. She could come back later with Holly to fetch it.

What a great day this had turned out to be!

Chapter 59:
Sunday, June 25, 2000

"If the dream is won—
Though everything is lost
We will pay the price,
But we will not count the cost."
—Rush, *Bravado*

Michel had an arm around Razor. Neither could see the casket for the tears that ran freely from their eyes.

Dreamer was speaking: "My daughter...Eva, who liked to call herself Jimmy, was..." He broke off and tried again. "Let me just say that Jimmy was a special person, one of those rare few who blow through the world like a benign hurricane, changing everyone they touch. She was like her mother in that..." He choked up, tried again, and had to stop.

Dawn joined her father and held him. Then, as one, Jimmy's brothers rose and embraced their father and sister. After several minutes, Dreamer got enough control to say, "Aw, heck... I can't do it. Go ahead and close it up!"

The casket was a simple pine box, as were all those of Dollar Ranch's dead. The enemy dead had already been bulldozed under an unmarked mass grave on what had become known as Anhel Hill. What pitifully few prisoners there had been were given canteens, some beef jerky, and told to leave and never return.

Jimmy rested in her box, looking almost normal, if a little pale. The knife wound was invisible beneath her clothes. The gauntlets Razor had given her glittered on her chest, where Jimmy's hands had been folded—one last silver gleam before the lid was nailed onto the coffin.

Razor herself had cleaned the gauntlets for Jimmy, as Jimmy had once done for her—though, by all accounts, Jimmy had acquitted herself much better than she had. Razor hadn't seen it, but Michel had been there. Jimmy had taken no fewer than twelve of the enemy out of the fight, after she and Dawn had run out of ammunition in their watchtower. Her last act had been to dive between Michel and an invader who was preparing to stab him in the back. She had deflected the blow, severing a number of the man's fingers in the process, but he'd had another knife...

Michel and Razor couldn't bear to watch as the box was lowered into the ground, and Dreamer wordlessly shoveled the first spade-full of dirt onto it.

Dawn stood over her sister's grave, looking up into the sky instead of down into the earth. Her suggestion of making belts for the Barretts instead of being stuck with the original five-round magazines had saved many lives—but not enough! Silently, Dawn bid Eva farewell.

Razor was wearing the rapier she had given Trish. It had been found, blackened but unbroken, in the debris at the top of Anhel Hill, and she now wore it everywhere she went. Her right shoulder was undamaged and she would learn to use the blade, in honor of her departed friends. She drew it now to salute Jimmy, and then turned to bury her face in Michel's shoulder, unashamed to lean on a man for the first time in her adult life.

About fifty feet farther along the slope, Scout, Penny, and Patty huddled close to Rosalia at a similar scene. Holly's casket was already closed, because she had been hit in the head.

The man-boy could not keep his tears in, but he steadfastly refused to release the wailing that he longed to let out. The girls stood by him, each holding one of his hands. While they too were crying, they had not become as attached to the brash redhead as he had. Scout couldn't even see for the effort he was putting into the struggle to contain his pain—for the second time!

Merlyn stopped in his rounds to thank Rosalia for her warning and her help. "I know it won't make the hurt go away right now, but try to remember what you and Holly did by coming here, and what you did all alone on your hilltop. You saved many lives!"

Rosalia's eyes were red-rimmed from all the crying she had done, but dry for the moment. She hugged Merlyn gently, avoiding the arm he had in a sling. "Yes, but... Do you know what I was telling myself while I hiked back from my hill? I was telling myself that we'd had a great day! Can you believe it!"

"It's a normal reaction to winning a fight..."

"If only I'd stopped him the night before, maybe this wouldn't have happened, maybe Holly, and Dreamer's daughter, and the others... Maybe they'd all still be alive!"

"Or, maybe Angel's second in command would have attacked immediately, and Major Tom would have found only ashes when she got here. Rosalia, do you really think you could be at peace with the memory of killing him with your own hands? Dawn's having a hard enough time, and she was a quarter of a mile away from the people she shot...and they were in the midst of an act of violent aggression! There's no use blaming yourself, or second-guessing history. We've suffered terrible losses—this valley will never be the same without Jimmy charging around on some piece of heavy equipment, but we've actually come through a major invasion rather well..."

Rosalia didn't answer.

"May I make a recommendation?"

"What?"

"Talk to Michel and Razor. They both know a thing or two about guilt, and have some interesting stories to share. I think they would, if you explain your hurt to them."

"I don't know them."

"Then get to know them. They are good people, and they can help you!"

"I'll... I'll think about it."

"You do that." He returned her hug and moved on to the next burial.

Chapter 60:
Tuesday, July 4, 2000

"My life goes on in endless song above earth's lamentations,
I hear the real, though far-off hymn that hails a new creation...
When tyrants tremble in their fear and hear their death knell ringing,
When friends rejoice both far and near how can I keep from singing?"
—Enya, *How Can I Keep From Singing?*

As the Dollar Ranchers awaited nightfall, the mood was still shot with somber overtones, but was generally more festive than it had been since the day of the attack. They were alive and they had won!

Three lines of picnic tables had been set up by the giant BBQ pit Jimmy had built in the central oval, and the common area of the little town was packed with people celebrating their victory. With most of the unpleasant after-battle chores behind them, the people felt a need to celebrate. It was not a wild party, but a more quietly joyful gathering of friends who had triumphed over tragedy together.

Anna, who had not yet really had a chance to speak at any length with Alexis, was asking about her trip home. The two were sitting beside each other across the table from Merlyn and John Allen. "So, the Englishman tried to fly his harrier back to Britain?"

Alexis nodded. "Yes, he thought he'd try his luck finding fuel at air strips Petrov showed him on maps, and head straight back to Europe."

"And what about the Frenchmen?"

"They came with us. The two computer experts decided to

stay in Silicon Valley, but the pilots came back to Deseret with the rest of us, and joined the Deseret Air Force. They'll probably stay there until more things are working again and they can go home."

"So how many decided to stay with the Mormons?"

Alexis grinned. "A lot of them, the ones that didn't stay in Silicon Valley. Captain Stewart fit right in. It's really tempting, you know. Deseret probably has the largest and most vibrant economy in the world right now. Everything is in overdrive there... All the building and repairing. And things are clean there. People have meaningful work, and seem productive and happy. Newcomers are adopting their religion left and right, and they are preparing to re-open their offices around the world. If this keeps up, the LDS faith will be the world's dominant religion in just a few years."

"Humph." Anna wasn't prejudiced about Mormons, but the thought of that much power and growth going on right next to them—and soon all around them—made her nervous. "We need to expand too. This little valley is too crowded with all the people we took in before the battle with Ejercito Dragon, and there are some abandoned oil and gas fields to the north and west of here. We should do as the Mormons are doing; move into unclaimed territory and invite neighbors to sign the Contract."

"As your chief of security and head of the Dollar Ranch Air Force, I agree. More territory will be harder to defend, but we need more land, and we need domestic production that we can trade with Deseret and other developing communities. Sitting on a bunch of oil and natural gas sounds to me like a good way to go!" She chuckled. "The Russians we left behind had the same idea. They decided that the Doomsday Device's power plant was actually a valuable asset. Once we made sure the third WOPR CPU was as frozen as the others and that the whole installation was basically harmless, they figured they could offer free electricity and attract people to live there. They're building a new city right on the spot."

"So," Merlyn interjected, "there was no civil government left in Russia either?"

"Not a shred. No military hierarchy either. No one to come and tell them that the bunkers were government property. It was kind of spooky in the bunkers—all the computers frozen up, so still, so quiet... But hey, if that's what they wanted, far be it from me to tell them otherwise!"

Alexis shivered at the memory of the machine that had caused so many deaths, and paused to wash down a bite of hot dog with some genuine pre-collapse Coca-Cola.

"Anyway, the Russians came to Petrov with this idea. He was very popular with his men and they wanted to make him mayor. He gave them his blessing, but becoming mayor wasn't his cup of tea, so I invited him to come back with us. It was a good thing he agreed, because I couldn't have fit all the extra fuel and people we had in the Blackhawks—and I doubt that the fishermen would have been as willing to go into the shipping business and help us get home, if Petrov hadn't assured them that it was okay to salvage the cargo ship. They were worried about someone from Moscow showing up and arresting them—probably still were, until we got to Alaska."

Alexis made a long face.

"What is it?" Merlyn and Anna asked it at the same time. Anna, being the closer of the two, placed her hand over Alexis'.

"Every big city I've seen since coming back has been destroyed. Seattle was a mess. Stokes said that lots of things caught fire— factories, fuel storage facilities, gas pipes, and the like—because they were abandoned without being properly shut down. Then, with no one around to clean up after a storm or put a fire out if lightning hit, more things went up in flames or got ruined. When it was obvious that the cities were not going to be bombed, scavengers and gangs of various sorts moved in to clean out all the food and supplies they could find. Some of them burned things down just because there was no one to stop them. Police stations, town halls, and federal buildings were the hardest hit, but the fires spread..."

There was a brief silence, broken by Merlyn. "Speaking of

Stokes, you never did say how he signaled your ship."

"Oh, when he spotted us sailing by, he tried to raise us on his radio, but Daniels was trying to raise McCord on military bands, so he didn't hear him." Alexis laughed. "He was afraid he might miss his only chance to get a ride, so he ran into the bathroom and ripped the mirror off the medicine cabinet! Pretty fast thinking, actually... But he did say he was an engineer."

"And you didn't find anyone else in Seattle?"

"We didn't find *anything* in Seattle. Some parts didn't look so bad, but everything was trashed, burnt, or stripped clean. It was a good thing that we found enough fuel in Alaska to fill the *Alexa Petrova's* tanks." Alexis was still mildly embarrassed about the naming of the ship, and grinned wryly. "We had to go on to San Fran without topping off. But you know, we kept close to shore and picked up two more families on the way. I think Captain Zaitsev is going to stick around the west coast, and go into the ferry business."

Merlyn had had friends in the bay area before The Collapse. "So, how was San Fran when you got there?"

"Burnt. Or trashed. So was Oakland, and most of the urban sprawl down to San Jose. I don't know why, but for some reason the Silicon Valley people never left their cities. Well, a lot of people did—including the government types who were afraid of being lynched—but the computer people stayed, and started building their new city right away. You should see the place. It's clean and sparkling, like a little Deseret, except that the people dress more like hippies. They don't have a government, exactly, but some kind of large scale mutual defense treaty among sovereign individuals— would you believe that they told us that one of them had pulled the treaty language off the internet years ago?"

John Allen took over the narrative, so Alexis could finish her dinner. "We finally got the fuel at the San Jose International Airport. We weren't sure what to trade for it, but when we told them that we'd gone to Russia to stop the WOPR on their behalf, they filled us up for free. A lot of our people—mostly ones who had been with us since before Y2K—liked it in Silicon Valley, and didn't think they'd get along in Deseret, so Alexis released them. One of the Blackhawks, several soldiers, and all of our computer people stayed there. When we finally got airborne, we followed I-80 back to Deseret. Sacramento was even more burnt than Seattle. Makes you wonder how things must be back east..."

All four friends stopped to ponder that unhappy thought.

"The east coast was one solid mass of people from Boston to Washington." Allen verbalized what all of them had been picturing in their minds. "There is no way that many people could live so piled up on one another without the technology and commerce that supported them. Now that I've met Michel, I know where some of them went... But I'd guess that a lot of small towns east of the Mississippi have doubled in size since The Collapse." He stared into the distance for a few breaths. "The east coast megalopolis must be nothing but thousands of square miles of ruins—it'll be a long time until it can be cleaned up."

"No doubt!" Again, Merlyn and Anna spoke simultaneously.

Alexis smiled ruefully. She had already heard jokes and whispered rumors about telepathy between The Owner and his partner, and was beginning to understand why. She hadn't really come to compete with Anna, and could now see that it would be impossible to separate her from Merlyn at any rate, but where did that leave her? She thought about John, guilt preying on her mind. She had to admit now, at least to herself, that she did love him, but she also knew that she loved Merlyn...and she had no idea what it was that Anna made her feel!

As if sensing her confusion, Merlyn slid around the end of the table and hugged Alexis, while Anna squeezed her hand and put an arm around the two of them.

John regarded the three quizzically and then in understanding. Now he knew why Alexis couldn't love him.

It hurt... Alexis had become very intimate, not just since that time in the helicopter in Alaska, but since she'd returned the Deseret people to their homes and had completed her mission.

Still, he'd accepted the risk, and he wasn't going to make a fuss. In an odd way, it was a relief to finally understand what was going on. It meant that Alexis really did care for him, but that someone else had gotten there first...

But what about Anna? Well, Merlyn wasn't married, so it was up to the three of them to work it out.

As if sensing his thoughts about her, Anna fixed Allen with her hypnotic gaze. Her direct look was made all the more mesmerizing by her almond eyes. He lost track of what he'd been thinking. Merlyn's physical closeness to Alexis and Anna's apparent lack of concern, or outright blessing of it, was disorienting. "So, uh," He tried to keep the conversation going. "Alexis let the last of her men go in Deseret... And..."

What was she looking at? Why did he feel as though she could see right into his mind? If half the rumors of mystery that surrounded Anna were true, he would probably never know.

He couldn't seem to get his words in the right order and had to break eye contact with her. "And, well... Some of the men didn't have anywhere in particular to go, but didn't want to stay in Deseret. At least, that's how Alexis sees it; personally, I think she's won their loyalty and they just want to stay with her. I know I—"

Allen broke off, took a gulp of his Coke, and changed what he was about to say. "So, the Okie and his co-pilot stuck with Alexis, like Old Petrov and some of the other men you've taken in to your security forces."

Merlyn and Anna nodded.

"We were still putzing around in Deseret when Alexis happened to overhear someone saying something about the radio distress call you put out. She went into overdrive, trying to get Okie's Blackhawk, her Apache, and Petrov's Hind all loaded up, fixed up, and fueled up. At first General Weber didn't want to replenish the Apache's weapons, or even give us the avgas. Boy, you should have seen Alexis then! I've never seen her so furious! She let him know what she thought about him not helping his own men to get home, even when we got ourselves all the way to San Francisco. She about roasted his butt, verbally speaking, and pointed out that she was leaving him with a Blackhawk he hadn't had before and that alone should be worth the trade... Well, you get the picture. I thought old Weber was going to have her arrested, but he couldn't pull a stunt like that—Alexis is very popular in Deseret for having gone to Russia."

Alexis' cheeks flushed with red. "I... I guess I lost my temper."

Merlyn and Anna laughed together. "We can imagine!"

Allen chuckled as well. "And after that, well, you know what happened when we showed up here."

An appreciative silence settled over the four, until Alexis jabbed Merlyn in the ribs playfully with an elbow. "So, Mr. Owner, I should think that the Dollar Ranch Air Force is worth something. Do I get to stay?" She laughed, and Anna joined her.

"Indeed you do, my Warrior Princess, indeed you do! And so can the rest of your crew." Merlyn kissed her on the forehead and stood up to survey the crowd. "I think most folks are done eating, and I want to say a few things to them before Dreamer sneaks off." He winked at his companions and stood on his chair, calling for silence.

There was some shuffling as people scooted closer. Michel and Razor moved to sit near Dreamer, who lifted his head to hear what The Owner had to say. Rosalia was with them as well, grief being something she had in common with the blond man. And wherever Rosalia went, Scout and his .22 were always at hand. After losing Holly, he had made it his mission in life to protect his remaining surrogate parent. And, of course, wherever Scout went, Penny and Patty were sure to follow.

"Friends, loved ones, and new arrivals." Merlyn's voice conveyed both joy and sorrow. "We have suffered a great loss, even as we have achieved a great victory. Those who gave their lives in our defense will never be forgotten, but they would want us to move on when our grief abates. They gave their lives that we might live, not to give us a reason to curl up and die inside. So, I want to take a moment to look to the future with you... But first, let me introduce you—for those of you who have not yet met them—to the members of the Dollar Ranch Air Force."

The crowd cheered wildly as Merlyn introduced the pilots, and especially when he introduced Alexis, whom everyone knew was responsible for having brought the helicopters in to help win the battle.

"Thank you! Thank you, it's good to be home..." Alexis cleared her throat hesitantly and decided to add only one observation. "From the air, I could see how disorganized the enemy was, even before we attacked. They thought they had you pinned down, and might have soon turned their attention to looting, but that would not have meant victory for them. Judging from the incredible sights I witnessed—not the least of which was a single girl mowing down man after man who was there to hurt her loved ones—I believe you would have defeated Ejercito Dragon without my help. But I'm really glad to have been able to thin them out for you and make it a little easier!"

The crowd cheered again, and Alexis sat down.

"The future!" Merlyn boomed at his audience. "The future spreads before us! Do you all realize that that so-called army came here all the way from California? And they came because honest peace-loving people like us were making it too dangerous for them to stay in California? Think about what that means!"

He gave them a minute to do just that.

"It means that we will probably never have to face such a threat again! Think about it... All over the world, gangs of thugs are probably starving, or getting mauled by people like us, people who want only to be left alone!"

There was some scattered cheering, but the crowd quickly quieted.

"Remember when I played that recording for Big Bob's gold coins? Well, as some of you know, we're hearing all kinds of things on the air these days. It seems that some of the folks sitting on oil refineries up in Wyoming are putting out Petro-Dollar coins, and the folks in Deseret are putting out Telecom Dollars on plastic cards. Brace yourselves for this! Remember the messages we sent to Deseret? Well, we eventually heard back from them. They turned us down, of course, *but they called me on the phone to tell me so!*"

There were gasps throughout the crowd, and several louder exclamations.

"That's right! I can't even remember the last time the phone rang—I think Goya almost had a heart attack!"

Scattered laughter could be heard throughout the gathering, and then Goya's voice called out: "I tought eet was an unleested number!"

Everyone had a good laugh, and then they settled down again.

Merlyn joined his friends in laughter briefly before continuing. "Folks, I can't tell you what the future will be like, but things are starting to come back together again. I honestly believe that we have survived the worst of the storm, and can now look forward to smoother and smoother sailing. So, in the future, when you are doing whatever it is you're doing, I want you to think back on the battle for Dollar Ranch with pride. A little sadness would be appropriate, but I think those we lost would want us to see that day as the day when the tide turned, and things started getting better again!"

The applause was not long, but it was heartfelt. It *was* time to get back to building the future!

AFTERWORD:
SPRING, 2002

"Let the truth of Love be lighted
Let the love of Truth shine clear
Sensibility
Armed with sense and liberty
With the Heart and Mind united
In a single perfect sphere."
—Rush, *Cygnus X-1 Book II Hemispheres*

Anna and John were taking their turn staying home with Osibisa, Alexis' one-year-old—whose father was obviously Merlyn.

Anna herself was expecting—due any day now, actually—and the brawl over the child's name was getting serious. She herself was partial to her mother's name, Yiing, but if Merlyn were the child's father, perhaps something African might be more fitting. On the other hand, Osibisa's name was African. It meant, 'criss-crossing rhythms that explode with happiness'—a meaning the child lived up to every day. Besides, John might be the genetic father of the little human preparing to emerge from her womb... How confusing!

Maybe she should ask some of her Mormon friends how large polygamous families go about selecting names for their children. Even though very few Mormons had ever practiced it, polygamy had never completely died out among certain splinter groups. The odd thing was that now that it was legal in Deseret, and polyga-mists could go about openly, the practice was dying out more quickly. Perhaps it had to do with the obvious success of the traditional 'family' lifestyle sanctioned and encouraged by the church, which now had more than a billion adherents worldwide. Or perhaps the women were realizing that, unless there were as many husbands as wives in a heterosexual polyamorous arrangement, it would be hard for them to get the love and attention they needed. Still, there were a few such families left, and some of them might be willing to share their secrets for managing the naming of children in plural relationships.

She decided to send an e-mail to some of her Mormon friends on the subject that very evening. Just now, she had to rescue the robot vacuum cleaner from Osibisa, who had discovered at an early age the wonders and joys of the electric screwdriver.

John came in from the afternoon ride—still a family tradition for The Owner and all his partners—even though Anna had stopped joining the others for the time being. He kissed her and bent over to put an ear on her belly.

"There he goes again—he's gonna give me a black eye!" He winked at Anna. "So, what's Tibetan for 'acrobat'?"

She laughed and pushed him away. "Let's not get into the Great Name Debate until Merlyn and Alexis return!"

"Okay, okay..." A fleeting look of worry crossed his face. "I hope they don't have any adventures on the way!"

"It's been a long time since anything has come up that they couldn't handle. I know you don't like the high tolls AHC charges, but you have to admit that they do keep the roads safe."

"It's more the way they moved in and seized the interstates here and the highways in what used to be Canada, Mexico, and other countries farther south. I know they weren't owned by anyone in particular, but it just seems... I don't know... A little too greedy."

"Well, that may be, but the roads were falling apart." They both knew that with no one maintaining the roads, cracks had been turning into potholes, and potholes had been turning into dangerous breaks in the pavement—in some places, bridges had been starting to come down. "If you ask me, it's a good thing someone took them over and fixed them up. AHC patrols those roads better than the police ever did without bothering people who are driving safely, just because they are going fast. They keep the criminals off the roads, they keep the restaurants and bathrooms clean, and the pavement was never so free of potholes before The Collapse."

John raised his hands in mock surrender. "I know, I know..." The last time he'd checked, there were more rest areas, more special lanes for people with sports cars, and more service stations that sold gasoline, electric quick-charges, and natural gas. "But geez, seven Telco-Dollars just to drive to Salt Lake?"

"At least you don't have to stop to pay the tolls." Computers subtracted the tolls from cards bought at vending machines and tossed on dashboards. It was anonymous and convenient.

"Yeah, but seven Telco-Dollars! I could buy two boxes of 30.06 for that and get some change!" John looked down to find Osibisa at his feet, apparently intent on making a cat's cradle out of his shoelaces. He picked her up and blew a raspberry on her tummy. The little girl squealed with delight and wiggled until he put her down. She toddled off to find something to take apart.

Anna loved the way John handled children. She'd seen the capacity in him right from the start—it was one of the things that she found most attractive in him. "I'll not deny that we seem to pay a lot when we drive on the interstates," she told him, "but we don't pay anything when we don't drive on them, and is it really more than we once paid in taxes?"

He laughed. "Well, you got me there! And you are right about the peace of mind. Between the safety of Deseret and the security provided by the American Highway Company, I can't say I really worry about anyone in our family traveling anymore. And Michel and Razor didn't have any problems on their trip to visit their friend in Costa Rica last winter... Hey, maybe we should all take a vacation down to Cancun after John Junior is born! Or, I hear the old navy ships that work for the ocean security companies have pretty much wiped out the piracy that flourished after The Collapse in the Caribbean, and the Disney cruise ship is back in business!"

"John Allen, even if this child has your genetic contribution, and even if it turns out to be a boy, I am not saddling the poor little guy with being a 'junior' anything. He gets his own identity!"

"I thought you said we weren't going to argue about names until the others got back!"

She stuck her tongue out at him and they both laughed. Osibisa joined in the laughter, just for the pure joy of it.

*   *   *

Elder Jared Christensen, newly of the Quorum of the Twelve, sat in his office contemplating the future. Much had happened since The Collapse—hard to believe that only a little more than two years had passed!

Ah, Brother Young, how I will miss your wisdom, and how inadequate I feel to fill your shoes...

He drifted over to his window and studied the gardens at the foot of the Church Office Building, almost thirty floors below. The flowers planted there and in Temple Square were of a hundred different varieties, each doing its own thing, but how beautiful they all were when seen as a whole from above!

Rather like the world these days, he mused. When the big governments of the twentieth century fell apart, nations around the world shattered into millions of fragments, each a community with an identity and culture of its own, a single species of flower in its own garden. And the collection, as seen from above, was the most beautiful thing on earth.

Of course, being living creatures, the people in those communities had struggled to sustain their lives. For most, that took the form of trading what they could produce for what they wanted. For a few, it had taken the form of violent predation on their fellows. How interesting that once there were no authorities to 'protect' the vast majority of people who were decent and hard-working, they had taken their protection into their own hands. The hard-working majority, who once lived in fear of the criminal minority, had risen up and all but wiped them out.

Enough wool-gathering.

Time to go to the meeting. Jared sighed. At first, he'd enjoyed these 'economic summit' meetings, when they heralded new growth and a rebirth of civilization. Now, they had become commonplace—boring. Perhaps he could get the Church to assign him to lead a mission to the new Moon colony when they were up and running...now *that* would be interesting!

Sighing again, he took the elevator down to street level and walked at a leisurely pace to the New Salt Palace, only a few short blocks away. Down several side streets, he could see more construction sites than he could ever remember seeing anywhere.

Well, it was to be expected, he supposed. Salt Lake City had become the de facto capital of the world, if indeed any one place could be called such. The nation-states that had fallen to the Millennium Bug had never arisen again. Today there were city-states, globe-spanning non-contiguous states such as Deseret, business concerns that might as well be countries, and even Sovereign Individuals—mostly powerful computer wizards whose services were without a doubt the most sought-after value in the world—who were nations all to themselves.

All of these new forms of social organization were interacting in harmonious—if somewhat voracious—competition with one another. In this environment, Deseret came the closest to being the equivalent of a twentieth-century 'superpower' and Salt Lake was its capital. In this new world, amazing things that would have been impossible a scant few years in the past were becoming commonplace. Communities and individuals were creating prosperity, not only rebuilding it in areas that had previously been governed by wealthy countries, but also *creating* it in areas that had known nothing but poverty for centuries. It was sobering, in this heady new environment of explosive worldwide growth, to realize that the people who were building the new Moon colony were a small group of high-tech gurus and engineers—based in what was once Equador, of all places!

Nothing was as it was before.

Jared wrinkled his brow. Maybe all the increases in productivity and wealth around the world were the result of the simultaneous near-extinction of the professions of *politician* and *bureaucrat*. He laughed at the thought, taking his usual place at the head table in the New Salt Palace Ball Room.

The usual faces were gathered around. There was the 'surfer dude' who represented the Autocracy of Silicon Valley. Two members of the four-way marriage that led the oil-rich Free City of Dollar Ranch were present—it was always a different two with them. There was the older man from Disneyworld in Florida—the only person present who insisted on wearing a suit and tie at all times. Three gentlemen were present from the gold mining company that had operations in what used to be Mexico, South Africa, and several other places. The elderly woman who was the CEO of the American Highway Company was in visibly better health than she had been at the previous meeting. And, of course, the sheik who represented New OPEC was there with a gaggle of attendants.

Jared smiled and waved at Admiral Al of the Pacific Protection Company, glad to see that he was in port. He wondered if he'd ever see the admiral who managed the shipping protection business in the Atlantic—that man was always finding some old navy ship that needed refitting and a new crew, and never had time for meetings anymore.

Jared wished he had as good an excuse!

There were many new faces as well. Jared wondered if the Global Cleanup Corporation had finally sent a delegation to seek new investors for the Cuban cleanup job. Ah, well... If not this time, then maybe next month—they were doing an excellent job, but potential investors would probably want to see how the profit margins on the east coast cleanup tallied up when the books were closed. Some of the new faces might be the representatives from Anonymous E-Cash, a company that was providing a major new impetus to worldwide trade. AEC's president had promised that someone would attend the meeting, but Jared had no idea what that person or persons might look like.

The meeting started late, as usual, and plowed through hours of reports, as usual. All the growth was encouraging, to be sure, but Jared grew more convinced that he needed a change in pace with each passing minute.

He took a glossy brochure out of his pocket and relived some of his boyhood daydreams. Those had been the days! Reading Heinlein, Asimov, Smith, and Hogan... Imagining himself living in a lunar colony, or plying the space-ways in his own starship!

Jared decided to talk to the Quorum of the Twelve about the need to take the Church of Jesus Christ of Latter Day Saints into space. Mankind was again looking into the future with heads held high and eyes opened wide. Jared wanted to be there on the frontier, watching it happen. Heck, it was worth a try!

*   *   *

Rosalia closed her eyes and concentrated on the heavy warmth of the wedding ring on her finger, then brought Dreamer's hand to her lips and kissed the matching one on his finger. "I came here following a trail I hoped would bring me justice...and maybe revenge. I got those things, but finding you has been even more important!"

"Aw, you only say that because you like my books!"

Rosalia pretended to pout and tickled him.

Dreamer laughed and pulled her close. "I came here to protect my family from Y2K problems. I thought I might find someone with a like mind here because, even though I knew it would be a small community, it would be built on the voluntary ties formed between people that have some important things in common. At my age, though, I never expected to find a wife who shared those important things *and* also happens to be the most beautiful young woman in the valley!"

Rosalia blushed. "Oh, you're not that old! And I'm not that young!"

"You know why I called myself Dreamer?" He kissed her, covering the scar over her right eye with his lips.

"No... I've never really questioned it. Why?"

"I'm a dreamer because I'm an idealist, like you. But more importantly, I'm a dreamer because even though I never really believed I'd find a woman who could fill the hole Eva left in my life when she passed away, I couldn't give up the dream that I might, someday..."

Rosalia knew he wasn't done, and gave him time to collect his thoughts.

"And you know what, you don't just fill a hole. By the time you came along, I'd pretty much filled that myself with all the things that are important to me. You're what I've been dreaming of, not because you complete me, nor because you're the first woman my kids have accepted, but because you *complement* me—you're my perfect partner!"

"Well," a tear escaped Rosalia's eye, "I'm glad you still feel that way after wearing that ring for a year."

Dreamer laughed. "I know it sounds naive, but I know I'll still be feeling this way in 100 years!"

They both laughed and Rosalia started packing up the remains of their picnic. "Holly would have liked you too... I wish you'd gotten to know her as well as I did."

Dreamer knew that Rosalia was tormented by guilt. She still wished she had stopped Angel when she was younger, or had put him out of everyone's misery the night before the battle for Dollar Ranch. He tried to shunt her thoughts off onto a different track. "Oh no! None of The Owner's crazy plural marriage stuff for me! Uh-uh. I may be old fashioned, but I'm perfectly happy with one wife and no husbands!"

"Oh, Holly wouldn't have..." Rosalia gazed at her husband.

"Then again, maybe she would have. You think Scout will end up marrying both of the twins when they get a little older?"

"Who knows? The girls are still kids, and they'll change a lot as they grow... But Patty and Penny sure do adore him! However it works out, I'm sure they'll always be close."

Rosalia was not fooled. She knew her husband too well to fail to notice it when he changed the topic. The subject of her guilt, and his insistence that she had nothing to feel guilty about, was the one thing they ever disagreed about. Rosalia thought he was just being noble—one of Angel's men had stabbed his daughter, after all!

But on this beautiful day, she did not want to argue. And maybe—just maybe—it was time to take Merlyn's advice and talk to The Advisor about her feelings. She had certainly held on to them long enough! And he certainly had helped many people deal with their grief after the battle with Ejercito Dragon. Maybe she should seek his counsel... She didn't really think it would help, but it would certainly please Dreamer if she made the effort.

*   *   *

Razor stood on the valley rim, holding The Advisor's hand. He had placed fresh flowers on Jimmy's grave minutes before, and now the two surveyed the valley together. Razor leaned against him, finding comfort in his solidity as she always did.

Odd, that he should feel so solid when he was going to die soon.

The Advisor's hair had started falling out, even before the battle with Ejercito Dragon. He'd misjudged the safety of driving so close to Kansas City only a day after the Atchison bombing, and then driven too close to Cheyenne Mountain without even bothering to close the vents on the armored car. The dosage he'd been exposed to wasn't lethal, and the truck's thick metal hide had protected him some, but not enough. His hair had grown back now,

wavier than it had been before, but it wasn't the radiation itself
that was killing him.

It was a cancer, diagnosed a few months before. It could happen to anyone, but Doc admitted that the radiation Michel had
soaked up had increased his chances for something like what was
happening. Neither Doc, nor the specialists from Deseret, were
sure how long The Advisor would last, but they didn't think it
would be longer than a year, maybe two, maybe less.

Somehow, even though everyone is headed for death sooner or
later, the probability of Michel's impending death gave extra weight
to his words. People listened to him, trusted his judgment, and
worked hard to implement his advice. For his part, he knew that
most of the things he was saying to the people who sought his
counsel were actually things he'd heard Natalie say. He'd learned
some important lessons about life after the turn of the millennium, especially lessons about guilt and self-doubt, but it was all
the things that Natalie had taught him that helped the most. Her
way of listening, her way of finding out what people really wanted
and feared, her way of encouraging people to become creative agents
in their own lives... He hadn't realized how much he'd learned
from her! His work now was his way of helping her to make a
difference beyond the grave, and it warmed him every time he did
it.

Razor was the one person who didn't treat him like a fragile
old mystic from a mountain peak in the Himalayas. The others
expected wisdom from him, so he didn't resist, but it was good to
have her to talk to...to *really* talk to, as he had with Natalie.

For her part, Razor ached every time she thought about his
condition, but she didn't let him see her pain. She knew how
important it was to him to be able to talk to her without the
conversation breaking down into tears. To finally find a man she
could love, only to have him... Better not to think about that!
When they did talk about it, Michel assured her that she'd find
someone else to love, in time, and whatever the gender, he was
sure that that individual would be a fine person...

The Advisor put his arm around Razor and they gazed up into the sky. There wasn't a cloud in sight and the limitless azure beckoned.

"Trish would be proud of me." The dancer-turned-entrepreneur leaned against The Advisor. "I never got my MBA, but I've started three successful businesses since coming to this valley. I've learned that using people in a coercive, manipulative way is not the alternative to being used by others; it's better to create something new... If only, just once, she could have spread her wings in this peaceful place!"

"Natalie would 'ave loved it too... But she also would 'ave reminded you zat even zough Trish only flew during ze storm, she would not 'ave flown at all, wissout you. You showed her what wings are for!"

Razor knew he was right. "And you know what's exciting?" She closed her eyes and spread her arms as though she were an eagle catching an updraft. "For the first time in the history of the world, I think most people are starting to realize that they too can choose to soar, if only they will dare!"